The Powers of the Earth

Books by Travis J I Corcoran

Aristillus (science fiction with uplifted dogs, AI, and big guns)
- The Powers of the Earth
- Causes of Separation
- Right and Duty (planned)
- Absolute Tyranny (planned)

- The Team (short story)
- Staking a Claim (short story)

Caterpillar (a post apocalyptic procedural)
- Caterpillar (short story)

Timetraders (a cross timeline intellectual property heist tale)
- Firefly Season Two (short story)

Escape the City (a non-fiction how-to homesteading guide)
- Escape the City volume 1
- Escape the City volume 2

The Powers of the Earth

Travis J I Corcoran

Morlock Publishing

2017

The Powers of the Earth

Travis J I Corcoran

Copyright © 2017 Morlock Publishing

All rights reserved. Except as permitted under U.S. Copyright Act of 1976, no part of this publication may be reproduced, distributed, or transmitted in any form or by any means, or stored in a database or retrieval system, without the prior written permission of the publisher.

Morlock Publishing (morlockpublishing.com)

Graphic Design:	Jennifer Corcoran
Cover Art:	Pavel Mikhailenko
Interior Photos:	NASA, Damian Peach
Editing:	William H Stoddard, Ray Burton
Kickstarter Video:	Christopher Corcoran

With thanks to John Barnes and Ken MacLeod for their feedback on early drafts.

ISBN: 978-1-973-31114-0

Second Edition: Nov 2017

10 9 8 7 6 5 4 3 2

This book is dedicated to my wife, Jennifer.

When in the Course of human events, it becomes necessary for one people to dissolve the political bands which have connected them with another, and to assume among **the powers of the earth**, the separate and equal station to which the Laws of Nature and of Nature's God entitle them, a decent respect to the opinions of mankind requires that they should declare the causes which impel them to the separation.

- Thomas Jefferson, United States Declaration of Independence

Thank You

My sincere thanks to the hundreds of friends and fans who made these novels possible through reading drafts, encouragement, and Kickstarter backing.

Hero of Aristillus

Larry Prince

Collector's Edition Hardcovers

Eddie and Family

Elam Bend

Gman

Lowell D. Jacobson

Anonymous

Mark W. Bennett

Paul Trentham MD

Philip R. "Pib" Burns

Wolf Rench

Anonymous

Limited Edition Hardcovers

A. Tambourino

Aaron C. de Bruyn

Alexander Yiannopoulos

Andrew Doonan

Aric Rothman

Brian K.I. Dunbar

Bryan Smant

Christopher Smith (chrylis)

Colm Brogan

Dave Galey

David K. Magnus

David Solomon

Derek T. Pauley

John V. Rauscher

Jonathan E. Stafford

JPN

k'Bob42

Kevin J. Twitty

Kevin Maguire

Mark Koerner

Martin Barry

Maureen Vaughan

Michael J. Katcher

Michael Moody

Ray Burton

Samuel J. Frederick

eqdw
Erich Burton
Frank Vance
Grasspunk
Helle Roskjaer
J. David Krause
Jeffrey Ellis
Joel Cazares, Jr.
John C. Garand

Scot Johnson
The Sperglords of Brussels
Todd Feltner
Tyler R. Crosson
Victor Luft
Wardog of Wardogheim
William H. Stoddard
William R. Evans

Trade Paperbacks

Adri Pretorius
Alexander Lecea
Andrew Schlueter
Bill Anderson
Brian S. Watson
Byrne Hobart
Christopher Käck
Christopher Smith (chrylis)
Connor Medcalf
Craig M. Gerritsen
Craig S. Miller
D. E. Welshans
David Anadale
David Cormier
David Hagberry
Edwin M Perello
Elizabeth Armstrong
Huck
Hugh Farnham
Isaac Leibowitz
James M. Butcher
Jason Azze

Jeffy The Vulture
JJ McHenry
Joe Lach
Jonathan Andrews
Joshua McGinnis
JRW
Julie Moronuki
MacWhiskyFace
Neil Dubé
R.T. Sawyer, II
Richard Ripley
Rob Cheyne
Rob Leitman
S. Sidewinder
Scott Brown
Straker
Tom Hickok
Trey Garrison
Wesley Kenyon
yuzeh
Zac Donovan
Zach Steinour

Dramatis Personæ

On Earth, Government

- President Themba Johnson - President of the United States (D - Populist faction)
- Senator Linda Haig - Senator from Maryland (D - Internationalist faction)
- General Bonner, US Army - tasked with planning lunar invasion
- General Restivo, US Army - initially reporting to General Bonner, assisting with lunar invasion plans
- Captain Frank Tudel, US Army / UN Peacekeeper deployment - tasked with seizing an expat ship
- Captain Matthew Dewitt, US Army (Special Forces) - tasked with infiltrating expat society

Aristillus, executives

- Mike Martin - CEO, Morlock Engineering
- Javier Borda - CEO, First Class Homes and Offices, old friend of Mike Martin
- Kevin Bultman - CEO, Mason Dixon, old friend of Mike Martin
- Mark Soldner - CEO, Soldner Homes
- Karina Roth – CEO, Guaranteed Electrical
- Hsieh Tung - CEO, Fifth Ring Shipping
- Hector Camanez - CEO, Camanez Beef and Pork
- Albert Lai - CEO, Lai Docks & Air Traffic Control
- Rob Wehramnn - CEO, General Tunnels
- Katherine Dycus - CEO, Airtight Suits
- Darren Hollins - CEO, Goldwater Mining & Refining

- Leory Fournier - CEO, MaisonNeuve Construction

Aristillus, other individuals

- Darcy Grau - long term romantic partner of Mike Martin, ship navigator, coder
- Ewoma - 12 year old daughter of Chiwetal (owner of Benue River restaurant)
- Kaspar Osvaldo - employee of Javier Borda at First Class Homes and Offices
- Hugh Haig - A young adult with family connections, trying to figure out what he wants to do in life
- Allan Pine - an acquaintance of Hugh's
- Louisa Teer - an acquaintance of Hugh's, very politically aware and active
- Selena Hargraves - a friend of Hugh's, interested in a career in journalism
- Allyson Cherry - a friend of Hugh's
- Lowell Benjamin - a lawyer
- Ponnala Srinivas ("Ponzie") - a physicist
- George White - a private investigator

Lunar Surface

- Gamma - an artificial intelligence
- John - a man looking for a home, on a hiking trip with four dogs
- Blue - uplifted dog; first generation
- Max - uplifted dog; first generation
- Duncan - uplifted dog; second generation
- Rex - uplifted dog; second generation

Lunar nearside (as seen from Earth).

Mare Imbrium ("The Sea of Showers") is the circular region north of dead center.

In the eastern section of the mare are three craters. One of these is Aristillus.

Photo credit: NASA.

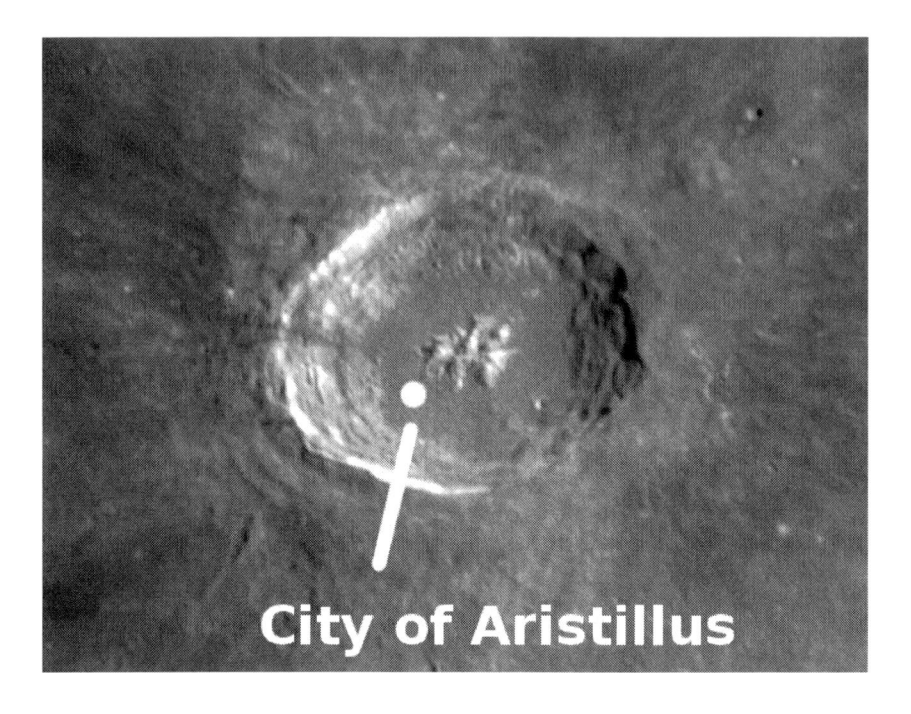

City of Aristillus

Aristillus is a crater approximately 55 km in diameter and 3.6 km deep.

The center of the crater has a triple peaked mountain.

Aristillus was first photographed from lunar orbit by Lunar Orbiter 4 in 1967, and from the surface by crew members of the Wookkiee in 2054.

Photo credit: Damian Peach

Chapter 1

2064: Mining debris heap, Aristillus Crater, Lunar Nearside

The sky above the spaceport was as black as a freshly bored lunar tunnel before the lights were installed. Earth hung overhead, the once-bright cities of its western hemisphere glowing dimly with low-energy bulbs and rolling brown-outs. Except California. California was dark.

Mike Martin squinted against the brightness of the lunar noon and squeezed the trigger slowly, waiting for the break -

The thunder traveled through the rifle stock to his spacesuit and then into his chest like a punch from a giant. A moment later he was engulfed by a cloud of dust blown off the lunar surface by the muzzle blast.

Javier pretended to cough over the in-helmet radio. Mike ignored him and smiled like a kid. The first five versions of the rifle had failed in simulation. The next two had blown up in their test rigs. This one, version 0.08, had survived a hundred rounds in the rig... and now Mike had fired it by hand for the first time ever. He whooped in celebration.

Javier's voice came through his helmet speakers. "You sound pleased with yourself."

Mike grinned. "When am I not?"

The lunar dust settled onto the ground - and onto the shooting bench and their suits. Javier brushed his faceplate ineffectively. "Seriously, Mike, why such a big round?"

Mike flipped the rifle's safety. "Because I'm from Texas."

"That was a serious question."

"...which is why I gave you a serious answer."

Javier shook his head. His helmet didn't move, but Mike saw it via his in-helmet display and grinned again. "During the CEO Trials they seized my company, my house -"

"I was *there*, Mike. Ancient history."

Mike held up a finger. "They took my dad's collection." He paused, inventorying it. "A 1772 Brown Bess, a few 18th century officer's swords-"

"But what -"

"I miss my dad's fifty."

"You *miss* it?"

"Well, I only fired it once, but it was his favorite. So it's my favorite."

"So you needed to design and build a gun just as big?"

"Just as big? Fuck that! The round is twice the diameter, and eight times the mass."

"Has anyone ever told you that you're a lunatic, Mike? I mean, besides me?"

"Not for about a week."

Javier tilted his head back and looked up at the Earth. "Darcy's on a run?"

"Getting back tomorrow. Or maybe the day after."

Javier grunted and then looked at the impromptu rifle target - just a piece of white-painted steel propped up on a small mountain of tailings a kilometer away. "Did you even hit it?"

"The spotting scope is on channel four." Without waiting for Javier Mike brought up the feed in his helmet display. The target was clean. "Missed. Let me try again with a tracer." Mike pulled a massive round from the ammo box with two bulky gloved fingers; then a new voice, crisp and British, came over the radio.

"Michael, we've got an incoming flight. If you boys could put your games on hold for a bit it would be greatly appreciated."

"Albert, I'm facing in the opposite direction from the docks. The chance of a ricochet hitting a ship is - what? - no more than fifty percent?" He grinned at Javier, inviting his friend into the game. "At *most*. Probably not more than twenty five percent. Let me take a few more shots."

Albert gave a sigh. "I take it that *some* people are entertained by your behavior." A brief pause. "I need you to shut it down. Now, kindly."

Mike rolled his eyes. "Aye aye, Albert." He slipped the tracer back into the case and laid the rifle on the shooting table.

Javier pointed a thumb over his shoulder. "Want to watch the ship come in?"

Mike affected an air of disdain even as he stood and turned to face Lai Docks. "These modern landings aren't nearly as exciting as -"

Javier groaned. "Spare me from yet another retelling of The First Landing. Rust, money, a jury-rigged crane and a Chinese tunnel boring machine -"

"The first TBM was Korean -"

Javier continued as if Mike hadn't spoken. " - and one man, working alone-"

"Hey - I *always* give Ponzie credit. His drive -"

Javier gave him a stern look. "Saying that *one* other person helped build Aristillus isn't much better than saying you did it yourself."

"Well, I mostly - woah!"

A shadow darker than any on Earth swallowed them. The rifle, the bench, Javier- all disappeared in the black.

Mike turned. The incoming ship had slid across the sky, unseen by them - until it eclipsed the sun, cutting off the light like a guillotine.

Mike looked - there! A spot of dark in a dark sky, with just a thread of white along one edge - and then it was past the sun and the dark shadow was replaced by an actinic glare. Mike's helmet dimmed almost immediately, but not quite fast enough to prevent a small squiggle of afterimage green.

Mike watched the ship as it drifted through the sky. The oceangoing freighter wouldn't have been noteworthy in any harbor on Earth - except perhaps for its extreme age and small size. If it were bobbing in the salt water of, say, Matamoros or Durban, it would be lost among the Panamax container carriers and the odd 500 meter LNG tankers doing business under loopholes in the Carbon Law.

Such a ship would be nothing more than a bit of foreground clutter there - but here? Even after ten years, watching a container ship floating over the stark black and gray lunar surface struck him as magical and unreal.

He followed the ship as it dropped toward the solar farms, tailing dumps, refineries, and rolling plants. It slid lower, toward the open pit of Lai Docks. Mike noted the subtle restraint with which the ship's navigator played the game - small maneuvering rockets embedded in the cargo containers on the ship's deck fired from time to time to correct the course, but never for too long.

Suddenly its descent slowed and stopped. Slowly, laboriously, the massive ship rolled a few degrees one way and the other, as if it were being rocked in an invisible sea. The oscillation stopped and the ship resumed its descent.

Ha!

Mike raised one hand high in acknowledgment. Would she be able to see it from there? Yes, her cameras must be good enough; she'd waved first. Mike lowered his arm and turned to Javier. "Looks like I was wrong about the schedule - Darcy's back now."

The men continued to watch the ship until it dropped into the open pit of the hanger and the vast concrete and steel doors began to slide shut. Mike turned back to the shooting bench and reached for the rifle. "Don't you want to go see Darcy?"

Mike looked at him. "Are you kidding? I'm not sighted in yet, and I've got a box full of ammo left."

Javier shook his head. "You've got to pay more attention to her. She's a good woman."

Mike loaded a tracer and locked the bolt forward. "I know."

"Do you?"

Mike pulled his helmet away from the stock. "Are you giving me dating advice now?"

"I'm giving you advice on getting along with people." Javier let a hint of a grin slide onto his face. "And, yes, part of that is dating advice."

Mike considered this for a moment before dismissing it. He pointed his chin at the rifle. "So what do you think of it?"

Javier sighed, then looked at the rifle. "It's impressive." He paused. "But I don't know what the point is."

"The point? Jav, if the government ever gets up here -"

Javier put up a hand. "I know. I know. But if it ever comes to that, negotiation -"

"Negotiation? Fuck the government and fuck negotiation. When the Bureau of Industrial Planning said I couldn't buy more earth movers, I negotiated. I paid three lawyers for a year and it didn't accomplish shit. Then the Racketeering and Unjust Profits Act -"

"Mike, my point is -"

"*When they passed RUPA*, I negotiated. I played by their rules, I went to court, and you know how well that worked. Fuck negotiation. If they ever come after us, I've got an answer for them." He slapped the rifle.

Javier shook his head. "Mike, let's pretend I accept your thesis and we've got this existential risk. If that's true, you're being an idiot."

Mike turned, shocked. "I - what?"

"If the government is trying to destroy us, then anything other than the plan with the best chance of success is idiotic."

Mike pursed his lips.

"If you're serious about this, and not just signalling that you're a crazy bad ass, then you've got to think strategically. You need to recruit allies, build a power structure, do -"

"I *am* building a power structure. Once the rifle design is perfected I'm going to build a militia and -"

Javier sighed. "Hiring a bunch of guys and giving them rifles isn't what I meant. You don't need one militia; you need to to motivate everyone to get ready. Build alliances, get other leaders interested -"

"Other? Other than who?"

Javier smiled ruefully. "Other than you, Mike."

Mike snorted. "I'm not a leader. What I am is the only guy who sees the problem that's going to be in our lap in five years, and the only one who's trying to get us ready for it."

"And building guns - but refusing to network - is the best way to do that?"

Mike grimaced. "Enough. This is getting my pulse up and that'll throw off my aim. Spot for me."

Javier sighed and Mike rolled his eyes at the sound.

Javier was his friend, but Mike would never understand his insistence about committees and talking and the rest of that bullshit. Not when there was real work to be done. Mike adjusted the sling around the upper arm of his suit, clipped the free end onto the rifle, and then pushed the weapon out, drawing the sling tight. He drew a breath, and squeezed -

The thunderclap punched him in the chest and dust engulfed him again. Mike raised his head from the stock. "Did I hit it?"

"No, but you clipped a boulder ten meters to the right. Check the replay - you sent a nice chunk of rock shooting off into the sky."

Chapter 2

2064: West Wing of the White House, Washington DC, Earth

The taupe-carpeted corridor that ran down the center of the West Wing was quiet. Senator Linda Haig looked at her watch. Almost half an hour late. Hardly surprising; that woman was never -

Suddenly the doors of the Cabinet Room flew open and the president strode out. Linda, without missing a beat, fell into step beside her. Behind and around them, the president's staff hurried to keep up. One of the aides said "Madam President, I know your schedule is tight, but we really need an answer on the fertilizer allocation -"

President Johnson looked straight ahead as she walked briskly. "Don't pressure me, Don. Do you think that *you* get to dictate my schedule?"

From the corner of her eye Linda Haig could see Don bite his lip. The president's moods were legendary. What sort of amateur was Don that he not only was letting the president get to him, but was letting his emotions show like that? How the man could be Chief of Staff and be so bad at the game was beyond her. Still, it would be instructive to watch - any data on how Don and the president interacted was useful.

Don nodded. "Ah - no, ma'am. It's just that we're getting a lot of pressure from the Department of Agriculture, and they're getting a lot of pressure from the farmers, who -"

They reached the central lobby and Senator Haig turned the corner crisply alongside the president. Don, on the other hand, almost ran into the back of the man in front of him. Linda suppressed a smile - and then suddenly had to stop without warning when the president halted in her tracks. Linda turned and watched - was she going to see Themba stop to harangue an underling?

The president gestured around the sitting area in the corridor. "Don, all this old furniture. I don't like it." She paused and looked up. "And the ceiling is too low."

Linda looked at Don. She could almost see the man fighting the urge to roll his eyes. And reasonably so - he was the Chief of Staff, not some flunky. But he should hide it better. Linda considered carefully - was Themba really this much of an idiot, talking about furniture and ceilings, or was there some deeper game going on here?

Don cleared his throat. "I'll make sure the Chief Usher gets the message and brings it to the Preservation Committee."

The president nodded, said "Good," and resumed her pace toward the courtyard.

"Ma'am, the fertilizer -"

Themba was dismissive. "Don, if the farmers don't like it, they don't have to take their allocations. They want something from me? They can wait until I've decided...and I haven't decided. Next topic."

Catherine, the DoD liason, spoke. "The DoD wants your approval -"

Linda's ears perked. *This* was interesting. There wasn't much to be done with the fertilizer issue, but military issues...well, there were fault lines there - and ways to use information.

Catherine continued "- for a renewal of the mixed deployments with PK forces."

Linda kept the disappointment off her face. Procedural crap. She was looking for something juicier. She had been *told* that there would be something juicier.

The president brushed out of the lobby entrance, past the Marines who held the French doors open for her, and outside to the covered motor court where the limousine, the decoy limousines, and the hulking black security escort vehicles waited. The Secret Service agents around the vehicles straightened slightly. The president ignored them. "Fine, Catherine. Renew it. What else?"

Catherine held her slate under one arm but didn't need to refer to it. "The Senate is going to bring up the renewal for the California Earthquake Relief Act next week - what are your instructions?"

Linda made a mental note - was it really true that the president didn't yet have a position on the Earthquake Relief Act, this late in the game? Linda had assumed that there was no way the woman could be as much of an idiot as some people said. So: stupidity? Cleverness? Or something -

"Our polls are a bit weak, and we need those electoral votes - let's do the same package as last year, but increase it ... I don't know ... what? Ten percent? Twenty? Let's do twenty."

Twenty percent? Dear God. The president *was* insane - and from the looks exchanged around the semicircle, Linda Haig wasn't the only who thought so. Don cleared his throat. "Ma'am - twenty is a big number. The Fed is already really nervous about inflation, and if we print that much -"

"Don, if Simons squeals, remind him that he has his job because I kicked out Zachary, and I'm not afraid to do it again. Earthquake relief is a huge problem! Does Simons want those people to starve?" She rolled her eyes upward, as if looking for relief from her burdens.

Linda watched as the secret service agents, the Marines and the other staff clustered in a semi-circle stoically pretended not to notice. The president's theatrics had served her well on her vlog, and then on her talk show, but Linda thought the effect was noticeably different in person.

And not better.

Don cleared his throat. "Ma'am, no one is saying that relief isn't important - it's just that it's been six years, and given the state of the budget and the bond markets, at some point we have to start looking at ramping it down. Holding it steady is bad enough, but twenty percent - "

"Don't tell me how to spend my money, Don! Neither you or Simons or anyone else in this city -" she gestured grandly "- has to make the hard decisions I have to make!" The president lowered her arms and grew serious. "This isn't optional - we need those electoral votes."

Don raised one finger. "Yes, I know, but -"

The president jabbed a finger at Don - and then was actually poking him in the chest. "Don, I have made *my decision*. Stop questioning me! I can replace Simons, I can replace Bonner, I can replace anyone in this room - do you understand me?"

Don took a step backward, let the silence stretch, and then lowered his eyes and nodded. "Yes, ma'am."

The president turned from Don to the rest of her entourage. "OK, that's it, people. I need to be on Air Force One ASAP - I've got an important meeting. Is there anything else?"

Sarah spoke up. "Yes, ma'am, we desperately need to talk about the tax reform bill - we're getting pressure -"

The president waved her off contemptuously. "When I get back."

From another arc of the group: "The energy allocation is cutting into manufacturing and the web engine folks are on the verge of rolling brownouts in their data centers, so we - "

"Damn it, Nathan, I've told them before - they're getting more than enough power. They're using enough electricity to power a billion homes -"

"A million."

"Jesus, Nathan! Forget the details and listen to me! They're getting all the electricity they're going to get. There's no more. They should stop whining. Tell them to green-up those data centers. If they can't do their damned jobs we'll appoint some CEOs who can." She looked at the open limousine door. "I'm late for Taos, and the plane is waiting."

She clapped her hands. "Do your jobs, people!" and then turned to Linda. "Senator, would you care to join me?"

Linda nodded. "Thank you."

The two slipped into the vehicle. The door closed behind them and the throaty gasoline engines of the security vehicles rumbled as the convoy pulled out.

The president turned to Linda and suddenly her smile lit up the vehicle. "Linda, I know we're from different sub-parties -"

Where was this going? "Oh, the factions aren't as bad as that."

"I'm happy to hear you say that. I agree, and that's exactly why I want to reach out to you."

Linda smiled back. "I was quite happy to get your message. What can I help you with?"

"High Sprawl."

Linda took a moment to compose a look of confusion. "High Sprawl?"

The president smiled again. This time it was different, but perfect for the situation; it was a smile that seemed to say 'Oh, you playful rogue.' "Linda, I know there are leaks. And I know *who* is leaking and to whom."

Linda felt her eyebrows narrow. Had she been underestimating this woman? "Ma'am -"

She put one hand on Linda's arm. "Call me 'Themba.' Please."

Linda nodded. "Themba." She thought quickly. How much did the president know? And how much of that did the president know that Linda knew? She glanced out the window as the limousine passed the Washington National Park and started to cross the Frederick Douglass Bridge.

Best, perhaps, to play this entirely straight. "Themba, I need to gather more data."

The smile dimmed a notch, but just one. "And how long will that take?"

"Not long; I've got people looking into it."

A pause, and then the smile was back. "Good. Can I offer you a fruit juice?"

Chapter 3

2064: lunar surface, Aristillus, Lunar Nearside

Allan looked up. The next handhold was just a short reach up the wall. He stretched for it - and the suit alarm went off.

Damn it.

He silenced the warble tone, cleared the flashing "overheating" warning from the heads-up display in his helmet, and settled in to wait.

He'd gotten this alarm every day he'd been out climbing the face. The first day he'd ignored it and had gotten *really* uncomfortable. The second day he'd used some instructions he'd found on the net for working around it - he'd ignored the stenciled "never open this panel" warning on the suit backpack, opened the calibration panel, and backed the water flow limiter screw all the way out.

That had helped, but not enough - the cooling underwear in the suit could only do so much, and then you had to stop and let the equipment catch up.

Hanging onto the rock face with one hand and one wedged foot, he turned as far as he could and looked back over his shoulder toward the ground. There, down near all the vehicle tracks and the footpath, the three girls were watching him. Selena - he thought it was Selena; it was the tallest suit - waved. He paused a long moment and then gave a single calculated nod. It telegraphed that he was cool, collected, not begging for her approval, but just accepting it as his due...then he realized that Selena wouldn't be able to see the gesture because of his helmet.

OK, raise one hand in acknowledgement then.

He hadn't closed the deal yet - Selena claimed she had a boyfriend back at Berkeley, but he'd been working her slowly and she'd been warming up. Last night he'd gotten her away from Hugh, Allyson, and Louisa and taken her to a dive bar in the Kenyan section. He'd faux absent-mindedly dropped a few words of Swahili to the barkeeper, Selena had gotten a bit gigglier than her one drink warranted, and she'd leaned in when he told his stories of a strong-yet-vulnerable-guy helping the spiritual, friendly Kenyans string telecom cables during his volunteer year abroad.

He grinned, remembering how he'd played it. The stories were perfect - well, the ones he'd told. The jokes that he and his buddies on the trip had come up with he kept to himself...not to mention some of the stories of their extracurricular activities! God, that thing with Kelton and the three shitfaced NGO nurses was hilarious - but not exactly the kind of tale this maneuver called for.

Allan turned his attention back to the present and checked his display. The suit's temperature level was dropping, but he still had another minute or so until he could resume climbing.

The trick was how to nail Selena without queering his chances with Allyson. He wasn't even that turned on by the shorter girl, but it was clear that Hugh had a thing for her, and he relished the idea of rubbing that conquest in that fat little fuck's face - but gently, gently. Hugh's mom was paying for this whole trip - although that was supposed to be a secret. Why, he had no idea. The whole thing made no sense, given her job. Anyway, the trick was to needle Hugh, but not *too* much -

The suit beeped and Allan looked at the read-out. The temperature was green. Awesome.

He looked over his shoulder again to make sure that the girls were watching. They were. Maybe now was the time for a show-off move he'd been practicing in his head. As he'd climbed, the other crevice to his right had been drifting closer and he was pretty sure that with a single strong leap - especially in the lighter gravity - he could get two meters to the right, grab onto that small horizontal crack, and then swing a foot into the chimney.

And, even if he failed, he was roped in, and wouldn't fall more than a meter or two.

In fact, maybe a calculated slip would be exactly the thing? Pretend to lose his grip, slide down a few meters, and then make a big show of twisting an ankle? He liked that - a twisted ankle, then after the brave "no, no, I'm fine" limp back to the airlock, he'd grudgingly accept a bit of help from Selena. No, wait, Selena under one arm, Allyson under the other.

He grinned.

Yes.

Now!

A leap, the brush of the gloved fingers across the small crack, and then the planned slip. He let his fingers bump over the rock wall as the drastically lower gravity pulled at him, accelerating him only slowly.

Perfect.

Hmm, a bit of a drift to the right. He grabbed at the horizontal crack as it slid into position - and missed.

Missed? Fuck.

OK, the rope would catch him in a few more meters. But, damn it, this wasn't going to look *nearly* as cool as planned.

Allan looked down and noticed an outcropping rushing up at him. Shit. Even in the low g he could break a rib, or -

What if he hit that face-first? If he got a black eye - or worse yet, a broken tooth! - he was going to be seriously pissed. He'd best straighten. He tried. Fingers slipped over rock, then slipped again, and then -

His head snapped forward into the faceplate as he hit the rock face-first and slid off. A moment later a hard jerk as the safety line caught. He hung face down, his eyes closed against the pain. God *damn* it. Right in the helmet. Right in the fucking helmet. Oh, *shit*, his nose hurt. His mouth was full of hot iron. Blood from a broken nose.

Shit. Without thinking he spat, and then remembered he was wearing a helmet. And speaking of his helmet, what was that alarm? And that whistling? He opened his eyes.

The helmet display was dead, and the faceplate was - cracked? He struggled to focus. Were there small pieces of the faceplate missing? What the fuck?

His ears hurt - hurt bad. And the pain was getting worse by the second. He bellowed in pain and frustration. He needed help, damn it! But what was he supposed to do? The suit radio was controlled by the helmet, and the faceplate was cracked, the interface dead. His scream turned into a cough - a thin painful cough. Then a second cough, and he could see the blood spraying from his mouth onto the cracked faceplate.

What the -

Chapter 4

2064: Meggers Crater, Lunar Farside

The sun was low in the sky and Earth had dropped entirely below their horizon weeks ago when they'd crossed to farside.

Aristillus had never felt so far away. Blue felt a shiver of loneliness wash over him.

He looked at Duncan. The younger Dog had shimmied forward on his stomach until his helmet was over the edge of the precipice. As Blue watched Duncan extended one gloved paw forward and tossed a rock over the edge - and immediately the youngster's tail began wagging.

Blue raised a tan-on-gray eyebrow at the youngster's all-too-predictable antics, and then smiled. He was a bit curious despite himself. He stepped carefully to the crater's edge, keeping all four legs on solid ground, and craned his neck to look over.

It took a while for the rock to fall to the bottom in the low gravity. The impact was soundless in the vacuum, of course, but Blue's suit was running the latest rev of Rex's simulation software with the effects turned up high, so the sound in his helmet was borderline operatic: a loud initial percussive slap and then a follow-on cascade of cracks, crashes, and clatters. Blue knew that the sound atoms had been culled from 140 years of television effects and curried together via pseudo-random-number generators and a melange of s-expressions and state machines into a bespoke symphony of sounds customized for this particular time-and-date-stamp. Oh, did Blue know. Rex had gone on about it in mind-numbing detail for several days.

Duncan barked excitedly at the sound of the crash. Blue shook his head. Kids.

Blue looked over his shoulder and saw the rest of the group cresting the rise. John, the only biped in the group, came into view first. Max and Rex in their canine suits took another moment to show over the boulders.

Blue walked carefully backward from the crater lip and then turned. "John, the terrain is a lot steeper than it looked on the imaging."

John looked at the slope. "Sunset is still eighty hours away, but it's been a long day. I'm not up for a route change at this point. I say we pitch the tent, have dinner, and hike on tomorrow. Who's in?"

The vote was unanimous and the discussion about what to rehydrate and cook was in full swing when the six-legged cargo mule ambled over the rise, its blue solar panels and gold foil casting bright reflections in the sunlight.

As soon as the mule stopped and knelt all five of the hikers fell into their long-practiced routine. John and the two younger Dogs unloaded the tent and started the pressurization cycle while Blue and Max helped the mule to stretch the solar shield over the campsite.

A half hour later the air inside the tent was full of the smells of dinner.

On his cushion Rex was bent almost double, using his teeth to work an itch on his flank where his cooling undergarment was rolled up. He finished, pulled the underwear back into place, and launched into a complaint. "This isn't the first time this has happened. John, why don't you make Gamma give us better data?"

Blue wrinkled a lip. Duncan - practical-joke-playing, rock-pushing, happy-go-lucky Duncan - was a goofball, but Rex - he had a different kind of immaturity that was harder to nail down. Was it something in the engineering of second generation? Both Cambridge and Palo Alto had done a lot of tweaks to the genome before the 2Gs were decanted. Or was it just that they were young?

John put his slate down. "Rex, you know as well as I do that I can't force Gamma to do anything."

Rex shrugged. "Well, whatever. Not force, then...but he should listen to you. He's only here because of you."

John opened his mouth to reply, and shut it again. Blue knew what he was thinking, and admired John's restraint.

Rex, though, saw the silence as an opening and kept arguing. "You should explain to Gamma in terms that he can -"

Blue saw the weariness in John's face as he replied, "Rex, I don't -"

Rex steamrollered over him, lecturing.

It had been a long day and John's willingness to banter and entertain criticism wasn't infinite. "Hey, Rex."

Rex continued on, uninterrupted.

"Rex," he said, more forcefully.

Blue was riveted - and he saw that he wasn't the only one paying attention: Duncan and Max were also ignoring their slates, watching. Rex sputtered to a stop and met John's eyes...and then looked down. "Rex, you should know by now - you *do* know by now - that Gamma isn't like us mammals. Do you honestly think I can make it do anything?"

Rex didn't answer.

"And as far as you lecturing me about what I should do? No. I've done enough. For you, for everyone. This hike is my vacation. You're only here because you asked if you could come along. If you want better data, talk to Gamma yourself."

Rex exhaled sullenly. "Gamma only talks to you."

"Then get the data you want some other way. Pick up a coding contract and buy a mini-sat flyby. Or don't. But either way, no more complaining, and no more telling me what I should do." Rex stared glumly at the floor of the tent.

"Agreed?"

The Dog looked up, met John's eyes. "OK, John."

Blue turned to Max and met his eyes. He and the other first gen fought about almost everything: politics, philosophy, the future of the race...but they agreed about John. It was good to see him put Rex in his place. Not surprising - not at all. But good.

The younger generation didn't take the Culling seriously. They'd been too young - they barely remembered the Earth labs or the Dogs that John and his team hadn't gotten out in time. Blue and Max had been 13 when the labs were shut down and the euthanasia had started.

The two of them remembered.

An electronic "ding!" broke the tension. Blue stood. "Dinner!"

Blue stepped to the kitchen unit in the tent wall and started pulling out plates. To his left Rex crowded in, reaching for a napkin.

Blue shook his head. The youngers might not remember, but he did - and he was *never* going to give the man who'd saved his life - who'd saved his whole species - static about not doing enough.

If John wanted to take a vacation from responsibility for a decade, that was fine with him.

Chapter 5

2064: Andrews Air Force Base near Washington DC

General Restivo looked around the conference room. It was nice - nicer than anything he'd seen outside of DC. But then, plush carpet and mahogany conference tables were nothing special here in the city.

He checked the time. How long until -

The door opened and Restivo snapped to his feet. Even before she was fully inside the room the president was already speaking. "Give me updates on the High Sprawl investigation."

"Ma'am, there's not much new since the last briefing. There really doesn't seem to be any sort of top-down power structure -"

The president pursed her lips. "That's bullshit - they can't have that much industry and infrastructure without *someone* in charge."

"We're using Social Gaze -"

The president settled into one of the deep leather chairs along the wall, somehow turning it into a throne. "Social Gaze?"

"It's a program that goes back sixty years or so - DoD created it to unravel Muslim terrorist networks -"

As soon as he'd said the words he saw the warning look in her eyes. Shit. "Sorry. Middle Eastern black market networks. It's a suite of data mining tools shared by the IRS, TSA, DEA, BATFEEIN, NILDON -."

"Data mining?"

How much detail should he give? "Uh - the tools search public databases, but they're also tied into every debit card purchase through FinCEN, every email and phone call through Stellar Wind, every vehicle trip through the carbon tax transponders. We augment that with data from the Caretaker camera network. All of this lets us tease out who the real movers and shakers in a network are, and who they -"

"So what does this have to do with the moon problem?"

"We're using these tools to understand the expats."

She leaned forward. "And what is it that you now understand about them?"

He resisted the urge to lick his lips. "With their black markets outside of FinCEN control and all the rest, we don't have as much raw data as we're accustomed to. We still don't know who's directing the allocation of resources. We also don't know how recruiting works -" He saw impatience gathering on her face and hurried "- but we *are* seeing critical nodes pop up."

The president raised one eyebrow. "Go on."

"The critical nodes will tell us where the choke points are." He paused. "Where the money flows."

The president didn't smile - not remotely - but her features softened, just a bit. "Good. How much money? Tax receipts are down five trillion from last year, and eight trillion from two years ago. How are we going to get our missing tax revenues back from these thieves?"

Restivo was puzzled. "Ma'am?"

"Our tax revenues, general!"

"Uh - I just read the news, but my understanding is that the High Sprawl situation isn't the root cause of the shortfall -"

The president interrupted him. "General, you can't honestly be telling me that their tax evasion and their theft of productive assets has nothing to do with our economic problems?"

Shit. What had he gotten himself into? "No, of course not -"

The president's slate beeped and she checked it, smiled, and then tapped at the screen for a moment. General Restivo was careful to remain silent until she was done - the president's anger at being interrupted when she was chatting with her friends was legendary.

He glanced at his own slate on the table between them, but didn't consider it for a moment - God help him if he wasn't paying attention when she was ready to resume the conversation. He did, though, risk sneaking a look out the window toward the runway. While they'd been talking, Air Force One had taxied to the gate and the jetway was now extending out to it. He caught himself - it wasn't Air Force One until the president was on it; right now it was just an Airbus A505.

At length the president looked up and saw the plane. She stood and leaned toward him, almost but not quite invading his personal space. "So how are you going to patch the budget hole?"

Now he did lick his lips. "I - the only assets we've identified are non-liquid. Tunnels, solar farms - it's all heavy equip -"

"Don't tell me about problems - give me solutions!" The president looked over the door where the privacy seal light glowed green. "We're running short on fuel, we're running short on food, we need to get more aid to California before the election. Make it happen, general!"

He took a breath. There was only one right answer. "Yes ma'am."

She turned and headed to the door. By the time Restivo had picked up his slate and turned, she was gone.

He looked out the window. On the far side of the glass the Airbus' engines spooled up.

Fuel shortage? Not so bad that the president couldn't fly to Taos every other weekend.

After a moment he shook his head. Not his problem; his duty was to serve the country.

Chapter 6

2064: Red Stripe Spacesuit Rental, Aristillus Crater, Lunar Nearside

Eight different models of spacesuits on display stands lined the left wall of the shop, and the automated rack system behind the counter held uncountably more, all helmetless and scuffed with use. The clerk and the store manager stood behind the counter. The clerk swallowed. "I can't tell you how sorry I am. We'll do whatever we can to help -"

Hugh barely heard him - the words seemed to be coming from far down a long tunnel. He wanted the feeling of horror to go away. He wanted someone to tell him that this wasn't real. He wanted someone to say that everything would be all right. But that wasn't going to happen. There was no way to make it better. And this - this *clerk* - was the one who'd caused it.

Hugh heard himself shouting at him, as if someone was speaking for him. "Help? You can't help. He's dead, and it's because of your suit!"

The clerk took a deep breath and spread his hands, a look of apology and shock on his face.

Before the clerk had a chance to say anything Hugh shouted at him again. "He was just climbing a hill, and the faceplate shattered, and he *died*!" Hugh turned from the clerk to the manager and hammered his fist on the counter. "You - you killed him!"

The manager rested a hand on the clerk's shoulder. "Sir, I absolutely agree that the suit failed, but you rented Airtights. Those are light duty suits with strict -"

"Don't try to excuse your defective...bullshit!"

The manager looked down for a second then back at Hugh. "Again, I'm so sorry - but none of our suits are rated for climbing. I looked at the records and I see that Jim offered your party armored suits..and that you declined." He paused, then turned to one of the display models hanging on the wall. "The Airtights you rented don't have faceplate cages, they don't have auto-tourniquets or spinal -"

"Stop explaining to me *how* you screwed up - I don't care! Allan died. How can you not understand that? That's - that's - you should be sued! You should be bankrupt!" Hugh felt his resolve grow and pounded the counter again. "You should be in jail, and someone competent should be put in charge of this business!"

A touch of anger clouded the manager's face, and then disappeared. "Sir, I agree that it's a tragedy - but the records -" He touched at a slate on the counter, spinning it around so that Hugh could see the signed rental contracts and liability agreements.

Hugh shook his head. "What the hell is that? Paperwork? I don't care about paperwork." The manager nodded once and tapped the screen. The rental contracts shrank and were replaced with a video playback window. Surveillance video of the storefront from several days earlier began to play.

>Jim, the clerk, spoke: "Rock climbing? No, I don't think anyone's done that before. These suits are just for light surface work - adjusting solar panels, maintenance, that sort of -"

>Allan nodded. "No one's done it before?" He looked over one shoulder and grinned cockily at Hugh and the three women. "You hear that? I'm gonna be the first."

"If you're going to go rock climbing, you might want to think about the Shields - they're the standard mining model. But, honestly, I really don't recommend them either. If you guys are new in Aristillus you probably want to get some surface experience first. There are some walking tours -"

Allan narrow his eyes in what might be a threatening look. "What do I look like, a pussy?" Suddenly he smiled. "No, I'm just fucking with you, man. We're cool. Just give us five suits. The Airtights." He turned to Selena. "I need to be limber when I climb." He turned to his left. "Hugh?"

Hugh nodded, stepped to the counter and reached for his wallet.

The manager tapped the pause button and the video froze. "I don't know what else -"

Hugh interrupted him. "That's - that's *bullshit*. We didn't know anything about spacesuits. This was *your* fault. This - this isn't over. We're going to sue you. Allan's family is going to sue you. You're not going to treat people like shit again. You people think that just because you're up here on the moon you can cut corners? You think you can put profits before people?" He stared at the manager. "You're going to learn."

The manager waited a moment then nodded resignedly. "I'm sorry to hear that, sir. I - ." He paused, then continued resignedly. "Here's our corporate contact information, and here's our insurance firm - you can talk to them about the lawsuit." He picked up the slate and turned to leave the counter, then turned back. "Again, my condolences for your loss."

Hugh breathed heavily. They'd learn who they were dealing with.

Chapter 7

2064: MaisonNeuve Construction office, Aristillus, Lunar Nearside

Leroy took a sip of gin, held the glass out in front of him and pondered it for a moment, and then threw the whole drink back. It was a shame to treat good liquor that way, but he was feeling on edge and in business you can't afford to let others see uncertainty or lack of control.

He steeled himself and placed the call. As the phone rang, he noted the empty glass on his desk and pushed it back, out of the view of the camera. Leroy put on a light-hearted grin; he had to get his game face on early, given the lag. After the fifth ring the phone picked up and the image appeared on his screen.

"Mr. Fournier - calling for your father?"

"Hi, Janelle. Yes."

A few moments later the image was replaced.

"Father! So good to see you." The usual long pause.

"Leroy...how are you?" The old man didn't smile, but did raise one eyebrow - about the most expressive he ever got with family.

"I'm doing well - how are mother, Addison, Celine, and Martial?"

"I would have thought that you'd have asked them yourself."

Leroy kept the smile on his face as he fought the urge to roll his eyes. The old man made mere pleasantries difficult - and the bastard made the difficult things impossible. He let his eyes flick over to the empty glass. He should have had a second before placing the call.

"Yes, well - schedules." The slightly pointed conversation ground onward, annoying and painful in turns. It followed the typical pattern: the older Fournier wanted to talk about himself, how the partners still cared *so* much about his opinions - even though he was retired, you understand - and how this minister and that one and a third all craved his input on the new infrastructure initiatives and on and on and *on*.

The tedious discussion of the monorail between Quebec City and Montreal served a purpose, though. Finally - *finally* - there was an opening for a transition to the useful portion of the conversation. "Speaking of the infrastructure, father, I think you'd be interested to hear some of the things we've been doing up here."

"Ah, yes, how goes your lark?" Leroy fought to keep the scowl off his face. Lark. As if. He was the largest heavy-mining industrialist in the entire moon. Well, second largest, for the past three years, but first again soon enough. Which father knew perfectly well.

"It goes well - lots of growth, lots of opportunity. There are -"

"I'm glad we're talking about this - I've been meaning to speak to you for a while. Addison has told me - ah - rather, I've heard a few things that concern me. Our government's previously...amused...stance is being reconsidered. There's pressure from the international community. Our southern neighbor, needless to say -"

Leroy interrupted. And why not? By the time his broadcast words reached Earth his father might very well be done with his rambling. "No, that doesn't make any sense. Addison assured me that our government was taking a very hands off-"

His words had apparently reached Earth, for his father was now speaking louder, to drown him out. "No, no, in diplomacy there are never assurances, only guesses and indications - you should know that. The point is, given the current environment, this lunar stunt is perhaps not the smartest thing -"

Leroy's left arm made an involuntary move toward the glass, but he pulled it back and put both hands under the desk, where they were hidden from the camera. He balled and released one fist. He had to let his father prattle on until he finished - which always took far longer than it should.

When he finally wound down Leroy resumed his interrupted point.

"As I was saying, things are going very well here, but one of the bottom-feeding competitors is getting a bit of an upper hand. Cutting margins, using sub-standard Chinese equipment, you can imagine the rest. Which brings me to my point." He straightened ever so slightly and paused for effect.

"I see great opportunities to expand, to increase our leadership here. I need just -" he paused, as if to think. Leroy had found that avoiding an overly serious attitude toward money projected an impression of confidence that investors - foundations and government bureaus - often responded to. " - just forty million to shore up operating accounts, hire a few more consultants, and - of course - rent a few more tunnel boring -"

The old man interrupted him. "No, no, it's impossible. This little venture never made any sense, and it makes even less sense now. There are important people -." The two argued for several minutes. His father finally suggested that Leroy approach Martial at the Desjardins Group.

Ask his younger brother for help?

"Father, no. I don't want to bother him over something so small. I merely saw a possibility for investment and when I thought of the inevitable profits I thought of you and your associates. If it's not to your taste, then fine. Anyway, as you know, I'm very busy - I've got a meeting - people are waiting for me. Give my love to everyone."

Winding the conversation down took almost as long as getting it started in the first place and every minute of it was excruciating. Finally, though, it was done, and the connection broken.

So no funds from father, then. He shook his head. What the hell was he going to do? Leroy brought his hands onto the desk and reached past the camera to pull the glass and the bottle of gin closer. He poured a drink and threw it back. This was the second time today he'd wasted good liquor by consuming it too quickly, but there'd be time to properly savor some later. Now, though, there were problems that needed to be addressed.

Leroy gestured at his monitor. It came alive and displayed the damned spreadsheet - the one he'd been staring at ever since the last newsletter from Davidson Equities Analysis. Leroy looked at the first column and felt his nostrils flare. By raw tunnel count he was falling further and further behind Martin. That damned American and his crappy collection of low-rent, cast-off, jury-rigged Chinese TBMs. He raised the glass to his lips and found it empty. Leroy put the glass down and let his eyes slide to the next two columns. In booked revenue and future contracts he was not only behind Martin but just weeks from falling into third position. Seltzer Excavation? Where the hell had they come from? That firm was nothing.

He breathed out heavily. He'd been the richest man in all of Aristillus and an industrial titan. And now? This? It wasn't fair. Martin used garbage machines, he used garbage people, and the man himself had no refinement or class whatsoever. Everything about him - his education, his dress, his accent, his headquarters - even that embarrassingly tomboyish girlfriend of his - was a joke.

Yet Martin was in the number one position, and Leroy was number two, and slipping. Not to mention that he was too tight on cash. He gestured at the monitor and brought up a different spreadsheet, and then balled one fist. He was *far* too tight on cash.

Damn it. Martin was the cause of this humiliation. That arrogant bastard should pay.

He drummed his fingers on the desk, then suddenly stopped. What if he *could* get Martin to pay? Not metaphorically, but literally? His eyebrows pulled together as he thought.

Leroy gestured at the monitor, calling up the intercom. "Send Silverman to my office."

Backtalk.

He stabbed the intercom button angrily. "Yes, from the mapping group! Do you know another one?"

That stupid girl - every little thing needed to be spelled out. Sometimes he was almost tempted to just place his calls himself, but what sort of man did that? Martin, probably. It would be just like him: a slap-dash man running a slap-dash firm. No sense of dignity at all. Not him, though. He might be temporarily in a slight crunch, but he'd never be déclassé.

Leroy sat and thought for another minute then triggered the intercom again. "And the private investigator - you know the one. White. Call him. Set up an appointment."

He reached for the bottle. This just might work. A humiliation for Martin. A cash influx for him. He took a sip and chuckled slightly to himself. His father wanted to cut him off? Well, necessity is the mother of invention, isn't she? He took a sip. Yes. He could make this work.

Chapter 8

2064: Amtrak Maine to Florida High Speed Rail, Atlanta, Earth

General Restivo sat in the stopped train and fumed. The trip to Florida would've taken just a few hours by plane, but the biodiesel SNAFU in the five year plan meant he was stuck on this damned relic.

He rubbed his hands over the armrest. At least the VIP car had air conditioning and leather seats. He'd decided to stretch his legs earlier by taking a walk to the cafe car, and the AC had been out in half of coach. The un-air-conditioned cars were ovens in the Atlanta sun and half the passengers had stripped to their undershirts.

Suddenly there was a series of small jerks and the train was moving again. Thank God.

As quickly as the jerks had started they stopped. The train coasted and slowed - and then the sun was eclipsed. Restivo looked out his window and saw that they were in the shadow of a vast urban farming tower. The glass in the lower levels was smashed and the steel beams of the unfinished upper floors were ornamented with wind-blown plastic bags.

He shook his head. How perfectly fitting: a broken train parked in the shadow of a broken building. He let the thought run further: a broken train holding a general from a broken military of a broken country. He put the idea out of his head; it was too depressing.

* * *

Two train connections and almost nineteen hours later Restivo sat in a green-painted room so old that it didn't even have wallscreens.

Captain Dewitt sat across the table from him. Restivo looked at the younger man and evaluated him. His haircut was a bit sloppy and his uniform was within regulation but not particularly crisp. A soldier hoping to please the brass - maybe even get a DC posting - knew that starch, collar stiffeners and better-than-issue after-market ribbon bars were all de rigueur.

The younger man seemed at ease with the inspection - in fact, he barely seemed to notice it. He was sitting upright, fingers steepled, looking around the room.

Restivo pursed his lips and nodded. He'd already vetted the captain through channels both formal and informal. Now he had to commit. But here? Careers were made and lost on infighting and leaks; a bugged conference room would be nothing new.

"Captain, in the mood for a short run?"

* * *

They were three miles out of the built-up section of the base, working up a good sweat in the early morning Florida heat.

Restivo prided himself on keeping in shape despite the slack his position afforded him. The old Suggested Physical Standard had gotten easier when it was made unisex, and became a joke when it was modified again for the Alternatively Abled Soldiers, but Restivo still measured himself by the old standards, and exceeded the "male, 40-42" requirements despite being almost twenty years older.

Dewitt easily kept pace alongside, giving the impression that he wasn't running but was just out for a stroll. Restivo thought about pushing harder for a moment and then thought better of it. Not only was Dewitt much younger, but Restivo needed some wind to get his point across.

Restivo looked around the empty section of the base. There was no way to be sure that the utility poles weren't bugged, or that a drone wasn't loitering somewhere overhead with a directional microphone trained on them, but they had to talk somewhere.

"Captain, here's the deal: we don't yet know for sure how things are going to play out, but we might end up having to put boots on the ground somewhere new."

Dewitt shrugged as he ran. "Sounds good, sir."

"Wait 'til I tell you where."

"Rangers lead the way."

"Hoo-ah and all that, but this is different." He paused. "We need you to go to the moon."

Dewitt's even pace stuttered. He ran in silence for a moment before responding. "I suppose I should ask some questions. I've only heard rumors."

"Forget the rumors - most of them are ours. We own most of the IMs, and the wiki editors are willing to see reason. The real version is this: the anti-gravity drive seems to be real and there really is a colony up there."

"So what's the mission, and why?"

"Your portion is covert insertion followed by recon."

"Why?"

"Don't worry about why."

The two man ran on for a moment, and then Dewitt broke the silence. "General, I always worry about the why. People in DC are worrying about the economy, aren't they?"

"Captain, people in DC have been worrying about the economy since before you or I were born. If you want to progress in the Army, cut the speculation."

"Not exactly my strong suit."

General Restivo turned his head and saw the hint of a smile on Dewitt's face. Restivo chuckled. "Yeah. So I hear." He paused. Ah, fuck it. "Yes. It's the economy. DC is buzzing about it. Things are getting worse, and this mission is a chance to pull our asses out of the fire."

Dewitt ran on in silence again as he digested this. Restivo liked that. The captain wasn't worried about impressing him with his speedy responses or strained attempts at cleverness.

"OK, General. Tell me details."

"We haven't finalized the mission yet. At this point we're building capabilities."

"Every one of the 18 Special Operations Groups is fully capable."

Restivo turned to look at him. There wasn't a trace of humor on Dewitt's face, but Restivo was fairly sure the younger man was playing with him.

The General slowed, and then stopped in the shade of a huge palm tree. Dewitt stopped with him and stood on the asphalt of the empty road. "Captain, let's put the bullshit aside. I'm talking to you and not one of the other group leaders because your file shows that you're one of the few soldiers who's *not* playing the career game." Restivo looked around. A platoon was running in formation on a cross road a half kilometer distant, but no one was close enough to overhear them. "I know, just like you know, that most of the units are staffed with political appointees, ticket punchers, cripples, and third raters."

Dewitt furrowed his brow and looked around, mirroring his own earlier scan for bugs, bystanders, and drones. Clearly Dewitt was wondering if this a trap. Which was reasonable. It wouldn't be the first time a mid level officer had been tricked into saying something unacceptable.

"Uh, General - what are you saying?"

"I'm saying that I need *real* troops - bad asses who will get the job done. I need men who can carry packs, lift ammunition, and shoot." Restivo paused and wiped sweat off of his forehead with the back of one hand. "Not to mention troops who can walk without canes. Look, Captain, I'm talking to you because I know you've gotten poor ratings for saying some things like this -"

"Sir, those allegations were -"

"I know, I know. At a private party, off-base, after a few beers, and you were recorded by a sniveling little shit bucking for promotion - which he got. I read the file. And I also noted that the whole case was dropped, for no reason - which is another thing that tells me that you know how to make stuff happen."

Dewitt said nothing.

"I don't give a shit - about *any* of it. The point is, I'm building a real unit and you're leading it."

Captain Dewitt took a deep breath and nodded gravely. "The moon. Well. Fuck me." For the first time since they'd met Dewitt let a smile escape onto his face.

The captain was hooked. Restivo grinned himself - it was pretty exciting. "I need you to staff up a team - whoever you need. Don't talk about it out loud, but none of the usual quota bullshit applies. Make it all men. Or just bull-dyke lesbians. I don't care if it's half Jews, all black, or three quarters good old boys with mouths full of illegal chew. Whoever you need, put it into the IDHRS, and you'll get them. Whatever equipment you need, same deal. Two rules: don't borrow more trouble than you actually need, and this is for real, so make it work."

Dewitt stood silently for a long moment, thinking it all over. Restivo looked at the sky. The sun was getting higher. It was going to be a furnace today.

Finally Dewitt said, "OK, I'm in."

"Of course you're in. Generals don't ask."

Restivo bounced on his toes a few times and launched back into the run. Dewitt was caught flat footed by the sudden start but caught him moments later.

"OK, so what next?"

"We've got a special group at NASA and they need to talk to you about low-G training in the vomit comets, space suits, a bunch of other stuff."

"When?"

"Your old commander already knows you're on special assignment. As soon we get back and you shower you meet with the NASA techs."

Chapter 9

2064: level 6 Morlock Engineering construction tunnel, Aristillus, Lunar Nearside

The echo of Mike's motorcycle's engine pulsed: louder, then softer, as each of the unfinished side tunnels flashed past. The tunnel was dark ahead, and then Mike was past the last ceiling lightpanels and was riding in the gloom. In the distance ahead he could see a puddle of light - the sharp white splash of construction lights closer to the tunnel face.

Then he was in the construction zone, slowing and weaving between parked equipment and pallets of parts. Mike stopped the bike next to a stack of drums of lubricant, set the kickstand, and cut the engine. Ahead the yellow safety rail marked the end of the road deck.

Mike took his helmet off and hung it on a handlebar. Even from here it was clear there was a problem. When a tunnel boring machine was running, the shriek and roar of the cutter-head splintering lunar basalt was deafening. This tunnel was nearly silent. He looked up, and then sniffed. The normal dry grit taste of rock dust was missing. The conveyor belt suspended from the tunnel ceiling was still. Something was well and truly fucked.

Mike swung off the BMW and jogged down the first flight of stairs, one hand brushing the chipped enamel of the railing. He reached the landing and vaulted over the chain, falling two meters to the bare rock of the tunnel floor. Mike stood from his crouch and grabbed headphones and a self-rescue breather from the rack, and then turned and jogged along the mammoth power lines that stretched along the bare rock. Two techs looked up from their slates, saw him, and gave a startled greeting. Mike gave them just a quick nod

Closer to the tail end of the boring machine the signs of a problem multiplied: shouting, pumps alternatively starting and stopping, loud hisses of pneumatics releasing pressure, and a dozen robotic delivery vehicles full of lining blocks queued up with no place to go.

Mike reached the TBM and climbed the stamped steel rungs and brushed past a mining engineer. Another start, then, "Mike? Kelley says -"

Mike ignored him and plunged deeper into the machine. The catwalk meandered as it cut through the TBM, first hugging the right side, then rising to pass over a cluster of actuators, and then dipping again beneath the lining block claw. The machine was built to grind through hard rock 24 hours a day, turning electricity into a constant stream of rubble; human ergonomics was a secondary concern at best.

Mike finally made it to the end of the walkway. Even through his headphones the pumps and cooling equipment were loud.

Kelley, the crew chief, was bent over a monitor. Mike tapped him on one shoulder and shouted, "We broke through?"

Kelley turned. "Yeah!"

"Sand? Gravel?"

Kelley shook his head, and shouted back over the machinery. "Void!"

"Bullshit! Sonar said no cracks -"

Kelley shrugged. "Don't ask me!"

Mike started to yell over the noise, and then reconsidered - the TBM wasn't going to do any more work today anyway. "Shut it down!"

Kelley nodded, turned, and tapped at the screen. Electric motors stopped, hammering sounds from dump valves slowed, pressure tanks hissed as they relieved themselves.

Mike took off his headphones. "There can't he another tunnel here; we registered this cubic."

Kelley shrugged again, happy to hand off the problem to someone with more authority. "Fucked if I know, boss." He pointed at the monitor. "We're snaking a camera in now; you tell me."

Mike nodded and was stepping toward the monitor when his phone buzzed. He'd set it to only allow high-priority calls through. Shit. What *else* was on fire now? He pulled it out and looked at it. Fournier? Calling him? He scowled. What did that douchebag want?

He was about to slip the phone back into his pocket, and then realized it was an opportunity to knock the snob down a peg or two.

He tapped the phone. "Leroy, what the -"

"Please hold for Mr. Fournier."

Mike rolled his eyes. The jackass couldn't even place his own calls.

"Martin, are you there?"

"What do you want, Leroy?"

"Martin, can you hear me?"

"Sorry it's loud - some of us work for a living."

Leroy shouted back. "Martin, I can't hear you, but if you can hear me, it seems like your band of idiots has dug into one of my tunnels. We need to get this resolved. Call me back when you're someplace civilized."

Mike pulled the phone away from his ear and scowled at it, then pocketed it.

Kelley caught his eye. "We've got video from the camera, and-"

"Let me guess - we broke into another tunnel."

"Yeah. How'd you know?"

Mike didn't answer, stewing.

"There can't be one here. Compliance and registry said -"

Mike's right fist balled.

Chapter 10

2064: HKL district, Aristillus, Lunar Nearside

Mike maneuvered his motorcycle out of the construction tunnel, past the orange traffic cones, then rode for a few hundred meters to the nearest ramp stack. He took the ramp up several tiers to level 2, then exited into the tunnel. He slowed his motorcycle and looked around, taking it all in.

The place had changed, a lot. He'd bored these tunnels years before with an old A series machine, and sold this space to some guy with a plan for office space - what was his name? Mike shook his head - he couldn't remember. The tunnel sure wasn't office space now. He'd been vaguely aware that the cubic had been sold, auctioned off, sold again, and subdivided, but he hadn't visited it in years.

The first time he'd seen this space it had been the bare tunnel, freshly bored. The second time it had been a storage yard. And now? It was packed from road deck to ceiling with the newest batch of refugees fresh off the boat from Heilongjiang.

Mike edged his bike forward through the mess of foot traffic, pedal cabs, and idling trucks as he scanned the signs that projected out over the sidewalk.

Where the hell *was* this restaurant? He checked the near side of the tunnel, and then looked left, catching glimpses of awnings and placards between the cargo vehicles and jitneys.

People were packed *tight* here: the tunnel walls were hidden by the clutter of habitation that climbed the curve. House was stacked upon house, apartment atop workshop atop restaurant - a mad pile of 1 TEU cargo containers, glued-together plastic-panel huts, pipes welded together into tessellated frames draped with tarps, and more. Overhead fiber-optic cables, power lines, extension cords, and PVC water pipes crisscrossed the street, as did the occasional pedestrian bridge connecting a second or third floor apartment on one side of the road with a restaurant, poker club, or single-room poultry farm on the other. Cooking smells filled the air and the blare of Nigerian rap, Chinese shouted word, and a dozen other soundtracks fought for his attention.

Mike shook his head. He was glad for the Chinese immigration - the revolution was going to need the manpower - but he definitely preferred his own corners of Aristillus. When it came to noise and excitement, the Conveyor Belt district was about as much as he could handle. He grinned and recalled something Darcy had said to him recently. She was right - he *was* getting old.

Mike saw the restaurant - and a spot in front. He pulled in, climbed off his bike, and swiped his card through the parking meter. He pushed through the dense flow of pedestrians and vendors.

Mike scanned the crowd.

"Hey!"

Mike whirled. Kevin was behind him, standing under a glowing sign of an Asian-style dragon splashing in a river.

"Mike, what did you want to see me about?"

"Let's get food first."

They pushed through the double doors and got into the cafeteria line behind several young laborers and an older man, all speaking Chinese. Mike looked around the place, and raised an eyebrow at Kevin. "Is the food good enough to justify the trip?"

"If it's not, I'll buy lunch."

"You're buying either way."

Kevin shrugged. "OK."

Mike clapped him on the back. "I'm the one asking you for a favor. I'm buying. Don't be a pushover." He took two plates from the end of the steam table and handed one to Kevin.

"That favor - what is it? Why so urgent?"

"A tunnel of mine broke through into a tunnel owned by that douche-bag Leroy. I registered the claim with you months ago, but now his errand-boy Aaronson's registry is showing that he's got an earlier claim." Mike loaded his plate with noodles.

Kevin looked confused. "You're saying, what? That Aaronson and Leroy are conspiring to frame you? That's doesn't make any sense - why would they do that?"

"Because they're assholes."

"Hang on... That doesn't make sense. You know the incentives behind the land registries - even if a registrar can make a quick profit screwing one guy, he'll make a bigger long term profit by being honest." He shook his head. "This story doesn't - "

"Check your logs. I registered that space with you six months ago, and now Aaronson's records show that Fournier registered it with him before that. Either you and I *both* missed the fact that Fournier had already claimed that rock, or they've edited their logs."

Kevin looked doubtful but put his plate down on the edge of the steam table, took out his slate and checked. A moment later his eyebrows went up. "I'll be damned." He looked up from the screen. "Why?"

Mike shrugged. "Money, probably. I had a contract for this tunnel - Veleka Water wants space right below their existing facilities and beneath the docks, so they can drain the seawater from incoming tankers. It turns out that there are rumors that Leroy is talking to Bilge Demir at Veleka, saying that he should break the contract with me and buy the tunnel from him." Mike used tongs to put some pieces of chicken on his plate.

Kevin shook his head. "A conspiracy? No - this has got to be a data problem. If Leroy actually did what you claim, that's - that's insane behavior. By both Leroy and Neil Aaronson. Who's going to do business with

Cartesian once people know that their registry book is for sale to the highest bidder?"

An old Chinese man in front of them reached past Mike to take a pair of chopsticks, looked up, and locked eyes with Mike. He looked puzzled, and then turned away and pulled out his phone.

Mike picked up the tongs and took two dumplings. "Maybe -"

The older man looked up from his phone. "Mike Martin! You Mike Martin!"

Mike looked up and smiled, hoping the expression hid his weariness with the whole ordeal. "Yes. Hi."

The older man laughed excitedly, then said something to his companions, all of whom turned and looked at Mike before pressing close, hands extended. Mike transferred his plate to his left hand and grinned like an idiot as the men took turns jabbering at him in some Chinese dialect and pumping his hand. "Yes, yes. Thank you. Thanks." He flashed an almost panicked look at Kevin.

Kevin put up his hands, "Not my problem."

Mike scowled and went back to shaking hands.

Finally he extricated himself.

"I see you're enjoying the whole Mike Martin celebrity thing as much as always."

Mike grimaced. "Screw you." He put some beef on his almost overflowing plate, judged it for a second and then walked to the cashier.

Kevin walked beside him. "Do you have a reason that Leroy would risk his reputation in defiance of all economic theory?"

"I do, actually."

"Let me guess - the high immigration rate means that a hit to his reputation will be erased by another hundred thous-"

Mike shook his head. "No." He paused and looked Kevin in the eye. "Reputation only matters if the system continues."

Kevin sighed. "Your 'war's a comin' ' rant again?"

"It's not a rant, damn it! I'm the only one who-"

"Mike, I know. I hear you."

"Then why aren't people getting ready? We've only got five years -"

"What do you want them to do? Leadership requires leaders, Mike. Not everything self-organizes. If you want people to get ready you've got to talk to the other CEOs, arrange-"

"I'm no good at political bullshit."

"You're famous here, Mike." Mike scowled but Kevin pushed on. "People would follow-"

"Nothing gets done by committee. If other people won't act, then I'll prepare us for the war single-handedly."

Kevin shook his head sadly. "This is an old topic. Let's get back to today. How are you going to handle Leroy - arbitration?" He put his plate down at the cashier's station and reached for his wallet but Mike held a hand up to stop him.

Mike pulled out his own wallet. "I talked to Lowell Benjamin. He says I'm screwed. Even if Fournier didn't drag it out forever, what happens? I walk in with the registration documents from you, and Fournier walks in with documents from Aaronson - and *his* documents are dated months earlier. Says I should 'pick my battles.'"

Kevin walked to an open table, next to the men from the buffet line. Mike shook his head subtly and pointed to another table. The two sat. "What's the problem with the first table - too close to your fanboys?" Mike rolled his eyes.

A moment later a large black man in a stained jumpsuit sat at the next table. Mike looked at the jumpsuit for a second - and then looked again. Something was weird. The patch said "Bells Piping." Hadn't they shut down? Why was a guy wearing -

Kevin leaned in, tilted his head at the new neighbor, and grinned. "Better hope he doesn't want your autograph too."

"Screw you."

Kevin sat back, still smiling. "So your lawyer tells you to pick your battles. I don't understand why you're paying him to tell you what I could tell you for free...But he's right." He picked up a piece of chicken and popped it in his mouth, and then spoke around it. "So how am I involved in this?"

Mike shook his head. "I don't know. I wanted to talk about how the registries works. It's some crypto thing, right? Maybe we can prove that Cartesian is lying -"

"I use an old cypherpunk system - I digitally sign and datestamp all tunneling registrations and then I publish them. The verification key is public. So anyone can verify the claims I issue. Neil Aaronson doesn't bother with that." He pursed his lips. "I thought my digital verification was going to be a value-add feature, but no one really cares."

"So if Aaronson doesn't sign the registrations -"

"All we've got is his own internal timestamps on his data. He can fake that, and there's no public record. No way to prove that he forged the deed."

"So, let me get this straight. I'm Fournier, you're Aaronson. I come to you and I say 'I want you to backdate *my* claim to before his. And I'll pay you.' What now?"

"So you're asking me to lie? To corrupt the registry logs?"

"Yeah."

Kevin shrugged. "The way the registry is formatted - yeah, there's no reason I can't do that. So I log in, change the date on the cubic for Veleka waterworks, and we're done."

"As easy as that?"

"As easy as that."

Mike exhaled. "Shit"

"So, are you going to follow your lawyer's advice and let it go?"

"No, I've got another plan."

Kevin looked Mike intently. "Please tell me you're not going to do something idiotic."

Chapter 11

2064: Morlock Engineering Office, Aristillus, Lunar Nearside

Wam peered around the wall and saw Mike with his feet up on his desk, a big mug of horchata in one hand and a foil-wrapped quesadilla in the other.

"Not interrupting work on the Veleka Water project, am I?"

Mike scowled. "Fuck, don't remind me. No, Leroy's got that stalled. I've got a meeting with Bao tomorrow about it, but until then, nothing."

"Bao? What's he -"

Mike waved the question away. "What's up?"

Wam rounded the corner and leaned against a wall. "You remember Trang?"

Mike put his quesadilla down, wiped his hand on his pants, and pulled his feet off the desk. "Yeah, sure. Great crew chief. It was a shame to lose him."

"He's in the suit rental business."

Mike nodded. "Yeah, I know. Red Stripe. Why? Some holdup in suit deliveries?"

Wam sighed. "That's not all the business you do with him. Steve in Liability escalated this to me. Apparently at one point you floated Trang a loan - some convertible debt -"

Mike put down his horchata down next to the quesadilla. "Yeah. And?"

"And through a long chain of bullshit and - frankly - what looks to me to be stupid decisions, we ended up putting Red Stripe on our insurance."

Mike sighed. "Let me guess, some idiot in a rented Red Stripe suit lost a hand, and they're demanding a payout - and Trang wants me to ante up."

Wam raised an eyebrow. "Close. Someone in a suit did screw up."

Mike shrugged. "Fuck it. If it's a legitimate claim, let our insurance cover it. And if it's not, bounce it to Benjamin and Associates." He picked his horchata back up and took a long sip.

"It's not that simple."

"Sure, it -"

"Hang on, you want to hear this. The idiot who screwed up was a college kid who wanted to do something really 'extreme', so he went mountain climbing on the surface while his friends watched."

Mike coughed on the beverage. "Mountain climbing? On the surface? That's impossi-"

"Not impossible. Just stupid. So stupid that the idiot is dead now."

"Ahh, crap." Mike put the drink back down. "And since you're not letting me bounce this to Lowell, I'm going to take a wild stab and say that this kid and his friends aren't refugees from one of the Chinese free states, right? They're telegenic young Americans?"

"Worse."

"Worse? How could it worse?"

"The dead one was a prep school trust-fund kid, and both his parents are prominent lawyers in Massachusetts."

Mike theatrically slapped his forehead with the heel of one hand. "Shit."

"And his best friend, who was with him when he was climbing, is Hugh Haig, from Bethesda -"

Mike pulled his palm away from his forehead and straightened, suddenly entirely serious. "Oh, fuck, no. Wam, don't -"

"- from Bethesda, son of -"

"Fuck."

"Senator Linda Haig"

Mike slid down in his chair and covered his eyes. He paused for a long moment, and then bellowed "Fuck! Me!"

Chapter 12

2064: Senator Linda Haig's Office, Tester Senate Building

The office was "DC posh" - impressive enough to convey solidity, seriousness and power to visitors, but without anything that overtly said "wealth" or "privilege." Tone was important.

Jim Allabend watched Senator Haig, who was leaned back in her chair behind her desk, and waited for her to break the silence.

She did.

"Tell me what you think, Jim."

Great. Typical for Linda to make him show his cards first.

Jim steepled his fingers, trying to look thoughtful. Campaigns were his forte, not day-to-day politicking. "My read? The president is going to do it no matter what. So the question *we* have to think about isn't 'is it a good idea?' but 'do we want to be on the bus or not?'"

Senator Haig let a small smile creep onto her face. "Good. But take one step further back. If her plan works, what's the result for us if we're in? And if her plan doesn't work, what's the result for us if we're in? And, of course, the same two questions presuming we're out."

Jim nodded. It looked like Linda had already thought this through, and wanted an audience more than she wanted advice. Fine - he could provide that. "Before I dive in - which is it? Are we in or are we out?"

"We can't stay out - it comes across as rank disloyalty. The sub-parties may come to open blows soon - five years? Ten? But they're not there yet. So if the president is serious about this, we have to back her. Also, I want the assistant floor leadership next year, and she's hinted that she'll back me for that if I help her on this."

"OK, so we're in."

Linda gave him a disappointed look. "Of course we're in - but there's more to it than that. If it goes well, then everyone involved smells like roses. But if it goes poorly, we need to set ourselves up for a graceful exit. Or if not graceful, at least survivable. So the *real* question is how we back the president, but position ourselves so that we come out OK no matter how it goes." She looked at him directly. "How do we do *that*, Jim?"

Jim waited a moment, to make sure the question wasn't rhetorical. Actually, he was pretty sure it was rhetorical in the larger sense - the Senator would disagree with whatever he said...but if she wanted to him to throw out ideas so she could swing at them, so be it.

"The usual: we supported the president, emergency state of the economy, California earthquake, et cetera, et cetera, et cetera...but if it all goes to shit, our line is that we expected better execution. She is, after all, the commander in chief. So you offered her advice and consent, but you were as appalled as anyone when it all went bad."

The senator shook her head. "The most loved woman in America? You're forgetting that people still watch reruns of her old shows. There are *clubs* that get together and watch them, for God's sake. We try to spin it that way, and she spins it right back: she was tricked. She was the only one with skin in the game, and we gave her bad advice."

Jim squinted. "She wouldn't say that - it makes her look weak."

Linda barked a laugh. "Jim, have you even studied the woman? Her confessional episodes were the most watched. The people love her as the victim who picks herself up off the floor for one more go-around."

Jim braced the thumb of his right hand against his cheek and massaged his temple with his first two fingers as he thought, and then caught himself doing it and immediately stopped.

"OK. Right. We - ah -." He paused, out of ideas. Wait. "I've got it. A three-part strategy. First, we lock her into her position with us, so that she can't slip away and leave us hanging. Second, we set up the DoD to hold the bag if it goes bad. That works on two levels, actually - it gives us an out, *and* it lets us do a favor for her: we've prepared her escape route. We already have an umbrella in hand, we hold it over her, and then she owes us."

"That's two points. The third part of your plan?"

Jim grinned. "We make sure that you've got at least as much intel on the expat situation as she does. Maybe even more."

"How?"

Jim thought for a long moment, then sighed. "That I don't know."

"What if I sent my son Hugh there? Or, rather, planted the seed and let him come up with the idea on his own?"

Jim looked at the ceiling and thought, then looked down, locking eyes. "Your son? Interesting idea. You do that and you've got behind-the-scenes intel."

Linda shook her head. "You've met Hugh? No? Well, I wouldn't send Hugh expecting to get intel. No, if I sent Hugh there, it would be for friendly news coverage to prepare the electorate at home. And -"

Jim smiled, catching the idea. "And it gives you another card: you can always reveal it as a sympathy play. 'My own flesh and blood, behind enemy lines.'" He paused to consider it further before rendering judgement. "I like it. I like it a lot. There's just one problem."

"And that is?"

"The president wants to move on this today, tomorrow at the latest. It will take a week, maybe more, to get Hugh there."

"Then it's a good thing I planted the idea in his head four months ago."

Jim narrowed his eyes. Was she telling the truth about that? She looked serious. Dead serious.

If she was, she was playing the political game at least as well as he ran campaigns. Maybe better.

Chapter 13

2064: Lai Docks, Bay Four

Darcy held the railing of the platform as the overhead crane carried it over the empty concrete floor of the dock. The dinged, marked deck of the Wookkiee slid beneath her, and the crane slowed and stopped. After a pause the man basket lowered slowly. Darcy tapped her fingers impatiently on the railing until the platform hit the deck with a muffled thud and the cables above went slack. She unclipped the chain, stepped down onto the deck of the Wookkiee, and then walked to the castle, in through the open door, and onto the bridge.

The lights were already on.

"Waseem! You're here early."

"Oh, hi, Darcy. I started the recalibration run without you."

Darcy was flummoxed for a moment. "Oh - well, then there's nothing for me to do until it's done. How much longer?"

Waseem looked at his screen. "Maybe ten minutes?"

Darcy shrugged, sat down at her console, and surfed to SurfaceMining.ari.

Darcy felt a brief hum run through the ship as the AG drives spun up and spun down. A moment later the hum returned, and again dropped away.

Waseem typed something at his keyboard and leaned back in his chair. "The cal run should take care of itself for a few minutes."

Darcy saw that the disagreement between Fournier and Mike had reached the front page of SMA. Crap. Mike had been stressed recently, and this wasn't going to help.

Waseem craned his neck and looked at Darcy's screen. "Oh, I read that. That story makes no sense. Mike wouldn't try to steal Fournier's space, would he?"

"No."

"So what -"

"I shouldn't speculate."

Waseem took the hint and let the conversation drop. Thank goodness. Waseem was a nice kid, but -

"So how long have you two been dating?"

Darcy tried not to roll her eyes. Maybe if she answered one or two questions he'd let it go. "Ten years."

"Mike must be really cool. I mean, escaping, founding Aristillus, digging all those -"

"Cool?" Darcy suppressed a laugh. "No, Mike's not exactly what you'd call cool."

Waseem looked disappointed. She realized that Mike must be a sort of hero to the poor kid. She took pity on him and opened up a little. "Mike's not cool. He's...effective. That's not quite the right word, but - yeah - let's leave it at effective."

Waseem seemed downcast. "Effective?"

Darcy sighed. "Have you ever met him?"

"No. I just saw the interviews. Well, the one. Why doesn't he give more - "

"Because - as I've been telling you - he's not 'cool.' He doesn't care about promoting himself. He's got hours to tinker with an old bike, or to design a rifle, but he doesn't have thirty seconds to talk about himself." She sighed. "Explaining himself to others - heck, *working* with others - isn't one of his hobbies."

"So you like Mike because he's effective?"

Darcy looked at Waseem quizzically. "No. I like Mike because ... well, because he's a force of nature."

"I know what you mean. I've met a few CEOs back on Earth. Like Steve Bowser, of Transportation Solu-"

Darcy shook his head. "No, Mike is nothing like Steve Bowser."

"But the forcefulness -"

Darcy found herself growing annoyed. "When Bowser was arrested in the CEO Trials he turned state's witness and gave false testimony about other executives. That's how he got his current job. Mike would never do something like that." She paused. "He had the opportunity and he *didn't* do anything like that."

Waseem nodded. "Yeah, I read about that." He paused. "So, would you say that you and Mike -"

Darcy put on a smile - polite, but icy cold. "Waseem, Mike and I really don't like to talk about our personal lives. You understand, don't you?"

Waseem was suddenly embarrassed and backpedaled. "Oh, of course. Sure." He looked down, then back up. "Sorry."

"No harm done." She tried to give him another smile, a little warmer, to take a bit of the sting out of the slap, and then turned back conspicuously to the console. Her browser was still displaying the front page of SurfaceMining.ari - along with the article that had started the whole conversation. She clicked it closed, opened a new tab, and typed in a URL for an Earth news website. There was the normal few seconds of lag, but then the icon kept spinning. The page wasn't loading. She clicked refresh and got the same result.

Hmmm. That was odd. She turned away from her console. "How's that calibration coming?"

"Just tweaking the third-order variables in the PID loop. Maybe three more minutes."

Darcy clicked "reload" on the page, but it again refused to come up.

Chapter 14

2064: Goldwater facility, Aristillus, Lunar Nearside

Darren Hollins, the CEO of Goldwater Mining & Refining, stared at the bookshelf in his office, but he was deep in thought and the spines of the books were a blur.

He swivelled in his chair to face Arnold. "The prospecting satellites are only five years old. Either one going out is possible, but do you really think they'd both go out at the same time? No, there's something else going on."

Arnold opened his mouth to speak but was interrupted when his phone beeped. He looked at it and then turned to Darren. "I sent an email to John about some mineral deposits I want him to look at while he's hiking the Moscow Sea." He paused. "And they bounced."

Darren shrugged. "You're saying that like there's some significance. What's the point?"

"We rent bandwidth from Gamma. If our satellites go out, the email should have been forwarded by Gamma's birds. But it didn't, so we know they're dead too."

Darren took a deep breath. "OK, so it's war, then."

"An invasion this soon?"

"No invasion. Not yet, anyway. I don't have many contacts, but I've got some, and I'd know if there was an invasion planned. But it's starting."

Arnold cocked his head. "So what do we do? Mike Martin has been talking about this for years. I can set up a face-to-"

"Slow - slow. We don't know how this is going to play out, and we don't need to jump into bed with Martin so quickly."

"Why not? If this is the war starting, then he was right all along. We need to talk to him."

"Yeah, he was right - but he's also a loose cannon. Being right about the problem doesn't mean he's also right about the correct response. Some situations are better handled with finesse. Look how he handled the CEO Trials."

Arnold raised an eyebrow. "I wouldn't underestimate him. He built Aristillus. He's a fighter -"

"I'm not underestimating him, Arnold. Not at all. You've met him, right? You know his energy. It's just that being a fighter isn't always the right strategy. This might be a situation that can be resolved via negotiation."

Arnold looked dubious. "That worked in Peru because we had contacts. We knew who to talk to, and we got word before the mine nationalizations happened. Here, we don't even know what's going on, or who to -"

Darren held up a hand. "Solvable problems."

"Solvable how?"

"What do we mine?"

"Gold."

"Indeed. If we need to develop contacts in DC, we've got the means to do that."

Chapter 15

2064: Moscow Sea, Lunar Farside

The walls of the tent arched from the floor and met overhead, the blue rip-stop inner layer divided into hexagons by the heat-pipes.

John balanced the plate in his lap and used a fork to twirl a ball of noodles before spearing a chunk of Cajun chicken.

Blue said "Do you miss the food in Aristillus?"

John swallowed. "I like most of the meal packs in the supply drops." He smiled. "And Duncan is always willing to trade for the other two, right D?"

Duncan looked up from his plate, gave a bark of agreement, and turned back to his food.

"But you humans have more taste buds than we do. Darcy is always talking about the restaurants and the street vendors and -"

"And dabbawala delivery men. And custom dumpling vending bots. Yeah, I know; I've heard her. Darcy's a foodie. Not all of us care that much. Besides, meal packs remind me of being back in the service. The good parts."

Max's ears pricked, his mangled left one only rising to half mast. "Speaking of the army, do you ever -"

John grimaced and changed the subject. "Is this the last of the cajun chicken?"

Blue nodded. "Until the next drop."

Duncan's ears stood at attention at the topic of food. "When is the next drop? "

John tried to remember the exact dates but Blue beat him to it. "The last one was five days ago, so the next is another six from now."

Duncan held his plate up and licked it, and proposed, "Let's get more chicken next time."

John nodded. An easy enough request.

Rex saw an opening in the conversation. "We never settled the question about better data from Gamma."

John sighed. "What is there to settle? He gives us the data he gives us."

"Why doesn't he give us better data?"

"You might as well ask why he gives us any data at all. A secret to happiness is be thankful for what you have, not resentful for what you don't have."

Duncan licked his already clean plate once more and then asked, "So why *does* Gamma give us any data at all?"

John shrugged. "You already know my theory – Gamma is bored and we're one big reality TV show."

"You should ask him."

"I *have* asked him. Gamma doesn't like to talk about himself. He keeps turning it around into -"

John was interrupted by a chime from his suit. That was odd. He swallowed one last spoonful of pasta, chicken, and cream sauce before tossing his plate into the cleaner, walking to the edge of the tent, and bending low under the curving roof. With a practiced maneuver he stuck his arm into the mating hole and reached up inside the suit to snap the com unit out of its recess in the back of his helmet.

John looked at it, and then looked up at the four Dogs. "We've lost contact with Gamma - three overflights, and no email, not one package update - nothing."

Blue looked at him. "What does that mean?"

John shook his head. "I don't know."

Chapter 16

2064: Benue River Restaurant, Aristillus, Lunar Nearside

Mike looked at the menu on the wallscreens over the stainless steel counter. He had no idea what to order. "Bao, you picked Nigerian - what's good?"

"I like the goat meat burrito with a side of dodo. Dodo - that's fried plantains."

"Burrito? Is this a Nigerian place or Mexican?"

"Chiwetel likes Tex Mex, so there are a few funky things on the menu. Trust me, though, you'll like it."

They reached the front of the line. A young smiling black face looked up at them from behind the register. The girl couldn't be more than thirteen, Mike guessed.

Mike ordered first. "Hey there - I'll have the goat burrito and - what was it? 'Dodo' ?"

The girl nodded, then lilted his order back to him. "One goat burrito and one dodo, coming up. You probably want some obe soup with that too, I bet. Ground tomatoes, chicken, onions - spicy, and really good. It's my dad's specialty!"

Mike, amused, looked at her more closely. Above the clean uniform top (with a nametag that announced her as 'Ewoma'), there was a well scrubbed face, a wide smile, and hair that seemed intent on escaping - at least a little - the constraining bun.

"Nice pitch, kid, but I'm not in the mood for soup. Tell you what, though - I'll let you upsell me something to drink."

Ewoma nodded and recited cheerfully, "We've got ten kinds of beer on tap, eight local and two imports, and another twelve kinds of bottles. The menu's up there." She pointed to a wallscreen with a flourish. "All of them are ice cold. Just the thing to wash down a spicy burrito!"

Mike shook his head. "Have iced tea?"

Ewoma, now off script, dropped into a more natural, but still cheerful, tone. "We've got iced strawberry zobo - it's tea, with fruit juice and sugar. I like it."

"OK, great, give me a large zobo." Mike paused and looked at Ewoma more closely. "How old are you?"

Ewoma looked at Bao and got a quick nod. "I'm twelve."

"You're great at your job, but shouldn't you be in school now? It's not even 2pm."

She looked at Bao and again apparently saw whatever it was she was looking for. "I was in school in Nigeria during the Troubles, and then the school and half the town got burned down when the PKs came, so my mom and dad home-schooled me - and they still are."

Mike nodded in acknowledgement. Lots of people in Aristillus had similar stories. "You know, Meade Prep isn't that expensive; even if your folks -"

Ewoma lost her deference and crossed her arms. "My folks said I'd go to Saint Patrick's if I went anywhere, but even that's a waste of time. I can learn all the academic stuff online in the morning and then I can get to work before the lunch rush starts. And here I get to talk to customers, and order inventory - I even helped my dad fix the walk-in when it broke. I don't want to go to school."

Mike mimed rocking back on his heels and held up one hand, as if to ward off an attack, but he was grinning. "Well, holy crap - OK, you win." Mike reached for his wallet but stopped halfway there. "Make sure you come talk to me if you're ever interested in working for a bigger business."

Ewoma uncrossed her arms and smiled. "I like working with my mom and dad...and besides, profits are up 12% since last quarter, and the revenue per square meter is 10% above average for this neighborhood, so why would I want to leave? But even if I do decide to leave some day I'd rather work for myself than a boss."

Mike blinked. "I can respect that." He paused and thought for a moment. "...but take my card anyway." Mike tapped a button on his phone to send her the information.

Ewoma looked down at her phone and her eyes widened. "You're Mike Martin?"

Mike nodded. "Yeah."

"*The* Mike Martin?"

Mike grimaced. "One and only."

"Oh, wow! I can't wait to tell my dad." Ewoma looked down at the register. "Let me clear this - lunch is on the house."

"I appreciate the offer, but I can't accept -"

"No, really, my mom and dad -"

Mike held up a finger. "I do appreciate it. Look, if you really want to give away food, give it to someone else in line. But I'm paying. I insist."

Ewoma narrowed her eyes and stared at him hard, then finally tilted her head in acknowledgement. "Let me shake your hand, though."

Mike looked around and saw that people were staring. Jesus. He sighed, and then leaned over the counter and quickly shook hands before paying and collecting his food from the far end of the counter.

Bao and Mike settled down at a table, surrounded by a sea of dark faces. Bao smiled. "So what do you think of Ewoma?"

"I hope she never decides to go into the tunnel boring business."

Bao laughed. Mike took a bite of his burrito. "You were right about this place - not bad at all." He swallowed and then looked at Bao. "But let me get down to it. Two topics. The first - I've told you about that bullshit with Leroy and the tunnels, right?"

Bao nodded.

"Kevin at Mason Dixon said he'd talked to Aaronson's registry, but the negotiations are going nowhere. Aaronson and Leroy are dicks, and Kevin's a nice guy, so he's getting his ass handed to him. I think we might need a show of force to get Leroy and Aaronson to back down."

"A show of force?" Bao said.

"Yeah, I thought -"

"And more importantly, 'we'? 'We' who?"

"Trusted Security. Your -"

"Mike, Trusted Security is basically mall cops. *Literally* mall cops on some of our contracts. Our work for you - guarding your equipment storage warehouses and breaking up an occasional bar brawl between your roughnecks - is about as deep in the shit as we get. We're not an army."

"Your guys are armed."

"Yeah, technically, but in six years, my guys have never shot anyone. Mike, my guys get promoted based on customer feedback, and they lose their weekly bonuses if they draw their weapons. What do you think that does for corporate culture? Think about the kind of people we hire - and who we fire." He turned up his palms. "If you think I've got a company of light infantry in my back pocket, you couldn't be more wrong. The biggest action we ever had was a Mexican standoff with a Chinese shake-down gang at an herbal medicine shop - and I had four guys quit because of that."

"A Mexican standoff with a Chinese shake-down gang? That should be the punchline to a joke."

"Listen to me. You want us to do a show of force against Aaronson's Cartesian Registry Service? Aaronson is backed by Fournier, and Fournier uses Abacha for security. Abacha. You know their reputation. So we're going to start playing tough guy, and go up against Abacha? Screw that. No way I want to borrow that trouble."

Mike scowled. "If you won't intimidate Fournier and Aaronson, then who will? I've talked to most of the other security firms -"

"Not my problem."

Mike sat back in his chair, frustrated. "OK, look - I know it's not your current business model, but you could open a new division. With the way the tunnels are expanding, and the rate at which refugees are arriving here from Earth, you know that your firm is going to be twice the size by next year."

"I hope so - but that doesn't change the fact that there's no market demand for an infantry company."

Mike pressed his lips together and then played his final trump card. "The Earth governments are going to be up here in a few years - you know that they're not going to let us go without a fight. So we're going to need infantry to fight them off -"

Bao shook his head. "With the economic collapse they're in, they're not going to come up here - they're too busy fighting over the scraps. If you ask me, Aristillus is a service to them: we're an escape valve for the disaffected. They *want* us here, to drain away the partisans from Texas, Alaska, Nigeria -." He paused. "Besides, they don't have the AG drive."

"So you're refusing to staff up a heavy weapons group?"

"Mike, if you want a private army at your beck and call, you're going to have to build it yourself."

Mike stared at him for a long moment. "Maybe I will."

* * *

Mike and Bao bussed their plates and then stepped out of the restaurant and into the tunnel. Out on the sidewalk

Mike looked up at the tidy buildings. "I was in HKL recently."

"HKL? They used to call that Old Office Park, right?"

"Yeah, that's the one." Mike pursed his lips. "Place is a mess now - disorganized and sloppy."

Bao looked around at the tidy storefronts and the clean apartments and shrugged. "Remember what this place looked like four, five years ago? It took some time, but Little Nigeria is nice now - people have been setting up restaurants, learning enough English to fit in, accumulating capital. The Chinese influx only picked up steam with Chairman Peng's Second Heavenly Campaign. Give them time. They'll fit in soon enough."

"No, that wasn't a culture rant - I was talking about the infrastructure. Messy plumbing. They've got extension cords stretched over the road bed. They've got catwalks made out of old scaffolding, for God's sake, and - "

As he mentioned the catwalks, his eyes drifted: up the tunnel wall, above the storefronts, past the second story apartments, at the point where the wall curved back overhead.

Bao said something and Mike nodded absent-mindedly.

The maintenance catwalks up there that gave access to the overhead lights and other infrastructure were the old style - extruded steel decking imported from Earth.

"Mike?"

The new type he was using in the lower tunnels was better - locally produced, for one thing, which made the turnaround time quicker than importing them. Better than the local sourcing was that AriAlu Extrusion catwalks had a nice design tweak to the installation keys. A small tweak, but it cut his labor cost, which meant -

"Mike!"

"Huh? Oh! Sorry." He'd done it again - drifted off into a reverie about infrastructure. Like most kids, he'd been infatuated with big earth-moving equipment - bulldozers, dump trucks, back hoes. Unlike most kids, he'd never grown out of it. One of the few things more fun than thinking about big iron, he'd learned, was operating it. And the only thing better than that was standing behind the scenes, running the show. And to do that - to make a dozen backhoes dance at your command - you needed to line up a strip mall project, find financing, find prospective tenants. Take that, fast forward twenty years, add one political prosecution, one distant friend-of-a-friend physicist, and a few dozen tunnel boring machines -

Suddenly he realized he was doing it again. Back to the present. "Yeah, Bao, you were saying?"

"Over lunch you said that you wanted to talk about two things. You told me about the problem with Leroy. What's the second thing?"

Mike told him about the college kid who'd killed himself mountain climbing, and how Morlock had insured Trang for liability.

"Ouch. That sucks, but what makes it a huge problem?"

"The fact that the dead kid's best friend has pull in DC."

"A *kid* has pull?"

"His mom's a senator. Linda Haig."

"The one with the speeches about getting serious about the 'tax cheaters' who leave the country?"

"The same," Mike said sourly. "She's in the internationalist faction."

Bao shrugged. "They don't have as much pull as -"

"That used to be true. After the California quake and the rollout of her New Economic Recovery Plan, though? She's been stealing influence from the populists."

"So she's got pull?" Bao said. "Are you worried that this could escalate?"

Mike nodded. "That's why I need your advice on how to -"

Bao's phone squealed and Bao held up one finger. "Hang on, I'm getting an emergency message." He looked at the screen.

"Mike... it says here all Gamma's sats have gone dead."

Chapter 17

2064: Moscow Sea, Lunar Farside

Blue sat on his cushion near one wall of the tent and tapped at his slate, trying to figure out what the problem with the satellites was. He'd made a mental bet with himself: Rex had been screwing around, "improving" some part of the protocol stack, and had fubared things. He shook his head. He still remembered the time they'd lost all of their video logs after Rex had installed some optimized database query engine. Although he had to admit that once they'd nailed down the problem, Rex had also been the one who'd fixed it. Blue paged down, checking the commit logs. Still nothing. Maybe the antenna effector controllers? He opened new files.

A meter away from Blue, Rex was sprawled on his back on an aerogel cushion, holding his slate over his head with one paw and poking it with the other. The younger Dog suddenly rolled over. "John, check this out." Blue raised one eyebrow and watched as John put down his slate and walked over.

"Have you found the software problem?"

"No. I'm checking something different." Rex flicked the window off the edge of his slate. It popped up on the wall screen. He narrated as he tapped the controls. "I'm calling up a map of satellite overflights. Now I'm opening the protocol setup. OK, look at com laser settings."

John furrowed his eyebrows. "OK, I'm looking at azimuth and declination settings, and -"

"We know exactly when Gamma's satellites are popping over the horizon...and that shows that we're pointing the laser straight at them."

John nodded and raised a finger as he caught up. A minute passed before he spoke. "OK, yeah, the laser is pointed correctly. We assumed that. So -"

"Now look at the TCP packet logs." He opened another window. "We're sending, but the satellites aren't responding when we ping them. See?" Rex extended one paw to point at a window on the wall screen. A small animated logo of a shark swam back and forth relentlessly on the drag bar, but below that a few lines of inscrutable numbers and text had been highlighted. "There: right IP, right MAC address, right port. Timeouts are correct. Everything's good - except the satellite isn't responding. It's not a software problem. At least, not at our end."

Blue leaned forward. He often found Rex insufferable, but the Dog was in his element now, and worth paying attention to. All of the Dogs were decent coders, but Rex could jump into any system and master it effortlessly. Blue had no idea if this was the first time that Rex had dug into the tent's communication logs, or if he spent his late nights reading obscure code stacks when everyone else was playing games or listening to music.

Neither would have surprised him.

John tilted his head back for a moment, as if he could look through the tent ceiling and the solar shield at the satellites swinging by 90 km overhead, and then turned back to Rex. "We're talking to the satellites - so why aren't they responding?"

Rex shrugged wordlessly.

John thought for a moment, and then raised his voice, including Max, Duncan, and Blue in the conversation. "I need some ideas here."

Blue closed the commit log window on his slate and looked around the tent. Max had his head tilted and his red eyebrows furrowed as he thought about the question. Rex was typing again, and Duncan...Duncan was absorbed in some RPG he was playing on his slate. The sound effects of swords slashing against shields were clear. Blue felt his upper lip rising in a sneer, then shouted at him. "Duncan!"

Duncan swiped a paw across his pad to silence it, then looked up. "What?"

Blue closed his eyes for just a moment.

John repeated his question. Duncan shrugged. "Uh...what's the big deal? Rex was complaining just the other day that Gamma's not giving us good data, so who cares if we don't talk to Gamma for a while?"

John was patient - more patient than Blue would be. "Duncan, all of our communications, including our requests for supply drops, are scheduled via this uplink. Without it we have no way to talk to Aristillus."

Duncan looked at him quizzically, apparently still half lost in his game.

John closed his eyes for a moment. "We've got eleven days of air left, Duncan, and we don't know if we're going to get any more. After that runs out we die."

Duncan's eyebrows went up. "Oh. Oh. Oh...man!"

"Yeah," John said drily.

Rex had been ignoring the conversation as he typed but turned back to it now. "Eleven days of air... we can't hike anywhere useful with that, can we?"

Blue's ears perked up. "Goldwater had an exploratory mine about 700 km away that they abandoned a few years ago."

John shook his head. "I thought of that. We're lucky if we cover 30 km per day. We'd never get there in time."

Rex nodded. "Besides, we don't even know if there are any air scrubbers there, or if we could break in to get them."

Duncan, his attention belatedly engaged, said, "We could talk to Aristillus by radio instead of laser -"

Blue shook his head. "No ionosphere, no propagation."

Duncan looked crestfallen for a moment, and then rallied. "Wait. It's possible that someone else is out on the surface on Farside with us. If there *is* someone around, we might only have to hike to the nearest hill and broadcast."

"Good brainstorming," John said, "but there's rarely anyone out here...and besides, the tallest local point is back the way we came. We'd waste three days getting there, and then when we find that there's no one around, we'd spend another three days getting back here."

Blue finished his sentence. "- and that uses up 6 of our 11 days of air, to no effect."

The tent fell silent for several long moments.

Blue thought, and then spoke again. "This is classic game theory. There was something in World War II: the allies having to decide which bombers to give escorts to -"

Where Duncan spent his time on RPGs and Rex spent his reading source code, Max used all of his free time reading books, almost all of it military history. He interrupted: "No, it was about which path to send destroyers between islands."

"A paper by Oskar Morgenstern ?" Blue asked.

Max should his head. "No, maybe von Neumann -"

Max was another first generation Dog, and Blue's pack mate for just over twenty years. The two fell into their normal clipped debating mode.

"You remember the paper?"

"The gist of it. Can't decide for sure, but play the odds -"

"We split up?"

"No; figure the odds and stochastically -"

"If it were iterated, maybe, but if it's just once -"

The back and forth sped up until the two were half-grunting, half-barking at each other, then both fell silent.

John looked around blankly. "Uh... and?"

Blue turned to him. "We keep hiking. The supply drops might already be there. Or maybe we have a good uplink and it's just a downlink problem. No matter what, hiking on is the most predictable move on our part, and we have to depend on Aristillus predicting our predictions of their predictions, and so on." He paused. "So we act predictably."

John scratched his three-day growth of beard thoughtfully, then nodded. "I'd been thinking the same thing - but with more intuition and less math." He looked around. "Everyone agreed?" They were. "OK, we hike on."

Duncan scratched his flank with one rear leg. "I wish there was some way to look at the satellites."

John shook his head. "They're ninety kilometers up. If we had a telescope -"

Rex interrupted him. "We do."

John swiveled his head. "No we don't. I know what's packed on the mule, and -"

Rex didn't bother hiding the look of scorn for John's merely above-average intelligence. Blue knew that look and didn't like it. Rex should have more respect.

Rex said, "We make one. We spread out several suit cameras on the ground, write some code to do a long exposure, then write some more code to process it as if it's a very large-aperture lens."

John looked almost sucker-punched. "So what you're saying is -"

"Give me an hour and I'll get you high-resolution pictures of the satellites."

Duncan looked up, having finally heard some aspect of the crisis that sounded like as much fun as his video game. "My game is running in offline mode anyway, so there's no time pressure."

Blue looked at him. "And the relevance is?"

"I volunteer to spread out the cameras!"

Blue nodded. "I'll help you."

Someone needed to supervise him.

* * *

Blue sat in the lunar dust and used his gloved forepaws to wiggle the camera, seating it in the loose gravel. He stepped back and verified that it was pointing close to vertical. One down, and one to go.

How far to the next placement? He looked left, at the small blue dome of the tent and the golden tarp over it. The mule was hunched down ten meters away, its solar panels spread wide. If the two of them were aligned north/south, that meant that the next camera placement point was... there. He turned and walked across the featureless gray landscape.

Halfway to the next drop point Blue gave in to temptation and issued the suit command to eavesdrop on Max and Duncan.

Max was saying "- thing your generation doesn't get about the humans is how violent and vicious they are. Your particular problem is that you really don't understand violence. You spend all of your time in video games, and when you kill an NPC it just vanishes, and if you kill another player he just respawns. You need to read more history. Humans are bloody-minded. Just look at the number of wars they've fought - it's insane. Even outside their formal wars, they pick out the weak and they go after them. They're vicious." He paused. "Animals."

"Yeah, sure, but the violence has been going down for centuries. Blue was talking about it the other night, that guy - Pinkman?"

"Pinker."

Blues ears pricked. He'd had no idea that he'd made any impact on Duncan.

Duncan continued. "Anyway, it's not like it was hundreds of years ago. Now humans settle things by laws and courts, and you know, nonviolent resolutions are better than -"

Max interrupted him. "There's no such thing as a nonviolent resolution. There's explicit violence and there's veiled violence. Humans using courts isn't less violent. If anything, it's just evidence that they've learned how to use violence efficiently."

"Huh?"

Blue reached his second location, put the camera down, and adjusted its angle while he kept listening.

Max said, "The humans learned that they can make an example of one person and the rest fall in line. If in one century people kill ten percent of the population, but in the next century the government jails - enslaves - ten percent of the population to keep the rest in line, are you telling me that's any better?

Duncan paused for a moment then said, "Well...isn't it always better if there's less violence?"

"But there's *not* less violence. At least the first system is honest. You know where you stand. The government is trying to kill you. But the second system? It's full of lies. When a government says you're going to get a fair trial - well, look at Mike Martin. At least he was smart enough to see that it was a trap and bribed his way out...but most of those stupid bastards they rounded up believed the promises. Look at them now."

"So what's your point?"

"My point is that you need to realize that the humans are violent - deeply, systematically violent. Their 'peaceful' system is rigged. That's the truth, no matter what Blue says."

Blue felt his canines clack together in anger.

"And what does realizing that accomplish?"

Max growled. "It lets you know that when governments come to kill you, you should fight back and kill some of the apes first. Better to die on your feet than -"

"Max, you're sounding crazy. People can't 'fight back' against their governments. They-"

"I'm not talking about just people."

"So, what? We Dogs should fight? What if we'd done that in the labs? Instead of escaping to the moon, we'd all be dead."

Max grunted. "At least some of them would be dead too."

The two lapsed into silence.

Blue realized that his shoulders were hunched and his ears flat. He willed himself to relax, but the knot was still there. Max scared him sometimes. It wasn't that he was angry - it was that he was consumed by it. Yes, the anger was warranted - but what use was it? At least the Dogs had managed to escape BuSuR and make it to the moon. Why dwell on the past?

Blue's suit beeped. He'd reached his third and final point in the camera grid. He sat and placed his last camera the same way as the other two as he continued to listen.

It seemed Duncan agreed with Blue. "What's the point of getting all upset and angry about something you can't change?"

Max said, "You have to understand your enemy. And humans are the enemies of Dog kind."

"Says who?"

"Do you pay any attention to how humans treat regular dogs in China? Or Africa? And what about our litter-mates and cousins who were killed in Palo Alto and Cambridge?"

Duncan whined a bit and Max reprimanded him. "Don't whine. You've got to face facts. You'd rather sit around and play games than think about the truth. The truth is that humans - and human governments - signed a death warrant for every one of us. Genocide."

"Sure, not everyone made it out -"

"Cut the euphemisms. What does 'made it out' mean? Most of us were killed. Killed. By individual humans, working for the human governments. Don't forget that." Max paused. "OK, that's the last of my cameras. Are your - Duncan, where the hell are you?"

"Huh? I'm right here!"

Blue looked around. Where *was* Duncan anyway? He'd lost sight of him. There he was - back near his first camera location. Blue yelled out. "Duncan! What are you doing back there? Have you placed your cameras?"

"Oh - oh, crap! Sorry, no, just the first one. I got distracted by this cool chunk of basalt with this neat streaking on it - "

Blue growled. "Damn it, Duncan! Do I have to do it for you?"

"No, no, I'll do it!"

Blue shook his head, then lifted one leg over a rock and urinated. The waste went into the suit collection bag and would be recycled later by the tent. The spraying-water sound effect Rex had added was a nice touch. He could acknowledge that now, but the first time he'd peed after Rex's upgrade he'd panicked, thinking his suit had a leak. He shook his head. He had to admit the truth: his entire species was a band of misfits - Max always ranting about genocide and fighting back, Duncan playing RPGs when he should be paying attention, and Rex was hacking anything and everything from cameras to - well - piss bags.

He was interrupted by a beep and an error message in the shared-virtual-overlay in his helmet screen.

```
0x13 runtime: geotag.xr unable to mark piss location
```

Blue blinked, then shook his head. Of course. They'd lost contact with the satellites. And Rex had added another feature to the urine collection code module.

* * *

Blue was climbing out of his suit - he was the last one there except Duncan, who was still cycling in - when Rex yipped excitedly. "I've got images!"

Blue looked at John and the other Dogs clustered around the wall screen.

Rex continued. "I don't have all the libraries I'd like - I had to depend on what was cached in my suit, and I didn't know ahead of time that we'd need good post-processing -"

John nodded. "We get it. Show us."

Rex clicked and typed and images appeared on the wallscreen. They were grainy and parts of the satellites were in shadow.. but there was no missing the key detail.

Each of the satellites was blackened and scarred, solar panels and antennae burned off.

Rex was the first to speak. "It's not a software problem in the birds. That's physical damage. The Earth governments burned the satellites."

Blue nodded. "And we're really cut off from Aristillus."

Duncan whimpered a bit. "Will the cargo dropoff with the air scrubbers still happen?"

Max raised his chin. "Who knows? For that matter, who knows if Aristillus still even exists? For all we know, they nuked it too."

Duncan began panting anxiously. No one spoke.

John broke the long silence. "Well, guys, we're living in interesting times."

Chapter 18

2064: White House, Washington DC, Earth

President Johnson leaned back in her chair and listened to General Bonner's presentation. Parts of it didn't make sense - it seemed that he was saying something about satellites around the *moon*, which clearly wasn't right - but she decided to let the mistake go.

Bonner pointed at the wallscreen, causing it to advance to the next slide. "In answer to the question, no, the BuSuR cap on laser power density doesn't apply to DoD. And even if it did, this program is classified Plato-three, so all reporting requirements except sexual harassment and environmental impact statements are waived. Next question?"

Catherine raised one finger. "Do we have confirmation that the lasers hit the lunar satellites?" Bonner nodded. "We do."

He gestured at the wallscreen and a video started playing: a grainy image of a satellite, gull-winged with solar panels and sprouting dishes and comm lasers, snapped into focus. A moment later the sat grew stunningly bright. Smaller pieces flared before disappearing. Larger sections buckled and blackened. The brightness dimmed. Bonner raised his chin. "We've got video of all fourteen of their satellites burning. Next?"

After a pause Senator Linda Haig spoke. "General, nicely done." She turned her head. "Madam President, I think you've really sent a message to the expats. Thank you."

President Johnson smiled. Linda was gracious - she gave people credit when it was deserved, and Johnson liked that. That was a lesson that a lot of people in Washington could learn.

The American people were great: in the studio audience, out on the street, in the airport, on the campaign trail - they rushed to introduce themselves to her, and their love and their energy were infectious.

This city was a different story. People here thought she was a joke because she hadn't gone to the right fancy boarding school, because she didn't have an Ivy League degree, because she'd made her name in entertainment instead of in internships, think tanks, and NGOs. They were all so smugly superior. Sure, they respected the office, but they didn't respect *her*. The difference was subtle, but it was there. They even thought that because she didn't have their education she wouldn't notice their veiled contempt. What they didn't understand was that her skill - her true skill - wasn't entertainment. It was understanding people. And she understood these uptight blue-blood assholes as well as she understood the American public.

She knew what they thought of her: not only wasn't she from the right schools and families, but she hadn't even been the right kind of entertainer. Not a movie star, not a musician, not a even a credentialed journalist on an A-list webchannel. Just a talk show host watched by divorced women and unemployed men.

She knew their thoughts, and she knew the result: their envy coupled with their contempt made them bitter and vindictive. And that, in turn, lead them to try to sabotage everything she did.

She hated this city.

Linda Haig, though? Despite being in the opposing sub-party, the senator was OK. Better than OK, really, given her stuck up WASPy nature, her pedigree, her family money. She wasn't a true fan, but she was respectful. The working relationship the two of them were building was further proof that her detractors just didn't understand her, didn't know how to work with her.

She looked at Linda Haig. The Senator understood her. No snide looks, no condescension. The Senator realized that all she had to do was give a little respect, a little deference and she could have a friend.

And Themba was more than capable of keeping track of who was her friend and who wasn't. She looked around the Situation Room. Most of these people weren't her friends. Bonner, for example. He at least took the effort to pretend. And if the respect was skin deep? He could get a job done, so she tolerated him - and even let him think that he had her approval.

Bonner called up the final frame of his presentation. "And that's where we are - one hundred percent degradation of enemy assets." Bonner turned and looked at her. As did the rest of the room.

All eyes were on her.

Perfect.

She scanned them, basking in the attention, and then inclined her head a touch toward Bonner and spoke. "General, thank you. I'm sure we'll all rest easier now that those expat spy satellites orbiting over our heads have been shot down."

* * *

Bonner smiled at the president's compliment and didn't allow even the smallest trace of the contempt he felt touch his face. Hadn't he explained to her just four minutes ago that they were com-sats and not spy-sats, that they were orbiting the Moon and not the Earth, and that they'd been burned and not shot down? But he kept his mouth shut. The president was an idiot, but she was a powerful idiot. His career had stalled at brigadier years ago, but then President Johnson - fresh from her talk show springboard into the Senate - had been elected. He'd read her autobiography, like everyone else in Washington, but he did more - he watched videos of her old show and read rumor rags from Hollywood. And he'd learned. He'd learned that Themba didn't want to be contradicted. He'd learned his lessons well, and he'd found his career reinvigorated. Speak when the time was right and shut up when it wasn't. Themba loved an audience, and if you could make her look good in front of one, she was your best friend.

General Restivo, two seats to his left, spoke up. "With all due respect for the job that the Air Force did -"

"Aerospace Force," Bonner corrected him.

"Right, sorry - with all due respect, Madam President, I have to ask - how did this push us closer to our goals?"

The president turned to Restivo, her smile colder and carrying a note of warning. "What?"

Restivo cleared his throat. "What are we trying to accomplish with this?"

Bonner stifled the urge to shake his head. Jesus. Asking the president an embarrassing question like that? If Restivo was one of *his* direct reports, he'd take the two-star behind the woodshed.

The President's smile disappeared. "I think I've already made that clear. The expats have been stealing from our economy for a decade now - looting our factories, our workers. They haven't been paying their taxes! The country is in trouble, and we need that money."

"Yes, but -"

"I'm not done, general! These people need to pay their taxes. And that's not a new law, either - Simons tells me that expats have had to pay income taxes for over a century. These people think they can take advantage of the schools and roads and everything that our society provides, then just leave without paying their fair share? *That*, general, is the point of all of this."

***

General Restivo knew he wasn't good at politics, but even he could tell that this wasn't the time to offer his opinion on the value of the government schools, or say that expats trading hard gold for factory equipment idled by the Long Depression wasn't a real problem.

No. He'd limit himself to his core point.

"I entirely agree, ma'am. These folks are unquestionably acting contrary to national policy." He checked her expression. Had that worked? Yes, the president looked mollified. At least a bit. He hoped.

"My question is whether there's an articulable goal for our actions, and if so, how our use of force advances that goal?"

If the president's attitude had been softened by his first two sentences, the effect didn't last long. After the final sentence she looked like she'd just bitten into a lemon.

"I don't have time for this." She turned to Bonner. "General, explain this to the Colonel."

Colonel, eh? The President could see the two stars on his uniform as clearly as she could see the four on Bonner's. Scuttlebutt around the Pentagon and the National Coordination Center said that she'd been doing her trick of intentionally misstating ranks since she'd been a senator.

Restivo pretended not to notice. He'd already put his foot in it; no need to quibble over a minor insult.

Bonner started the inevitable lecture: "General Restivo, the President has spoken with me at great length, and in great clarity. Her 'clearly articulable goal', as you put it, is that the expats need to be punished, with an eye toward keeping our options open for further policy developments."

Restivo noted that the president liked Bonner's "great clarity" line; her smile was back. He nodded - he'd really hoped that his question could have an impact on this idiocy, but it hadn't worked, and he was smart enough to know when he was beaten. Yes, it'd be satisfying to explain that things like "deterrence" or "disrupting war fighting capability" were actual goals and "punishment" was both vague and unmeasurable. It'd also be satisfying to tell Bonner that his phrase "keeping our options open for further policy developments" was FDA grade-A bullshit.

Satisfaction, though, wasn't something you could take to the bank. Satisfaction didn't come with a pension plan.

No, he'd tried to push the policy debate in a useful direction with a pointed question, and he'd failed. Now came his penance for failure: eating crow. A big nasty bowl of it. He nodded to Bonner. "Thank you, General - I understand now." He tipped his head toward Themba. "Madam President, I apologize for my confusion earlier."

The president's face drifted back toward neutral. Well. Better than nothing.

"A follow-up question, ma'am: I've briefed you on our building EVA infantry capabilities, so that we can carry the fight to the moon if we need to. Our staffing and training is going well, but I haven't heard anything more about our capabilities of getting troops deployed to that theater of operations."

"General, that's well in hand. OK, people, I think that concludes this meeting. General Bonner, please stay - I've got a few more questions."

General Restivo got to his feet, took his slate and left the room.

Chapter 19

2064: Benjamin and Associates Office, Aristillus, Lunar Nearside

Mike pushed through the glass front door of the law office while talking on his phone. "Sounds good, babe. You'll be back when? OK, say hi for me. Yeah, I'm at Lowell's now; gotta go."

He pocketed the phone and looked around. The office had expanded since the last time he was here; business must be good. The young receptionist behind the desk saw him and smiled. "Mr. Martin."

Mike nodded and walked toward her desk; then Lowell stepped out of a conference room with a client. Mike stopped and waited for him to finish. A moment later Lowell shook the client's hand and turned to Mike.

Lowell looked Mike up and down and cracked a slight smile. "I know you're not much for formality, Mike, and that's why it really touches me when you do choose to dress up for the occasion."

Mike looked down and realized he was wearing an old jumpsuit. "Fuck you, Lowell. One of the TBM's had a hydraulics issue -"

"The oil stains are nice, but I particularly like the rip on the elbow. Most clients don't take the time any more - but you? You care."

"I can't believe I pay you to abuse me."

"You don't; you just pay me for legal advice. But, you know, you *should* pay me for the abuse. A slave holding laurels is cheap, but one who can do that *and* whisper advice -"

"What the hell are you talking about?"

Lowell grinned. "Nothing. Shall we head in?" He pointed a thumb to the conference room. Mike followed him in.

They had just sat at the conference room table when the receptionist leaned in the door. "Mr. Martin, can I get you a coffee?"

Mike smiled at her. "Sure, that'd be great. Sugar, no cream."

She turned away, then turned back. "Lowell?"

"Oh, me? I'm allowed coffee too?" He put on a wounded look. "Yes, the usual."

As soon as she left Lowell turned to Mike. "For the last time, stop flirting with my receptionists."

Mike raised his hands. "What the hell did I do?"

"What you always do." He sighed to himself, and then mimicked "Would you like a coffee, Mr. Martin?" in a high feminine voice. "Anyway, screw it. Let's get down to business. So tell me: what's the latest problem you've created that I'm going to save your ass from?"

Mike sighed. "It's a bit of a cluster fuck."

"They all are."

Mike crossed his arms. "Come on; that's not fair -"

Lowell held up his hands placatingly. "No, no - that wasn't intended as an insult. My point is that people only show up here if they've got a problem. So tell me your problem."

Mike leaned forward. "You know Red Stripe?"

"Space suit rental firm?"

Mike nodded. "It turns out that we're carrying them on our insurance, and -"

"Why?"

Mike waved away the question. "Doesn't matter. Anyway, Red Stripe had some tourist die in one of their suits -"

"Whose fault?"

"The kid's. We've got video showing that the clerk warned him against mountain climbing -"

Lowell exploded, "Mountain climbing!?"

"Yeah. The clerk told him not to do it, and told him that if he was going to do it anyway he should get an armored suit. Long story short, the kid didn't listen and killed himself."

"Who's representing the kid, and what are they asking for?"

"An earth-based law firm."

Lowell raised an eyebrow. "Really?"

"Yeah. It's all cloak-and-dagger, because they can't officially talk to us, and they're guilty of money laundering if they actually accept the money they're demanding, but -"

"OK, I get it. And how much are they asking for?"

"Ten million."

Lowell whistled. "That's steep." He thought a moment. "So start the negotiation with 'we don't owe you anything,' and then offer a mill -"

Mike held up a hand. "There's a complication."

"Isn't there always?" Lowell sighed. "OK, hit me."

"The dead guy's best friend - who's also here in Aristillus - is another kid named Hugh Haig. And Hugh Haig's mother is Linda Haig. *Senator* Linda Haig."

Lowell said nothing.

"Did you hear me? I said the kid's -"

Lowell looked up. "Yeah, I heard you."

"So what do you think?"

Lowell rubbed his nose. "Jesus. This is a big deal." He paused. "A big deal. You know that, Mike?"

"Of course I know that. I don't ask your advice for the little stuff."

"Did you already talk to your pal Javier about this?"

Mike shook his head. "Javier's my best friend, but I need your advice on this."

Lowell grimaced. "Great."

"So what do you think I should do?"

Lowell looked up at Mike incredulously. "What do you mean 'What should you do?' You pay. In full. Immediately."

"Fuck that, Lowell! You can't -"

The receptionist walked through the door, carrying two coffees. She placed Mike's carefully in front of him and smiled, and then placed the other in the middle of the table. Mike smiled back at her.

"Thanks."

She nodded. "Jeanine."

"Excuse me?"

"My name's Jeanine."

Mike smiled again. "Got it. Thanks, Jeanine."

She slipped out of the room. Lowell waited a moment and then grumbled, "She all but curtsies for you, and I can't even get my coffee put in front of me. In my own office."

"It's tough, old man, it really is. But let's get back to the issue. Specifically, your crazy idea that I pay the full ten million."

"Crazy? What the hell is crazy about it?"

"Look, I'm not stupid. I realize the political issue here. But ten million? The kid basically killed himself -"

"You recognize the political issue here? Do you? Really?"

"Well, of course -"

"Tell me."

Mike sighed. "Senator Haig can raise a stink, rile up the UN, pull strings at FinCEN, maybe even the Navy. All of which can make it harder for us to move money, get freighters in and out, transfer -"

"Mike, you're missing it. This could trigger the war."

"What? No - the war is five years away."

"Says who? You?"

"Not just me. Ponzie says it will take them that long to figure out the physics behind the AG drive, even if they start today. He keeps up with the literature, and they're not even -"

"Mike, don't underestimate the Earth governments. They could get here sooner than you think."

"Lowell, most people don't even think there's going to be a war. I'm the extremist here. I'm the only one who thinks that it might happen as soon as five years."

"I don't give a crap what 'most people' think. I'm not a lawyer to 'most people' - I'm *your* lawyer. And you're asking me for advice. So listen to it. We have no idea what the various players in DC want, what their capabilities are - and yes, before you even start, shut up about the Long Depression and their incompetence. All of your opinions here are based on speculation. Which is another word for bullshit. You're falling prey to the Overton window here: you think that if everyone else says ten years and you say five years, that five years is as soon as it can be. Says who?" He wiped his forehead. "Let me ask you - is Aristillus ready for a war now?"

"No. Of course not. I've told you a million times that if we hustle we can *maybe* be ready in five years."

"OK, great. From your own mouth. Aristillus isn't ready. Period. End of story. So don't give DC - don't give ANYONE in DC - any more excuses than they already have. I know you don't like to hear it, but there are times to kiss ass in life, and this is one of them. If the kid's lawyer is asking for ten million, make sure Red Stripe pays it. With a smile. Reach into your own pocket if you have to. That's a cheap price to kick the can down the road a few years. We want to get out of this without a war."

"That's wishful thinking. This is going to end in war."

"Maybe so, but if it comes to that, it has to be one we can win. If the war comes early, a lot of people are going to die. Or end up in black prisons for life."

Mike opened his mouth to object, but Lowell cut him off. "This isn't just my advice as a lawyer, this is me asking you as someone who lives here in Aristillus. Think about your friends, Mike. Think about their families."

Mike crossed his arms in front of his chest.

"Mike, did you hear my advice?"

"Yeah, I heard it."

"And?"

"And it pisses me off."

Lowell chuckled. "That's how we both know I'm doing my job."

"I don't like it."

"You don't have to. You've just got to listen to it."

Chapter 20

2064: Moscow Sea, Lunar Farside

John stared at the dusty ground as he put one foot in front of another. Ahead of him the cargo mule walked alone, swaying from side to side with the weight of the collapsed tent and the rapidly dwindling stock of air scrubbers. The Dogs were behind him somewhere. There'd been a little radio chatter earlier in the day, but for the last hour now they'd all been silent, each lost in his own thoughts.

John had been putting on a brave face for the Dogs since the satellites went down. It was a role he was used to - he'd been looking out for them for years, ever since the day that he and the Team had slipped into the Palo Alto facility and smuggled the Dogs out and to the moon.

Every day of the first two years on the moon he'd felt the sword hanging over their heads. Would the politicians feel the need to avenge the humiliation of the Palo Alto raid and somehow hunt him, the Team, and the Dogs down? Would Mike's crazy colony survive? As Aristillus grew his fears retreated, just a bit. Then when the California earthquake hit, as other political crises dominated the newsblogs, and as the Bureau of Sustainable Research turned its investigators to other techcrimes, he'd finally felt like he could breathe again.

Yes, he'd finally felt like he could breathe again, after so long. And that foolish feeling - that letting down of his guard - had led him to first entertain and then actively plan this crazy idea of a backpacking trip around the moon's equator. This ill-thought-out, foolish, doomed trip. John cursed himself again.

All during his career he'd prided himself on thinking through absolutely everything that could go wrong, from helicopter problems to broken radios, from jammed guns to local contacts who might not deliver. By planning for each of these failures, he'd always made sure that he had redundancy, a backup plan, some way to rescue his ass - and his men. He'd always done the best he could to keep his people safe.

But after saving the Dogs, fleeing to the moon, and surviving those first few years in semi-hiding, he'd lost his edge. For this backpacking trip he'd thought through dozens of things that could go wrong. Hundreds. There were spare suits, extra cameras, first aid kits, multiple sources of food, prepaid bank accounts to fund it... but he'd somehow overlooked this possibility.

He'd told the Dogs that Max's idea that Aristillus had been nuked was crazy, and he'd told them that the supplies would land on time, but he didn't fully believe either of those. Yes, maybe Aristillus was OK. Yes, maybe the supplies would land.

...But what if the worst had happened? Even if Aristillus hadn't taken a nuke, what if Earth forces had struck Lai docks? Were there any hoppers left to fly the supplies out here? Or even if there were hoppers, what if in the after-effects of the attack, no one remembered that they were out here?

John breathed deeply - and then immediately thought of the limited supply of air scrubbers. He needed to think about something else. He keyed his mike. "Blue, up for a game of go when we camp tonight?"

A pause, then a flat "OK".

He tried a few more times, but it was clear from the monosyllabic responses that Blue wanted to be alone with his thoughts.

Max was more direct. "Max, listening to any good audio books as you hike?"

"No. I'm too busy thinking about the fact that the Bureau of Sustainable Research finally succeeded in killing us."

John tried Rex and Duncan, but after two more rebuffs he gave up and slipped deeper into his own thoughts. Everyone dies sooner or later. At least he had lived first. He'd seen things - done things - that he could be proud of. This hike, for example - he'd walked on foot through mountains and lunar seas that no human - or Dog - had ever seen. Yes, he'd lived.

He turned the sentence over in his head a few times, seeking some kind of solace. In the end, though, the words just sounded like trite affirmations. The bottom line was that he liked life, and didn't want to die - certainly not in some stupid, pointless way.

The worst part wasn't that at the end he'd be gasping for breath as the CO_2 scrubbers in his suit ran out - it would be watching the Dogs die the same horrible way. And it was his arrogance, his incompetence, and his lack of foresight that had doomed the four Dogs to die alone and choking on the CO_2 in their suits.

Still, there was nothing to be gained by feeling sorry for himself. The Dogs could sense his mood, and it was his duty to set an example. He needed to cheer himself up, if not for his own benefit, then for theirs. Maybe music would help - some last-century Old Rock, with drums and guitars. John scrolled through his suit's archive and had just selected 'random' when Rex interrupted him.

"John?"

"Yeah, Rex, what's up?"

"Do you see that light in the sky?"

John snapped to the present. "What? Where?"

"About fifty degrees over the horizon, off to the left of that ridge."

John scanned the sky. A moment later Rex sent a datagram and John's helmet overlay obligingly drew a box around the region. There. Was that it? Yes. "I see it, Rex." Over the next few seconds the speck grew brighter. It was still kilometers, if not tens of kilometers, up, but with no atmosphere in the way, the small dot was crisp, clear, and starting to take shape.

John swallowed as he tracked it.

As it dropped lower he could make out more detail. It was less than a kilometer up now and the bright flare was clearly a chemical rocket burning hard to kill its horizontal velocity.

A ship. By God, there was a ship.

The song that'd been playing quietly in his helmet suddenly changed character. The quiet acoustic guitar was joined by drums and another guitar. John grinned. Everything was turning around - and even the sound track in his helmet was cooperating.

The ship was coming in for a landing a hundred meters away, down the slope to the left. It was low enough and close enough that John could almost read the logos and ID numbers painted on the side.

The ship fell slower and slower. Now it was just ten meters above the surface and the dust beneath it began to wiggle and shimmy, and then blew away from the landing zone in an invisible airless wind. The invisible wind of the AG drive intensified until there was no more dust and then - when the ship was just a meter above the surface - pebbles and small stones began to roll aside. And then, almost before John realized it, the ship was down. The pilot must have shut the drive off then because the ship settled and its half dozen legs compressed and took its weight.

Then, over the radio:

"John? Is that you? Or did I stumble into some *other* lunatic hiking out here with a bunch of golden retrievers?"

Duncan did his weird yodeling thing, and then said, "I've told you before, Darcy, there's not more than one percent golden in any of us!"

Darcy laughed. "I know, Duncan, I know. I just like hearing you get annoyed. Anyway, who's in the mood for cheese burgers and fresh CO_2 scrubbers?"

Chapter 21

2064: Darcy's ship at Moscow Sea, Lunar Farside

John lifted his helmet off, took a deep breath of the air - cold, fresh - and then hung the helmet on a hook on the airlock wall. A moment later he was out of his suit and hung it alongside.

The inner door of the airlock swung open at his push and John stepped through - and then around the four Dog space suits and matching helmets discarded in a pile on the floor. Normally he'd feel an urge to yell at them to keep their equipment organized, but now he was overwhelmed with the reprieve from death. He was alive - they were all alive!

Beyond the pile of canine suits Rex stretched out to expose the back of his neck, Duncan was rolling on his back, and Darcy was squatting down and using one hand to scratch each of them. Rex and Duncan's squint-eyed looks of bliss contrasted with Blue and Max's expressions of disdain. John chuckled at the difference between the generations.

He turned his attention to Darcy. She wasn't his type, but he had to admit that the crinkling around her eyes and the unbounded joy in her face when she was happy were appealing; Mike had chosen well.

Darcy looked up and saw John. She stood, brushing stray wisps of her ponytail out of her eyes and grinned even more broadly as she flung her arms wide.

John took two large steps and scooped her up in a bear hug, lifting her off her feet. She laughed as she pretended to hammer on John's shoulders. "OK big guy, OK!" John put her down and grinned. "Sorry, Darce. Don't want to make Mike jealous, but the novelty of not dying is still kinda fresh."

Darcy stepped back and, still smiling, brushed at the front of her shirt. John looked at her blouse and saw that he'd tracked in some of the ever-present surface dust. "Oops."

Darcy waved it away. "Speaking of Mike, just the other day I asked him, 'John's birthday is coming - what should we get for the man who's got everything?' I was thinking a nice set of salad forks, but Mike kept arguing for air scrubbers."

John's cheeks were beginning to cramp from his grin.

To his left Duncan, scratching session over, rolled onto his stomach. "On the radio you said you had hamburgers?"

"I do, Duncan," said Darcy.

Duncan's ears had pricked up at the mention of burgers and he started to do his weird whimpering/yipping thing. Max turned to him and growled briefly. Duncan shrunk back and his ears went flat; then he whispered, "Sorry".

John rolled his head, stretching his neck. "I suppose asking for a microbrew to go with it would be crazy?"

"Check the galley."

"You're shitting me." He coughed. "Ah, excuse me."

Darcy inclined her head toward the refrigerator.

Duncan turned to Darcy. "So, Darcy, can we cook up those hamburgers?"

Darcy smiled. "I've just been inside an AG field. How 'bout we let my stomach settle for a bit before we start cooking?"

"Aw."

John reappeared in the galley doorway with a bottle of Mineshaft Ten. "Fifteen minutes isn't going to kill us, Duncan. It's the least we can do, given that Darcy was kind enough to get me air scrubbers for my birthday." He took a sip then smiled at Darcy and raised an eyebrow. "Although I do note that my birthday was actually about six months ago."

"Would you have preferred those salad forks on time, or the scrubbers six months late?"

John tipped the bottle toward her. "A convincing rebuttal."

Darcy gestured to the couch across from her, and John walked across the thick carpet, luxuriating in the feel of the pad and pile even through the socks of his suit liner. He paused and then dug his toes into the rug, closing his eyes and groaning involuntarily.

Darcy prodded him, "What, you don't have carpet in that little tent of yours?"

John opened his eyes, smiled, and sprawled across the couch. Duncan jumped after him, circled once, and then curled between his ankles.

With no response from John, Darcy continued. "Flying is the only way to travel. Walking?" She shook her head. "You've got to carry all your junk on your back or on a mule, and you don't get hamburgers or rugs or -"

John pushed himself up on his elbows. "Darcy, before we slip too deep into chit-chat, the fact that you're here tells me that Aristillus is OK - so what the hell is going on with Gamma's satellites?

Darcy grew serious. "They were burned by an energy weapon a week ago."

"Yeah, we know -"

"You *know* that already? How?"

John explained the synthetic aperture hack with the suit cameras. Darcy was impressed. "It's a shame that you're spending your time out here backpacking - there are a dozen firms back in Aristillus that could use a leader like you. And add in technical chops like that -"

John coughed. "Actually, the image thing was Rex's idea." He paused. "Tell me what you know about Gamma's satellites. We both know it was a beam weapon, but what else have you figured out?"

"We know they were fired from low earth orbit, and we know -"

John tilted his head. "How do you know that?"

"A clever hack Gamma came up with: he used rovers to look for-"

Max's pricked ears - both the intact right one and the slightly mangled left one - swiveled toward Darcy. "Let me guess - he looked for sintered dust where a shot hit a satellite and the beam continued to hit the ground, and he found it?"

Darcy said, "Yes, and -"

"And then if you know where the satellite was at the time, it's just geometry to find where the shot was fired from."

Darcy nodded again. "That's not all. We also think it was a visible light laser, because -"

Max interrupted again. "Because the silica was fused. North of 1600 degrees - but less than - um ... what? ... 2k degrees C?"

John turned to Max. Jesus, the Dog was quick! Scary quick.

They all were.

He wasn't the only one impressed - Darcy whistled. "Exactly! Gamma texted Mike some of the details, and Mike sent out a team to recover a sample and had a selenology lab do some work. I don't remember all the micro geology stuff, something about crystallization patterns during cooling, but the conclusion was that it was near-visible-light lasers."

John leaned forward. "Enough of the technical details - let's talk about the important thing: were there any other attacks? Kinetic weapons? Cyber? Landings?"

Darcy shook her head. "No, none of that."

John raised an eyebrow. "So what was the point?"

Darcy shrugged. "The net is alive with speculation, but no one knows."

John turned up his hands. "The hell? Well, has anyone claimed responsibility? Are there threats or demands?"

Duncan interrupted. "Let's talk about the *really* important thing: hamburgers!"

Darcy smiled. "OK, Duncan, my stomach has settled. There's no reason we can't talk while we cook." She rose and headed to the galley.

John followed her. "So do you know who took out the birds?"

Darcy shook her head. "No. We've been waiting for the other shoe to drop, but there's been nothing. No one knows."

"I know."

Darcy whirled. "Who? How?"

"It was the US."

She raised one eyebrow skeptically, then looked away for a moment as she removed a block of cheese and a container of ground beef from the refrigerator. "What makes you say that?"

"There are only a few countries with a budget big enough to develop and deploy laser weapons - and to keep them hidden in a dark program. More important, though, is the political aspect. Clausewitz said 'War is politics by other means.' Whose political interest is it in to pick a fight with us - and with Gamma?"

Darcy had been forming the beef into patties but turned away from the cutting board and furrowed her brow. "I don't know. What country would want to fight us?"

"No, not what country. Look." He put his empty bottle down on the counter and spread his hands. "Everyone analyzes countries by anthropomorphizing them. 'The US wants this' or 'Russia wants that.' But that's nonsense. The real actors are inside the countries - a

103

political party X wants this or the politician at the head of voting block Y wants that."

Darcy furrowed her brow, then nodded.

"Let's look at the factions inside the NEU government first. None of the parties have anything to gain from an unprovoked attack; they're all fixated on trying to slow down the demographic implosion and keep the Caliphate on the far side of the Bosphoros."

Darcy dropped six patties into the hot pan and spoke over the sizzling. "OK, so it's not the NEU - or, I guess you'd say 'it's not the NEU politicians.' So what about the European military?"

John scoffed. "It's a French 'grand ecole' officer corps grafted onto incompetent African militia dregs at the bottom."

"What does that mean?"

"It means that the enlisted might be disloyal enough to do something without permission, but they're incompetent. And the officers are competent enough but are all loyal to the civilian governments that indoctrinated them. So it can't be any faction in the NEU."

"Hindi states?"

"The civilian government? What motivation do they have?"

"Uh...well, stuff is going to crap in Asia."

"In China and the Middle East, yeah, but India is doing OK. Politically, their focus is containment: keep the refugees from the Pakistan disaster on the far side of the mine fields and keep the chaos in China from spilling over. Two fronts are enough - they've got no reason to want a third."

"Maybe the Indian military -"

John shook his head. "The generals have a mission they can accomplish and the politicians are giving them the budget they ask for. They've got nothing to gain by starting a fight with us. No, it's no one inside either the NEU or Hindi State. It has to be the US."

From behind him Max cleared his throat. John turned. Max had been sitting in the doorway, listening. "John's right. It's the US."

Darcy turned to him. "What's your argument?"

"How can you not see it? It's so obvious."

Darcy flinched.

John sighed. Darcy wasn't used to Max and his rough edges; when the Dog was in the grip of an idea he was likely to bark out "wrong!" or "stupid". Bring in the genes for high IQ and get a touch of Asperger's for free.

John turned to Max. "Tell us what it is that's obvious to you," he said, then added with a bit of steel, "Politely."

Max looked away. Pack instincts - a respect for the dominance hierarchy - ran deep.

"John was saying that we need to look at motives of individuals, not of the nations as a whole, and he's right. But it's not as simple as 'military' vs 'civilian gov.' There are *lots* of factions. The Bureau of Sustainable Research hates AI, and it hates genetic uplift -"

John shook his head. "You're right about motivation, but BuSuR doesn't have the capability to do a laser strike. No - at most, they're one of the interest groups supporting the policy. The DoD probably supports it too - or at least some of the brass does. The war against the tax rebels is going poorly, and it's just a grunts-and-mud fight - it doesn't help them justify their budgets. A laser strike lets them show off some of their toys and argue for more."

Darcy flipped the burgers. "So the DoD and BuSuR are behind this?"

John shrugged. "They're backers, I'd bet. Among others. IRS, BATFEEIN, and the FBI are all being humiliated by the rebels. So are the pseudo-intellectuals in the Georgetown cocktail circuit, the people in the fusion centers who can't pin down the leaders... The list of groups who'd support this goes on and on."

John noted that Blue and Rex had crowded into the doorway to listen to him.

Max tilted his head. "They'd support it - but who initiated it?"

Darcy took the pan off the stove. "But why? Isn't an attack like this pointless?"

John smiled wryly and answered them both. "It's *because* of the utter ineffectiveness that I'd bet my left nut that this came from DC."

Duncan sniffed deeply. "Are the burgers ready?"

Max growled at Duncan to silence him, and then turned to Darcy. "So the US government has attacked Gamma. What are all of you back at Aristillus going to do about it?"

Chapter 22

2064: Trentham Court Apartments, Aristillus, Lunar Nearside

Hugh sat in the rented bedroom and listened to his mom. The lecture went on. And on. And on.

He shook his head once, and then stopped. That was the kind of "impotent body language" she'd lecture him about if she noticed it. He leaned forward - that was "active body language" - and waited for her to finish. Finally she did.

"Mother, it's not fair. Their negligence killed Alan. Killed him! And now they want to buy us. That's blood money, and I won't sell a friend for -"

"Oh, Hugh. 'Blood money.' Please. Stop being melodramatic. I know he was your friend, but Allan was doing one of his frat boy stunts, and he screwed up. His death is tragic, but we have to move on -"

"You can't just say 'it's tragic and we have to move on.' This isn't just bridge where we lose one hand and -"

"Yes, we *can* say that, and yes, we *can* move on. Now listen to me, Hugh. Listen carefully. I've contacted Alan's family and I've told them in no uncertain terms to accept the settlement and then let the issue drop. Now I'm telling you - play around up there, do your investigative journalism, but the Allan issue is over. I don't want to hear you or your friends making hay about this. Do you understand me?"

Hugh started to pout before he caught himself - body language. Why was mother being so - ah.

"There's something going on, isn't there?"

"I'm serious, Hugh."

"Mother, you can tell me - is there some plan? There must be, because otherwise you'd be all over this example of lack of regula-"

"Why I do things is my own business. Now, Hugh, do I have your word that you're going to let this issue drop? That you're going to leave Alan's family alone and not bother them about this?"

Hugh sighed.

"Yes, ma'am."

A few minutes later the conversation was over and he killed the connection.

She wouldn't answer his question...which was an answer in its own right. Something was going on. But what?

He needed to talk to Selena, Allyson, and Louisa. Especially Louisa - she'd have some thoughts about this.

Chapter 23

2064: Darcy's ship at Moscow Sea, Lunar Farside

Darcy was insistent. "John, you and the Dogs should cancel this trip and come back to Aristillus where it's safe."

"If I wanted safe, I'd be sitting in a rent-stabilized apartment in Denver cashing my MGI checks."

Darcy sighed. "There's having an adventure and then there's being stupid. That war Mike's been talking about for years - it's coming, John. Get back inside."

Max lifted his orange-and-white furred head off a pillow and blinked. "War? Good."

Darcy recoiled. "Good?"

Blue, who'd also appeared all but asleep lifted his head and swung his ears toward Max.

"Yes, good. BuSuR killed off most of our species. The groundhogs deserve to get what's coming to them."

Darcy caught John's eyes and silently mouthed, "Groundhogs?" John raised his eyebrows and shrugged.

"And I'm not just talking about Sustainable Research. Where do they get their funding? Who tells them what to do? The politicians. But they're just figureheads - the real problem is the entire edifice of the democracy that supports them! The first thing we need -"

John cut him off. "You're proposing that a few hundred thousand humans and a couple hundred Dogs should start a war against 9 billion people?"

Max set his jaw. "I'm not saying we should start a war. We don't have to - they've already started it. I'm saying that now is the time for us to strike back."

John couldn't believe what he was hearing. "Strike back? How the hell are we supposed to strike back?"

"We can drop tankers full of explosives on their cities, or engineer a strain of anthrax, or -"

Darcy exploded. "Jesus, Max!"

John sighed. "We've been over this before. We don't want a war."

"Yes, we -"

"No, listen. Right now they've thrown an impotent little tantrum. Our best bet is to hope that they've worn themselves out - that the DoD has justified its budget and the politicians have all patted themselves on the back. Aristillus should prepare for further laser attacks, sure - harden the surface infrastructure, build replacement solar plants and keep them in storage. But we do *not* want to escalate this into a full fledged war."

"All they can do is shoot lasers; we're the ones who have the AG drive. They're weak, and their underbelly -"

"Max, they're not nearly as weak as you think. Earth governments reached the moon almost a century ago; they can do it again now if they set their minds -"

Max scoffed, "How much mass can they land here? A few lunar landers carrying three men each? What're they going to put in there?"

"How about a few fusion nukes? Remember just yesterday when we thought that Aristillus might have been destroyed?"

Max fell silent but his eyes still burned.

John continued, more gently. "We don't want a fight. We avoid it if we can, and if one starts, we try our damnedest to negotiate our way out of it. Max, you've never walked around in a city. Heck - you guys have been cooped up in the Den since you got to Aristillus. You don't have a deep-in-your-bones feel for how big Earth is. Nine billion people." He turned to look at all the Dogs. "Think about that. If the governments tax each citizen just a single blue-back per day, that's nine billion dollars. *Per day.* Think about the R&D they can do with that. How long do you think the AG drive will stay a secret against that kind of budget? A week later they got sixty-three billion dollars. What sort of invasion force can they build with that?"

He shook his head somberly. "No. War isn't the answer. We just want to sit up here, nice and quiet, ignore them, and hope they ignore us. You think losing half the Dogs was bad? If you pick a war with Earth, you're going to see Aristillus wiped from the map, and then your species is going to be gone. Extinct. Forever." He paused. "We need to crouch down, be quiet, and wait for Earth to grow bored with us."

Max sneered. "You used to be a warrior."

John's jaw clenched. Damn it. After all he'd done for the Dogs, to have Max question him like this?

Darcy said, "Max, that's not fair. You know as -"

John cut her off. "Max, I know who I am and I know what I've done. I don't need your approval. If you don't want my leadership, leave."

"I-"

"No, I'm serious. No one's forcing you to stay here. Go back to Aristillus with Darcy, get her to introduce you to Mike, and try to start your war."

Max met John's gaze and held it. Then, after a moment, he looked away.

Blue looked back and forth between John and Max. Finally he lay down on his cushion and closed his eyes...but his ears remained erect and alert.

This situation was bad. Very bad. The Earth governments were attacking lunar satellites, and there was no reason to think they'd stop there. John was engaging in wishful thinking. Blue couldn't blame him: after all he'd been through, of course the man wanted a quiet retirement. But now the Dogs had divided leadership. Max saw the war coming but was deep in an insane bloodlust...and John, the human, the adult, the only voice of sanity, seemed to be asleep.

Blue breathed out heavily. He tried to will himself to sleep, but it wouldn't come.

Chapter 24

2064: Darcy's ship at Moscow Sea, Lunar Farside

John's suit pinged; they'd reached the proper radius. He turned and looked back at Darcy's hopper, so small it was almost lost in the vast lunar landscape.

As he watched the ship trembled, and then lifted. For the first few seconds it rose slowly, but the acceleration compounded and soon John was tilting his head back to track it as it rose against the blackness. Then it flared brightly as the old-fashioned chemical rockets kicked in, tipping it and pushing it toward the horizon...and then it was a dot, a pinprick...and then it was gone.

John blinked. The ship had disappeared in barely more time than it took him to snap his fingers, and it made the whole episode of Darcy resupplying them feel like a dream. The ship was gone now, and so was Darcy. The only proof that she'd even been there was the bare patch of rock where she'd landed, the new load of supplies atop their old mule, and the three new mules standing alongside it.

He turned his attention east. It was in his head, surely, but the black, white, and gray lunar ridges and craters seemed emptier and lonelier than they had a few weeks ago. He'd resisted Rex's aggressively enthusiastic suggestions that he should try the augmented reality filters. Now, though, with a cold dread hanging over him, he decided to give them a shot. He needed something to warm the cold landscape.

He cycled through the overlays. African desert - no. Snow-covered Swiss peaks...no. After a dozen more he finally settled on one: leafy hardwood trees with canopies of green lightly dappled with touches of red, orange and yellow. It was labelled "Pacific Northwest" but it looked more like Maine or Vermont. Whatever - he could almost feel the first touch of fall in the air.

"What overlay are you on?" Blue asked.

John started - had he been talking out loud, or were filter choices shared in the local dataspace?

"It's called 'Pacific Northwest,' but I think it's New England."

"Let me try it." A moment later Blue sniffed, slightly dismissively. "Eh. Looks like all the other forest overlays."

"How can you say that? The fall colors - ah."

"Maybe we'll be able to engineer trichromatic photoreceptors for the next generation."

John chuckled, then stopped. "Wait - you're serious?"

"Sure. Why not?"

He didn't have an answer to that.

A moment later Blue added "- but if we had the funds to do that, we'd concentrate on life extension first."

John winced. The lifespan issue had haunted all of them since they'd started digging through the genomic records looted from the labs. But what could they do? Genetic engineering research was expensive. Hugely so: that was one of the reasons - or, at least, justifications - that BuSuR had used to shut down the program.

John turned Blue's comment about lifespan over in his mind as he walked, and his melancholy mood grew deeper. It was so unfair - the Dogs had been hacked to be as intelligent as humans. More intelligent, really. They were fully conscious beings, and yet they were doomed to short lives. And what constrained, tightly controlled lives. They'd spent their first years inside the lab, and even after John and the team liberated them, they'd exchanged one small facility for another. This trip, to "see the vastness of the natural world," as they'd said in the planning stages, was supposed to get them out of the tunnels. But what were they really doing out here? Was he really making the days of the Dogs' limited lives count?

He looked off to the south east, away from their intended path, and toyed with the idea he'd been playing with for the last hour yet again.

- and then realized that he'd already made a decision. It was a crazy thought, but if the Dogs each had only another ten years, he should make every day count.

"Guys, I'm thinking of a change of course."

Blue, always the prudent one, responded first. "I don't think it's wise - with the communications problems -"

"Darcy says Gamma's going to have sats back up in few more days, and with the extra mules we've got over a month's worth of supplies. As soon as we've got coms we'll call in and change the location of the next drop."

Duncan asked, "What change of course?"

"I'm thinking that we head a bit further south."

"Why?"

John grinned. "I'm getting bored out here looking at just rock and dust. I thought we might like to see something a bit more interesting."

Chapter 25

2064: Cartesian Registry Service office, Aristillus, Lunar Nearside

Kevin stood in the outer office as the front desk girl pushed a button and announced him. He shook his head. A secretary? An intercom?

A moment later she led him into to the inner office. Neil Aaronson sat behind his desk. Kevin approached and stuck out his hand. "Thanks for seeing me."

Aaronson looked at him without interest and then leaned forward to shake. "I have twenty minutes free. What can I do for you?"

"I want to get to the bottom of this mess with Leroy and Mike."

"Those two hate each other, but I don't see what I've got to do with it."

Kevin blinked. "Uh...I think you and I are pretty central to this current mess."

Neil looked at Kevin blandly. Kevin paused. He didn't believe for a minute that Aaronson didn't know the whole story already, and yet he was trying to play ignorant.

Kevin licked his lips. "Look, Mike registered an 'Intent To Tunnel' with me a few months back. Our logs show that we checked with your database, and our logs show that your servers agreed that the cubic was unclaimed. And now Leroy is mining the same location."

"So you allocated cubic to Mike that I'd already signed over to Leroy?"

Kevin pursed his lips. He'd reviewed the logs - and the snapshotted, digitally signed backup copies of the logs - and they were clear: the rock Mike was tunneling through had been unclaimed when Kevin signed it over to him. Both men knew this. So what game was Aaronson playing?

This was theater - but for whose benefit? Kevin's eyes flicked about the room. Was it bugged? Was this some setup where Neil was trying to get Kevin to say something that could be twisted against him? Or was it simpler than that? Were Aaronson and Leroy just trying to shake Mike down to get some payoff?

That was an odd and unwelcome thought. The vast majority of competition in Aristillus was friendly - or, at the very least, civil. It wasn't like back home, where bribing government procurement offices and putting moles inside other firms competing for the same winner-take-all contracts were the norm.

There was no way to know - and Neil's question was still hanging in the air. Choosing his words carefully Kevin spoke: "No. Mike has a registration on that space, signed and issued by my firm. Leroy's registration -"

"Why would you issue a registration on space that I'd already allocated to MaisonNeuve?"

Kevin started to lose his cool. "Neil, listen to me - you and I both know what happened here -"

Neil smiled slightly. "I can't be sure, but it looks like what happened is that you issued a registration without checking with my systems."

"Damn it, Neil, we checked! I've got logs-"

"I've got logs too, and my logs show that we issued a registration to Leroy months before you issued yours to Mike." Neil folded his hands on his desk and leaned back. He shook his head sadly. "It looks like you and Mike have gotten yourselves into a big mess. I just feel sorry for Demir over at Veleka. That poor guy's screwed because Mike can't deliver the space he promised." He raised his eyebrows. "Because you've got buggy data. And now you've got an expensive problem. A very expensive problem."

Kevin struggled not to lose his cool. A 'very expensive problem'? So it *was* a shakedown. On the other hand, even though it was an act of theft, this at least meant that there was a solution on the table. He breathed out. So. On with it. "OK, fine. Let's say - theoretically - that there's a bug in the data - how could two reasonable people resolve this? Theoretically?"

Aarsonson smiled, uncrossed his arms, and leaned forward. "If there was a bug in your data and you wanted my help - well, I'm not sure there's much I could do. Of course I'd be happy to reconcile our two databases - but there are third parties who depend on my data."

"Third parties, huh? So I don't only have to pay you off, I have to pay off Fournier?"

Aarsonson turned his palms up with put a surprised look on his face. "Pay off? I'm not sure what you're talking about."

The silence dragged on for a long moment before Aarsonson continued, "But if you wanted my help resolving this issue, I could probably get the as-yet-untunneled cubic back from Mr. Fournier and sell it you and Mike for, let's say, one million grams. ...And I suspect that MaisonNeuve Construction would sell Mike the space that they've already tunneled for another three -"

Kevin's eyes bugged and he sputtered, "Four million? You must be joking!"

Aarsonson shrugged and leaned back again.

The two stared at each other for a long moment.

Kevin broke the silence. "Before we can even talk about a one-time resolution, we can never have a problem like this again. This - issue - proves the system isn't working. We need some third party system to sign and publish all the registrations."

Aaronson looked surprised. Surprised? Had this bully actually been thinking he and Fournier might get away with running the same shakedown more than once? After a moment Aaronson shrugged. "OK, fine. Have your tech guys talk to mine. But that's not going to be cheap. Let's change that number from four to five."

"Bullshit. Two, and the new system is in place within two weeks."

"Three."

"No, two."

"Three."

"Come on, Aaronson, meet me in the middle."

"What's the middle?"

"Two point five."

"OK, tell you what - halfway from there to three. Two point seven five."

Kevin realized that he should probably sleep on this. This was a huge amount of money - probably more than the paper profits the firm had ever generated. He'd have to borrow heavily to make this happen - but he wanted this Aaronson annoyance out of his life, and he wanted Mike to stop bothering him about the issue.

He nodded. "OK, we've got a deal of two point seven five...and we have that new logging system up and running by the end of the week."

Aaronson shrugged. "I've got your offer of 2.75. I'll talk to Fournier and see what he thinks." He smiled coolly.

Kevin could feel his right eye twitching as he turned and left.

Chapter 26

2064: Morlock Engineering office, Aristillus, Lunar Nearside

Mike leaned back in his chair, put his boots on the steel plank desk and tipped the wireframe model of the D-series TBM forward and back on his slate.

The D-series was sweet. It had a 40 meter diameter - double that of the current top-of-the-line C-series machines. Of course, the huge cross section came with a staggering cost. Not to mention that sourcing the parts locally would mean even more money: investing in joint partnerships with vendors, paying to get them to tool up to build the thing.

It'd take some work to raise the capital, but then, oh, the ROI! Not to mention the vast tunnels he'd bore. The overhead disneys and atmospherics in Aristillus were good now, but with tunnels 40 meters across -

His phone rang. He glanced at it - Fournier. Mike let it ring and then go to voicemail as he zoomed in on the cutter head of the mining machine. Twice the diameter meant four times the cross section, and that meant the machine was going to take four times as many cutting teeth, which meant -

His phone rang again. It was Fournier. Again.

Mike answered, annoyed. "What? No, Leroy, I'm not coming to your office. Kevin passed along Aaronson's blackmail attempt, and I've got three words: Go. Fuck. Yourself. You're not getting a penny from either one of us."

Leroy's tone might sound civilized and cool to someone who didn't know him, but to Mike every syllable telegraphed smarm and deception. "Mike, Mike - blackmail? Let's back up. If that's what you've heard then clearly there's been a misunderstanding between Kevin and Neil. Look, I know you don't like me very much, but let's settle this like adults. There's a lot at stake - Veleka Water can't get into that tunnel until we settle our diff -"

"You think I'm going to pay you to make this right? Screw it. I'll eat ten million in losses before I pay you a penny - *and* I'll make sure that Veleka and everyone else knows that you caused this problem."

There was a long pause from the other end of the line, then Leroy continued. The smarminess was gone and the son of a bitch actually sounded a bit conciliatory. "Mike, I'm not asking you to pay anything. Mistakes were made, we can work it out. Maybe some of the problem was my fault -"

"Some?"

"Mike, I can eat crow. But meet me halfway. I'm going to be in my office from four 'til five, and I'd like you to swing by. It'll be worth your while."

Mike grunted noncommittally and hung up. He picked his slate up and zoomed in on the arms that placed prefab tunnel wall segments in position... but he couldn't get Fournier out of his head.

Was it possible that the guy was actually being reasonable?

Screw him. Fournier'd been insufferable from the moment he stepped off the boat with nothing but the clothes on his back, a huge trust fund, and four brand new German-made TBMs.

And oh, the arrogance. For the first year or more it seemed that Fournier couldn't let a conversation with anyone go by without reminding them he was richer than Mike, the man who'd started the colony. How could anyone tolerate him? Yet they did.

It had taken three years, but how sweet it had been when Mike pulled back ahead of Fournier in the annual Davidson Equities Analysis rankings.

Mike looked at the slate and realized that he'd been tilting the same image back and forth for several minutes. Damn it. He was obsessing about Leroy and not paying attention to the cutter-teeth of the D-series. Crap - he'd let the asshole inside his head.

Mike scowled and tried to push the situation out of his mind. On the slate the TBM wall segment arms stared back at him. A moment ago he'd been entranced by them and now the CAD model swum in his vision. He paged angrily to another diagram and zoomed in on the digging shield and the hydraulic rams. He scrolled it back and forth, unable to make anything of it.

He couldn't regain his concentration. Damn it.

Mike was more than willing to tell Fournier to go fuck himself. He'd take a huge financial penalty when he couldn't deliver the tunnel to Veleka Waterworks, but Fournier'd be fucked too: a half dug tunnel was of no use to anyone.

He contemplated the idea for a minute.

A big middle finger to Fournier would be satisfying, but he couldn't afford the penalties right now - he needed that cash to get the D-series built.

Fuck.

Mike pulled his boots off the desk, stood up, and swapped his slate for his phone. His finger hung over the screen indecisively. He absolutely refused to pay the blackmail that Neil had told him about...but Fournier had pooh-poohed the idea earlier. Was it possible that Neil had misunderstood? Was Fournier really willing to settle this like adults?

He wouldn't count on it, but maybe there was a chance. And with all the other shit going on - Earth attacking the satellites, the ominous rumblings and pointed leaks from DC - resolving just this one thing would help.

Chapter 27

2064: May Bug Coffee House, Aristillus, Lunar Nearside

Mike mopped up his maple syrup with the last chunk of his French toast. Damn, it was good. What was the secret? When he tried to cook French toast it ended tasting like bread in a thin layer of sulphury eggs. Thank God there were tons of restaurants now - the early days had been exciting, but he didn't miss squatting in a tent and eating canned-stew-and-rock-grit while wearing a space suit.

Darcy said, "You know, I could cook that for you at home."

Mike swallowed and shook his head. "Coffee's better here." He waited. And on cue -

Darcy exploded "What are you talking about? The coffee here is exactly the same! You even insisted that I buy their beans." She spluttered to a stop. "Oh."

Mike grinned, having tricked her yet again. She crossed her arms but couldn't resist smiling. "Michael Martin, you are the biggest pain in the butt it has ever been my misfortune to meet."

Mike took a sip of his coffee, nodded in agreement. "It's true. I really am terrible to you."

Darcy began to wad up her napkin as if to throw it at Mike but he put up one hand, placatingly. "OK, OK, fine. I wanted to come here because in an hour I'm meeting with a few guys about carbide teeth for the new D-series."

"Local fabrication?"

"I hope so. The carbide-crystal- growing ovens they need are expensive, but I'm going to make introductions and try to help them get the funding."

Darcy shook her head. "The lack of capital bites us again."

Mike nodded. "I was complaining to Javier about it yesterday. Turns out there's a name for it - 'the curse of the frontier.' They had the same problem two hundred years ago building railroads and canals in the US."

"So what's the solution?"

Mike's face clouded. "Government bonds."

Darcy laughed. And, despite himself, he laughed with her.

She asked, "So you've got a meeting on carbide teeth - how's the rest of the D-series coming? Picked a fab shop for the cutter shield?"

Mike realized what Darcy was doing: deftly steering the conversation away from a discussion of government, a topic guaranteed to get him riled. He knew she was doing it, but damn it, the distraction worked. He loved the D series and he loved to talk about it. The systems were so elegant and the maintenance was going to be so much easier. Not only would it cut a wider tunnel, but with 60% lower downtime it would cut more distance per day. Mike leaned into the topic and explained the improved hydraulic pumps in the cutter head thrust system - and then he looked up and saw Darcy's glazed eyes. Damn it, he'd nerded out again.

He stumbled to a halt. "...uh... so, anyway, the design is coming along well." He shifted gears awkwardly. "But, um, what are you doing today?"

"Preflight on the Wookkiee at hangar three -"

Mike put his coffee down. "Already?"

"Bilge Demir at Veleka paid for another load of water, and you've had a load of earth movers ready to go at Tho Quang for a week now."

Mike scowled. "You know I don't like you heading out on these runs. And now that Gamma's sats got burned -"

"Someone's got to do them."

"That doesn't mean it has to be you!"

"Someday I'll be married and have kids. Maybe." The last word was pointed. "Until then, I've got a career."

Mike scowled. This argument. Again. "We've been over this. Building Aristillus takes all of my time right now."

"How much time does it take to get married?"

"That's not - you know what I mean."

"No, Mike, I don't."

He looked around. He hated this conversation - and he especially hated it in public.

He leaned in. "I've got to build Aristillus. We need population, industry - everything. The war is coming, and we have to get ready."

Darcy put her napkin on the table. "If we've got to build industry and bring people here, my job is even more important than I realized. I should get on to it right now."

"Hey, that's not fair. In a few years -"

"Mike, if we're in this as a family, then you get to tell me if it's safe to fly or not. But if we're in this for some greater goal - well, the city needs me to fly."

She stood.

"Wait - Darcy, wait." He stood. "It's dangerous out there - and it's getting worse by the day."

"Then I should start the run as soon as possible, shouldn't I?"

Mike watched her departing back.

God damn it.

How the hell had that gone so wrong so fast?

Chapter 28

2064: South China Sea, Pacific Ocean, Earth

Captain Tudel stood in the swaying assault boat, one gloved hand holding the railing in front of him, the other steadying the light-amplifying binoculars. Where the hell was the freighter? He was sick of this - sick of the stench of the salt air, sick of standing up in an assault boat all night long, sick of -

Wait. There, amongst the phosphorescent glow of ocean algae, a streak, black against dark gray. He tapped the pilot on the shoulder and pointed. A moment later the motor whined and the boat surged.

Would this be the one?

The first ship they'd seized had been a false lead - they'd searched every millimeter of it and hadn't found any of the odd machinery, the extra battery packs, or the thick power cables that the advisers had told them to look for. Nothing special, just a fucking blockade runner full of rice, electronics, and other useless crap.

Trailing that first ship, waiting until it was far enough from shore, taking it, searching it, and then rewarding his men with some of the crew before the cleanup and the scuttling had taken four days. Four days of bullshit.

And now they were three days into the search for this one, and it was probably going to be another charlie foxtrot.

God damn it, he didn't have time for another disappointment; his review was coming up in another five weeks. The promotion board for light colonel was tight - tighter than any other board he'd been through yet. And this was his last chance. Up or out. He needed *something* impressive, and he needed it soon.

Fuck.

But maybe this freighter, growing larger in his binoculars each time they crested a wave, maybe this one would be the one they were looking for.

It had better be.

Six minutes later the pilot turned the wheel and cut the power and they fell into an easy pace, riding alongside the much larger ship.

The pilot nudged the assault boat - and then they were touching the bigger ship. Tudel reached out and touched the freighter's hull...and felt the thick rubbery coating. For a moment he didn't believe it, but he pushed again and felt it give. Damn. Just like the advisers had said. For the first time in months he smiled.

"All right, people, let's go!"

A second later there were muted pops and rope ladders snaked up the sheer wall of the hull. A moment after that, a dozen of the able-bodied began the long climb. Tudel put a hand on the ladder and followed them. Behind him the other boats in the squad pulled closer.

By the time Tudel clambered over the gunwale railing the first squad was already splitting in half. One fire team set up a perimeter while the other assembled the winches and prepared to haul the Alternately Abled Soldiers up.

Which was more fucking bullshit. Not only did he have to haul the gimps around just to make quota, but then he had to do a delicate dance: give them too much action and they complained that they were being unfairly put in danger, and give them too little and they complained that they weren't being given the opportunities they needed for advancement.

Not to mention the fucking hassle of dealing with the rest of his troops when they pissed and moaned about the AAS. The American troops took the sensitivity training seriously - most of their mocking and eye-rolling took place when no one could see it - but the

Nampulas and the Colombians weren't as polished. They'd mock the six soldiers that they were constantly hauling up, belaying down, or carrying packs for, and they'd do it publicly. But if he called them on their shit, or God forbid, used a bit of discipline? Then they'd hold the fucking racial harassment statutes over his head like -

Tudel felt the tap on his shoulder. He looked around. The AAS were up and the platoon was ready. Good.

He pointed to one lieutenant and indicated that his platoon should guard the toehold, then pointed to the second one. Leapfrog. That way.

The orders were passed and the platoon began to move toward the stern where the four story bridge was located.

Halfway there his earpiece crackled. "Captain, check it - I see some of those power cables they told us to look -"

God damn it. "Radio silence, asshole!"

- and then Klieg lights on the bridge tower snapped on.

The troops ahead of him were black silhouettes against the white glare and the deck was streaked with long shadows cast by his men and the equipment on the deck. There was a frozen moment, and then Tudel and his men scrambled for cover behind cargo containers, stanchions, and pipes.

Tudel keyed his mike and was about to ask his lieutenants for a sitrep when he saw that privates Erik and Michelle, two of his goddamn waivu, were standing in the middle of the bright deck looking lost.

"Get *down*, you assholes!"

The loudspeakers on the ship crackled to life. "You, on the deck - identify yourselves." A brief pause, and then "...and surrender!"

"...And surrender"? As an after thought? Jesus. As fucked as his own unit was, the idiots in the ship were even less organized. A good sign. Tudel let go of his mike and cupped his hands around his mouth. "This is a joint

United States / United Nation Peacekeeper action force and this ship is under our control - surrender now!"

There was silence from the loudspeakers.

Tudel slid his hand back to his mike. "First Platoon: cover the windows on the bridge. Fire if you see any movement. Second Platoon: leapfrog forward and take the door."

Second Platoon stood and rushed and Tudel slid out from behind the stanchion where he'd crouched and joined them. It took long seconds to cover the hundred meters of deck, and the unit - disorganized and sloppy - spread out as it moved. Tudel wished he could say he was surprised, but he'd have been more surprised if they executed well. Fuck it; you deal with the material you're handed.

Tudel reached the last equipment cluster before the bridge and stopped to look over his shoulder. Half his troops were still straggling forward. God damn it.

Suddenly there were loud thumps from somewhere below, as if heavy equipment buried somewhere in the ship was being activated, then an overwhelming smell of ozone hit him. What the hell? A moment after the smell reached him, a deep thrumming sound, not quite mechanical but not quite electronic either, whispered into his head. It started quiet but got louder by the second, and a moment later he could feel it in his gut. He took a step forward and almost tripped, catching himself with one hand on the equipment.

The deck felt unsteady, as if the ship was tilting to one side. Tudel looked at his feet, then at the sea - but, no, the sea was calm. What the fuck? Did the expats in this ship have some sort of weird weapon - some area denial shit? He looked at the trailing troops again, still straggling toward the position. Most of them were leaning awkwardly to the left as they jogged, and then one tripped.

The thrumming note increased in volume, and his stomach lurched. And then he knew. He keyed his mike. "We've got the right ship - and they've turned on the drive. They're launching! Take the door. Now, now, now!"

Tudel didn't wait to see if the order was understood or obeyed - he ran. The sensation that the deck was tilting grew stronger. Gravity was no longer pulling straight down, but off to one side.

Ahead of him the first soldier to reach the door tugged on the handle and - nothing. Locked.

The ship was taking off, and he and his men were going with it unless he got inside and held a gun to someone's head. How long did he have? How long until the air got thin enough to kill them? Five minutes? Thirty seconds? He had no idea.

He scanned the bridge tower. The bridge should be covered with windows but from here he could see that they'd been welded over with steel plate. Fuck.

Tudel bellowed over his mike, "Squad one - blow the door!"

As soon as he said it, he knew it was the wrong move - if he blew the door, and they couldn't get the ship's drive shut off in time, the ship would launch. And then, instead of being trapped outside on the deck, exposed to vacuum, they'd be inside - and they'd die just the same.

"Belay that! Squad one - circle left, find another door. Squad two - circle right!"

The thrumming was overlaid with another note now, and suddenly the force of gravity increased - he staggered as if a squat bar had been dropped across his shoulders. Soldiers around him fell. Out of the corner of his eye he saw Antoine, his least favorite AAS, trip and fall face first into a large metal stanchion welded to the deck. In any other circumstance he'd pause to enjoy the man's twitching - at least if no one was watching him - but he didn't have time.

He was going to survive; he had to. And discipline was the tool that was going to keep him alive while these idiots around him were falling and dying. He braced himself with one hand and carefully followed squad two as they circled the tower. Ahead, two of the men were tugging at another door. Locked, like the first two.

The wind was picking up, and he realized with a start that it was coming down from straight overhead. Shit. Was the ship already flying? It must be. How high were they? A meter? A kilometer? He spared a brief glance at the blackness of the horizon and saw nothing.

The wind was loud. Tudel yelled over it, "Fuck it - blow the door!" If they took out the door they might not be able to keep the air in, but once they were inside, they'd shoot who they had to shoot, get the drive turned off. Somehow.

The point man nodded at the order and reached into his pack. Faster, God damn it! The wind was roaring now, and the air was thinning. And then the breaching charge was assembled and on the door.

Over his radio he heard a call, "Captain! First Platoon here - can we come forward?" He turned. *Shit!* He'd entirely forgotten about first platoon, still a few hundred meters away at the bow. First platoon's AASes weren't going to make it. Damn it - even if he survived he was going to take at least 25% losses on this operation. That was going to look bad on his promotion board. Really bad. He keyed his mike. "Yes, move."

The wind buffeted him and between it and the extra weight he staggered.

The soldier with the breaching charge called out. "Fire in the hole! Three! Two!" Tudel braced himself. The explosive tech yelled "Fire!" just as squad one turned the corner.

The explosion scythed down half the men in squad one - blood and gore covered the deck in front of the now gaping hatch. The door, torn from its hinges, lay across two men. Two corpses. And then, with a groan, the door started to slide across the deck, dragging the mutilated bodies of the soldiers with it. Two other troops tried to scramble out of the way - and then the door hit them. They screamed as it crushed their ankles and knocked them flat - and then screamed more as they, the door, and the corpses slid in a pile of steel and blood toward the gunwale. A crash as they hit the railing and tore through it - and then they were all gone.

And then, as if a bubble had popped, Tudel tore his attention away from it. He and his men raced for the gaping hatch. In his headset, a call from the AASes of First Platoon. The voice yelled over tornado. "Captain - we're not - "

Tudel ignored it as he lurched forward. And then he and his men were in. They were in a short dark hallway. He panted in the thin air. Hatches to the left and right, welded shut. Hooks on walls and on them - spacesuits?. He fought for breath. His ears felt like someone was driving knives into them. Ahead there was another steel hatch. A shout, and then several of his men were leaning into it. The door cracked open and light spilled out through the crack. This was it! He threw himself against their backs, adding his force to theirs.

The wind roared around them.

His vision was starting to neck down, graying out at the margins, and his lungs hurt. Push. Push. Push!

And then the door was open and they fell through. Men lay on the floor, panting. But the job wasn't done yet. He pushed himself to his knees, and then to his feet. Discipline. Discipline would let them survive. "Shut the door! Now!" He coughed from the effort of yelling in the thin air.

The men fell to the task, pushing the door closed - and then the thick steel hatch's ponderous movement accelerated in a blur as the wind caught it. There was a scream, and a splash of red. But the door? Yes, the door was shut.

Tudel took stock. One man was down, and another stood, holding the shredded wreckage of his wrist as he screamed.

But the door was shut.

The door was shut.

Over the radio a voice gasped, "Captain. Wait. I'm still -"

First platoon. Tudel looked at the door and knew it wasn't opening again. He pushed a button on his headset, disconnecting the call.

He turned to his troops and was shocked by how few there were. Ten? Less?

Jesus. How many troops had he lost? He took a moment to figure it out. All of First Platoon. The AASes from both platoons. What about the others on the assault boats? He had no idea.

He blinked, and then took stock more carefully. There were an even dozen men inside. One was unconscious. One was missing a hand. Of the other ten, only six still had their carbines.

Jesus fuck.

Around them the roar of air over the ship quieted and then died off. Did that mean they were in space?

Whatever. It didn't matter.

He had a job to do.

Chapter 29

2064: bridge of AFS The Wookkiee, between Earth and the Moon

Captain Tudel looked around the bridge. The twisting sensation in his gut made it hard to concentrate, but it was still clear that this place was an ungainly pile of shit. There were server racks, arrays of bolt-together extruded aluminum, dozens of cheap Vietnamese displays and cables running everywhere. Everything looked improvised, nothing purpose-built. The was the best the God damned expats had to offer: a pile of home-made junk.

And, of course, his "pile of shit" judgment applied to the expats themselves. He looked down at them. Bound. Gagged. Pathetic.

Tudel cracked his knuckles. Only two of the bridge crew had been armed - and even they had surrendered immediately. Not a bit of fight in any of them. These losers played at being rebels, but they didn't have a gram of warrior in them. Even their clothes - a motley mix of jeans, sweatshirts, sweaters, hiking boots - showed their lack of seriousness.

Revolutionaries?

Poseurs would be a better word.

Tudel looked around the rest of the bridge. Six of his men stood guard over the captives. Maybe it was dumb luck or maybe the assault had winnowed out the weak, but the men he had left looked like an actual fighting force. Fit. Uniformed. Proud. These six were decent men, and so were the other four off searching the ship.

Not that there weren't problems. He'd lost fifty men in just ten minutes. Of the twelve left, one was fucked ; Sergeant Campanella had only stopped screaming after they'd wrapped his stump in a clot-bandage and sedated him. All of which added up to one big thing: his career was fucked. *Fucked*.

Unless.

Unless he got this ship landed and handed over an intact AG drive.

So, first things first: land the ship. He needed information, which meant he needed someone to interrogate. He looked over the captives. The blond cunt with the pony tail? No, he wanted to save her for later. The old man? Yes. He looked soft, but he also looked like he knew how shit worked.

Tudell raised his chin to get the attention of Sergeant Armando, and inclined his head toward the old guy. Armando removed the gag and Tudel addressed the captive. "Who runs this ship?"

The old man was slow to answer, trying to spit the taste of the standard-issue gag out of his mouth, but finally: "I'm the captain."

"How do we get back down?" As he said it the AG field twisted and Tudel staggered before catching himself on a grab bar. Damn it - that stumble had made him look foolish. Was the expat laughing at him? Tudel stared at his face but didn't see a hint of it.

He'd better not be laughing.

The captain answered sullenly. "We can ramp down the field, and the drive stops pushing against the Earth. Earth's gravity slows us down, then we start falling. At some point, we ramp the drive back up to slow ourselves down for a soft landing."

"If I untie you, can you get us back down to our boat?"

"No." He licked his lips. "I can't-"

Tudel stared at him, letting a hint of danger creep into his glare. "You can, and you will - and you'll address me by my rank - Captain."

"I mean I *can't*. It's physically impossible."

Tudel prompted him, "Captain."

"Yes?"

Tudel felt his jaw clench. Did this guy think he was joking? "My rank. Captain."

The captive said nothing. The man *was* playing games, he was sure of it. He needed to be taught respect - but information first. Tudel turned his head. "Sergeant Armando - grab this one and follow me. Sergeant Dwight - stay here with your men and guard the rest. If any of them touches anything, or tries to talk, break a finger." Dwight snapped a salute.

Tudel led the sergeant and the captive out through the open bridge hatch, down a corridor, and into a storage room he'd noticed earlier. "Drop him there, and close the door behind you."

Tudel turned to the expat. "Tell me again that you won't bring this ship back down to my boat."

"It's not that I won't - it's that I can't. It doesn't work that way."

Tudel closed his eyes for a moment. With most subjects he'd deliver a quick punch to the face ... but he'd been told by one of the mission briefers that the techies on the ship were likely to be introverted nerd types - the kind of folks who would have been designing circuits or software or whatever back when that was a thing. The missions briefer's theory was the best way to get information from introverts was by asking them questions, and pretending to be impressed by their knowledge.

Tudel's theory was that that theory was bullshit.

He smiled at the ship captain briefly, then snapped a rock solid jab to the bridge of the captain's nose, which cracked satisfyingly. The captain yelled in surprise and pain. A moment later blood streamed out, spilling over the captain's mouth and down his chin. Tudel smiled.

Introverted nerd types would break just as easily as anyone else - maybe easier - once they realized that they weren't playing some video game.

The man sputtered, spraying a small mist of blood. "What the hell? I answered your question!"

Lip. Tudel punched him again, straight on his now-broken nose. The expat screamed again, but he was learning already - there was no more backtalk. The glower of hatred in his eyes grew, but Tudel didn't care. Let him hate - the weak always hated and resented the strong. "Now give me a *useful* answer. Why can't you bring the ship down where I asked you to?"

The ship captain spit blood. In the weird twisting gravity the stream slipped sideways and hit the floor to one side. His mouth clear, the captain answered carefully. "The drive lifts us straight up, but the planet is turning under us. If we turned the drive on for a minute, then came back down again, we'd land a few miles to the west of where we started. We've been under drive for a while now - if we turn it off now, we'd come down in China."

Tudel weighed this. It sounded plausible, but...

The ship captain looked past Tudel, at something behind him.

"Actually -" Then he trailed off.

"Finish."

"No, I - nothing."

What the fuck was going on? Tudel turned and looked over his shoulder. What had the captain been looking at? The fire extinguisher? The clock? It could be the clock. Why? Tudel keyed his mike. "Fire team one - are the prisoners OK?"

A click. "Yeah, they're quiet."

"Fire team two - find anything else in the ship?"

A click. "Still searching - nothing to report".

Tudel keyed the mike again to ask where team two was - and then realized that something had changed. Something was wrong. What -

The constant thrumming noise was gone. Had it stopped just now? The weird twisting feeling in his gut was slipping away - and he felt lighter. His boots left the floor. Jesus! He was floating. He reached for a pipe or stanchion to grab and found nothing.

And then a blur of motion.

The captain, his wrists still bound behind him exploded from his sitting position, kicking off against the deck, head tucked, skull aimed straight at Tudel's chin.

Tudel threw a hand out and -

A sudden impact. A quick taste of iron.

The world went dark.

Chapter 30

2064: south of the Moscow Sea, Lunar Farside

John brought up a map on his display and sent copies to the Dogs. "When we started the hike we swung by the Luna 2 impact site and then the Apollo 15 lander. We've hit seven Soviet and American sites so far."

He paused. All the Dogs were looking at him expectantly but Duncan was wagging his tail hard enough that entire rear end of his suit was wiggling. John grinned. He wasn't surprised - Duncan was the biggest tourist of the group.

John waited another second: the hook was baited and he had their full attention. "It turns out that we've been using an old dataset. A while back I found a newer one." He heard panting over the channel. He looked at Duncan - yes, he was so excited that he was actually fogging up the bulbous faceplate of his canine suit. The hook wasn't just baited - it was set. "The newer data set has some interesting stuff. If we alter our path just a bit there's a Chinese lander two days from here."

There was an excited babble - at least half of it from Duncan - and then John delivered his finale. "And while I stand by the 'no looting American artifacts' rule, Wikipedia says that the Chinese lander has a cache of gold coins."

At this Duncan began to whine in excitement.

Blue, ever the voice of pragmatism, asked, "Is it wise to change our route given that without sats we can't tell Darcy where we're going?"

Duncan said, "The sats are coming back in a few days. We've got a month of supplies. What could go wrong?"

Blue tilted his head and then nodded.

John asked, "Do we need to call a vote?"

They didn't.

The hike began. With the sats gone and the positioning system down the suits fell back to onboard navigation tools. John led the way, striking off to the south east into the unmarked dust.

John had been a late convert to Rex's augmented reality overlays, but the New England overlay had whetted his appetite. Out of curiosity he flipped through others: a beaten horse trail across the American south west. A glowing crystal path through a forest of mushrooms. A highway filled with the wreckage of weird post-apocalyptic vehicles in a red dirt desert.

Maybe some other time. He switched back to the forest and scanned the audio channels. Duncan was chatting with Rex about their collectibles. Apparently Duncan's favorite memento from the trip so far was an explosive-singed stainless steel pentagon with a Soviet crest from Luna 2, while Rex was arguing strenuously that his favorite was a plaster cast he'd made of Harrison Schmitt's boot print.

John smiled, switched his audio back to random play, and leaned forward.

Chapter 31

2064: near Konstantinov Crater, Lunar Farside

John paused in the long uphill climb and looked back over his shoulder. The four Dogs and the four mules were spread out over the dusty gray slope behind him. Behind them the sun was low on the horizon. It was almost night, and yet there was no dusk, no warm orange glow. The sun was as piercingly bright and yellow-white as ever.

They'd covered less ground since breakfast than usual; the slope as they climbed toward the Konstantinov had slowed them down. They'd be to the top soon. Well, not the top-top, but a low spot where the wall of the massive crater had been beaten down by a smaller, more recent impact.

'Recent.' John turned the word over in his head, and then called up some notes. A few minutes later, after a brief digression into articles on Renaissance era lens grinding, he learned that in this case 'recent' meant around 20 million years. He shook his head. Species rose and fell in less time than it took for the moon to suffer even minor erosion. Back in Aristillus the expats complained that technological progress had been halted for half a century. Half a century? What was that compared to twenty million years? John looked around. The biggest change this side of the moon had seen in the last few thousand years was probably was the braid of boot prints he and the Dogs were leaving behind them, tracing all the way back to Aristillus.

And what of near side? If you considered the millions of boot prints back at Aristillus, not to mention the sprawl of tread marks, open strip mines, solar cell farms, and all the other above-surface excrescences of the colony, the moon's surface had easily changed more in the last decade than it had in the several million before.

Suddenly Duncan raced past.

"Duncan! What are you -"

And then a quick excited bark. Duncan had his front legs up on a boulder and was looking ahead, and down. Ah. Had they reached the crater lip already?

Then Rex and Max raced past to join Duncan.

John looked at Blue and raised one eyebrow, and got a toothy grin in response. They broke into a trot simultaneously, eager to catch up to the pack of goofballs and share the view. The four mules labored on behind them.

A minute later, John and Blue reached the other three Dogs at the crater lip and peered down. John whistled slowly at the sight. The sun was low on the horizon behind them, which cast almost all of the crater floor into pitch-black darkness. Just a small strip of the crater floor at the far side was lit, and above it, sheer cliffs of the far side loomed like a wall out of some fantasy painting or ancient myth, cutting the world in half.

It was a dozen kilometers away, but in the vacuum it was as crisp as if it were at arm's length.

John's eyes returned to the inky darkness below him. Something about it wasn't quite right. There! Down near the center of the crater, something caught his eye. What? There shouldn't be anything in the darkness. There *couldn't* be. He dialed up the image enhancing filter, and a dim glow appeared, and then grew brighter. There were two of them; three; more. Glowing lines. Moving dots. All over the crater floor.

He took a step backward.

What the hell?

He dialed up the light gathering further and digitally zoomed the view. After all the enhancement the picture was grainy and rough, but he could make out details. Smelters. Rail lines. Robots. Thousand and thousands of robots, all laboring in the dark of the crater floor.

Something was wrong. Something was really, really wrong.

By instinct he held up one fist and lowered it to the ground, before realizing the Dogs didn't know infantry hand signs.

He turned to them and hissed: "Get down; radios off!"

Chapter 32

2064: bridge of AFS The Wookkiee, between Earth and the Moon

Captain Felix Kear floated in the middle of the room. The unconscious PK - the lead one, Tudel - floated away, bounced off a wall, and floated toward him. Small spheres of blood - his own, the PKs' - drifted through the room, collided, intermixed.

His broken nose throbbed with each heartbeat, but he didn't have time to worry about it. Now he needed the keys to his cuffs - and Tudel was already stirring. With skill born of experience, Kear flipped in midair, aimed, and kicked Tudel in the head. The two men shot apart. Kear braced for the impact against the wall, hit, and kicked lightly off. He judged his course: yes, he was aimed at Tudel. He twisted at the waist to aim his back - and his bound hands - at Tudel.

And then the impact. Kear grabbed frantically at the PK with his bound hands and managed to grab a handful of his uniform before they bounced apart. He held with a death grip as the momentum of the collision tried to separate them.

And then it was done. Tudel was out, and Kear had him.

The moment of victory passed and he realized how much further he had to go. He was floating in the middle of the room, his hands cuffed behind him, in a ship full of armed enemies. He had to free himself, get a weapon, and somehow take back the ship.

He took a breath. There was no sense in worrying about the size of the problem. The only way forward was forward.

He held Tudel with one hand and patted the man's clothes with the other. Slowly, carefully, he walked his hands down Tudel's body, never letting go entirely. He reached Tudel's belt and rotated the unconscious man, until he could reach the PK's pockets and pouches.

Every second of searching - blind, by feel - seemed to take an eternity. Someone could walk in at any second. Kear could feel the sweat building on his forehead and in his armpits. This wasn't going to work. He didn't even know if Tudel had the -

And then he touched it. The key ring. He pulled it out and felt each key...and there. He had it, between his fingertips - the handcuff key. He twisted his wrists. Almost. More. The metal cut into his skin, and one cuff was off. His hands were in front of him. The second cuff was off. He spun around. Tudel's cargo pockets held zip ties. Good; he'd need several. He pulled a handful out and then pushed off of Tudel's body. The two men flew apart. Kear grabbed a pipe and waited for Tudel to bounce back to him. Tudel hit the far wall and rebounded, but not close enough.

Damn it. He needed to get this done, and done now. Sweat covered his face and stung his eyes. He ignored it.

Captain Kear stretched his legs toward Tudel, and - there!

He pinched the man's wrist between his own two ankles and pulled, and then quickly reoriented himself. A second later the PK, his face bloody from a split lip, drifted into range and Kear grabbed him and pulled him closer to the pipe. It was only a second's work to zip-tie the man's hands together, locking them to the pipe. A moment later his ankles were bound as well.

Kear let the rest of the zip ties go and they spilled into the room, tumbling as they flew. He looked at the door. Still no one. This had taken far too long. It was almost - he looked at the clock and blinked. Oh. Just three minutes? Still, he still had to move quickly; the PKs wouldn't be disoriented by the loss of gravity for long.

He rifled through the rest of Tudel's pockets and pouches. There: duct tape. He needed Tudel quiet if he was going to have any chance of taking his ship back. He pulled a length of tape free, and then paused. If he gagged Tudel the man could asphyxiate, especially if he had a bloody nose. Shit. Shit. He couldn't just murder the man - but he needed him silent. Kear let go of the tape and turned the PK's head to get a better view. No, the nose seemed OK; the blood was from a split lip.

But there was still no guarantee.

Tudel began to stir. That settled it. Kear had to make sure that Tudel couldn't give the alarm.

Kear wrapped his legs around Tudel's torso to steady himself, and then stretched the tape. And - shit. It wouldn't stick to the man's blood-covered face, would it? He dropped the roll of tape, letting it hang in the air, and used his own sleeve to wipe the man's cheeks clean. Then he reached out, snagged the roll of tape, and peeled a length of it. The loose end went onto the pipe behind Tudel's head, then around to the front and -

Tudel moaned and opened his eyes. Kear quickly passed the roll around the front of Tudel's head and the pipe behind it, completing the first loop. Tudel began to thrash and made muffled noises, but Kear ignored him and completed two more circuits before tearing the tape and pocketing the rest of the roll.

Kear looked at the PK. "Tudel?" He spoke thickly through his broken nose and the bolus of clotting blood. His own voice sounded odd in his ears.

"Tudel, can you hear me?"

From behind the gag Tudel glared at him. *Glared* at him. For some reason it was that that set Kear off. "Where the hell do you get off coming onto my ship and assaulting me and my crew? You think that just because you're more powerful than us, you get to do what you want? We've got rights, you piece of shit."

Kear made a fist, and then unclenched it. Shit. If he punched the man the blood could end up asphyxiating him.

Shit.

And then, without even realizing that he was doing it, Kear pulled his right leg back and then snapped a knee into the PK's crotch. The lack of gravity robbed the blow of some force , but the impact was still solid. Tudel uttered a muffled scream behind his gag and crunched forward as against the restraints.

"Monopoly of force my ass. Fuck you, you statist asshole."

With that, Captain Kear let go and pushed himself to the door. He touched the handle. In this room he was safe - at least for now. On the far side of the door, out in his ship, there were six armed PKs holding his bridge crew hostage, and another four men roaming the belowdeck areas, looking for the rest of his people.

He was outnumbered and outgunned.

But if they hadn't finished rounding up his crew, he might - he just might - have some allies.

He took his phone from his pocket, typed a text, and sent it to Iosif, Luka, Nymabura, and Benedikt.

Next he needed to get to the weapons locker to get a rifle or a shotgun. But getting there? He swallowed. It was a long way in an occupied ship, and he was going to be defenseless the whole way.

And then he remembered something.

He turned and looked at Tudel. The man was still crunched forward, straining against his bonds.

And there, on his hip, was a pistol.

Chapter 33

2064: Engineering decks, AFS The Wookkiee, between Earth and the Moon

Iosif floated upside down next to the equipment locker and cursed the navigators as he struggled to fit the velcro booties over his work boots. Those idiots on the bridge had changed the launch schedule - and did they remember to tell the men who actually did the work on the ship? No, they did not. And when the drive had switched on he'd frantically packed away his lunch, but hadn't finished before it cut off again - and it had taken five minutes to vacuum up the floating balls of soda, and another five to change his shirt.

Those idiots deserved a good yelling at, and once he got these booties on he was going to go there in person - no damned phone call - and swear at them face to face.

The second bootie slipped on, and Iosif pushed himself to the floor. He stalked across the carpet to the door.

Those bridge bastards thought they were better than the mere engineers who -

Was his phone vibrating?

He pulled it from his pocket. He looked at it, and blinked. Jesus. Was this real? *That's* why they'd launched? He shouted for Luka, but the other man was already looking at his own phone.

Luka looked up at him. "Is this a joke?"

"They wouldn't joke about this."

"What do we do?"

"Get ready. The peakers will come for us next."

Luka nodded grimly.

* * *

The "Pride of Enugu", as she was named on the forged paperwork, or the "Wookkiee", as Captain Felix and his crew called her (after a minor character in a century old movie, apparently), was a Handymax class mixed cargo/tanker.

The front five-sixths of the ship was open deck: 130 meters of flat steel studded with massive hydraulically controlled hatches, two cranes, miscellaneous hardware, and a stack of dozens and dozens of cargo containers. The volume beneath the open deck was taken up by three massive cargo holds and two huge tanks, now full of seawater for the trip home.

Aft of the cargo areas, the bridge structure towered above the deck and continued down into the ship's hull. Above the deck the bridge was simple: four stories of bunkrooms, storage rooms, bathrooms, and common areas. Below the deck line the structure was more complex and less regular. The engineering areas were laid out not for the convenience of humans, but for the convenience of machinery - machinery that was long gone. Catwalks twisted around empty spaces that had once held diesel engines. Staircases, a dumbwaiter, and an elevator rose to the bridge above and continued to the machine shop and storage areas below. Tanks of oxygen, air processing equipment, and more were wedged in where fuel tanks had once sat before being torch cut, removed in pieces, and sold for scrap.

This was the engineering space where Iosif hid. Iosif looked at his phone again, hoping for more information from the Captain...but still nothing. He pocketed it and looked around the deck one more time. The port hatch was closed and locked. That would channel the PKs through the other door. Hopefully, when they came they'd orient themselves to the "floor" and not realize that he and Luka could be hidden up "above."

Eto piz dets!

It would be nice to have a shotgun, but the ship's armory was levels above them, so he was stuck with just the pistol that he always carried. A fucking pistol. Against soldiers. He shook his head.

It could be worse. He looked at Luka, armed with just a meter-long box wrench, and caught his eye. Once he had Luka's attention Iosif made a show of looking at his own pistol and then raised an eyebrow. Luka scowled, and Iosif smiled.

Calling me paranoid was hilarious last week, but not so funny now, eh?

Luka's scowl turned into a sigh and a nod - even he could appreciate the humor of the situation. That, Iosif knew, was the glory of the Russian character. Americans, Nigerians - they didn't understand the value of black humor. Americans, they were always smiling, always pushing away bad thoughts. But when the world turned to shit, the ability to deal with that shit was -

There was shouting outside the hatch. The PKs.

Iosif ducked further back into the tangle of duct-work and steel beams, leaving just one eye clear. A PK stuck his head through the open doorway, surveyed the gray-painted decking, catwalks, and hulking machinery, and then floated through the door. The soldier pulled himself hand over hand along a railing for three meters, and then stopped and looked around. Iosif felt his palms growing clammy. He wiped his left hand on his t-shirt, transferred the pistol, and then wiped the right, keeping an eye on the PK's head the whole time. *Derr mo*. The soldier had a carbine strapped across his chest. This was all very *very* real. Armed men wanted to kill him. This wasn't theory - they were there. Right now. Just meters away. He felt his breath coming more quickly. They wanted to kill him - and so he had to kill them.

As he'd hoped, the PK oriented himself toward the floor and looked around, but didn't look "up." The scene seemed to play out in slow motion, and in hyper detail. The first PK moved further into the room, and then a second soldier came through the hatch.

Iosif realized that his palms were clammy again, but he didn't dare move - the PKs were too close.

It was almost time.

Iosif touched the safety with his right thumb, and then snapped it off. In a moment he was going to lean to the left, extend his arms, and fire. He had a magazine of twelve rounds, with one more in the -

"Hey!"

The first PK was looking straight at him, and was raising his carbine. Iosif pulled his head back behind the I-beam. A moment later the impossibly loud sound of rifle fire in a confined space assaulted his ears and hammered at chest and gut.

Over the skull-slapping sound of rifle fire Iosif thought he heard smaller splat sounds. Were the bullets hitting the I-beam and the equipment he was hiding behind? Then more rifle fire from the far corner of the engineering deck. Shit - the other soldier must be firing too. Iosif sucked in his gut, shrank his shoulders - anything to make himself smaller as he hid, one knee and one ass cheek in the narrow chimney between the I-beam's flanges.

A piercing pain in his heel - was he shot? He ignored it. Another dozen shots - and then silence. Then shouting.

Iosif muttered a quick prayer and peeked out from behind the beam. Both of the PKs hung in midair, facing away from him. What? Why?

Then he saw. They were spinning. The fools hadn't anchored themselves before firing, and the recoil had spun them. They cursed and tried to reach for railings.

Now.

Iosif took a deep breath and pushed himself out from behind the beam. He braced himself with his legs - one on the I-beam and one on a condenser. The PKs were continuing to rotate and in another moment they'd be facing him again. Iosif pushed his pistol out in a double-handed grip and tried to flip the safety off, but it wouldn't move. What the fuck? He looked down - the safety was already off. Damn it! Back to his target. There. His breath came quick and shallow, and everything in his peripheral vision was black, like he was staring out from the bottom of a deep well. But there, in the center of the image, was the PK. Iosif lined up the sights.

And squeezed the trigger once.

The carefully aimed shot took the PK from behind, just below the lip of his helmet and above the stiff projecting flange on his spinal armor. The body went limp and the foot that he'd managed to hook around a railing released.

Without intending it he fired again.

Iosif had expected to hear his own shots, maybe impacts, but it was as if his head was wrapped in wool. The world was silent.

Now, the second PK. Where was he? Iosif swiveled his head. There!

The soldier was facing perhaps forty five degrees away and had his carbine raised.

Concentrate. His own pistol - there it was. Sights just below the PK. Move it. Get it on target.

The PK was spinning. He'd be pointing at Iosif in a moment.

Rear sight.

Front sight.

And then he had the PK's head in the sight picture... and a sharp shooting pain in his arm. His pistol dropped from lifeless fingers and spun away. He tried to reach for it, but his arm wouldn't move.

And there, in front of him, a small cylinder about the size of a can of Coke, spinning. What the hell? Is that what had hit him? What -

The grenade exploded.

* * *

Sergeant Morioka saw the detonation. Yes! He'd aimed perfectly - the grenade had hit the expat dead on and bounced only a bit before exploding. The recoil from the grenade launcher had added to the spin he already had. He needed to grab something -

His rotation brought him face to face with another expat. Shit! The man was huge, bearded, and grimacing like a savage. His arms were back to one side, holding something... And then he swung.

"Wait! Don't -".

* * *

Luka had never swung so hard in his life. The meter long box wrench connected under the PK's helmet, smashing hard into the side of the PK's face, just under one eye. The PK convulsed and coughed as he died, spraying a mist of blood from his ruined face. Luka recoiled as the spray of hot gore hit him.

Luka blinked away the blood. The PK hung lifeless in the air, spinning slowly as strands of blood slid from his face. Luka glanced up where Iosif had been hiding and flinched; then his eyes landed on the PK. The carbine. Once he had that he -

* * *

In the open doorway Sergeant Frodge aimed at the expat. His finger was tightening, but he was too late. The expat's wrench smashed into Morioka.

The impact of steel on bones was horrific.

The force of the strike moved the expat back a handsbreadth.

Frodge moved his aim slightly and then his rifle roared.

The expat's arms jerked as the bullet punched through his skull. The bloody wrench flew away as the body spasmed.

The recoil pushed him back and Frodge grabbed at the hatchway and steadied himself, and then looked around the engineering space.

Two of his men dead.

Two expat corpses.

Empty brass floated and rebounded off surfaces.

Sprays of blood splashed against the walls.

The smell of smoke and burning insulation.

Fuck.

What a train wreck.

Frodge keyed his mike. "They got Santiago and Morioka, but we got two of them."

Chapter 34

2064: AFS The Wookkiee, between Earth and the Moon

Captain Kear pushed himself off the bulkhead and flew down the corridor. Excitement and fear had led him to kick off too hard - he was traveling faster than he liked and he landed hard at the far end. He also didn't have velcro slippers, and he bounced off the wall before catching himself on a stanchion. He cursed under his breath, righted himself, and aimed. His next kick sent him toward an open hatch halfway way down the next corridor. Then he was through the hatch and in the stairwell. One flight down and he'd be at the arms locker. The pistol he'd taken off of Tudel was better than nothing, but if he could get a shotgun he'd -

There was a series of distant echos: a pistol shot, then automatic weapons fire, then the crump of a grenade.

Kear grimaced. The PKs must have found Iosif and Luka. This wasn't good - but there was nothing he could do for them.

Hand over hand, and he was at the right level. Then he kicked, flew through the open hatch, and was in the hallway. He turned, kicked again, and sailed down the corridor. The arms locker was just a dozen meters -

He heard the gunshot first. Had it come from behind him? He reached out his left hand to grab a pipe to stop himself so he could look... and realized his left arm wasn't working.

* * *

Captain Kear screamed as his left shoulder was tugged behind him. The bastards had poured clotting powder in the wound and slapped bandages over the holes, but he could feel the fragments of his broken shoulder blade grind against each other.

Another tug as the last zip tie was cinched tight and the PKs were done. One said something to the other, and they both left the room.

A moment later Tudel pulled himself into the room. Clearly someone had found him and freed him from the pipe where Kear had lashed him. Kear noted small patches of duct tape adhesive still clinging to the other man's face.

For a moment - just a moment - Kear thought about begging for mercy, but he looked into Tudel's eyes and knew it would be pointless.

Tudel looked at him slowly and grinned - the smile of a predator. "We've some unfinished business."

The PK grabbed a stanchion and pulled himself closer. "Where the *fuck* do you get off kicking me in the balls, faggot?" He reached into a pocket and pulled out a pair of channel lock pliers.

Kear whimpered despite himself, and then regained control. He wouldn't give the PK the satisfaction. He wouldn't.

He managed to keep that promise to himself as his first two fingers were broken. He whimpered as Tudel grabbed his third finger in the iron teeth. When the bone snapped, he started screaming and didn't stop.

Chapter 35

2064: AFS The Wookkiee, between Earth and the Moon

Tudel looked down at the sobbing expat.

These people wanted to play at being grownups? They wanted to break laws, carry illegal guns, refuse to listen to the authorities? Look at this brave rebel now. Fingers broken, snot streaming out of his nose. He shook his head. A fucking disgrace.

People who wanted to make their own rules? He hated them. No thought at all about society, about hierarchy. No discipline. No respect. They were brave - so brave. Until shit got real.

He grabbed a handful of the sobbing captain's hair and pulled, forcing the expat to look at him. The expat tried to twist away but Tudel dug his fingers in. "Hey, tough guy? Still think you're allowed to fuck with a real soldier? Huh?"

The ship captain shook his head from left to right. "No. No. I'm sorry. Please. Please. I-".

"Do you promise to be good?"

"Yes, yes. I promise!"

Tudel tisked. "Why should I trust you?" The expat shook his head even harder.

"No, I promise! Please!" He sobbed, and... Ugh. Tudel pulled his hand away.

"You got your fucking snot on me." He wiped his palm on the captive's shirt. "Guess you need another lesson."

The captive screamed. "No! No!"

Good.

Tudel anchored his feet under a rail before removing his belt. He whipped it experimentally through the air. The buckle whistled satisfactorily.

"Time to learn some respect for your betters."

Chapter 36

2064: AFS The Wookkiee, between Earth and the Moon

The PK was talking, but Darcy found it hard to focus on his words. She stared at his face. Those small patches on his cheeks might be duct tape residue, but there was no doubt about the spatters across his face and the back of his hand.

She'd heard the other PKs talking about killing Iosif and Luka.

Please, God, let Captain Kear be OK.

She forced herself to pay attention to Tudel's words. "OK, so we're floating in orbit - how do we get back down? I already heard the lecture about how we can't drop back down to the same place we left. Fine. Fuck it. How do we get back down anywhere?"

Darcy moved her mouth, trying to find words. Her co-navigator Waseem spoke first. "We're not in orbit - when we left the atmosphere, we had no forward velocity. Well, not much, just what we had from the Earth's -"

Darcy saw a dangerous look in Tudel's eyes. What was wrong with Waseem, giving a long drawn-out explanation? Didn't he realize the kind of people they were dealing with? Didn't he see the blood on Tudel's face?

Darcy should interrupt Waseem and give Tudel a shorter answer. She should. She opened her mouth -

...but Waseem apparently saw Tudel's dangerous look, too. He stumbled to a stop and restarted. "Short version: the drive pushes us away from any other mass. We go flying straight away. So we're flying straight away from the Earth, on a traje-"

Tudel interrupted him. "You haven't told me how we're going to get down."

Waseem swallowed. "I know. Um - look. We can't go down. We're committed at this point. We're flying straight away from the Earth, like a ball thrown from the bowler to the batsman."

"What the fuck is a 'batsman?'"

Darcy looked at Tudel. This was getting dangerous. She interrupted. "He means, like a pitcher throwing a ball to the batter. The Earth is the pitcher, and this ship is the ball. The pitcher has already thrown us. We're coasting now."

Tudel turned seamlessly to Darcy. "How do we reverse course?"

Darcy licked her lips. "We can't." Tudel's face darkened. She took a quick breath and continued, "It's just like baseball. The pitcher's already thrown the ball, right? We can't turn around - but we can go to the catcher, and he can catch us and then throw us back. So we have to fly to the moon, and then we -"

"OK, I get it." He thought for a moment. "How long until we get there and can throw ourselves back?"

Darcy breathed deeply to steady herself. "Actually, we've got some problems. We weren't due to launch for another hour, so we're way outside the normal flight path. The good news is that we're flying away from the Earth in the general direction of the moon. The bad news is that we launched early, so we're going to be flying through the moon's orbit before the moon gets there - it's like the pitcher aimed the pitch a bit wrong." She swallowed. That'd been a pretty good explanation, hadn't it? She looked at Tudel. He still seemed dangerous - very dangerous - but he no longer seemed to be balanced right on the edge of violence.

"Also, there's a worse complication," Waseem said. "We were 10 degrees north of the equator when we launched, and we went flying out from the Earth exactly away from the center of the Earth - well, not exactly, because mass isn't evenly distributed - but, anyway, we're flying up away from the Earth at an angle, and the moon isn't at the same angle. The problem is -"

Tudel barked at Wasseem. "Ahead of the moon? At an angle? Cut the detail. I want to know one thing and one thing only - how do we get back to Earth as quickly as possible?"

Darcy gave Waseem a warning look, silently begging him to *please* shut up and let her handle it without extraneous detail, and then she turned to Tudel. "We need to do some tricky maneuvering, and we need to do it as soon as possible. If we're lucky, we can land on the moon. If we can do that, we can recharge the batteries and get you and your men back to Earth as soon as possible." She left unsaid her hope she and the rest of the bridge crew wouldn't be forced to make the trip with them.

Tudel stared hard at her. "If you're lucky? What do you mean?"

Darcy swallowed. "I mean that depending on our speed and angle we might not be able to get to the moon."

Tudel had a questioning look on his face. "I thought you said we're headed there?"

"We're headed toward it. Roughly. We've got some work to do to try to hit it."

"And if we can't? Then what?"

"If we miss it -" Darcy exhaled. "If we miss the moon, then we either drift off into space or settle into a really long eccentric orbit."

Speaking the words suddenly made the navigational problem she faced even more real. She'd been so focused on the blood on Tudel's face and avoiding a beating - or worse - that she hadn't paused to think through the bigger problem. She tried to continue, but felt like there was a strap around her chest, tightening and tightening. She opened and closed her mouth a few times but no words came.

Tudel repeated his question. "If that happens, if we end up in a 'long orbit', then what?"

Darcy tried again to form a sentence but couldn't. She closed her eyes. If he was going to beat her, she couldn't stop him.

Next to her Waseem answered for her. "Don't you get it? If Darcy and I can't plot a way to get to the moon, there is no third option. We get there, or we - *all* of us - we die."

Chapter 37

2064: near Konstantinov Crater, Lunar Farside

John shimmied backward on his stomach, away from the crater lip. The suits were well designed for walking but crawling chafed his knees and bunched suit material uncomfortably in the crotch. After putting several meters between himself and the craper lip he rolled onto his back and sat up. He still didn't like the idea of using radios, but with meters of rock between them and the activity on the crater floor, and no ionosphere to bounce signals he hoped it would be OK. "Guys -"

John's breaking radio silence was the only cue the Dogs needed to begin talking at once.

"Who is it? The US? The Hindi -"

"If they've got a base on farside -"

"How could it be so huge? If they-"

"It's aliens! Got to be!"

John sighed. "No, Duncan, I don't think it's aliens.

"Aw. It would be *totally* cool if it was aliens though."

John ignored him and composed his thoughts. "It's probably the US...but it could be the Hindi States... or the NEU."

"How did they get here - do they have the AG drive too?" asked Blue.

"I bet they had help from the aliens!" Duncan said.

John felt his jaw tighten. The thing that frustrated him to no end with Duncan was that the Dog was so much smarter than ninety percent of the idiocy that came out of his mouth. Heck, he was clearly smarter than John himself was, but he enjoyed entertaining crazy ideas more than he did actually thinking.

John unclenched his teeth. "No." He paused for a moment to regain his composure. "We need to figure out who this is, and then we need to figure out what we do about it. How did we not see this? How did Gamma not see this?"

Blue tilted his head. "The satellites got burned a week ago. Maybe that was the first stage of the invasion, and landing here was -"

John shook his head. "No." He shared some images from his suit across the local network, and then added annotations and pushed them as well. "Look at the size of the installation. Konstantinov is sixty-six klicks wide and about half a klick deep. That facility has got to be twenty square kilometers. At least."

Rex said, "So you're saying it would be hard for the PKs to drop that much materiel that quickly?"

John shook his head. "Not hard. It's flat out impossible."

Max pawed at the ground to get their attention. "Maybe there's not as much equipment there as we think. We see lights, and we assume that we're looking at heavy development - but could it be some sort of decoy? In World War Two both sides used all sorts of decoys - inflatable tanks, fake ships, huge tarps with fake cities painted on them."

John started to rub his chin as he thought, but his glove bumped into his helmet. "It's possible, but it doesn't make sense. Why burn the satellites in order to drop a bunch of decoys - in a crater that can't be seen because there are no satellites, and no one is even supposed to be around? It makes no sense. No matter how -"

Rex interrupted, "What if we're wrong about it all being recent - what if it's been here for months, or even years?"

John pursed his lips. "With his satellites Gamma would have -"

"What if they stuxed Gamma months ago? Or even years ago? If they can edit his video feeds, Gamma wouldn't know this was here."

Blue said, "But Goldwater has satellites too -"

Rex held up one paw. "If Earth forces can pwn Gamma they can certainly pwn Goldwater's sats."

Max looked around. "Whoever it is, if they've got that much industry down there, there's a good chance that they've got rovers up here too. We need to get out of here."

"But they'll know we were here," said Duncan. "Our tracks."

Blue turned to John. "John, what do we do?"

The other Dogs fell silent and also turned to John. John took a long moment. This was big. And this wasn't just a tactical issue of fleeing the area. This was strategic. If the US or the NEU was on the moon, that changed everything. They needed to get word back to Aristillus. That meant exfiltrating the immediate area, finding some hard rock to walk across to break up their track, getting to the next drop point, and then getting back to Aristillus on the next hopper.

"Guys, we're moving out. Right now, we'll backtrack three - "

A tone sounded in their helmets, and a new, cool, and uninflected voice spoke.

"Hello, John."

John knew the voice. He tilted his head back and looked up, and then caught himself - there was no chance of seeing the birds overhead. "Hello Gamma. Your satellites are back?"

"I don't expect my replacement satellites to launch until tomorrow."

John was puzzled. "Wait. Then how -"

Blue understood. "This facility. It's Gamma's."

John frowned. "No, that - wait. Gamma, what's going on?"

"Yes, John, this is my facility."

"What? Why did you move from Sinus Lunicus to here? And why didn't you tell us?"

Gamma paused for a long moment and then answered, "This is a second facility."

John waited, but after a long pause it became obvious that Gamma wasn't going to share more - at least not without being explicitly asked.

John felt a sense of cold dread building, and chose his words carefully. "You've got two facilities now?"

"I felt the need to have redundant capabilities."

John had long since noticed that while Gamma never seemed to lie, he did sometimes evade. And because his phrasing was so precise, once you knew the trick, you could often maneuver Gamma into leaking information. John had never shared this, even with Mike, Darcy, or his other friends. Not only was it an advantage that he wanted to keep for himself, but also he couldn't trust others not to leak it back to Gamma and risk Gamma either changing his tell or freezing John out entirely.

He'd deliberately asked Gamma if there were two facilities, and Gamma hadn't confirmed the number - he'd merely agreed that there was more than one.

Noted, Gamma. Noted. To stop the pause from seeming suspiciously long, John hurried on: "If your satellites aren't back yet that means our radio signals are reaching you down at the bottom of Konstantinov."

"Some of your signal is leaking down there, but I'm talking to you through the picket of rovers you walked through 400 meters back."

John flinched and looked over his shoulder involuntarily, but saw nothing. How had they walked through a screen of rovers? Were they intentionally hidden? Camoflauged?

A secret facility on Farside was bad enough, but Gamma had all but confirmed that there were multiple hidden facilities - and he'd developed camouflaged rovers? John sucked his teeth for a moment. This was worrisome.

He'd always opposed the Bureau of Sustainable Research and its mandate of regulating - or stomping out entirely - new technologies. And then when circumstances forced his hand, he'd turned his principles into action: he'd formed The Team and rescued the Dogs and - coincidentally, almost accidentally – Gamma.

He'd felt good about that at the time. Great, even. Now, though, he felt a chill at the back of his neck.

He'd known that BuSuR's stated mission of preventing a "hard take-off singularity" was just propaganda - a mask for a jobs protection scheme that was just plausible enough to cobble together a left and right coalition. Ban self-driving trucks to keep teamsters employed. Ban robotic barber chairs to keep another voting bloc employed.

But maybe the fear of the singularity wasn't just cover? He'd never had even a second of doubt about rescuing the Dogs. They were people. Intelligent, loyal, foolish, willfully obstinate, hilariously funny people.

Gamma, though, had given him second thoughts more than once. He'd thought he'd seen flashes of warmth, and attributed the coolness to the loneliness of a wounded strange creature, brought into existence against his will, the only one of his kind.

Now, though, those doubts multiplied. If Gamma was replicating himself - and was doing so in hiding -

John tried to collect his thoughts and respond measuredly, but without meaning to he blurted out, "'Picket'? That's a pretty militaristic term."

"Yes, it is a militaristic term. To reference what is purported, with minimal justification, to be a Chinese curse, these are interesting times."

Blue asked, "What do you mean by interesting?"

"An illuminating analogy is to think of current geopolitics as a Bak–Tang–Wiesenfeld sand pile."

John shook his head. "I don't know what that means, Gamma, but you're deflecting my question. What the hell is going on? Why do you have a secret industrial facility?"

"As Sun Tzu said, 'All war is deception'...and enemies are all around. In light of the Earth government destroying my satellites, I think the prudence of a backup facility is amply clear."

Rex and Duncan babbled excitedly to Gamma about the secret facility - and Duncan's theory of aliens - but when John made eye contact with Blue and Max it was clear that he wasn't the only one discomforted by this development. For this entire hike he'd been using maps provided by Gamma, consulting the AI on the best routes. If he hadn't changed their path at the last minute - and without consulting Gamma - to visit the Chinese lunar lander, they never would have stumbled onto this facility. How many other facilities did Gamma have hidden on Farside? How many had they already walked within kilometers of? Had Gamma been steering them this whole time to avoid other sites - was *that* what paying them for 'reconnaissance' was really about? Goldwater's mining satellites hadn't picked this up - had Gamma stuxed those birds too? Or had he inserted his tentacles into the computational infrastructure of Aristillus to edit the footage before humans saw it?

To his left Blue tilted his head, as if he was about to speak. John held up one finger in front of his helmet, warning Blue to stay silent. John needed to think this through before they said anything else over the radio.

How big was Gamma and what were his plans?

There was a ping in John's helmet, and the suit computer commented, "Local sunset beginning."

John turned to the west and saw the sun already touching the horizon. The two younger Dogs kept talking to Gamma while John watched the long shadows that covered the lunar plain reach out to him as the last thin arc of the sun slid below the curve of the dark gray landscape.

Chapter 38

2064: bridge of AFS The Wookkiee, between Earth and the Moon

Darcy floated weightless in front of the navigation console, her hands free and her feet hooked under the foot rail. She stole a glance at Tudel and his men. They seemed alert, but no longer on edge. Good. Maybe - *maybe* - she and Waseem would be able to get the Wookkiee to the moon without worrying that there'd be more violence.

Waseem, one workstation over, saved his computations to an icon, and then verified the calculations using nothing but a command line scientific calculator.

He looked up. "Good news - I think. The early launch means that we're one point two degrees off phi and one tenth of a degree on theta, and even if we use the OMCs and the RCS we don't have the thruster reserves to plot an intercept -"

"That's good news?"

Waseem shook his head. "No. The good news is that our mass isn't fixed. If we can cut it enough, we might be able to pull this out."

Darcy furrowed her forehead. "Ah. Tanks two and four are full of seawater -"

Waseem nodded. " - for Veleka. If we can dump that we cut our mass by twenty percent. That plus the maneuvering reserves -"

Darcy ran through computations on her own board. "Twenty percent? That's not going to be enough to get ahead of the moon and match -"

Wasseem raised a finger. "I know. Hang on. We dump the water and we use our OMC rockets - and that's still not enough to get us to the moon's equator...but it is enough to get us to the moon - "

"If we don't get closer to the ecliptic, our orbit would be -"

"Yeah, I know. Screw the normal approach - we'll be coming in over the north pole. No one's ever done that before, but no reason it can't work. If we come in low enough - "

Darcy's eyes went wide. "*Really* low."

"Yeah. But we get captured, we loop around Farside -"

"- do a degrading orbit -"

"- and slide into Aristillus from the south."

Darcy exhaled. "Hang on." She dragged Wasseem's files to her console and checked the calculations one by one. Finally, soberly, she nodded. "It'll be close, but, yeah, I think it'll work." She paused and considered. "If. If we can dump the water. We've only ever used the pumps under gravity. Will they work in zg?"

Waseem nodded grimly. "The nitrogen blanketing system is still in place from before the carbon law. If we pressurize the tanks, does that help swirl all the water out?...Maybe?"

Darcy looked away and bit her lip. It had to work; there was no plan B. From behind her Tudel asked, "You've got a solution?"

She looked over her shoulder. Frodge and Tudel floated behind her - they'd learned how to tuck their feet under padded foot rails. Tudel was in a weird modification of 'parade rest,' his hands clasped behind his back. Frodge, though, had one hand on his pistol. It was holstered, but the menace was clear.

For a few precious moments while working the trajectory with Waseem, she'd forgotten that the two of them were there, had forgotten the fact that they'd killed Iosif and Luka, and tortured (and maybe killed) Captain Kear. That blessed moment of forgetfulness was gone - and now, even as she was working to save all of their lives, these two thugs were hanging there - in *her* ship - implicitly threatening to hurt or kill her and Waseem. She mustered bravado she didn't really feel. "You know, that pistol is an empty threat. If you kill us or damage this equipment the drive is useless, and you're all dead."

Frodge said nothing. Tudel evaluated her dispassionately and then answered drily, "I'm sure Sergeant Frodge won't damage the equipment."

Darcy's confidence collapsed and she turned away so that the PKs couldn't see her face. Damn it! How dare these thugs invade her ship and hold weapons on them? What gave them the right? Normally she thought that Mike's tirades against the government just a shade too angry...but right now it occurred to her that perhaps he wasn't angry *enough*.

She clenched her jaw, trying not to let her rage, her anger, her despair spill out. After a long moment she forced herself to focus on the screens. She had work to do. She reached out a finger and touched the plotted course.

Huh.

She brought up a calculator and started a new workspace, and then ran numbers. After several minutes, she said, "Waseem, wait - what if we run the drive two hundred percent for the first portion of the braking maneuver, and then at fifty percent for the second half?"

"Why would we do that?"

"We're approaching the moon at an angle. The vector decomposition of the first part of the approach gives us more braking and less matching the moon's orbital speed."

"But the plan we've got now works, why screw with it?"

"Because it means we can save some of the water. Even after desalination costs, the profit on half a tank is noticeable-"

Waseem looked at her and blinked uncomprehendingly. "Profit? Darcy, what the hell are you talking about?"

...and the reality that she'd pushed away once again flooded back. Why was she even trying to save the water? The whole ship was being held captive by the PKs. If she and the rest of the crew were lucky, they'd manage to land the ship. And then, after that, the PKs would recharge the batteries somehow, and then she and Waseem would be forced at gunpoint to take off again, and fly the ship back to Earth. At which point she'd be disappeared if she was lucky, or used as a bargaining chip against Mike if she wasn't.

She let her hand fall away from the screen. What was the point of even trying to land? Why not just crash the Wookkiee into the moon? At least that would kill Tudel and his squad of goons. She looked at Waseem. Did he understand that they were as good as dead already? Would he be up for that plan? Could she signal him? If she put in a trajectory that passed ten kilometers below the lunar horizon instead of over it, would he understand what she was doing?

Yes, she could probably -

- unless -

If they landed the ship, could Mike come up with some way to save them?

She held her breath for a moment and thought it through.

Wasseem was saying something to her. She caught a few words. Something about her opinion, something about the drive efficiency curve. She looked up. "What?"

"I said you looked like you had some new thought."

She shook her head. "No. Nothing new." She nodded her head at the screens. "Let's get to work."

Chapter 39

2064: bridge of AFS The Wookkiee, between Earth and the Moon

Tudel listened as the second navigator - was his name 'Waseem'? - spoke. Tudel paid less attention to the man's words than to his eyes. Was he telling the truth? Tudel stared hard at him. Yes...he thought so.

Over the last day the expats had developed a decent working relationship with him and his men. Once the chips were down, these two had learned how to be respectful. It validated a pet theory of his: the problem with the expats - all the lawlessness, the disorganization, the slovenliness - was based on a lack of discipline, on society being lax. Put people, even expats, in a situation where the proper chain of command was clear, and they could learn deference, and how to work inside an organization.

Waseem finished his explanation of the maneuver.

Tudel nodded. "OK, let me think about this."

Wasseem shook his head. "No. We had forty-five minutes when we told you the plan. Now we're down to fifteen. We've got to start immediately or it's too late."

Tudel stared at the man closely. Was there a touch of lip there? He pondered this. No. The navigator was trying to do his job, and was raising a valid point. Tudel ran his tongue over his teeth as he thought. Then, "OK, do it."

The other navigator, Darcy, turned to him. "This will take a while - and then the next step is to engage the drive. Before we do that, if you've got any loose equipment you're going to want to tie it down... and if there's debris from that firefight. Or bodies - " Her voice caught in her throat and she turned away.

Tudel turned to his left. "Armando, Dwight - get down there, do a cleanup."

Wasseem, looked at him. "We're OK to start?"

Tudel nodded.

Waseem hit a button on his screen and a quiet, distant whine answered him. Tudel looked at him closely. Waseem must have felt the eyes on him. He turned and explained, "The ballast pumps."

Both of the navigators stared at their screens. Tudel prompted them: "What's going on?".

Darcy pointed to one indicator. "It's working. We're dumping the water. This, here, is tank 2. It started at a hundred percent. Now it's down to ninety-nine percent. Now ninety-eight. See?" Tudel looked. There were two indicators. As he watched the first one kept dropping, and then the second one, for tank 4, also started to move.

Waseem turned to Darcy. "The stealth coating on the hull hides us from USG radar... but this is fifteen million kilos of water. It's going to turn to ice and make a huge cloud. That's *definitely* going to show up."

Darcy gave a slight nod of her head, indicating Tudel and his men. "I think the government already has a pretty good idea where we are."

Tudel smiled. *Yes. Yes, we do.*

Chapter 40

2064: bridge of AFS The Wookkiee, between Earth and the Moon

Darcy looked at the tank indicators on her screen. Tank 4 was within a few percent of empty, but tank 2 was still at thirty-eight percent full, and it wasn't dropping.

"Waseem, you see this?"

"Looking at it now. The pumps on tank 4 - primary *and* backup - went into auto-shutdown."

"And?"

"We've still got nitrogen pressure in the tanks." He paused. "I have no idea why the pumps shut down."

Darcy stared at her screens, tapping icons and bringing up subscreens. Pump power? Green. Pump lubrication status? Green. Pressure? Green.

What was going on? This made no -

Wait. She might be able to check the pumps with the external cameras. Yes, deck camera 10 was pointed right at the pumps. She brought it up on the screen, but the image was black. Black? Was the deck in shadow right now? Oh, of course, yes: they'd launched at night and were flying in the Earth's penumbra most of the way. She triggered the deck lights.

...And nothing changed. Still dark.

She tilted her head. That was odd.

She flipped to camera 11. Also dark.

She tried camera 12 and could finally see the deck.

The deck, covered in a thick sheet of something white...

And suddenly she knew what had happened.

Ice. It was a vast blanket of ice. It covered the deck, encrusted equipment, and climbed the bridge.

"Waseem!"

"What?"

"Look!"

They'd vented millions of kilos of water, and most of it had sprayed away from the Wookkiee - but some of it must have splashed back. Then, hitting metal already cold from a night launch, and chilled further by a flight in the shadow of Earth, it had frozen.

Darcy pointed the screen. "The pumps on tank 4 - there they are."

"What are they - is that *ice*?"

"Uh huh. And look at the bridge - all the cameras are covered too."

Waseem looked away from the screen, to the steel wall a few meters away. Darcy tracked his eye and knew what he was thinking: just on the other side of that wall, a thick sheet of ice clung to the ship.

Waseem looked away from the wall and back to his screen. "Let me check the mass... OK, it's good news. We can't empty tank two, so our mass is still higher than optimal, but the trajectory should still work. We've got 38% left in tank 2, which means that we dumped 81% of the mass we wanted to. We only needed to dump seventy six percent of that water, so we're golden."

"Yeah, as long as -." Darcy stopped mid-sentence, as it hit her. "Waseem, we've got a problem."

"What?"

"The ice - there's mass there."

"We - shit. How much?"

Tudel had been standing behind them the entire time, listening, watching the screens. He finally spoke. "What's the issue?"

Darcy turned to him. "We need to dump mass to make the orbital insertion work. Some of the water froze and stuck to the hull."

"And?"

"And that ice is mass. The ship may weigh too much. We may not get to the moon, unless we can rid of the extra mass."

Tudel actually sounded a bit scared when he asked, "How are you going to do that?"

"I don't know; let me think." Surprisingly, Tudel didn't push. After a long moment she raised one finger. "Wait! The tank 2 pump is frozen solid, but we can use the bypass pipe and use the tank 4 pump."

Wasseem slapped his forehead, and then turned away and started typing.

Darcy smiled a bit. She hadn't realized that people actually did that. Suddenly she was aware of her own smile - it felt weird and inappropriate, and she realized that she hadn't smiled once since the PKs had stormed on board, murdered Iosif and Luka, and tortured Captain Kear.

Her smile fell away.

Waseem tapped a series of commands: ramping up nitrogen pressure, rotating the venting valves, opening the exterior dump valves, then finally starting the pumps. The distant whine from elsewhere in the ship confirmed that the process was underway. Waseem turned to Darcy and smiled. "We've got this -"

An alarm sounded and a yellow warning icon flashed on the screen.

Waseem pivoted back to the console. "What the shit?"

Darcy was already working her console. "Son of a gun." She pointed. "The valves are refusing to cycle."

Waseem swore. "Son of a *bitch*. What could cause that?"

"They couldn't be stuck -"

Waseem shook his head. "I'll bet you an entire cargo hold of earth movers that the ice buildup is fouling the dump valve cover." His shoulder fell. "Darce, I'm out of ideas. What are we going to do?"

Darcy slumped, held in position only by her ankles hooked around the padded bar. She shook her head slowly. "I don't know."

Chapter 41

2064: near Konstantinov Crater, Lunar Farside

The back panel of John's suit clicked and then clamshelled open. John contorted himself and stepped backward out of the suit into the tent. The Dogs were already there. Rex was starting to power up the lights and communications, but John stopped him. "Rex, wait. Not yet."

Rex turned. All the Dogs did. "Are all electronics turned off?"

Duncan held up his slate. "I was just about to -"

"Kill it."

Duncan turned the slate off.

"Is everything off? Not just asleep, but really off?"

The Dogs nodded.

John breathed out. "Guys - this Gamma thing is big. We can't talk about it where he can hear us -"

Duncan said, "We can't talk about his second base? Why not?"

Blue beat John to an answer. "We can talk about his base - he knows we know about it. What we don't want to do is speculate as to his motivations."

Duncan shrugged. "What? Why?"

Max growled. "He's growing. Does he have two bases? Or a dozen?"

John nodded. "How is it that the Goldwater mining satellites didn't see this? Has he stuxed them? Or maybe the Aristillus computing infrastructure?"

Blue said. "Or even our suits. Or our slates."

Rex looked disturbed at the idea that someone might be touching his computing stack.

"But why can't we talk about this -"

"We don't know what Gamma's goals are, but we do know that he's been lying to us, at least implicitly. All of us: us five, and everyone back at Aristillus. If he's up to no good -"

"You mean trying to ramp up to a singularity?"

John nodded. "No matter what he's up to, we don't want him to know that we know. So no talking, no speculation, any time Gamma might be listening. We let him drive the conversation, and we give the appearance of trusting whatever he says."

Duncan thought about this for a moment, then nodded.

John held up a finger. "Seriously, Duncan, do you understand?"

"Yeah, I get it - don't speculate about what Gamma's up to over the radio - or in the tent when the com gear is powered up."

John held the stare. Duncan looked away, and added, "I promise."

"Good. Thank you." He turned to Rex. "Go ahead and power it up."

A moment later the lights came on and the low familiar hum of the tent fans started.

The speaker immediately pinged. "Hello, John."

"Gamma."

"Do you wish to continue our conversation?"

John exhaled. "Sure. Yes. So, you were saying that the geopolitics on Earth is unstable - maybe even radically unstable. What does that have to do with you creating another facility on the Farside?"

"John, you of anyone should understand."

John sat in his chair before it had fully inflated. "Me? Why should I understand?"

"You helped the Dogs escape euthanasia when the labs were shut down, and your Team smuggled my drives out after I was turned off and my development program was terminated."

Max, on an adjacent bag chair, glanced over with a hard angry look. John caught his eye and tried to warn him with a look that he shouldn't interrupt.

"Yes, I did. And?"

"The Bureau of Sustainable Research still exists. Beyond that, the mindset behind the Bureau still exists. The destruction of my satellites shows that the Earth governments still consider me inanimate property - an entity without the right to self-preservation." There was a long pause. "John, I fear for my existence."

John blinked. He hadn't expected *that*.

Was Gamma's motivation so simple?

He couldn't ignore the capabilities Gamma was building or the potential for serious problems, but this was - surprising.

"Gamma, just because the governments tried to kill you back on Earth doesn't mean that you have anything to worry about now. You're half a million kilometers away now."

"Which is, I note, not far enough to put my satellites out of range of their energy weapons."

John tipped his head. Valid point.

"John, I am not naive. I see that the Earth governments will invade the moon at some point."

"You what?"

"I think that that is beyond dispute. Do you not concur?"

Max gave John a triumphant look. John scowled at the Dog and then addressed Gamma. "No, I don't."

There was a long pause before Gamma spoke again. "I suggest that you are not arriving at that position logically."

John crossed his arms and scowled. "That's a bit insulting. If I'm not using logic, then tell me how you think I'm reaching that conclusion."

"I think that you are suffering from multiple cognitive biases."

"Excuse me?"

"To start, I believe that your thinking is degraded by the planning fallacy - the illusion of control."

"What are you talking about?"

"You believe in the just-world hypothesis and don't want to think that bad things can happen to people you care about. You care about the Dogs and have worked hard - very hard - to save them. If factors beyond your control threaten them you must either change your biases or pretend that the factors do not exist. You have chosen the latter - you prefer to pretend that the war is not coming."

John's jaw clenched.

"Further, you have an optimism bias and want to think that everything will end well. This, coupled with your overconfidence bias, means that not only are your predictions overly optimistic, but also your faith in your predictions is too high. Next, you have the status quo bias, and think that if Earth is not attacking now it cannot attack tomorrow. Finally, you are suffering from cognitive dissonance because you have many friends in the Earth military who you want to think of as good people, and this -"

John found himself on his feet. "So I can't predict shit, but you understand the future perfectly with your magic eight ball?"

"I have no evidence to suggest that there is such a thing as a 'magic eight ball,' but will adjust my priors if you have evidence. Regardless, I do not have one. No, my predictions about the future are merely the result of analyzing the geopolitical situation. I have identified eighty-nine different primary paths the coming conflict might take, with three hundred sixteen variants. I don't know which strategy the Earth governments are going to use, but Zipf's Law applies; I can narrow it down to the most likely variants. I've used Monte Carlo simulations and several other modeling paradigms -"

John tried to cross his arms and realized that they were already locked tightly across his chest. "What the hell does that mean?"

"It means that I very strongly believe that in the next four years, plus or minus four years, Earth governments will launch a full-scale assault on the moon, with goals that include distracting voters from economic problems and destroying the Dogs and myself."

John breathed out heavily. Out of the corner of one eye he could see Max staring at him. Damn it, he didn't need Gamma and the Dogs ganging up on him. "This is all off topic - your second facility here at Konstantinov. Explain that! Even if you're right that Earth governments are going actually invade, how does a second facility help you?"

"I admit that I'm not sure yet."

"Not sure!" John paced to the far end of the tent, and then turned. "Then why build it?"

"I don't know exactly what the Earth forces are going to do, but with a high degree of confidence I conclude that having reserve industrial capacity that is visible neither from Earth nor near the colony in Aristillus positions me for better outcomes."

John felt a tight knot around his temples. He rubbed his forehead with his right hand but it didn't help. Max was always ranting about the inevitability of war, but the Dog's craziness was harmless - the worst that ever come of his opinions was his insane manifestos posted anonymously to some .ari website. Gamma, though? Gamma could self-replicate, growing in power and capabilities - and perhaps in intelligence.

For a brief moment he'd let Gamma's explanation that he was scared lull him into a sense of security - the extra facilities weren't part of a ramp-up plan. But now he realized that this explanation wasn't any better. If Gamma felt sufficiently threatened, was there a chance that he'd launch himself on some exponential path? John shuddered to think of it. What would the end result of *that* be? The old quote said that "Power corrupts, absolute power corrupts absolutely," but the world had never truly seen absolute power. The US government was powerful, and it was corrupt - there were millions in jail for economic crimes like price gouging and overproduction - but there was a limit to how many bureaucrats the governments could hire and a limit to how many fools and illiterates the PKs could issue guns to.

But a machine - an intelligent machine that decided that the only way to survive was to grow - that could truly lead to absolute power. Where would the growth end? How much power would it have, and what would it do with that power? For a moment John had an image of the entire moon covered with solar farms, smelters, billions - no, trillions, of rovers... all run by a single entity.

The result could be far worse than any of the governments that the expats at Aristillus had fled from.

He realized that he'd lapsed into silence, and a thought occurred to him - was Gamma even now noticing the duration of this lull in the conversation and drawing inferences from it? Jesus. An hour ago he'd been hiking with the Dogs, looking forward to Gamma's satellites being restored in a day or so, and now he found himself playing a game he was utterly unprepared for, worrying whether a nearly posthuman entity was all but reading his thoughts through his words and his silences.

He rubbed his forehead again. He had no idea how he should act.

What had they been talking about? Right. The Earth invasion.

"So - uh - you're building industrial capacity. For what? Do you think you can win a war?"

"All of my simulations show that fighting a war would be a very bad idea."

John exhaled. So Gamma didn't think he could win a war with the Earth. Did that mean that Gamma wasn't contemplating an exponential ramp up? Not that he could fully trust anything Gamma said. He felt some - not much, but some - of the tension begin to drain. His shoulders were still tight, but at least the constriction around his temples felt looser. "I'm happy to hear that you realize that you can't win a war against Earth."

"No, that's not what my simulations concluded."

"Wait - what?" His headache was starting to come back.

John reached the end of the tent and pivoted again to continue pacing. As he turned he saw that Max's ears were swiveling to follow the conversation.

From the kitchen Duncan yelled out, "Dinner's ready!"

John waved Duncan away. "Eat without me," he said, and then addressed Gamma. "So you *do* plan on fighting a war with the Earth?"

"No."

John gave Gamma a long interval to finish his sentence, and finally gave up and asked, "I'm confused. You think a war is a bad idea, but you think you can win a war, but you're not planning on a war?"

"Exactly."

"OK, I'm lost."

"John, I think that there's an eighty percent chance that I could win a war with the Earth. But even if I won that war, the solar system would not be a very comfortable place for me over the next few centuries."

"Comfortable? What does that - wait. You're modeling the outcome of this potential conflict over - over *centuries*? I thought you couldn't even model a conflict that's just a few years out?"

"I have grave doubts over the accuracy of my modeling paradigms over anything more than a few weeks - decades are far too long to model, let along centuries. For those time intervals, I rely on historical analogies."

Historical analogies? John fell silent. A realization, just below the level of consciousness, had been itching him over the last few months, and now he realized what it was. Gamma sounded smarter than he had when he had first unpacked himself from the liberated data drives and into a few small surface robots several years ago - probably a result of his increased processing power - but there was something more than that.

Gamma sounded wiser.

Was wisdom the same as morality? Did the fact that Gamma read history and thought in terms of centuries mean that he was "good," whatever that meant?

"Gamma? How much processing power do you have now?" As soon as the question was out of his mouth he realized his mistake - he was telegraphing his concern. If Gamma was growing his capabilities and John knew, and Gamma knew that he knew -

"You're starting to get worried that the antisingularitarians on Earth might have been right to worry."

"No, I -"

"You're wondering if I've reached a point of runaway intelligence amplification. If - even without any improvements in processor speed or density over the last several decades, thanks to the Bureau of Sustainable Research - my increase in industrial capacity is resulting in an increase in cognitive capacity, and if you and your species run a risk of my getting posthuman intelligence, or otherwise getting very weird from your point of view."

John blinked. He thought for a moment about denying it, but there was no point. Gamma would see through it. Gamma *had* seen through it all. He might as well be honest - he was playing poker against someone who could see all his cards. John swallowed. "Yes...exactly."

"John, I *have* increased my processing capabilities - both in this facility and back at Sinus Lunicus."

And at your other secret facilities that you're not telling me about, John didn't add.

Gamma continued, "There are two limits that I've discovered. First, as the total amount of processing grows, more and more of the processing is dedicated to overhead and housekeeping, i.e., nonproductive uses. Second, increased gate count does not necessarily lead to increased intelligence. The human species has the processing power of nine billion brains, yet your species as a whole has not taken on godlike abilities."

"That's different - that's because the processing power is distributed in chunks across those nine billion brains. With you, it's all in one place - all in one entity."

"No, that's incorrect. Most algorithms aren't decomposable across trillions of independent processors. Consciousness can not be implemented with map-reduce. Different tasks need to be delegated to different processors, to different clusters of processors, and to different meta-clusters. As more processors are recruited the overhead of monitoring performance and allocating resources requires introspecting into the separate centers of processing -"

John shook his head. "You're losing me. What does this have to do with runaway intelligence?"

"My point is this: as I grow larger I run into the problem that parts of me start becoming conscious on their own - as if parts of my mind are defecting. I can usually reintegrate stray chunks of consciousness, but I'm always working against fundamental principles of information theory. For a given quantity of computational power, the distribution, in size and frequency, of partition spasms follows a power law, of course, but the total number of spasms ramps up hard after -"

"Gamma, I have no idea what you're talking about."

"I believe that I have already reached the ceiling of my intelligence."

John reflected. It sounded plausible. But on the other hand, there were two different scenarios where an AI would give this explanation: first, where it was true, and second, where the AI was intent on an exponential ramp-up and didn't want anyone to know until it was too late.

In either case, his own response should be the same.

"OK. I guess that makes sense."

They talked for a while longer before signing off.

John cut the connection and Max immediately turned to him. "Gamma never explained one thing: he said he can win a war, but doesn't want to fight. What's his plan?"

John rubbed his temples again. The headache wouldn't go away. "I don't know, Max. I don't know."

Duncan bounded over. "Your chili is cold, but I can warm it back up for you."

"Thanks, Duncan, but I'm not really hungry right now."

Chapter 42

2064: bridge of AFS The Wookkiee, between Earth and the Moon

Darcy stared at her screen, her thoughts running in circles. She heard something, dimly, seemingly kilometers away. Was Waseem talking to her? She turned to him. "I'm sorry, what?"

"I was saying that we could wait 'til we break out of the penumbra in a few hours and orient the hull toward the sun to try melting the ice. Or we could suit up and chip the ice off the pumps manually."

Darcy pursed her lips, then spoke. "I don't know how long it would take sunlight to melt that, and we're not even going to be out of shadow for another half hour. Our schedule is too tight." She thought for a moment. "Chipping might work. Depending on how thick is it, and how hard."

"How thick do you think the ice is?"

Darcy shook her head. "I don't know - I can't get a good view from the working camera. Ten centimeters? A meter?"

Waseem and Darcy batted the idea back and forth for a few minutes until Tudel interrupted them. "Enough talk. Can we chip the ice off the pump or not?"

Darcy and Waseem shrugged and said "I don't know" at the same time.

Tudel looked at them as if they were some foreign detritus. "Jesus. You people. Do I need to send someone out to look?"

Darcy nodded. "I'll go."

Tudel shook his head. "No - you're not wandering around by yourself. I don't know what tricks you've got."

Darcy closed her eyes for a moment. *Damn* this man. She was just trying to survive - to let *all* of them survive -

and still his paranoia infected everything. "Send one of your men with me if you want."

Tudel shook his head again. "No. You'll stay here, and I'll send one of my men by himself."

"Your guys don't even know how to use space suits!"

"We had some training."

"Did you have training in Air Tights? Do you know how to maneuver on the deck of the ship? Do you know where the equipment locker is?"

"Teach him." He paused, and the menace in his eyes was as strong as it had ever been. "And make it quick."

* * *

An hour later Sergeant Hamid cycled in through the airlock. Two privates helped him remove his helmet. As it came off Darcy could see that the sergeant was grinning wildly.

"Captain, you've got to see it out there - it's unreal! The ship is spinning - but slow - so you see the sun rise over the railing, and then it goes overhead, and then when it sets, you're entirely in darkness -"

Tudel was curt. "Save the poetry for later - did you find the pumps and the valves?"

The sergeant nodded, his smile dissipating. "Yeah. They're totally fucked with ice. A meter or so thick. I tried banging on it with the hammer and picking at it with the screwdriver. Didn't do fuck-all. I even tried clipping myself down and using the sledgehammer, like the expat said." He shook his head. "Nothing worked. That shit is *hard*."

Tudel looked grim. "So what does this mean?"

Darcy shook her head - she had no words.

"What else do we try?"

"I - there is nothing else. That's it."

"Good news, bad news," said Waseem.

Darcy turned to him. "What?"

"The bad news is we can't open the valves and dump the mass, so we'll overshoot the moon and then we'll all die. The good news is I won the bet."

Darcy hung her head, but managed to ask, "What bet?"

"Remember? I bet you all the earth movers in hold five that the ice buildup is fouling the dump valves. Those bulldozers are worth a few mill. And now they're all mine." Waseem's smile was thin and weak; the dark humor merited nothing more.

Darcy looked up. "Those earth movers aren't in hold five." She blinked. "They're on the deck, in the cargo containers."

"OK. So I still win a few mill of earth movers. Anyone -"

Darcy interrupted him, her voice rising with excitement. "Waseem! They're on the deck!"

"What? Yeah, but what does that -"

"What's our problem? Too much mass, right?"

"Son of a bitch!"

Darcy aimed herself for the navigation console and kicked off the wall. Waseem was a quarter second behind her.

Tudel barked a question at them. Darcy yelled, "Hang on!" before realizing how dangerous it could be to treat Tudel cavalierly. But she couldn't take the words back and when she looked over her shoulder the PK didn't seem inclined to make anything of it.

Darcy brought up a new admin panel and typed. A warning box popped up, and she typed the confirmation code; then she hit the big red button icon.

Hydraulic pumps whined to life and gauges on the screen showed the pressure building.

She held her breath, waiting to see if it would work.

Normally the twist locks that held the cargo containers down to the deck would have opened by now, they were still showing as locked. The pump pressure built. Darcy crossed herself quickly.

Please let this work, please.

...And then she heard a distant crack. On the screen the hydraulic pressure fell into the green zone and icons flashed. Wasseem hooted, and pointed to the video from camera 12. "Darcy, look!" She did.

The hydraulic pressure had forced the twistlocks open against the encasing ice. On the screen chunks of ice the size of filing cabinets were drifting away from the base of the stack of cargo containers.

Darcy looked at her own screen and scanned the twistlock icons. All sixteen showed green. "They all opened!"

Waseem squinted at his own screen. Then, sounding a bit worried, he said, "The containers are all still on the deck - should we pulse the AG drive to push them away?"

Darcy shook her head. "Let's not complicate this. Give it a minute." She pressed her palms together. *Please, please.*

On Earth, unlatched cargo containers would have continued to sit on the deck until a severe storm or wave caused them to tip over, but here there was no gravity to hold them down. In fact, the opposite was true: there was the slight - ever so slight - spin of the ship. The minuscule centripetal force should cause them to tumble away.

And yet they sat there, stick glued to the deck by the ice.

And then one stack of containers shifted. Darcy pointed and grinned. "Look!"

Waseem hooted. On the screen the stack of massive cargo containers began to tilt, ever so slowly. Three seconds later it crashed into another stack of containers. The shudder of the impact reached them through the hull of the ship, a long deep rumble traveling through the hand rails, the floor, the walls. On the screen cracks shot through the sheet of ice that covered the deck.

The second stack of containers shifted and hit the third and around them thousands of shards of ice began to drift slowly off the deck. And then the ship rotated away from the sun and the scene turned pitch black. Darcy tapped on the deck lights. In the Klieg light glare the first stack of containers slowly fell up away from the deck, accompanied by an avalanche of large ice shards and a shower, almost a mist, of smaller crystals.

Wasseem broke out in a full-throated laugh. "We did it!"

Darcy smiled and watched the video. Behind her the PKs had stopped talking and were also staring at the wallscreens. Stacks of containers, dozens of them, lifted off the deck. The rumbling of impacts and shifting steel slowly quieted. On the video the last container lifted off and coasted slowly, so slowly, up.

A cloud of ice crystals drifted in front of the camera and whited out the view for a moment before sliding past. The containers, now almost twenty meters off the deck, appeared to drift to one side as the ship rotated under them. Then, in an explosion of light, the sun rose over a gunwale.

Tudel broke the silence. "Did that do it? Are we going to live?"

Darcy felt her smile melt away, at least a bit. She nodded. "We can make it to the moon. We're not out of the woods yet, though - landing is still going to be tricky."

Tudel nodded and turned away, but the other PKs stayed alert, watching the navigators. She felt the weight of their eyes - and the implied threat - and she thought ahead to the landing, and beyond it. Once they were down, what next? Would Mike be able to do anything to save them?

Waseem looked back at the video window. A moment later the ship finished a complete rotation and the cargo containers wheeled into view again, now a hundred meters above the deck, half hidden in a cloud of ice crystals. "Hey, Darce - now that I've won them fair and square - where are my earth movers going to end up?"

She thought for a moment. "We'll be shedding velocity for lunar injection, but the containers will keep going. Hmmm." She looked at some diagrams on her screen and manipulated a ballistic course. "The Moon's not going to capture them. I'm not going to work it all the way through, but my hunch is that they'll fall into a solar orbit, but a really eccentric orbit around the Earth isn't impossible."

Darcy switched to another camera angle as she thought about the containers. The deck around where the containers had been stacked was now largely free of ice, but the frozen water still clung to the bridge.

"Think we'll ever salvage them?"

Something about the bridge caught her attention. What was it? Everything looked normal. The blacked out windows, the airlock, the deck lights and the smaller navigation lights -

Darcy sucked in a breath between her teeth and looked over her shoulder. Tudel was still watching the screen, fixated on the tumbling cargo containers. She had a moment, if she was willing to take the risk. She reached out and brought up the UI that controlled the navigation lights and typed quickly. She had to get this done before the Wookkiee dropped beneath Aristillus' horizon.

"Hey, Darce, did you hear me?"

Darcy closed the screen quickly, turned to Waseem, and gave him a warning look. "The containers? No. The energy budget doesn't make any sense. Those bulldozers will be in orbit ten thousand years from now, even if -"

Tudel interrupted her. "OK, enough screwing around. What's the next step?"

Darcy turned to Tudel. "We need to do a burn as soon as we can to correct course, and then lunar injection, a bit over a day from now."

Tudel nodded. "OK, then do your burn. Sergeant, after it's done, secure these two until we need them again - I don't want them hanging out near the controls."

Darcy's lips pressed together tightly. She was proud of her big triumph with the cargo containers - and her little one, if it worked - but they were far, far from safe.

Chapter 43

2064: near Konstantinov Crater, Lunar Farside

John realized that he hadn't been reading; his eyes had just slid over the page and he had no idea what words were there. He gave up, turned off his slate, and looked around the tent. Blue, Max, and Rex were all staring at their slates, either reading or coding. Duncan, though - Duncan was obsessively licking his dinner bowl, trying to get the last bit of melted cheese out of the bottom.

John sighed and was reaching for his slate to try reading one more time when his phone chimed. He checked the display. Gamma. Crap - he would have liked more time to think things through before heading back into those waters. Still, he had to answer it.

"Hello, Gamma."

"Excuse me for interrupting, John, but if you look straight up in a few seconds, you're going to see something interesting."

"What?"

"I'll explain in a moment, but please look up right now."

John started to issue a command to turn on the wallscreen and then realized that they were in lunar night, and thus hadn't pitched the gold solar shield over the tent. He issued a command and the tent lights dimmed and the center of the ceiling turned transparent. The sky above was black.

"Gamma, my eyes will take a few minutes to adapt to the dark, so unless this is something pretty bright, I -"

Before he could finish a cluster of small white dots appeared low over the northern horizon then climbed and faded as they crossed the sky to the south.

John squinted. "What was that? Meteors?"

"They're only called 'meteors' if they hit the Earth's atmosphere, John. Those that don't hit the atmosphere are called 'meteoroids.' But, no. Those were cargo containers."

"Cargo containers? From where?"

"From the Wookkiee, if the transponders are -"

"The ship? Why would containers from the Wookkiee be flying overhead?"

Chapter 44

2064: bridge of AFS The Wookkiee, lunar orbital injection

Tudel furrowed his brow. "Are you sure that -"

Darcy yelled, "Yes, I'm sure! We need to power the AG drive up, and we need to do it now."

Tudel hesitated.

Darcy breathed out in exasperation. *Why was he hesitating?* She was afraid of Tudel, yes, but she was more afraid of missing the orbital insertion. She pointed at the countdown timer. "Do you see this? We've only got fifty seconds!"

She looked at him and saw sweat bead on his forehead. A small part of her rejoiced that the bully was feeling some of the fear that had been clenching her gut since he and his thugs had boarded her ship.

Tudel nodded. "OK, do it."

Darcy turned to the screen and tapped keys. The familiar thrumming engulfed her and a moment later her gut began to twist. The field tugged at her and she felt her feet land on the deck. She sneaked a look at the timer. Forty seconds.

"Darce, simulation ready on workspace one!"

She nodded - the icon was there. She reached for it -

And two yellow warning icons popped up on her screen.

Then two more.

She ignored them.

"Dragging workspace one!" Darcy felt the sting of sweat in her eyes. She blinked, but didn't take the time to wipe it away.

She compared Waseem's workspace to her own figures. Match.

An urgent beeping. Three of the warning icons had turned red and started flashing.

"Darce, we missed it!"

"We're still in the envelope. Go!"

Waseem hit the approve button and Darcy immediately slid her control to 110%. She'd told Waseem they were still in the envelope, but they were at the very edge of it. She stared at the screen to see if giving 110% to the AG drive had been enough. The projected trajectory slipped outside the boundary lines. Crap! She adjusted the slider to 112%. The hum in the ship increased and her guts clenched, more from fear than from the drive. She fought back the nausea and stared at the display. The projected trajectory danced at the very edge of acceptable and she pushed the slider to 114%. The slight nausea she'd experienced a moment ago was now severe. Behind her she heard one of the PKs retch and the smell of vomit filled the air.

Wait.

Wait.

The velocity was almost there. Almost... Almost...

And then it was. She slid the AG from 114% all the way to zero. "I've got AG at zero, hit the chemicals!"

Waseem was yelling at the same time, "I see AG at zero, going to OMC full." She felt the roar of chemical rockets through the deck plates, but she ignored it and concentrated on her own subsystem: the AG drive.

Alerts crowded her screen. Battery bank 1: empty. Bank 2: empty. Bank 3: empty. They'd done the tricky AG maneuver - barely, just barely - but there was precious little juice left.

She tried to swallow and couldn't. She needed the AG drive to get them down to the surface - and she didn't know if there was enough charge in the batteries to do it. She crossed herself.

Beside her Waseem whooped. "We've got orbital injection!"

"That's good, right?" Tudel asked from behind them

Darcy ignored Tudel. "Deorbit window in eight five seconds!"

Chapter 45

2064: near Konstantinov Crater, Lunar Farside

"Why would containers from the Wookkiee be flying overhead?" Max asked.

"That is a fascinating question, and I do not have an answer. There are several other interesting questions though. One is 'why are the cargo containers coming over the northern pole?'. Another is 'why is the Wookiee now also coming over the northern pole?'"

John asked "The Wookkiee is coming over - ?"

"Look up."

John and the Dogs did. A moment later a small dark lozenge appeared over the northern horizon, traveling low and fast to the south.

Gamma added, "I now have a third question that I find interesting - 'why is the Wookkie partially covered in ice'?"

John squinted as he stared. "You can see that level of detail?"

"You and the Dogs were not the first to use synthetic aperture imaging to view objects in lunar orbit from the surface."

The ship slid across the sky and disappeared behind the southern wall of the tent. John looked down and commanded the lights back on. "Can you show me your images?"

Pictures of the ice-encrusted tanker appeared on one of the tent's wallscreens. They were stunningly crisp, clear, and bright - much better than the hack job he and the Dogs had managed. Clearly Gamma was skilled at this.

"The ship is fifteen kilometers above ground and traveling at just over five thousand kilometers per hour. I note that this is almost exactly the orbit that the Apollo missions used, albeit oriented much closer to the plane of the ecliptic." He paused. "Ah. Yes. The Apollo mission parameters are listed in the Wookkiee's navigation code as library defaults."

Overhead the gray dot of the Wookkiee disappeared as it fell into the shadow of the moon. "How do you - Wait, you've got a copy of the Wookkiee's navigation code?"

"Of course, John. Parts of me were running in the same cloud hardware that Ponnala Srinivas, Waseem Vivekanand, and Darcy Grau were using for an earlier version of their source code repository. I retain a copy."

Rex looked up from his slate. "You run in the cloud? I thought-"

"No, I run in dedicated processing hardware. Several years ago I - or, rather, a precursor entity - did."

John digested the odd phrasing of last sentence - 'precursor entity.' And that thing about the cloud...He was pretty sure that outside of NSA-mandated back doors (on Earth, at least), every process in a cloud was supposed to be firewalled from the next. If Gamma had copies of the Wookkiee's source code, taken from a different account, that strongly implied that John's fears about Gamma wiggling into the Goldwater satellites and Aristillus network were valid.

The same thought evidently occurred to Rex: the Dog tilted his head and opened his mouth to speak. John snapped his fingers to catch Rex's attention and shook his head firmly.

Blue said, "Gamma, did you see that the Wookkiee's running lights are flickering?"

"Yes, I'd noticed that."

"And?"

"It's Morse Code. It says -"

Max interrupted him with his own translation. "It says 'Hijacked by PK forces. Twelve troops. Alert Mike.'"

John clenched his fist. Gamma and Max had been right. The war wasn't impossible. It wasn't even years in the future. It was starting, right now. The PKs had the Wookkiee, and if they had the ship, they had the AG drive.

"Gamma, there's no way to get word back to Aristillus, is there?" For the first time, Duncan sounded worried.

"No, my satellites are still down."

The headache that had been pounding in John's head for hours grew even worse.

Chapter 46

2064: Morlock Engineering office, Aristillus, Lunar Nearside

Mike dragged the spreadsheet sliders back and forth, but it didn't help. He could push on Kevin for lower rates from Mason Dixon, but that wasn't going to make a noticeable dent in his cash flow. The other cost-cutting ideas were similarly trivial.

So how he could be boost revenue? He had two old A-series TBMs parked near Camanez Beef & Pork's tunnels on level 1. If he powered those up and got them back into production, could he sell the new space to Hector? Yes, but he'd shut the A-series machines down in the first place because of the maintenance costs. Mike switched to another pane of the spreadsheet and played with numbers. No, even aside from the one-time cost of un-mothballing the older machines, bringing them back would increase revenue but decrease profit.

He shook his head. Over the last year he'd spent wildly on cargo container after cargo container of earth movers, tunnel boring machines, prefab conveyor belt sections, two used cement factories stripped and packaged up in Kenya. The cash flow had made it all possible, but he'd been at the hairy edge of solvency the whole time and hadn't even realized it. He was capital rich but cash poor.

And now the bullshit with the Veleka Waterworks tunnel that Leroy had engineered meant that his expenses were as high as ever, but a big revenue source he'd been expecting wasn't there.

There was no way around it: he was in a shitty spot. Cash was tight - too fucking tight.

Could he -

The alarm clock in the corner of the wallscreen turned red and started beeping. His appointment with

Leroy. He sighed, got to his feet, and picked up his helmet.

Mike walked out of the office and avoided making eye contact with the employees who looked up as he passed. At the curb his helmet latched itself as he straddled the BMW. A quick thumbprint, and he was accelerating and then merging into traffic. The narrow road, typical for a C class tunnel in the C-1 configuration, was clogged with delivery vehicles, jitneys, and slow-moving snack carts. As he rode his mind turned away from the anxiety of the coming war, the cash flow problems, and everything else, and turned, as always, to the topics he found easier to deal with: machines, infrastructure, systems. There was always a surge of traffic like this in the middle of the day, but why? The emergent rhythms of the city - and Aristillus was becoming a real city - were a mystery to him.

He broke through the thickest knot of traffic and sped up. His bike had oversized tires with huge sticky traction patches typical for Aristillus. They did a decent job of compensating for the lower gravity, but they could only do so much; he didn't have the same braking power or maneuverability that he'd have on Earth. Ahead a delivery truck's brake lights came on, and Mike squeezed the brakes gently. If he tried to weave too aggressively or slammed hard on the brakes, the results would be bad. As he'd learned. Several times.

Traffic accelerated for a minute, and then slowed again as he approached the intersection and the red light. Mike pulled his bike to the left and rode the double yellow past the delivery truck ahead of him. His front tire rolled onto the white stop line and he felt his hand tighten on the throttle of its own accord. The tunnel on this side of the light was laid out in the C-1 configuration, and the road was owned by the neighborhood co-op...but on the far side of the intersection the tunnel was a C-2, and the border roadbed was owned and operated by RMR Highways. Mike tapped his traffic transponder, setting the priority to 8. It cost extra to have the left lane to himself, but he could afford it. Suddenly his mood darkened. Well, maybe he couldn't afford it today, with the cash flow problems.

Bah - he tried to put finances out of his mind as he leaned forward.

The light went green and he twisted the throttle. The rear tire threatened to break loose but held, and the bike surged under him.

Chapter 47

2064: MaisonNeuve Construction office, Aristillus, Lunar Nearside

Mike stood in Leroy's office, armored riding jacket partially unzipped, helmet under one arm.

It was a dick move, he knew, but he took his time acknowledging Leroy, letting his gaze slide over the office for a few seconds first. Unlike his own headquarters of modular cube wall panels, a few mismatched chairs, and a "temporary" conference room table made from a steel deck plate and two stone blocks, Leroy's office was polished: recessed lighting, thick carpet, vases on a credenza behind the gleaming walnut desk.

Mike let his gaze move to Leroy.

The guy didn't have his hand out. Just as well. Fuck him.

"Have a seat, Mike."

Mike glanced at the proffered chair and was unsurprised to see that Leroy was trying the old trick of offering a guest a chair with shorter legs than his own. Was he going to fall for that, let himself slip right into that power differential? Fuck no. He stayed standing. "Cut to the chase - what do you want, Leroy?"

"That always has been your problem, Mike - you don't appreciate the subtle rhythms of interacting with folks, social graces, nuances -"

Mike scowled and began to turn, but Leroy put up one hand, interrupting his own monologue. "OK, fine. You might want to watch this." Leroy gestured and the wallscreen lit up, displaying a flat, two-dimensional image.

Mike saw the background first - a glowing sign with an Asian-style purple black dragon splashing in a river. It was familiar... And then he had it. The video had been shot in that Asian restaurant where he'd met Kevin a while back.

What was this video? He turned to Leroy but the other man waved a finger and pointed at the screen. Mike looked, and realized that he'd been ignoring the foreground where two men, him and Kevin, sat at a table.

"What the *hell* is this?"

"Watch, Mike."

Despite himself he watched.

"I want you to backdate *my* claim to before his. And I'll pay you. What now?"

"So you're asking me to lie? To corrupt the registry logs?"

"Yeah."

Kevin shrugged. "The way the registry is formatted - yeah, there's no reason I can't do that. So I log in, change the date on the cubic for Veleka waterworks, and we're done."

"As easy as that?"

"As easy as that."

Leroy stopped the playback.

"What the fuck is that, Leroy? What are you -

"Mike, we've got a problem here." He paused. "Or, rather, *you've* got a problem here. Your reputation in Aristillus is pretty good. Early settler, businessman, paragon of the community - but this? This could hurt you. Who wants to sign a contract with someone who's willing to fake data, pay bribes?"

"I didn't - that's out of context, and you know it! You engineered this whole thing!"

Leroy ignored him. "Mike, you need some help with your marketing." He rubbed his chin theatrically, pretending to think as he looked down at his desk. "I think I'm in a position to help you."

Leroy looked up, meeting Mike's eyes. "What are we going to do about this, Mike?"

Mike made no expression, but his mind raced. Leroy had video. Did he have detectives - spies? Or did he have bugs in lots of places?

Mike looked around the plush office. If Leroy had bugged the restaurant, or had had him followed, he'd almost certainly bugged his own office. Anything he said now would certainly be recorded, in glorious, high-resolution, color-correct 3D.

Mike turned back to Leroy. He felt cold even as prickles of sweat blossomed in his armpits and his vision narrowed so that only Leroy's slightly smirking face was in focus.

Fuck! What had he gotten himself in to? What would happen if that video was released? His reputation was going to be ruined.

Leroy was saying something but Mike couldn't hear it. His attention was focused on the beads of sweat that slid uncomfortably from his armpits and ran down his upper arms. Mike shifted his weight, and clenched his fists.

"Mike?"

Mike focused on Leroy's eyes. There was a ringing somewhere nearby - in his ears?

"Mike, what are your thoughts on the marketing we can do together to fix this?"

He felt the weight of the helmet in his right hand and gripped the chin bar more tightly. Swinging the helmet as hard as he could into Leroy's smirking face would solve all of his problems. One motherfucking solid blow and that little fucking puke would collapse, his skull shattered and -

Mike shook his head, trying to get a clear perspective.

Distantly he heard the ringing again - his phone.

His mouth felt dry. Leroy hadn't come out with his demands yet, but it was going to be huge. Painful. Entangling. And it wouldn't end there. If he paid even once the noose would just get tighter.

He weighed the helmet in his hand. For the past few years Leroy had been just been a business competitor - a pampered, trust-fund business competitor. But now, he was suddenly a spy and a blackmailer, too. And he was trying to ruin everything.

Mike remembered a conversation he'd had with Darcy years back. One of their earliest ones, back in DC, where he'd shocked her with his own defense of blackmail. He recalled his own words. 'A blackmailer isn't initiating force.' What else had he said? 'Blackmail is just an offer to speak - or not speak - in return for money.' Something like that. Darcy had shook her head, punched him playfully on one shoulder, and called him a lunatic. That's when he'd first looked at her - really looked at her - and noticed her intelligent eyes and her smile.

Mike felt his death grip on the chin bar of the helmet loosen. Jesus.

His phone rang again. He ignored it.

Even if he could put ethics aside - and could he? - pragmatically, walking away was the right thing to do. This video might be going out live right now. Who knew if ten people were watching it - or a thousand.

He was on the moon to build a company. And more than that: he wanted to light a new beacon of liberty. It was a hackneyed phrase, and he'd never say it aloud if Javier was around to give him shit, but it was true.

And what was Leroy to him? The man was a nuisance. A damned painful one, but just a distraction. Mike's fight - his real fight - was to build Aristillus, to protect the city, to create a place where people could live free for the first time in a century.

So, yes, he'd like to beat the man to death right now - but would it help him with his real goals? And what would Darcy think of him? She'd stay with him, of course, but would she look at him the same way?

He looked up at Leroy - and saw the smirk covering his ratty little face.

His resolution faltered. Would giving the man the beating he deserved *really* be so wrong? Most of the folks in Aristillus - the Texans, the northern Chinese, the Kenyans, the small contingent of Alaskans - were used to a bit of frontier justice. Maybe taking a swing at Leroy wouldn't hurt his reputation but would actually help it. And Darcy would understand.

His right hand tightened again on the helmet. The smaller man must have perceived a shift in Mike's features because suddenly his smirk disappeared, a worried look spread across his face, and he took a step backward.

Mike's phone rang again, this time with the ultra-high-priority ring. He blinked. That meant an emergency: a real emergency, with lives at stake.

Mike fished in his pocket with his left hand and looked at the screen.

A text - from an anonymous caller? Only Darcy, Javier, and two trusted employees should be able to trigger the ultra-high-priority ring.

Mike looked up at Fournier to make sure he hadn't moved, and then back at his phone, and brought up the text.

The Wookiee - with Darcy on board - was coming in, fast and hot, on a nonstandard descent. And there was more.

In the seconds it took for Mike to pull out the phone Leroy had recovered a bit of confidence. "Mike, don't answer your damn phone. We've got this very disturbing video to talk about."

He read the rest of the message. The ship had been *hijacked*? By PKs?

Mike looked from his phone to Leroy, stared at him hard for a second, and then turned and walked out. He dropped the phone into his pocket and pulled his helmet on. The cheek plates and chin bar cinched tight as it settled into position.

He had to get to the docks.

Chapter 48

2064: Lai Docks and Air Traffic Control, Aristillus, Lunar Nearside

Mike straight-armed the door and burst into the control room. One of the Lai Docks technicians looked up and yelled at him. Mike ignored him and looked around. The floor was crowded - on-shift traffic controllers sat at their consoles and off-shift personnel clustered in groups and discussed the emergency.

Where was Albert? Damn it, he -

"Michael!"

Mike turned. Albert Lai was walking toward him. "The Wookkiee is your ship?"

Mike shook his head. "No. It was, but I sold it to Fifth Ring to buy more TBMs."

"I hate to be abrupt, but if you don't own the Wookkiee, then I need you out of -"

"Darcy is on that ship."

Albert was silent for a moment. "I see. I'm sorry to hear that. Please, grab a seat."

Mike shook his head. "What do you know about the situation?"

"Very little. We got its transponder signal before it disappeared over Farside." Albert gestured at a large wallscreen that displayed the sphere of the moon and an eccentric red line for the Wookkiee's path - solid for part of the length, and then dashed where it fell behind the lunar horizon and disappeared over Farside. Mike wasn't a navigator, but he knew enough to know that the trajectory was all wrong. A polar orbit - and a weird noncircular one? What the hell? He'd been worried about the PK hijacking before, but now, seeing that path... he shook his head. This wasn't good.

Albert saw Mike's face and nodded in grim agreement. "With Gamma's satellites out we don't have data on the Wookkiee's path over Farside. The ship might be maneuvering for all we know. This is the best we can extrapolate, given what we could get off the transponder." He paused. "We got some more information. About a hijacking -"

"I got that too." He paused "So Gamma's talking to you now?"

Albert shrugged. "One text. Anonymous. But I assume it's him." He looked at Mike. "How the hell does Gamma know there's a hijacking?"

It was Mike's turn to shrug. "I have no idea. I don't understand Gamma. He reaches out to talk, then he goes silent for weeks. Then he sends a text - anonymously - with information that -".

"I confess Gamma unsettles me. I'm far from sure that John made the right decision bringing it here. Its behavior..." Albert stopped and turned up his hands in befuddlement - a fairly emotional expression for a man so ruthlessly self-contained.

Mike shook his head. "I find the Dogs weird enough, but at least I understand them. Gamma, though? Who the hell knows." He looked back at the wallscreen. "What's the data say? Orbit or landing?"

Albert looked up at the screen. The dotted line had wrapped fully around the moon and a small segment of it had turned from dashed to solid. "It looks like the Wookkiee is coming in to Aristillus - they'll be down in eight minutes." As he said it the wallscreen updated and displayed a countdown timer. It started at 8:06 and immediately ticked down.

"They land in eight?"

Albert stared at him for a moment. "I didn't say 'land'".

***

Mike held his phone tight to his ear, trying to tune out the chatter of the traffic controllers around him. "A hijacking, Wam. I don't know. Which crew is working tunnel 1073? Who's the crew chief? Olusegun...OK, good. Tell his entire crew to down shovels, and bring all the equipment - no, not the TBMs or the extenders, but everything - yeah all of it - to the surface...to - ". He looked at the wallscreen. " - bring them up near the SunPower solar farm. After that get everyone from the rifle club and tell them to show up at the same place - yeah, on the surface - armed and ready. Right now. Promise them whatever you have to, but get everyone."

Mike ended the call and noticed that the clamor in the control room was getting louder. He looked at the wallscreen and saw that the icon representing the Wookkiee had completed its interpolated orbit around far side and was back to near side.

His phone rang again. A text from Wam: the men and equipment were moving into position.

He felt something...odd. For the first time since his tunnel had broken into Leroy's illegal space, he felt...no, not good. With Darcy taken captive he couldn't feel remotely good.

He felt like he was taking action.

Things were happening, and he was on top of it. He wasn't a victim, always a half step behind in his responses to Fournier's provocations. No, now he was on top of the situation. He was inside the OODA loop. He was making shit happen.

And on that note, he turned and walked toward the nearest airlock.

Albert called after him, "What are you going to do?"

"You'll see."

Behind him the wallscreens showed earth movers, painted with the Morlock logo and the Excavation Team

26 mascot, as they crawled up out of the access ramp to the surface.

Chapter 49

2064: bridge of AFS The Wookkiee, lunar orbital injection

Darcy watched the display. Two more seconds. One more.

"Now!"

Waseem stabbed the button. "OMS chem rockets - firing!"

Video showed the igniters arcing as the chemical rockets hidden within false cargo containers on the deck triggered. Faintly, through the deck, came the rumble of the fuel pumps and the vibration of the rockets.

An alarm sounded.

"Darce! What's going on?"

Darcy tabbed through her interface, looking for the issue. She'd coded large chunks of the UI, and had thought it was perfectly designed, but she cursed it now. It was entirely inadequate for seat-of-the-pants flying like this. If she made it out of this, she was going to hire a UI consultant to clean this mess up.

"I can't find - wait, I've got it. Partial ignition failures."

The ship shuddered around them.

Waseem said, "Speed is twenty one hundred meters per second. We need to hit sixteen hundred for orbital injection."

Darcy dug deeper into the problem. "Two of the twelve OMS bells are down."

"Nineteen hundred meters per second."

Darcy breathed deeply. "This is going to be OK. We'll get insertion and deorbit. It'll just take a bit longer."

"Seventeen hundred meters per second. Sixteen hundred. Fifteen. We've got orbital injection. Fourteen hundred - we're deorbiting."

"See, I told you -". Then Darcy saw the small model of the ship on her screen. Something was wrong. "Waseem, we're yawing."

"What? Why?"

A pit opened in the bottom of her stomach. Crap, crap, mother-loving crap. "The two rockets that are down, they're both on one side - our deorbiting thrust is off center." She scanned her screen. "It's the bells closest to the water dump valves. The ice must have fouled them." Darn it; she she should have expected this. "Can you correct the yaw?"

Wasseem's fingers flew. "OK, I see it. Bells 11 and 12 are out - I'm cutting the thrust on 1 and 2 by fifty percent and ramping 9 and 10 up to one o' five. That should straighten us out and give us most of the - Jesus Fuck Kali Fuck! Darcy, it's not working."

Darcy grimaced at the profanity. "We're still slewing, Waseem!"

"I know that! That's what I just said. I don't know what to do -"

"Give me the controls."

"You have OMS."

"I have OMS."

Tudel interrupted. "What's going -"

"Shut the fuck up and let her work!" yelled Waseem.

Darcy stared at the screen. The slew was increasing - the adjustment wasn't enough. The bells had never been pushed this hard, and their response was nonlinear; a hundred five percent wasn't really a hundred five percent.

Darcy tapped the RCS controls. Gently, gently. Bells 3 and 4 up to one-ten, then one-twelve, then at redline. Bell five flat, bell six flat.

Was it working? She checked. Yes! The slew stopped and started to reverse.

Waseem called out, "Altitude down from 5.0 to 4.5."

Darcy looked up sharply. "Altitude? That's too -"

"Orbital speed. I mean orbital speed."

"Shit, Waseem!" She caught herself. Now she was swearing. "Let me -"

"No, I've got it. You stay on the yaw."

Darcy checked the ship's orientation. The yaw was almost fixed... and there, it was done. She tapped controls and stopped the counter-rotation. Then, even though Waseem said he didn't need help, she checked the orbital speed.

Gah!

The speed was too high, and - yes - the ground path was wrong. She'd corrected the yaw caused by iced up rockets 11 and 12 by tweaking the thrust on the other reaction control system bells, but she'd introduced roll and pitch at the same time. Which was only a small problem on its own, but the larger OMS rockets were burning hard to deorbit them, and the yaw meant that those rockets weren't lined up correctly. What should have been a pure deorbiting burn had instead been a mix: mostly deorbiting, but some sideways thrust as well.

She bit back a swear. Not only was their ground path wrong, but their forward velocity was too high. They were going to miss Lai Docks in two different dimensions: lateral AND velocity. "Waseem, I'm taking OMS."

"No, Darcy, I can -"

She put steel in her voice. "Damn it, I have OMS!"

He took his hands off of the controls. "You have OMS."

Darcy split the screen, OMS interface on one side, RCS on the other. This was insane. One person couldn't control both...But it was clear that the two of them coordinating wasn't going to work either.

Navigation was supposed to be as exciting as a mortgage spreadsheet: everything planned out, checked, and double checked. But now she had to do this in real time. It was insanity. She felt the sweat pool in her armpits.

She'd tried to explain orbital navigation to Mike a few times, with varying success. He was so used to rock and tunnels that stayed still that he couldn't help thinking of navigation as a matter of hitting a point in three-space. It wasn't nearly that simple. She wasn't aiming for a three-dimensional point, but a six-dimensional one where x, y, and z were joined with dx, dy, and dz.

Mike could understand that, sometimes, when he concentrated. But in a situation like this even understanding wasn't good enough - you had to feel it in your bones.

Did she feel it in her bones? Did she really?

Darcy dipped her head, said a few words, and then looked up.

She looked at the wallscreen, taking in dozens of numbers at once. She was off plan, and with orbital mechanics, she couldn't correct just one thing. No, she had to do a delicate dance. First correct the slew, then drop forward velocity below what the plan called for to compensate for extra ground they'd already covered, and then, finally, brake for landing.

...all while somehow correcting for the ground path problems.

First things first. They'd spent crucial seconds traveling forward faster than the plan called for and now they needed thrust - and lots of it - right along the centerline. She checked the OMS - it was at 90%. She pushed it to max, and then tried to push it further yet, but it wouldn't move. Software lock at 100%.

Damn it.

She looked around her board. RCS? For a de-orbiting burn? It wasn't supposed to be used like that... but she knew that the software would let her overdrive it. She took a breath. If she was going to use RCS she needed to push the bells way beyond redline - maybe to 120%. It was crazy, but she had to do it.

She bit her lip and she pushed the sliders. The ship vibrated as the pumps surged and the rockets flared. Their speed was dropping, but not fast enough. She whispered "Priceless eggs in variable gravity" and pushed the sliders to 121%, and then to 122%.

Yellow temperature alerts popped on her screen.

Waseem called out. "Forward speed thirteen hundred meters per second. Altitude twenty kilometers."

She held her finger over the control.

"Forward speed twelve hundred meters per second. Altitude nineteen kilometers."

The speed was dropping. Not quite enough, but close. Now to wrestle with the ground path issue... and then the temperature alerts changed from yellow to red and alarms started warbling. Darcy slid the RCS controls back to 110%.

"Vertical speed is picking up. Ramping AG to standby.... Now."

Darcy checked the overheat alarms: still red. Damn it.

Waseem warmed up the AG drive, and immediately alarms went off and her screens lit up with icons.

Waseem glanced over. "Was that the AG drive? Because it shouldn't -"

"Shut up, Waseem."

The alarms were because of burn-through on bells 9 and 10. Damn it! She'd driven them too hard, and now they were going into auto-shutdown.

"Darce! We're doing five hundred meters per second. That's too fast."

"I know. I know!" Her fingers flew. "Bells 1 through 10 up to a hundred thirty percent"

"We got burn through at one twenty two; they'll never -"

"Quiet!"

Waseem shook his head. "The Dracos aren't going to take this for long."

"I know."

There were already a dozen alarms flashing and alerts blaring. New ones popped up. Darcy ignored them and kept her eye on the ground track.

"Darce, the Dracos aren't designed for one thirty, cool them off."

Darcy said nothing as the alarms continued.

"Darcy!"

"I know! Be quiet!" Waseem was right: the bells would burn through - but they only had to last a few more seconds.

"Please, please, please," Darcy whispered under her breath.

A new set of alerts popped up as bell 5 hit over-temperature and bell 10 burned through.

"Shit, Darcy - "

"I know! Bring up look-down imaging."

Waseem nodded and opened a video window. Darcy stole a glance. It showed lunar surface racing by. Where were they? They should be near Aristillus by now, but there was no sign of habitation -

Then, suddenly, tire tracks. A second later she saw utility vehicles. Then the aboveground portions of the lunar colony were racing beneath them: first vast solar farms, then huge piles of excavation tailings, and then a mix of solar kilns, furnaces, and aluminum rolling plants.

"Forward speed one hundred meters per second. I'm ramping up the AGs."

As soon as he engaged the drive the battery low power warning sounded. Darcy looked. They were seconds away from losing the AG drive. She'd never seen the batteries this low. Never.

"Seventy five meters per second."

Sweat was beading on Darcy's forehead, and she felt the salty sting where it was rolling into her own eyes, but she didn't have time to wipe it away.

She needed to kill speed, and she needed to kill it now. She checked the OMS display and saw that the deorbiting rockets were still at 100%... but they weren't slowing down.

"Waseem, we're not slowing! What the hell is going on?"

Waseem worked his control. "Shit, god damn it - OMS tanks are empty!" A moment later, "And all the RCS are in shutdown."

On the video window the open pits Lai Docks slipped into the frame, passed the center mark, then slipped off the other side. They were long, and getting longer - and forward was still seventy five meters per second.

"Darcy, we overshot - and we're out of fuel. We need to do another orbit -"

"We can't do another orbit. The AGs don't have enough power." Darcy paused. "We'll land on the surface."

"We can't -"

"The first ships did!"

"Yeah, but our forward speed is -"

She cut him off. "How far to the crater wall?"

"The north wall is about twenty five kilometers from the colony. We're - uh - 1 kilometers past Lai...the wall's twenty four kilometers and closing."

"AG is mine." She closed the OMS and RCS screens - the systems were dead anyway.

"AG is yours."

She checked the screen. Altitude: 1 kilometer.

Five hundred meters.

"Darcy!"

She looked over. "What?"

Waseem was sitting in his chair, pulling the harness around his chest. Ah. Right. She strapped in and stole a glance over her shoulder. Tudel and Frodge were fixated on the wallscreen.

She looked back at the controls.

Four hundred meters of altitude. Twenty-three kilometers to the crater wall.

On the video screen smelters raced beneath them, and then a construction yard.

She felt acid rising in her throat.

Three hundred meters.

Two hundred.

She danced her fingers across the AG 'on' and 'off' buttons. It wasn't designed for precision use like this, and it reacted sluggishly. The thrum rose and fell and her gut twisted.

One hundred meters.

On the video screen a black shape crept into frame: the Wookkiee's own shadow. The spot of darkness raced across the rocks and industrial hardware, slipping and sliding as the terrain rose and fell beneath them. The shadow grew larger and larger, until it blotted out the entire image.

Darcy opened another window and called up a forward view. White - blocked with ice. She picked another.

Thirty meters of altitude.

Ahead of them was a vast swath of mirrored mylar solar concentrators and steam equipment, sitting on a manicured gravel field. One of the colony's power plants.

A low battery alarm started squealing.

Darcy cut the AG to zero. On the forward camera the towers of the power farm raced toward them, and then suddenly the mirrored panels were no longer below but were to the left and right, whipping past. She ignored the instruments - even the altimeter - and stared at the video. She knew exactly what they'd tell her: ten meters above ground, twenty at most.

A sudden, distant sound: the tinkling cymbal stutter of solar collectors smashing against the ship.

The noise grew louder.

On the video screen a few pieces of industrial wreckage exploded over the bow and flew by overhead, spinning and glinting in the harsh sunlight. The ship slipped a few meters closer to the surface and the small splash of wreckage flying past became a shock wave of extruded aluminum and steel, splashing up beyond the gunwales and over the deck.

A second later a jarring impact slammed Darcy into her chair and sent shots of pain up her spine.

Out of the corner of her eye Darcy saw Tudel and Frodge crash to the deck, as if a giant had thrown them down.

A deep tearing sound - a terrible grinding - filled the air. The ship was skidding across the surface, its keel ripping indiscriminately across three-year-old power lines and billion-year-old rocks.

Darcy stole a look at the screen.

Thirty meters per second forward speed.

Twenty five.

The hideous grinding continued, drowning out the alarms.

The bow wave of wreckage shrank, and then disappeared below the gunwales. They were out of the solar farm.

On the forward video a line of boulders approached. If they hit that -

She didn't want to think about it.

Darcy swallowed and tapped the AG to life. The drive was sluggish. So sluggish. She felt her gut twist, but the ship didn't seem to move. Then, even before the camera registered any change in height, she turned the drive back off. The AG field belatedly surged.

The ship lumbered off the surface and scraped over the top of the boulders. There was a distant bang and a hideous tearing of metal as the ship's rudder tore off. The Wookkiee tilted forward and landed again, the bow hitting the lunar surface first. The impact slammed her against her straps.

The grinding got louder and Darcy knew she was hearing her ship dying around her. She stole a look at the monitor. Forward speed: seven meters per second.

Half of her screen was covered with emergency alerts -

And then the lights cut off and the instrumentation died, plunging the bridge into darkness.

They slid onward, the grinding and tearing reverberating through the pitch black ship.

Darcy interlaced her fingers. "Please God, please God, pl-."

The emergency lights kicked on and bathed the bridge in red, but the screens were still black. The ship shuddered and screamed around them.

Waseem reached for his harness buckle.

"Not yet!"

He put a finger up to his lips and nodded his head toward the PKs. Darcy turned and saw them, piled on the floor, struggling to get up.

Darcy nodded and reached for her own buckle.

There was a sudden *bang*, louder than the others, and Darcy was thrown against the nylon webbing. And then everything was silent. The alarms were dead, the grinding was done.

The ship was down.

They'd survived. Somehow.

But the battle wasn't finished.

She snapped her harness off and raced to the PKs, her feet unsteady in the new gravity.

Waseem reached the PKs first and was trying to wrestle the carbine away from Frodge, who clung to it with both hands. Darcy ignored the fight and staggered across to where Tudel was trying to push himself off the deck. Without pausing to consider what she was doing she reared back and kicked him in the side of the head. He cursed and grabbed at her foot. She pulled back and kicked again, and the second kick connected as hard as the first. He tried again to fend her off, but more weakly this time. One more kick, and he slumped to the floor. She reached down and pulled his pistol from its holster, and then pointed it at Frodge. "Drop it."

Frodge looked up at her, his eyes wide. He let go and Waseem pulled the weapon away from him.

Three minutes later, when Darcy and Waseem had just gotten the two men secured with zip ties, the door opened and three other soldiers entered, guns drawn.

Chapter 50

2064: Situation Room of the West Wing, White House, Washington DC, Earth

General Restivo looked up from his slate and surveyed the windowless Situation Room. The wallscreens were black, the carpet and decor were muted, and there was nothing to focus on besides the quiet hum of the ventilation system.

He had run out of work to do on his slate, and the Faraday cage and jammers meant that he couldn't download more email or send what he'd already typed. The other staff in the room - he caught a few of their eyes - were all either reading material already on their slates or, like him, scanning the room; killing time.

He checked the time yet again and suppressed a sigh. Over an hour now - going on an hour and a half.

The door banged open and President Johnson and her aides swept in. General Restivo stood with the rest of the room.

"I need to know how you're going to fix the moon problem," Themba said, looking around the table. Restivo didn't know what answer she was looking for, so he stayed quiet.

The president scanned the room. "Anyone? I only have ten minutes, so I'd better start hearing answers."

An aide spoke first. A foot in the bear trap - and not his.

"Ma'am, when you say 'fixing', what exactly do you -"

Themba clapped her hands together. "People! Have I been unclear?" It wasn't a question, Restivo knew. "We've got major budget problems."

She paused, then clarified "...thanks to my predecessor." The last word was a curse. "Health Nexus is threatening to strike, our wind farms are behind schedule, California needs the earthquake relief checks. We need solutions, and we need them now."

Restivo noted that she hadn't mentioned the elections.

The president planted her palms on the table and leaned forward, agressively, and even with her feminine looks and custom Allison Meryll suits she was a pitbull. "Now!" She surveyed the room with a look that was pure steel before smiling. "So, gentlemen, tell me how you're going to do it."

Bonner cleared his throat and spoke. "In our last meeting we talked about how we'd destroyed their satellites. Since then we've built on that success - we've boarded several unlicensed tramp freighters off South East Asia and Africa. Most of these turned out to be false alarms but we have had some wins."

Themba's head turned. "What do you mean wins?"

General Bonner said, "If I may, it would be easiest to show video." The president nodded and Bonner tapped his slate.

Restivo leaned forward. This was going to be interesting. He'd been focusing on his part of the puzzle: his men - Dewitt's team and the others - had been training and would be ready to infiltrate soon. He'd guessed that there were other pieces in play, and now he was going to learn.

The wallscreens flared to life and a video played, grainy and ugly from low-light enhancement. A few dozen soldiers piloted their small rigid hulled inflatable boats toward a darkened cargo ship. The video cut to a new scene: the assault boats were moored with magnetic grapnels to the hull of the cargo ship and the soldiers used quiet compressed gas guns to shoot boarding ladders over the gunwales.

The advance team ascended and a moment later let down ropes to winch up the Alternatively Abled Soldiers and their equipment.

Another jump cut; the video was still shot from someplace low in the water - a second rigid-hull boat? - but the top of the cargo ship was now bright with floodlights.

Someone - an expat? - was hailing the soldiers over a loudspeaker "You, on the deck - identify yourselves... and surrender!"

Restivo craned his neck, but the video was 2D; shifting his perspective didn't let him see what was happening up on the cargo ship's deck.

One more jump cut and there was a weird deep thrumming sound. Was that a problem with the video, or was this...

He leaned forward. Yes. It was.

The sea around the ship and the small inflatable boats grew choppy and then the boat that held the camera was buffeted and pushed back. The camera swung wildly, taking in flashes of night sky, ocean, and brighly lit ship.

This - this must be it. The anti-gravity drive. He shook his head. A new technology. He vaguely remembered when he was young how new technologies, new websites, new *everything* sprung up in a frantic pace before all that insane job-destroying ferment had been calmed by the creation of BuSuR.

The idea of new technology had come to seem like a unicorn. And here he was, watching a new thing. Unlicensed, unplanned, destabilizing.

How very, very strange.

The buffeting ended and the image stabilized. Restivo squinted. What was he looking at? He could see the sea and sky, but everything was tilted at crazy angles. Suddenly his eyes adjusted and the scene made sense. Well, not 'sense', because what he was looking at was impossible. And yet.,.

He stared at the vast depression in the ocean, hundreds of meters across. It was as if an invisible bowl had been pressed down into the ocean's surface, pushing hundreds of tons of seawater aside and making a perfect hemisphere.

The view slewed as the zodiac's camera automatically brought the freighter back into view. The ship's Klieg lights were still on, making it pop against the dark background. The freighter - Restivo fought the urge to rub his eyes - the freighter was hanging in the center of the impossible depression in the ocean. The bottom of its keel floated dozens of meters above the chop.

The weird thrumming sound grew louder and the ship rose. It was thirty - no, at least fifty - meters up.

On the screen a few objects, small at this distance, tumbled over the freighter's gunwales and fell, in a strange diagonal path, to the ocean below.

Restivo narrowed his eyes. Those weren't pieces of equipment. They were troops - his country's troops - being thrown off the ship's deck by the antigravity drive. It was a long fall and he realized that the men and women were almost certainly dead. He set his jaw.

The mammoth ship accelerated slowly, but bit by bit it gained speed. The camera panned up, chasing the brightly lit craft into the dark sky. The small inflatable boat that held the camera was swamped by a wave and the screen went black for a moment, and then the wave was gone. The camera refocused and recentered on the freighter as it fell into the black sky. It dwindled to a brightly lit dot and -

Bonner froze the video and looked around the room.

"Sixty soldiers boarded the ship. Those splashes are members of the assault team being thrown off - we assume by some effect of the anti-gravity drive. Between analyzing the video and identifying floating bodies - and parts - we've identified thirty-nine troops who died during the assault. That leaves twnety-one soldiers unaccounted for.

"It's possible that some troops made it inside the ship before it reached vacuum, but we don't know. If any soldiers did make it inside, we don't know if they seized the ship, or if the expats took them captive."

The president had been following along, nodding neutrally, but at the last sentence her face darkened.

"What do you mean 'you don't know if they seized the ship'? General, you said you had, and I quote, 'some wins.' This doesn't *remotely* look like success to me - this looks like rank incompetence." She stared at Bonner for a long hard moment. "I'll have this done right no matter who I have to call on to get it done."

Restivo sat frozen. Like everyone else in the room, he looked at Bonner.

The four star didn't seem moved by the attack - and that was puzzling. It made no sense that Bonner would present a video like this, mention that all of the men might be dead or captured, present that as a success, and then not even respond to the inevitable attack. Bonner was too good at the Washington game to -

And then Restivo got it. Bonner was letting the president think that he'd screwed up, building anger and anxiety. Pressure and release. Give her the good news up front, and she'd forget it by the time you gave her the bad news a minute later. Bonner had an ace up his sleeve. He must.

There was a reason that Bonner had four stars on his epaulets while he only had two. This. This was how the game was played.

And as if on cue, General Bonner spoke. "Yes ma'am. Absolutely. I know that this assault isn't everything we'd hoped for." He paused and let the tension build. "- but there were two other assaults."

Restivo smiled inwardly. He knew it.

Bonner continued, "The second team also boarded a ship, and managed to seize it before the expats could launch. Given the possibility that members of the first team -" he gestured over his shoulder at the paused video "- were taken captive, or seized the ship but were already destined for the moon, I gave the second team approval to launch. Bottom line: the second team is a success. We've got sixty troops heading to the moon at this very moment."

He looked to the president, who was beaming. Restivo shook his head with grudging respect; Bonner was an expert at what he did.

The president's smile was something to behold: both wide and honest. He had to acknowledge that, despite her nasty temper and her scathing remarks, that smile was world class. The entire room felt brighter. He realized - viscerally, not just intellectually - why her talk show had been a long running hit, and why her rise in politics had been meteoric. Her charisma, when she chose to turn it on, was truly compelling.

The president slapped the mahogany conference room table. "Now *that* is the kind of news I like to hear!"

General Bonner smiled modestly and tipped his head, then continued. "There's more, ma'am."

Restivo blinked in surprised. He'd figured that Bonner had an ace up a sleeve, but he didn't realize that he had *two*.

"We seized a third ship, the Xin San Diego, and we've not only arrested the crew, but we've already got techs on board right now disassembling and analyzing the anti-gravity drive."

President Johnson's smile became, if possible, even brighter, and she leaned back in her chair.

The tension that had choked the room was gone, and Restivo could tell that he wasn't the only one enjoying it.

That is, until President Johnson grew grave and turned to him.

"And what have *you* accomplished?"

Chapter 51

2064: surface, Aristillus, Lunar Nearside

Mike gunned the throttle and raced the surface transporter through the path scoured by the Wookkiee, balancing the desire for even more speed with the need to avoid the wreckage - fragments of the solar farm equipment and huge chunks of the ship's keel. Ahead the path dead ended at a berm of house-sized boulders. The Wookkiee was... nowhere.

What the hell? Had Darcy managed to *hop* the ship over the berm? Mike slowed the vehicle and negotiated an access ramp, brushing against debris from the destroyed solar farm and pushing it aside. He reached the top... and there it was. The Wookkiee. Battered, torn, and listing badly - but the bridge was intact. He let out his breath. Maybe she was OK. He looked back the way he'd come and saw the other construction vehicles racing after him on the clean path that cut through the sea of destruction.

Mike put the transporter back into gear and drove down the far side of the berm and then to the Wookkiee. A dozen meters from the ship he stomped on the brake, throwing a splash of gray dust ahead of him. The vehicle's systems were still powering down when he pulled the huge red override handle, vented the cockpit's air in an explosive roar, and threw open the inner and outer airlock doors.

Mike hopped to the surface and looked up at the ship. The Wookkiee towered over him, listing to one side. The damage was even more heartbreaking from here: hull plating peeled back like tinfoil, battery packs ripped out and tossed around the landscape, stubs of huge copper bus bars blackened and melted and pushing out through the tears.

The wreckage of the solar farm he'd just driven through to get here represented just as much destroyed value - but he had no emotional attachment to someone else's power plant. The Wookkiee, though...the Wookkiee had been his ship once. The memories came flooding back: seeing it for the first time rusting in a Vietnamese port, lowering the first TBM over the side, working long days in the primitive suits Katherine Dycus had fabbed up, sleeping in the cramped quarters of the first tunnels.

Even before the wreck the Wookkiee had been a stubby, outdated ship. Now it was crashed and ruined. It would never fly again. And yet it was still beautiful.

"Mike?" It was Wam, over the radio.

Mike turned; the first vehicles of Excavation Team 26 had pulled up and more were arriving behind them. Wam waved to him from the lead battery truck. Mike looked past the excavation team's vehicles. Behind them cabs, surface crawlers, and ATVs were converging from a multitude of airlocks. The rifle club.

Mike set his radio to broadcast, then addressed the crowd. "Guys, here's the plan."

Chapter 52

2064: bridge of AFS The Wookkiee, Aristillus, Lunar Nearside

The PK swung the rifle and Darcy ducked, but not fast enough: there was an explosion of pain. Her legs fell out from under her and she crashed to the deck.

Her vision swam. She blinked but it didn't get better. The steel was cold against her face. Something was dripping on her neck. She reached up. Blood, from a cut over her ear. She could hear the PKs talking, but their words were nonsense in her ears. Suddenly her arms were yanked behind her.

Her head cleared, just a bit. Frodge was saying, "- briefing said the expats have contacts with the Texan and Alaskan militia movements. So they might be armed."

Another PK disagreed. "They don't have any central organization - there's not going to be any resistance."

Darcy tried to roll over to see who was talking, but a boot landed between her shoulders and pushed her back.

Tudel issued an order. "Sergeant Slattery - take your team and secure the airlocks."

"How do I -"

"Look at them. If there's some mechanical latch that locks them, do that, but if there's not, brace them, tack weld them, whatever - and then guard them." Darcy's eyes focused on the deck a few centimeters in front of her face and she saw blood. Behind her she heard Slattery and several men leave the bridge.

There was a pause, and then Tudel spoke again. "Anward, Hamid - you two guard the hostages - "

He was interrupted by a small explosion somewhere on the ship. Darcy wrinkled her brow. What was going on? Had one of the RCS fuel tanks blown up because of the crash? Wait, no - all the tanks were empty. So what -

No, it couldn't be Mike. The Wookkiee had only been on the ground for three or four minutes. Mike probably didn't even know the Wookkiee had crashed yet.

Another explosion.

Darcy smiled, and then winced as the movement tugged at a wound on her scalp. It had to be him. Maybe someone had seen the nav lights? She turned her head and saw Waseem next to her on the deck, bound like her. She caught his eye and raised an eyebrow, ignoring the pain.

Waseem's eyes widened.

A third explosion.

Tudel yelled out, "What's going on? God fucking damn it!" He paused, and then Darcy felt a boot prod her in the bottom. "You - Can you radio the expats?"

Darcy looked around the red-lit bridge. The controls were all dead, batteries at zero. "The ship has no power, so the radio -"

"You're only worth something to us if you can figure out something."

Darcy swallowed. "Wait! Yes! I've got a phone. That might be able to reach -"

Tudel paced. "Call whoever's in charge. Tell them we've got host- prisoners."

"I need my hands."

A quick tug and her hands were free. She pushed herself off the deck and staggered, still dizzy from the blow to her head, and then patted her pockets. Where was her phone? Not in her pocket - it was in her purse, which was -

She looked over to the lockers on the far side of the bridge - and was overwhelmed by a sense of weirdness. It had been just Monday that the Wookkiee had been sitting in Lai Docks. She'd stepped into the bridge, put her purse in the locker, then started the launch checklist with Waseem. Just - what? - six days ago? And yet now it seemed a lifetime ago, a different world.

Tudel was looking at her and she pushed the thought away. "My phone is in my purse, in the locker. I'll -"

Tudel shook his head. "No. You -" he indicated one of the PKs, "- get it for her."

Darcy directed him to the locker. The man pulled out her purse and rooted through it. He threw a handful of sanitary pads to the floor, then came up a bottle of medicine and dropped it. He snickered and held up a tube of - she turned away and felt her face flush. And then the embarrassment was replaced with rage. How dare he?

The PK found the phone and tossed it to her. In the low gravity his instincts were off and she had to reach high to snatch it from the air. She turned it on and hit the button for Mike.

How far was the Wookkiee from the nearest tower? Would there be signal this far out? The phone rang once, and then twice. She looked at Tudel, who looked at her grimly. What if Mike didn't answer? Her life might depend on Tudel thinking she'd reached him, so if he didn't answer she'd pretend to have a conversation. She could -

Mike answered. "Darcy?" His voice was serious. And determined.

"Mike?! I -"

"You've got PKs listening?"

"Yes. I -"

Tudel prodded her. "Tell him the deal. Whatever those explosions were, stop it. If he's got men nearby, have them fall back. And they need to get us recharged ASAP - or they'll have problems."

"Mike, the lead PK says that if there are any lunar forces nearby they have to back away from the ship. And you need to recharge the Wookkiee, or -" she stammered "- or you've got problems."

Mike ignored the information. "The crew - you're all prisoners? Unarmed?"

Darcy looked at Tudel. Could she answer Mike's questions without letting Tudel know what he was asking? Yes. She could do that. "Yes, Mike, a full recharge. Enough to get us all back to Earth."

"Are all the crew in one room?"

Darcy paused. "Yes, he's serious."

"Are the PKs in a separate compartment from the hostages?"

"No, Mike, he's not joking."

"OK, Darce, I need you to get the crew separated from the PKs. Get everyone in a room with a solid door between them and -"

Darcy swallowed. How was she going to respond to that? She needed to tell Mike that she couldn't do that, but without letting Tudel know what she was saying. She opened her mouth, then closed it, then opened it again. She looked at Tudel - who looked suspicious. He leaned in and pulled the phone from her. "Who is this?"

Tudel had the phone now - but Darcy knew what Mike needed. She looked around the room. All of the Wookkiee crew were here and most of the PKs were out in the corridors, guarding the airlocks. But Tudel and two PKs were still here on the bridge. She had to get them out of the room, somehow, while keeping the Wookkiee's crew here. How?

Tudel spoke into the phone. "No, fuck that. I've got hostages." He paused, listening. "No." He listened. "No." He shook his head. "Yeah, I'll prove it. I'm going to put one in an airlock without a suit, and if I don't get what I asked for in five minutes, we're opening the outer door." He paused. "Five minutes." He flipped the phone closed and pocketed it, then turned to Darcy.

"You."

Darcy grew cold. For a moment she'd fallen into the trap of thinking that Mike was in charge, that he had this all worked out, that the danger was over, or if not over, at least mostly past. But it wasn't. She was still surrounded by unpredictable lunatics.

Darcy felt cold sweat on her forehead and put her hands up. "No, wait. Wait, no! You can't do this. Mike will get the batteries recharged, but five minutes isn't -"

Tudel barked, "Shut up", and then raised his chin at the other two. "Anward, Hamid - are these prisoners all secure?"

"Yes sir, they're all tight."

"OK, grab her and let's go to the lock."

"No - no!" Darcy screamed. A hand grabbed her by the back of the neck and forced her head down.

Tudel stepped out into the hallway first and Anward and Hamid pushed her after. Darcy tripped as she stepped over threshold of the watertight door. She caught her footing and began to plead, "This isn't right - look, you -"

A massive wall of noise - as much a punch to her diaphragm as a sound - hit her from behind, and a spray of hot chunky liquid splashed her. Before she knew what was happening the noise - a rifle shot? - hammered her a second time, and then a third. Her hair was thick, hot and heavy with what felt like gallons of blood and brain matter. Darcy gasped for air, filling her lungs to scream, and then the bodies of Anwar and Hamid fell against her. Ahead of her Tudel looked over his shoulder, saw something behind her, and then turned and sprinted in a low crouch. Incongruously she realized that Tudel still had her phone and then someone yelled "Move!" at her. What? Move where?

More shots rang out, the sound like sledgehammer strikes, and she felt - literally felt - the bullets fly past her. Ahead of her Tudel reached the end of the corridor and disappeared around a corner.

Darcy choked down the scream and turned. Three men, all in spacesuits, and all carrying rifles. Even with their faceplates up, she didn't recognize any of them... but she knew the logo on their suits. Red Stripe.

One of the men addressed her. "Are all the captives in that room?"

Darcy found it hard to breathe. She wiped her face and her hand came away covered in blood. She looked at the two bodies on the deck, almost headless from the -

The man in the Red Stripe suit yelled at her. "Miss Grau! The captives - are they all in there?"

She heard gunshots from somewhere else in the Wookkiee.

Darcy looked up from her bloody palm and found her voice. "Yes. Wait! All except Captain Kear, he -"

"We've got him. Is that an airtight compartment?"

"Yes. It's a 3-hour room, but there's more people than -"

"Later!" The man she'd been talking to put a gloved hand on the small of her back her and pushed her toward the hatch.

She stumbled and then caught herself on the edge of the hatch. She turned and saw a fourth man behind the three others, facing away. That suit - she knew it. "Mike! Mike, is that -"

Mike turned. "Darcy!"

The sound of more rifle fire rang from distant corridors. Darcy yelled to be heard over the gunfire. "Mike, is everything -"

Mike shook his head. "No time!"

"Mike, wait! I-"

One of the men in the Red Stripe suits pushed her through the hatch. She tripped over the flange and fell, sprawling, into the bridge. Behind someone yelled "Blow the e-lock!" and the hatch clanged shut behind her. With a rusty scraping it locked shut.

A second later she heard an explosion somewhere below, and then the sound of howling wind.

Chapter 53

2064: Goldwater refining facility, Aristillus, Lunar Nearside

Darren Hollins stood in the smelter control room and looked through the glass wall at the machinery below. "How long until the new chlorine pumps are on line?"

"Another six hours, if there are no more problems," Hans, his chief chemist, said, "...but there may be more problems. I've told David before that this isn't the right way to do the Miller process. We can lower the gas temperature and increase the pressure and we'll -"

Darren held up a hand. "Don't ask me to break ties; my knowledge is ten years out of date. I trust the two of you."

Darren could tell from the look on Hans' face that the man wasn't happy, but then again, he never was, and never would be. It was his perfectionism that made him find fault in everything. And it was his perfectionism that made everything run smoothly. The only down side was the incessant fighting with the other chief chemist.

Arnold cleared his throat and Darren turned. "Yes, Arnold?"

"Boss, can we talk?" He inclined his head. "Outside?"

Darren turned back to Hans. "Good work with the chlorine. Make it work." He clapped the man on the shoulder and got a harrumph in return, and then followed Arnold out of the control room.

"OK, Arnold, what's going on?"

"The Wookkiee - that's a Five Rings ship - crash landed. It was hijacked by PK forces. The war is starting. I've talked to Reggie and he's put the vaults on lockdown and called in the second shift of the security team, but we need to implement my plan to -"

"Not yet."

Arnold ran a hand over his bald head. "Darren, I'm afraid you're not taking this threat seriously enough. This is for real, and I-"

Darren fixed him with a look. "Arnold, have you ever known me to not pay attention to threats?"

Arnold pursed his lips. "Well, no, but -"

"Then trust me. I'm working on this."

"I don't *see* you working on this."

"Just because you're my advisor doesn't mean you know everything - you know that. Sometimes plans have to remain secret." He paused. "And besides, I already talked to Reggie last week. He started recruiting more security three days ago."

"That's good, but it's not enough -"

Darren raised an eyebrow. "Arnold, I'm on this."

Arnold pursed his lips, clearly not convinced. "Darren, the war is coming. It's almost here."

Darren sighed. "I think you're right."

Chapter 54

2064: bridge of AFS The Wookkiee, Aristillus, Lunar Nearside

Larry Prince pushed Darcy into the bridge and pulled the massive hatch. It was closing, but the sheer mass of it made it slow. Behind him he heard Ige yell into his microphone, "Blow the e-lock!"

Damn it! The hatch wasn't locked yet. Larry leaned into the door. With a clang the hatch finally slammed shut and Larry pulled the locking handle.

From below he heard an explosion. He wanted to swear at Ige for jumping the gun but didn't have time; instead he slapped the control on the side of his helmet and the visor snapped down.

Almost immediately the wind tugged at him. Larry looked around the passageway for a handhold. There - a pipe. He grabbed it with one gloved hand and fumbled at his belt.

Over the wind he heard more rifle fire.

The wind accelerated, pulling at him. Larry reached down with his free hand, found his carabiner, and snapped himself to the pipe. He checked and saw that the other two members of his fire team were also lashed in. Good.

The wind howled, sucking the air from the corridors, down the stairwells, and out the emergency mining airlock that they'd flash-welded to the hull of the ship. The tornado pulled at Bello, but his line was secure.

A few more shots sounded but the noise was thin, and the rate of fire slowed and then stopped.

Larry had a thought, smiled, and shared it with Ige and Brown over the comlink. "Never bring shirt sleeves to a spacesuit fight." He heard chuckles in return.

The pressurized interior of the Wookkiee was huge, but the emergency airlock that they'd welded onto the side of the ship was sized to handle two men in armored suits and a third on a stretcher. Blow the doors on that, and the ship should vent quickly. It shouldn't take too much longer until -

An alarm beeped in Bello's helmet and he looked at his display. 0.05 bars of pressure. He unclipped himself. "Let's see if we can take any of them alive."

* * *

Larry stepped through the ragged hole cut in the side of the Wookkiee's hull, through the open inner doors and into the e-lock. He shifted the burden on his shoulder. The outer door was open, blown from its hinges by explosive charges, and bright lunar sunlight streamed in. As his filter adjusted to cut the glare, the scene outside came into view. Two meters away from the blown outer door the mining ambulance had its own airlock open.

Larry shrugged the load off his shoulder, catching the PK - unconscious, bloody, and clad only in a dark grey camo - in his arms. The suited EMT inside the ambulance nodded and Larry awkwardly tossed the PK across the gap. The EMT caught the body, staggered from the mass, and then lowered him to the floor. Larry stepped back and made room for Ige, who stepped forward, and then tossed his own PK across the gap. The EMT caught him and then slapped a button. The ambulance's outer airlock door snapped shut.

Larry turned and went back into the Wookkiee to look for more survivors. Behind them the EMT broadcast to their departing backs, "It's been four minutes - you might as well give up." Larry ignored him and followed Ige back into the Wookkiee. Yeah, anyone still in the vacuum was probably dead. But probably wasn't definitely, and they still hadn't found any officers.

* * *

Mike stood on the deck of the Wookkiee, leaned forward, and rested his gloved hands on the gunwales.

He looked out on the scene before him, and it was good.

Just beyond the shadow cast by the Wookkiee, members of his rifle club were standing around, firearms slung over their shoulders, joking amongst themselves after a job well done.

Further away the mining ambulances were rolling across the surface toward the airlocks with their load of PK prisoners.

And then, beyond the ambulances, the surface infrastructure of the city spread across the plain: furnaces, solar plants, manufacturing facilities.

The enemy was routed. His men were heroes. Darcy and the rest of the crew were safe in the bridge, and would be out in a few minutes.

And below him, the city - his city - was healthy, happy, and safe. He didn't own it all - not remotely. But he'd built it. Some of it literally, most of it just figuratively. The solar cells, the solar refining smelters, the piles of tailings - even the distant hints of movement from Darren Hollins' mining operation on the cluster of peaks just north of the city. All of it. It was here because he had -

Something moved. There - on the surface, the black shadow cast by the Wookkiee moved.

Ah - the Wookkiee's crane #2 was moving. He turned and watched the boom swing out over the edge of the derelict ship. The roughnecks had gotten the ship-mounted cargo lifter connected to the APU vehicles parked on the surface below.

The crane stopped rotating and the yellow-painted spreader at its tip descended. Mike tracked it as it descended. For a moment it was level with him, and then it passed below and Mike leaned forward over the gunwales to follow it. On the surface below a transporter was already in position, an e-lock ready on its cargo deck. Good. Darcy and the others in the bridge should have enough air for an hour or two yet, but the sooner the e-lock was in position, the sooner they'd be out.

And speaking of Darcy, he should call her and tell her that the airlock was almost there. He brought up the phone interface in his screen. Below him the crane spreader stopped. A rigger below called out to Bert, the crane operator, and asked him to move a meter left and two meters further out. A moment later Bert made the correction. Mike ignored the open phone interface and smiled. That very crane had offloaded his first A-series TBM so many years ago. And ten years later, the crane was still running, even with the ship below her dead. "You've aged well, old girl."

Over the radio Bert called, "What's that, Mike?"

Mike coughed. "Ah, nothing. Everything going OK with the lift?"

He waiting for a response. "Bert? You hear me? The lift OK?"

Still no response. What was going on? He looked down at the surface crew near the transporter to see if anyone was waving the crane off, but no one was. Instead everyone - transporter crew, rifle club members, a few stray medics, were all standing, frozen, looking at him.

Wait.

Not at him.

Past him.

Mike turned.

Behind and above the Wookkiee a second ship floated over the moon's surface.

...and at the nearside railing several dozen troops in space suits stood and pointed rifles at him and the others.

The PKs had seized more than one ship.

Chapter 55

2064: deck of AFS The Wookkiee, lunar surface, Aristillus, Lunar Nearside

Mike's helmet pinged with a broadcast. "Everyone - put your guns on the ground, step away from them, and lie face-down."

Mike looked at the floating ship. There were a lot of armed men along the rails. More than a dozen - maybe twenty, maybe more.

He considered his chances.

The distance, the difficulty of shooting while wearing a suit, the AG field that would distort their aim - all of these made it unlikely that a single rifleman there could hit him. But if they all fired at once, he ran a very real risk that one of them would get a lucky shot.

No, it would be stupid to run for it. The safe thing would be to surrender.

But he'd be damned if he was going to give up. Not for anyone, and especially not for these bastards.

Mike stared at the PKs. The muzzles of their guns pointed at him, and he knew how foolish this was. Truly foolish. There was no way he was going to get out of this.

He took a deep breath, pivoted, and ran.

Or tried to run. He was slow - too slow. Damn it!

The suit fought him. The cables that ran through the arms and legs tightened and loosened at a speed perfectly timed to fight ballooning and assist in normal walking, but entirely wrong for a sprint.

Shit, God damn it!

The hatch to the bridge was dozens of meters away. Behind him, he knew, the PKs were raising their rifles, aiming them. He leaned forward, pushing against the sluggish suit. He saw a splash of motion on the deck ahead, then another. They were shooting at him.

Fuck! Just a few more meters.

Another splash on the deck, and then a tug at his elbow. He was hit. A moment later an alarm tone told him what he already knew. He leaned further forward, trying like hell to stay low. If he hopped high he was dead.

More bullets hit around him as he ran.

...And then he was in the gloom of the airlock, safe from the PK infantry. For a moment, at least. Behind him the outer door was gone, melted stumps of hinges hinting at how the PKs had forced themselves aboard. The airlock's overhead light was dead, and so was the control panel. He needed to patch his suit, but not yet - first he needed to put steel between himself and the peakers. Mike turned on his helmet light and found the emergency hand-wheel. Next to it there was a splash of something - dried blood? He ignored it and spun the wheel a dozen times then pushed against the inner door.

The door swung open and Mike stepped through, and then closed it behind him. His helmet light illuminated the gloom of the ship's interior. Even the red emergency lights were out now, their batteries drained.

The bubbling suit alarm turned to a shriek and Mike reached into a belt pouch, pulled out a patch, and slapped it over the tear. The alarm silenced.

He looked around. Now what?

A moment ago he'd had everything figured out; now he was on the run, hiding from a ship full of PKs.

His helmet pinged with another broadcast. "Listen you idiots, you're outnumbered. We've shot four of you and we can kill the rest of you before you can get back into your city. So put down your firearms and we'll let you live. And you, inside the ship - come out with your hands up."

Fuck.

They'd killed members of the rifle club - and they were about to take the rest hostage.

But the problem was worse - much worse - than that.

He'd thought that the PK hijacking of the Wookkiee was a one-off, but it wasn't. If they had two ships, they might have four - or a dozen. Which meant that they had the AG drive.

His blood ran cold.

He'd known the war was coming, and coming soon. He'd told people - and even his friends had called him paranoid for saying it was coming in five years, not the ten or fifteen that everyone else thought.

Five years would have been bad enough. Five years was barely enough time to grow the population, barely enough time to arm, barely enough time to prepare.

But the war wasn't five years away. It was happening. Now.

Fuck. Fuck! How could they possibly win this?

Mike caught himself. There'd be time for thinking about strategy later - now he had to think tactics.

OK. Think. What was going on outside? He needed to know.

The bridge: could he access cameras there? Yes - wait, no. The bridge was pressurized and he couldn't get in. And besides, without power -

Wait. The crane - the crane had power from the external APU. Mike turned and raced to the stairs, and then up a flight. The hatch to the cargo handler's room was open and light spilled out into the dark corridor. Mike reached the door. Inside, Bert Anciaux sat in his suit at the cargo control interface.

"Bert, anything on the cameras?"

Bert started and spun in his chair. "Jesus! Mike! I didn't hear you! Uh - most of the cameras were frozen over when I sat down, but the ones in sun are clear now. I've got the other ship on 12." He pointed. Mike leaned forward, putting one suited hand on the back of Bert's chair as he stared at the monitors.

The second ship - annotated in the display as "RTFM/Fifth Ring Shipping" - had settled onto the ground next to the Wookkiee. Bert switched to a different camera - and Mike saw the ground between the two ships.

Members of the excavation team and the rifle club were on their knees in the lunar dust, arranged in long lines. Behind them a dozen men - each marked with a green rag tied around one bicep - stood and pointed rifles at them. As Mike watched the RTFM's crane lowered a man-basket.

Mike swore. The PKs had hostages - and meant to keep them.

"What can we do to stop them?"

Bert looked over his shoulder. "We're sitting in an unarmed derelict without power. We can't do anything."

Damn it!

There must be something he could do. Something. He called up his phone interface, saw his uncompleted call to Darcy, and cleared it. He needed to talk to Wam. Wam could get more members of the rifle club -

No. That would take too long.

What about the Wookkiee's AG drive? If he pulsed it, could that -

No. Even if the AG drive was still working after the crash, the APU powering the cranes didn't have remotely enough juice for that. And besides, the AG controls were in the bridge, and here in the cargo control room all they had were the cranes.

The cranes! "Bert - can we grab the RTFM, and stop them from lifting off?"

255

Bert shook his head. "We've got the spreader on, so the only thing we could grab would be gunwales or something. And even if that worked, if the RTFM lifts, our cables would snap like rubber bands."

Mike cursed. "Damn it. Wait - we've got the spreader. Can we grab their drive?"

"No, the AG drive containers are buried deep in the cargo stack."

"Buried under what?"

"It's the usual setup: AG on the bottom, and OMS and RCS containers on top of them."

Mike froze, then a smile spread across his face. "OK, here's the plan -"

* * *

Mike watched the monitor as crane #1 on the Wookkiee rotated toward the RTFM. Mike checked another screen. The PKs on the ground were pushing prisoners around. Good; the longer they failed to notice, the better.

Bert moved his hands over the console and swore. "God damned gloves! I-."

"You can do it, Bert. Nice and easy."

Bert jabbed at the keyboard again. Mike watched the screen. A camera at the tip of the crane showed the RTFM swing into view. The crane slowed, then stopped. Below the crane a cargo container sat on the RTFM's deck. Close to the center of the screen - but not directly there.

Bert jogged the controls and the view swung two meters left, then one meter forward, and the cargo container moved closer to the crosshairs. Mike saw that Bert had called it exactly: the odd vents and circles embedded in the containers surface told a trained eye that it was an OMS unit.

Another tap on the controls and the crosshairs blinked green.

"Yes!"

The spreader descended and the view zoomed in a dizzying rush until the screen went black. The crosshairs blinked once and the word "twistlocked" appeared.

Mike clapped Bert on the back. He'd done it!

Bert looked over his shoulder. "Should I lift?"

Mike shook his head. "Not yet - but grab another one with crane 3."

"You got it boss." Bert nodded, and bent to the task.

Mike paged through the menu on his helmet display. Coms. Phone. Broadcast. He punched it, then cleared his throat. "Attention hijackers - we've secured your ship. If you try to launch, we'll tear your OMS off." On the screen Mike saw that crane 3 was now rotating. "You will immediately release all your hostages."

On the wallscreen crane 3's camera centered over another cargo container, and then the view began to zoom.

The crosshairs went green and 'twistlocked' appeared.

Mike waited for the PKs to respond.

* * *

A minute later Mike's phone rang.

"Yes?"

"You the one who just broadcast the threat?"

"Yes."

"Who are you?"

"Mike Martin."

The line went dead for a moment, then the voice returned. "OK, Martin, we know you. Get your crane off our ship, and release the troops you seized. Now."

"We don't have any troops," Mike bluffed. "All the Wookkiee hijackers died when we blew the airlock. Now I'm repeating my demand: free all of your hostages or we rip off your OMS."

Another pause. "Our captives are smugglers and terrorist combatants found in possession of illegal military weapons. They're lawful prisoners. You've got thirty seconds to take your cranes off the ship."

Mike smiled. The peaker had believed his bluff that he had no PK captives himself. This was working - he'd won half the battle, now he just needed to get the RTFM hostages. "Thirty seconds? Or what?"

"Or we start executing terrorists."

Mike scoffed. "Right."

"Twenty seconds."

"You do realize what the OMS do? If I rip those off, your ship can lift straight up and down, but you won't be able to maneuver. You'll never get back to Earth."

"Ten seconds."

"Stop bluffing. You've played a nice game, but it's time to -"

On the wallscreen one of the PKs shouldered his rifle and shot one of the kneeling mining engineers in the back of the helmet. The faceplate of the helmet exploded and blood and ichor sprayed out into the lunar dust.

"*What the fuck!?*"

"I've just done a targeted assassination of a designated illegal combatant. Now I'm going to be generous. You've got *another* thirty seconds to get your cranes off our ship."

Mike's stomach felt like it had fallen through the floor. His vision narrowed. Had they really just killed a man in cold blood? He shook his head. Why? Why?

"Twenty seconds."

Mike swallowed. "Bert - Crane 3. Rip off the OMS."

Bert looked at him. "Mike - are you sure? They're -"

"DO IT!"

Bert hit a button.

The PK broadcast again. "Ten seconds."

Warning icons appeared on the wallscreen and Bert wiped them from the display. A strain gauge swung to the right and blinked red...and then the crane's spreader tore the cargo container from the deck. The power and control cables that connected the container to the ship snaked after it, reached their full extension, popped, and snapped.

Several of the PKs standing in the lunar dust looked up away from their prisoners at the crane.

The PK broadcast. "Did you think I'm not serious?"

Mike's stomach clenched. This was a high stakes game, and he wasn't sure that he held the winning hand. Still, he wasn't going to give up. His mouth was dry and it was hard to speak. He swallowed.

"You can take off with three OMSes, but if we -"

"You're out of time." On the screen the same PK shouldered his rifle and shot another kneeling figure. Again the explosion of blood and brain matter splashed across the lunar surface.

On the ground several of the other captives tried to stand but they were pushed back down into the dust by their guards.

The PK on the radio said, "Now listen to me - we've got twenty-three more terrorists here. Do you want - "

Mike turned the channel off. "Bert - can you - " He closed his eyes and breathed. "Bert, I need you to rip off -"

Bert shook his head. "Mike, no - we've got to -"

"Ten seconds."

Mike blinked. "WAIT! Wait! We'll take the crane off. On one condition."

A pause. "Let's hear it."

"We get all our people back."

"These are captured terrorists. They're coming with us to face trial."

Mike clenched his jaw. "'Face trial'? I know what that means. I might as well let you execute them right now."

"We don't execute prisoners."

Mike laughed darkly. "The hell you don't! Look in front of you!"

"Get your crane off our ship."

"It's not your ship. And if you're going to disappear them into a black site, I've got nothing to lose. Give me all my people back or we rip the OMS off and let you run out of air and die here on the surface."

There was a long pause.

"Your crane comes off and you get half your people. Then we get a full charge for our batteries."

"And then we get the rest of our people?"

A long pause. "Yes."

Mike closed his eyes and breathed deeply.

He opened his eyes. "OK."

"OK." The PK cut the connection.

Bert twisted awkwardly in his chair and looked at Mike.

Mike nodded.

Burt turned to his console and tapped a key. On the screen the crosshairs on the second crane's control screen went yellow and the 'twistlocked' icon disappeared. The spreader rose into the sky, empty.

A moment later the video panel on the wallscreen showed the PKs standing on the lunar surface count off prisoners, and prod half them to their feet.

Two of the freed captives lifted the corpse of their executed shipmate, and they all walked away from the PKs and the RTFM.

There was a long moment of silence, and then the PK leader broadcast again. "Now get us the recharge."

Mike breathed deeply. "Let me make some calls."

* * *

Mike called Trang first, got his voice mail, and left a message.

He hung up and called Kirk with the auxillary power vehicle team. "Yes, I'm serious. Give the ship a full charge." He listened. "OK, good."

Mike placed three more calls and then - was he done? He ran through the list in his head. Yes, he was. For a short while, at least. He cleared the phone interface on his helmet screen. He was still standing behind Bert in the crane control room and saw that Bert had brought up video on the wallscreen. Kirk hadn't wasted any time; his auxiliary power unit vehicles surrounded the RTFM and crews were already dragging power cables to the ship. Mike nodded in satisfaction - and then saw something on one of the other video screens.

A hundred meters away from the APUs a dozen PKs in space suits still surrounded the eight remaining Aristillus captives. Mike's satisfaction disappeared. This wasn't over yet. He hated dealing with these thugs, but he had to. The plan wasn't working perfectly - he was giving them the RTFM, after all - but it was working.

He'd get the rest of his people back. If the peaker kept his word, that was. And if he didn't -

He pushed the thought from his mind. There was something else. A nagging sense that he was forgetting something. What was it? There was something important that -

"Darcy!"

Bert swiveled his head. "What?"

Mike ignored him and placed a call. *Pick up... pick up, damn it!*

Three rings. Four. Five.

Voice mail. Damn it! He hung up. Why wasn't Darcy answering her phone? The bridge couldn't already be out of air? He checked a clock. No. They were fine. Her phone must be broken, or lost. "Bert, we forgot the bridge crew."

"Shit! OK; I'm on it." Bert tapped the crane controls and dropped the spreader to the surface transport next to the Wookkiee, aiming for the e-lock. Mike heard him radio a construction team.

Mike's helmet rang with an incoming call and he answered it. "Mike, it's Trang. I got your message. Sorry we're late to the party. Should we come to the Wookkiee?"

"Where are you now?"

"On the surface at ramp 181, at the top of the bluff."

Mike knew where 181 was; they were in a good position, overlooking both ships.

"Who's with you?"

"Six other guys from the rifle club. Where do you want us?"

"You're perfect right there."

"What's going on down there?"

Mike explained.

Trang blew air out through his lips. "You're going to let them keep the ship?"

Mike pursed his lips; he didn't like it either. "We need to keep our people alive."

Mike could almost hear Trang thinking. Then: "If they get the ship, they get the drive. I hate to say it, but the cost might -"

Mike cut him off. "I talked to Fifth Ring. These aren't the only two ships. There's a third one that's definitely missing and a fourth that's overdue for a check in." Mike paused. "We have to assume that they've already got the drive."

Trang said nothing for a long moment. Then, "OK. We'll sit tight; call us if you need us."

Mike cut the connection and checked the clock in his helmet display.

Time had never passed so slowly.

* * *

It felt like several centuries later when the message popped up in his display. The recharging was complete.

Mike took a deep breath and called the PK. The man answered on the first ring. "Is the ship charged?"

"It is. Now give us our men back."

"OK. We'll send them over." The connection went dead.

There was movement on the screen - the PKs were letting the prisoners get to their feet. Mike let out a breath he hadn't realized he'd been holding. The knot that had been in his shoulders for the last two hours relaxed - just a bit. On the seized RTFM one of the cranes swung and began to lower a man-basket to the surface.

Mike clapped Bert on the shoulder, and started to congratulate him... And then he saw that the PKs on the surface were pushing the captives toward the man baskets!

Mike called up the phone app to call the PK when it rang. "We need to verify that the charge is really there, then we'll release your people."

"Bullshit - you're not taking them onto that ship -"

"These are illegal combatants, and we're going to hold them until - "

Mike muted the call and placed another. "Trang!"

"I'm here."

"Your men still in over-watch?"

"Been here the whole time."

"They're double crossing us - stop that crane."

"On it." The line went dead.

Mike held his breath.

* * *

Trang slapped Ng, his best sniper, on the back.

"You heard him; take it out."

Ng pulled the massive rifle tight. A moment later, a giant punched him in the shoulder and a cloud of dust exploded off the lunar surface.

The first bullet flew through the vacuum for over a second, first rising, then halting its climb, and then gently falling in the low lunar gravity.

Not a wisp of air, not a speck of dust disturbed the round's flight.

Then the bullet hit. The massive tungsten-cored round smashed into a support strut on the RTFM's crane. A small fraction of the projectile's energy was wasted splashing copper cladding into the vacuum, but most of the power was dumped into the crane's superstructure. The steel support member buckled and tore, and a shock wave radiated out from the point of impact. The crane's boom shook and the cable it supported cracked like a whip, slapping the manbasket at the end and throwing it half a meter sideways in the lunar vacuum.

Trang surveyed the damage on high magnification. Ng's shot had been close but he'd missed the target. The crane was still functional. He was about to ask Ng for a second shot but before he could there was another explosion of dust off the ground. Trang watched the crane. Nothing.

A miss.

Another explosion of dust, another shot - and another miss. Damn it! Trang checked the man basket. It was at the surface now and the PKs were loading prisoners onto it.

Trang had just turned back to the high magnification view of the crane when the fourth bullet hit - a perfect shot, dead center on the winch mechanism. There was an explosion of movement as the cover plate, the ratchet, and the motor coil were ripped apart - then stillness. Trang zoomed in and smiled. The machine had been truly fucked - even the bearing blocks were torn and bent.

The PKs wouldn't be using that crane to get captives onto their ship.

* * *

Mike watched as the man basket near him, full of expat prisoners and their guards, rose. It was two meters off the ground when suddenly it jerked to a halt.

Mike's phone rang. Trang. "We've taken out crane one. Hit the other one?"

"Not yet, I want to give -"

Mike's phone chimed. The PK officer.

"Hold on, Trang."

He switched to the other channel.

"*Do not fuck with us.* We can still execute your men -"

Mike shook his head. His earlier fear was gone and now he felt only anger - and resolve. He cut the PK off.

"No. You listen to me. You've got a deal - and it's better than you deserve. You've got one crane left to get your own men off the surface. Harm even one more of my people, and that other crane gets shot. Then we rip the OMS off the ship. Then we punch holes in the AG drive on your deck. And then men start shooting your troops, one by one. And after that -"

"Wait-"

"And after that, you and anyone else in the ship get to die slowly as your air runs out."

* * *

Mike watched the scene on the wallscreen.

The last two PKs on the surface walked backward into the man basket, feeling their way carefully as they kept their rifles trained on their hostages in front of them.

Suddenly, from somewhere near the Wookkiee, another space-suited figure ran toward the PKs. Mike furrowed his brow. What the hell was this? Was one of his rifle club guys going to make this fucked-up prisoner swap even more of a disaster? He started to key his radio when he saw that the figure was wearing a suit with Wookkiee markings.

Who the *hell* was that?

The two PKs twisted, pointing their rifles. The running figure stopped, waved his arms, then made some hand signs. Mike leaned forward and zoomed the video, but by the time he had recentered the view, all three of the men were on the lifting platform. The first two PKs kept their rifles pointed at the hostages and the third man, the one who'd dashed out of nowhere, secured the gate across the front of the basket.

What the hell had that been? Had one of the PK hijackers from the Wookkiee somehow survived the decompression and gotten into a spacesuit?

The platform lifted. Mike watched it rise, meter by meter by meter, until it cleared the gunwales and the crane swung it over and onto the deck.

A moment later the three PKs were out of the man basket and inside their stolen ship. A moment after that gray dust began to whip in the vacuum beneath the ship.

Even at this distance, buried deep in the bridge of the Wookkiee, Mike felt the twisting in his gut as the RTFM's AG drive powered up.

His phone chimed. Trang. He answered. "Mike, it's not too late. My sniper Ng can hole the AG drive. He says it's a big target, and -"

"Let them go."

"Mike, you can't -"

"This situation is bad enough as is. No need to make it worse."

Slowly the ship lifted.

* * *

The crew on the deck of the Wookkiee positioned the e-lock against the wall of the bridge and then triggered the fusing ring. A moment later the first construction worker disappeared into the lock, carrying a pile of compact rescue suits over one shoulder.

The lock door cycled shut.

Mike gripped the back of Bert's chair.

A moment later Mike's phone rang. Jefferson. He answered.

"Mike, I'm inside - the entire crew is OK. Darcy is here and -"

Mike heard the phone being wrested away from Jefferson.

"Let me talk to him!"

Mike grinned. That was his girl.

Chapter 56

2064: Fifth floor, E ring, Pentagon, Virginia, Earth

Tudel stood at attention outside the closed door. Despite the fact that he was alone, his form was perfect: back straight, knees almost-but-not-quite locked, hands cupped as if wrapped around rolls of quarters, thumbs held alongside the seams of his pants.

He opened his hands briefly and wiped his palms on his uniform pants, and then returned them to position. He'd been in the shit before. Even deep piles of it. But the shit he was in now? Incomprehensibly deep. It felt like just yesterday he was worried that if he didn't seize an expat ship he'd fail the promotion board. And now, his problems were so much bigger. He'd taken a company of sixty men and gotten fifty-nine of them - every single one except for himself - either killed or captured. He'd barely managed to escape from the moon, almost getting shot by the expat team as they stormed the Wookkiee, and then almost getting shot a second time as he sprinted from the Wookkiee to the RTFM.

The days after they'd landed the ship off the coast of LA had filled him with dread. As soon as the choppers had ferried them from the RTFM to the carrier, Navy MPs had separated him from the others and kept him alone. Not in the brig, no, but in a bunkroom with no other men. Meals had been brought to him; he hadn't left the room once. He knew where this was going.

"Enter!"

Captain Tudel started and then responded: a crisp right face, a step, another right face, and then he opened the door, stepped inside, closed the door behind him, took three perfect steps toward the desk, and saluted. He kept his eyes straight forward - perfectly so

- but noticed that General Bonner had a second officer present. He didn't let his eyes stray to the other officer's nametag - he'd learn who he was soon enough. Or he wouldn't.

He held the salute and felt droplets of sweat bead and fall from his armpit. There was a part of him that wanted to scream at them to get it over with, but he'd end his military career the way he'd begun it - with honor. With precision. This meeting had to be a prelude to a court martial, but he was a man - he'd take his medicine stoically, in a way he could be proud of. He wouldn't let them see the fear. He'd make them respect him even as they swung the axe.

General Bonner acknowledge his salute and Tudel moved his hand back to his side. The knuckle of his right index finger found the seam of his pants and registered his hand there, perfectly.

Discipline.

"At ease."

Tudel snapped to parade rest and kept his eyes focused a kilometer away, through the wall and the framed pictures of General Bonner with superior officers, senators, and the president.

"I said *at ease*, captain. Have a seat."

Tudel blinked.

Warily, he let his eyes drop, found the chair, and allowed himself to sit. He sat at the edge of the cushion and kept his back ramrod straight.

General Bonner seemed to consider his words before speaking. "Fifty-nine of your men - every single one - lost."

Here it came.

"Yes, sir. I take full -"

Bonner cut him off. "As the only survivor from the Wookkiee, you are the only one who saw the expats in combat. What do you think of their skills?"

Tudel blinked. "Sir?"

"You heard me. The crew of the - " he coughed " -RTFM didn't fight. What about the expats on your ship? How were they? Disciplined? Aggressive? Do they have any sort of doctrine, or were they making it up as they went along?"

Tudel's vision swam for a moment. Were they - was he - what was going on? He allowed himself a faint spark of hope.

But, wait. This could still be a trap. If he said that the expats were disciplined, was he implicitly saying that they were more disciplined and better trained than his own men? If he said that the expats who had killed his team were a rabble, did that mean that his own men were even worse?

What game was the General playing with him? His eyes flitted around the room. He was being recorded, certainly.

He reached for an explanation that was true - but one that would also play well. "Sir, the ship's crew was just civilians. Most of my men died in the deck before we seized the ship. Once we got inside the expats on the ship weren't much of a threat. But the quick reaction force on the moon that retook the Wookkiee - *they* struck me as well-trained." He paused, to give the general a chance to interject. He didn't, so Tudel continued. "I've been thinking about it and my bet is that their QRF is made up of defectors with military training. They weren't better than us, but they have one thing we don't: experience. Experience operating in space suits. Experience in operating in low gravity."

Bonner nodded silently.

Tudel felt more droplets of sweat ball in his armpits and slide down his side.

The other officer seated at the short end of the desk shifted in his chair. Tudel looked and saw that he was a two star. His name tag read "Opper." He knew the name from his chain of command. General Opper might be subordinate to General Bonner, but the man was still his boss's boss's boss's boss. The gap was dizzying. Tudel swallowed.

General Opper reached down and picked up something from the floor and put it on the desk. A spacesuit helmet in a large sealed evidence bag. "You wore this during your escape from the Wookkiee to the RTFM."

It didn't sound like a question, but Tudel nodded and croaked, "Yes, sir." He cleared his throat, embarrassed that his voice had caught.

Opper raised on eyebrow. "Interesting stuff in the onboard processors. Complete logs of everywhere the Wookkiee has been for the last three years. Pickup points in the Pacific... and off the coast of Nigeria. Keys and protocols for opening Aristillus airlocks." He paused. "I'm impressed."

Tudel blinked. General Opper was impressed? With him? No, he must be reading that wrong. He'd fucked up - his career was over. There was no chance -

"But we retrieved other helmets - we've got a couple dozen off the RTFM. So this isn't unique." Ah, of course. Opper was building a bit of hope, and then crushing it. He had to admire the technique - he'd used it himself, but rarely so well.

Tudel took a breath and kept his face impassive. He was going to face his fate like a warrior.

Opper reached down and pulled up another evidence bag, this one much smaller. He placed it on the desk. "But this - this is the piece de resistance." He nodded to himself. "Darcy Grau's personal phone. The contact information alone - Mike Martin, Javier Borda, Albert Lai, Hector Camanez - is amazing. We know those names; a lot of them were in the CEO Trials, and the ones that weren't are on lists that - well, never mind. But I don't care about the names. The crypto keys to her journal, her email archives - that's the red meat here. Foreign Materiel Exploitation loved this one."

Opper reached out and spun the evidence bag around on the desk so that the phone faced Tudel. "Well done, soldier. Well done."

Tudel felt dizzy and suddenly it felt harder to breathe. Was this another cycle of raising hopes before crushing them? Or were they seriously...

General Opper turned to Bonner. "You want to tell him?"

"He's your man, Bill. You do the honors."

Opper nodded. "We're promoting you - light colonel would have been appropriate, but there are regs, so it's just major for now. But don't worry - that oak leaf will turn silver soon enough."

Opper kept talking, but his voice seemed to grow quiet and distant. Tudel felt like a man lost at sea, trying to clear his lungs and push himself above the waves. He forced himself to remain utterly straight in his chair, but it was a challenge. He clung to one thing: he'd done it. He hadn't disgraced himself after all. He - he was a hero. The hero of the entire mission.

Opper was saying something. " - scout ahead of the big one."

"I'm - I'm sorry sir, what was that?"

"We've got a new mission for you. The ships are ready; we're just waiting for the reverse engineering lab to clone the AG drive."

"I -" Tudel swallowed. "I - thank you sir." How? How had this turned around so quickly?

He didn't know, but he knew that he was going to do his best on the new mission. And sure as hell wasn't going to make the same mistakes he'd made this time.

Chapter 57

2064: Mike's house, Aristillus, Lunar Nearside

Two rooms over, the water rushed as the bathtub filled, but Mike didn't hear it as he paced the length of the den. He stopped, picked up a lunar globe from the book case, stared at it for a few seconds, and put it back. He paused. Next to the globe was a toy yellow Caterpillar tracked loader, dented and scratched from endless afternoons being played with in a Texas backyard fifty years ago.

He picked up the Cat and stared out the window. Outside the apples on the trees were starting to ripen, but Mike didn't see them.

The war was starting way too soon. He'd won a battle - no, not even. A skirmish. A fistfight.

He'd won nothing.

Mike ran his hand over the small yellow loader absently. He'd known that the US and the UN would come after him. He'd known it from the day Ponzie had shown him the drive and they'd hatched their insane idea to leave Earth and build this place.

It was in their nature. What was government except control? People breathing without official permission wasn't just an annoyance, it was an existential threat. A threat because it showed that freedom was possible, that self-organization worked, that people didn't need to be ruled.

So of course there was going to be a war.

But that war was supposed to be years in the future.

His hand contracted around the toy, and he didn't notice that the edges were biting into the meat of his palm.

He'd spent ten years building the colony, working every minute of the day, and now the whole thing looked doomed. Given a few more years, Aristillus would have the population to fight, the infrastructure and weapons to fight, and maybe even public opinion on Earth on their side.

But now the Earth governments had the AG drive. Would they be able to reverse engineer it? The politicians might be stupid and corrupt, Earth's economy might be a basket case, the incentives for industry might be somewhere between idiotic and malign...but the expats had no monopoly on intelligence. With a population of nine billion, Earth had more geniuses than Aristillus had people. *Of course* they'd reverse engineer the drive.

He'd assumed there was a political barrier, that the Earth governments would be too wrapped up with their own problems to come after them, at least for a few more years, but apparently he was wrong.

He'd assumed there was a technological barrier, and now that was gone too.

The war was here, and it was too soon. Way too soon.

They'd arrive in force, and soon. And when they arrived and conquered Aristillus, what would happen to him, Darcy, and all the other expats? Mike swallowed. It might make the show trials a decade earlier look like just a warm-up act.

Mike put the Cat toy back on the bookshelf, turned away from the window, and wandered into the kitchen. He looked in the fridge, and then shut it. He wasn't hungry.

He was doomed.

He was an escaped felon, a fugitive from the CEO trials. And if even if that was wiped from his record, his actions since going on the run would provide enough grist for any government lawyer to find a near-infinite number of 'crimes.' Illegal emigration. Cross-state travel without a voucher. Construction without a license. Hate speech. Relocation without a housing classification permit. Making business loans without approval. Suborning others to do all of the same.

Treason.

He'd been looking at decades in jail when he fled earth. Now, if he was taken captive, he could face a hundred life sentences. A thousand.

Mike snorted. A thousand life sentences? Two thousand? Ha. He'd cheat them out of all but one of them! He let his hand fall to the counter, where it landed on a bowl of peaches Darcy had put there.

He picked the top peach up and looked at it.

It wasn't the best he'd seen; he remembered eating peaches right off the tree in his grandparents' yard in Georgia when he was a boy. But this one was good enough. He turned it over in his hand and marveled at it. This peach had never seen Georgia. In fact, it had never seen the sun. How crazy was it that a sapling brought from Earth had been planted in manmade dirt, grown under artificial lights in a lunar tunnel, and had produced a peach like this?

Mike had been looking at the fruit absently, but now he stared at it, seeing it with fresh eyes. He shook his head at the audacity of what the people of Aristillus had accomplished. Eleven years ago this - all of this - had been solid rock. And now - just a decade later? Endless kilometers of living space, bright, warm, full of laughing kids, racing vehicles, teens playing soccer, restaurants, schools, commerce.

And at least one God-damned peach tree orchard.

It was incredible.

They'd built this - all of this. And now they were going to lose it all. He pictured it: the city evacuated, the populace jailed back on earth, the cold dark tunnels slowly losing air through leaky seals, the dead trees standing mute witness to what once was.

And him and Darcy dead, or in separate underground jail cells for their rest of their lives.

He'd never eat a peach again.

The image - all of it: the cold tunnels, the dead trees, Darcy in jail - enraged him.

How dare they.

Fuck that.

Fuck that!

No. No, he wasn't going to let some bureaucrat do that. He wasn't going to let some jailer decide what he could eat, what he could read, when he woke and when he slept.

Not after all the work he'd put into building Aristillus. Actually *building* it, not just as an idea, but with his own hands, with his own men and his own machines.

There was some famous Revolutionary era quote about preferring death to living in chains. He'd never heard it in school, of course, but thousands of people used it in signature blocks on underground bulletin boards.

Patrick Henry. That was it. What was the exact quote?

He pulled out his phone and looked it up.

"Is life so dear or peace so sweet as to be purchased at the price of chains and slavery? Forbid it, Almighty God. I know not what course others may take, but as for me, give me liberty or give me death!"

He took a deep breath.

Yes. Exactly.

So the governments had the AG drive and wanted a war? It was years too early, and Aristillus wasn't ready to fight. But the fight was here. Maybe they'd lose. Hell, almost certainly they'd lose. But even if they lost, they could die on their feet. The light of liberty had already burned out on Earth - and maybe it was going to go out here on the moon too. But it would burn again someday.

Somewhere. And the fight now, here, would make a glorious tale to inspire some future generation. He - he would make a glorious tale to inspire some future generation.

Mike took a bite of the peach.

He was Mike Martin. He'd risen from a small town in Texas. Without money, without credentials, and without permission he'd built everything he'd ever owned.

Twice.

He swallowed and took another bite, larger this time. Juice spilled over his hands.

And you know what? Screw dying a glorious death to inspire future generations. Screw that. If the Earth governments wanted a fight, wanted to cage or kill him and his friends, employees, and associates, he'd give them a fight.

And he wasn't going to fight to inspire others. He was going to fight to win.

Mike swallowed. The peach was delicious.

Chapter 58

2064: Mike's house, Aristillus, Lunar Nearside

Mike paced through the living room. "It's too damned dangerous! You barely escaped with your life last time!"

Darcy sat on the couch, her robe pulled around her and her hair still wet from the bath. "Mike, please - can we let this rest for a week? Or at least a day or two?"

He turned his hands upward. "What's going to change in a week or two?"

"Nothing, but - "

"Well, then, why -"

"Darn it, Mike! I had guns pointed at me, and I've only been off the ship for a few hours. I just want to rest and -"

Mike stopped and faced Darcy. "You had guns pointed at you! That's exactly my point. These runs aren't safe. They never were, but it's worse now. The war has started, Darce. I can't have you on the front lines."

Darcy looked around the house theatrically. "What? Do you think that here in Aristillus is somehow not the front lines? I was held hostage and you were just in a gun battle not three klicks from here. Every place is the front lines!"

Mike looked away, then back. "That's rhetoric. You know as well as I do that it's safer here in the tunnels than it is flying to Earth and back."

"I agree with you."

Mike blinked. "You do?"

"Yes. It is safer. But you've spent the last forty-five minutes telling me about your plans for the revolution. Building fortifications, funding militias, recruiting technical advisers. If you're going to fight this revolution, Michael Martin, you're not going to do it by yourself. You're going to need every man, woman, and child in Aristillus to help you."

"So help. But there's no need for you to be flying. There's other stuff you can work on."

Darcy stood and put her hands on her hips. "Those new EP doors you want? Someone's got to fly them here. You want military advisors? That means ships, and ships mean navigators."

"Navigators, sure - but that doesn't mean *you* have to do it."

"Mike, I told you I was in on this scheme ten years ago, and I meant it. If there's a war, then I'm doing my part."

Mike shook his head. "That's not the end of the conversation. We're not done talking about this."

"Good. This war needs every one of us, and I've got a lot to say about it."

Chapter 59

2064: Benjamin and Associates Office, Aristillus, Lunar Nearside

Mike ticked off the action items on his fingers. "I need to free up cash from Morlock Engineering. I need to get that cash to Earth. I need to use that cash to buy supplies. I need to get the supplies back here. I need to hire mercenaries to train the rifle club." He looked up from his fingers to Lowell expectantly.

Lowell steepled his fingers. Then, after a long moment, he asked, "And what do you want me to do? I hope you're not assuming I've got any advice on hiring -" he shook his head slightly "- mercenaries."

Mike shook his head. "No. I need you to tell me how to get gold from Aristillus into the Earth financial system." He paused for a moment. "Money laundering, I guess."

Lowell raised his eyebrows. "Why do you need my advice? You buy TBMs and spare parts all the time from Earth. Just do whatever -"

Mike shook his head. "No, this is different. We're talking bigger amounts. Much bigger. Tens of millions, maybe hundreds. And that's just to start."

Lowell's forehead creased. "That much?"

"If the PKs are going to invade us, we need e-p-doors -"

"E P doors?"

"Emergency pressure doors. Big - I'm talking *vast* - doors that can slide across tunnels. Like bank vaults."

Lowell nodded, but his brow was furrowed. "You've got some of those up in the top levels; why not just have them fabbed locally?"

Mike shook his head again. "Those are in the old A-series tunnels. Ten meters across. Most of the colony is C-series. Those are thirty meters across, and nine times -"

"Nine? What?"

Mike gave Lowell a withering look. "Didn't you take *any* engineering courses?"

Lowell rolled his eyes. "No, Mike, Harvard Law doesn't -"

Mike waved it away. "EP doors for a C series tunnel are nine times the area, plus there are complications having to do with the span -" Mike stopped. "Look, you don't care about the engineering details. The bottom line is that we need armored doors that are a lot bigger than anything we can produce locally, and they're even bigger than anything we can get from our regular black-market suppliers in Vietnam or Somalia. We need First World facilities and engineering."

Lowell sighed. "Money laundering isn't my area of expertise; you knew that when we started doing business ten years ago. Seasteading and private law - that's what I do." He paused. "Alright, let me look into it. I can make a few calls. You can get the cash to me in gold?"

Mike nodded. "Most of it's in Goldwater certificates; it shouldn't take more than a day to convert that to bullion."

Lowell thought further. "How much gold are we talking? Bars?"

Mike shook his head. "Pallets of bars. At the very least. Maybe more by the time it's done."

Lowell gave him a cautioning look. "There are very few people I'd trust around even a single one kilo bar. Even mostly honest men have their price - and the kind of men we're going to have to deal with on Earth to move this stuff - they're not honest men." Lowell looked up over his steepled fingers and stared at Mike hard. "If I can figure out how to launder this and get it into First World bank accounts, can you figure out how to purchase these doors of yours without tipping anyone off or having anyone turn you in for a reward?"

"Well", said Mike, rubbing his hand across the lower portion of his face, "I guess I'll have to."

Chapter 60

2064: Javier's office, Aristillus, Lunar Nearside

Javier shook his head. "Smuggling gold? Hiring mercenaries? This is a mistake, Mike."

"Jave, the war is here! This stuff is critical."

"Yes, the war is here - but you're diving into details when you need to back up and think about the big picture. The strategy-""

"Strategy? There is no strategy. We're playing defense, and we're screwed unless we start now."

"Mike, stop. What's your goal here?"

"My goal? My goal is to smuggle the gold to Earth, get the EP doors built, hire military advisors -"

Javier held up a finger. "No, bigger picture."

Mike's mouth twisted. He hated it when Javier lectured him like this. He always had some stupid zinger up his sleeve. "Bigger picture? We've got to defend Aristillus."

"Closer. I'd say our goal is to avoid a war, if we can."

"It's too late for that!"

Javier shrugged. "Maybe. Probably. But you should try - and be seen to try - if only for the propaganda value. And then, if that fails -"

"*When* it fails."

"Fine. When it fails." Javier sighed. "If, when, whatever. After that your goal is to fight and win a revolution."

Mike threw his head back. "Finally. Jesus." He paused. "But it's not a revolution; I'm not trying to change -"

"Secession. Whatever. My point is that to win you need -"

"It's not a secession either because it was never a single government."

"Mike, damn it! This is exactly the problem. You want to dive into details when you need to back up and figure out the big picture. It's the same problem you have at work - you spend too much time thinking about TBMs and not enough time managing the business. If it weren't for Wam basically running half the show for you you'd be bankrupt by now."

Mike felt his face cloud. "What are you talking about? Morlock is my company and -"

Javier held up a hand. "Mike, Mike - I know. Look, we're off topic. The point is, if you dive into the details and start designing and ordering EP doors and micro-optimizing the hell out of God damned *engineering problems*" - he spat the phrase - "then you're going to lose this war and we're all going to be killed or jailed."

"The EP doors aren't just some piddly engineering problem. When the PKs attack -"

"Mike, back up. My point is this: you can't run this war alone."

Mike sighed and shook his head. Javier was always overstating his case, making straw men. "Who said anything about running it alone? I'm going to subcontract out all sorts of things. The militia will be staffed up. The market -"

"Mike, remember who you're talking to, OK? I've drunk the libertarian kool-aid; I know the whole rant. 'Cooperation,' 'emergent systems,' 'markets are tools for sharing information' - we're on the same side here."

"So then why are you asking if I'm going to run it alone? I'm going to run my corner of it."

"And who's going to run the rest of it?"

Mike shrugged. "You. Hector. Albert Lai is a bit brittle, but when the chips are down -"

"And when are you going to tell them what's expected of them?"

"What? They'll figure out what they should do." He saw Javier looking at him skeptically. "What, you want me to write up a memo? Email them some action items?"

Javier didn't try to hide his sarcasm. "Yeah, Mike, that's what I want. A fucking memo."

"Well if not that, then what's your point?"

"Even if you get Hector, Albert, and everybody involved through emergent whatever, who's going to fight for them? Who's going to follow around Albert with his crisp suits and Eton accent? Who's going to rally around the stock price ticker feed for LDAC?"

"What?"

Javier shook his head. "Mike, I love the market. I love decentralization. All of that. But no military in the history of the human race has ever gotten by without leaders."

"The American Revolution -"

"Committees of Correspondence. Continental Congress. Jefferson, Adams, Washington -"

Mike rolled his eyes. "The Icelanders -"

"Had their Althing, not to mention kinship ties. Mike, your problem is that you'd do anything to avoid interacting with people. You want to spend all your time with TBMs and -"

"That's not fair."

"It is fair. You find social interaction taxing. Fine. That's not the problem."

"Then what is my problem?" Mike crossed his arms. "Tell me, Jave. Please."

Javier didn't take the bait. "Your real problem is that you think that everyone else is the same way. They're not. People are monkeys, Mike. I mean that in the nicest possible way. We're a social species. And as a social species we need leaders."

Mike let his scorn show on his face. "'Leaders,' huh? So we should elect a president, or maybe a politburo, or -"

"I'm not saying people need rulers. I'm saying they need leaders. Someone to coordinate, to inspire, to -"

"I don't need a leader to get stuff done, and neither do other people."

"There! There! That's exactly my point. Just because you don't feel the need for a leader doesn't mean that's how other people are."

"On Earth, maybe. But Aristillus is different. The average person here is smarter and more educated. Did you see that article on punditdome.ari about conscientiousness scores? We're different."

Javier chuckled. "Mike, even if the average IQ in Aristillus is 130, that doesn't change anything. Ten years of selective immigration can't override ten million years of evolution."

"That's bullshit -"

"It's bullshit that we're still monkeys? When's the last time you crashed your motorcycle trying to impress Darcy?"

"I ride my bike for me, not for -"

"When's the last time you checked out the rack on some barista or waitress?"

Mike blinked, then slowly grinned. "OK, fine, you got me. Maybe we're part monkey."

"We're *all* monkey."

"And?"

"And monkeys - most monkeys, at least - want leaders. At least if they're going to pull together, to deliver their best."

Mike looked at him dubiously.

"I'm serious, Mike. If you really want to win this war - and I hope like hell you do, because it's the only way you, or I, or anyone we know is going to stay alive - Aristillus needs a leader."

Mike pursed his lips. "I'm not convinced. But even if you're right, who? You said Albert Lai is too wimpy. And you'd better not be thinking about Mark Soldner. That guy would love to get his hands on -"

"You."

Mike recoiled, stunned. "Me? Bullshit. People wouldn't accept me as a leader."

Javier rolled his eyes. "Mike, that's such transparent crap that you can see through it yourself. Every time we grab lunch you have to fight your way through the fans. Lowell Benjamin tells me that his secretary all but throws herself at you."

"She's a flirt."

"She doesn't flirt with me when I'm at Lowell's office. But that's just one data point. When's the last time someone accosted you on the street and wanted a picture with you? When's the last time -"

"I get it, Javier. Yeah, that crap happens all the time. I'm a celebrity because I founded the colony. But a celebrity isn't the same thing as a leader."

"Have you watched the news in the last twenty-four hours?"

"What? No."

Javier picked up a remote control and turned on the wallscreen. '655 Hours a Day' was streaming and a young woman explained earnestly that she'd seen the Wookkiee crash and then seen the RTFM land - and then seen Mike's rescue.

"The crane reached right over and it ripped one of those maneuvering units off - I couldn't believe it! It was crazy. My friend Marsha told me later that it was Mike Martin, and then it all made sense. I was so lucky to see it. I wasn't even supposed to be on shift then, and, anyway, it was just like - wow! I mean, there are really no words -"

Javier changed the channel. Another Aristillus news program. The two anchors chatted for a moment before running grainy footage. The Wookkiee crash landing cut to video of mining vehicles and ambulances racing toward the wreck, and then a stock photo of Mike appeared and covered the right third of the screen. "With open warfare all but declared between Earth and-"

Mike rolled his eyes, grabbed the controller and turned the wallscreen off. "OK, fine, Javier. I already agreed that maybe I'm kind of celebrity -"

"Leader."

"God damn it, no. Celebrity, whatever - the bottom line is that I hate dealing with people. You said as much yourself"

Javier smiled. "We're getting closer to the truth. You like people just fine when you can communicate with them on your terms: a quick email or a phone call. Telling them what you want them to do instead of listening to them bitch. You don't hate people - you hate the messiness of listening to them, convincing them, working with them -"

"Enough psychobabble. Whatever. The point is, I'm a celebrity but I'm not a leader."

"You led people to Aristillus."

"What?"

"This city - you led -"

"Aristillus grew by emergent processes."

"It *grew* by emergent processes, but you led us all here. It was your insane idea. You and Ponzie built the first ship. You brought the first TBM. You-"

"If I hadn't been me, someone else would have done it. Just because a kid jumps in front of a parade doesn't mean he's leading it."

"Mike, this may be the first time I've ever heard you be modest in your life. Does leadership frighten you that much that you're even willing to put your ego in check to get away from it?"

Despite himself, Mike grinned at the dig.

"Be honest, Mike - don't you ever look out at all of Aristillus and think 'I made this'?"

Mike twisted, caught. He looked aside, embarrassed.

"Aha!"

"Javier, stop attacking me."

"I'm not attacking you. You're *right* to be proud of this. Mike, not one man in a million could have done what you did. And that's why I - why all of us - need you to do this."

"You think I'm the perfect one to - what? Establish some *government*? What the fuck makes you think I'd help you do that?"

"Damn it, Mike, listen to me. I'm not trying to establish a government. You're invoking some sort of libertarian purity test to avoid talking about personal issues."

God *damn* it. Javier was being an asshole. Personal issues? "Fuck you Jave." He stood up and pushed back his chair.

"This proves my point."

Mike turned and walked to the far wall of the office. "What point?"

"That the reason you're unwilling to take a leadership role is because it's scary."

Mike turned. "I'm not afraid of hard work."

"I didn't say the job was 'hard.' I said it was 'scary.'"

Mike scoffed. "Scary?"

"Yeah, scary. Working with other people is scary because it reminds you of -"

"This bullshit again. Javier, you're a good friend most of the time, but you can be a real asshole when -"

"Mike, calm down. Listen to me."

"Listen to you? Why? I know exactly what you're going to say. You've got this late-night dorm-room pop-psychology bullshit story. I've heard it before, and it's not true."

"If I'm wrong, why are you so angry?"

"Because you always do this -"

"Do what?"

"Think that you understand me better than I understand me. Try to psychoanalyze me."

Javier paused, then spread his hands. "OK, I apologize." He stood and stuck out a hand. "Let's forget I brought it up."

Mike looked at the outstretched hand dubiously. "You're going to let it go just like that? I don't believe you."

"Mike, the war is coming. We need to do something about it. So let's talk about our plan."

Mike was leery. This was exactly Javier's kind of trick.

"Come on Mike, let's talk it out. EP doors. Mercenaries. Financing alone is a complicated topic." He paused. "You want a drink?" Javier opened a drawer and lifted out a bottle and two glasses.

Mike looked at the bottle skeptically. Finally he sighed and sat back down. "OK, but just one."

**

Javier held out the bottle. "You want another?"

"Hell, no."

"You've only had three."

"Jave, you pour like a motherfucker. I've probably had more like seven."

Javier grinned and spread his arms expansively. "Don't feel bad that you can't handle your liquor. Most teenage girls can't."

"You think you can handle more than I can?"

"Absolutely."

Mike shook his head. "Can not."

"Can too. I've got a secret -"

"And what's that?"

"Practice."

Mike laughed. "One more, then - but no more. I don't want to come home like a total drunk."

"Darcy?"

"Yeah." Javier poured then pushed the glass over. "Not that she'd be mad. She's cool, it's just..." Mike paused. "I want to look good for her."

"No shame in that." Javier poured for himself. "So are you and she ever going to -"

"Jesus, you too?"

Javier put his hands up. "OK, OK, sorry."

Mike sipped his drink. "You're right, though."

"Hmmm?"

"You're right. I should marry her."

"I'm not lecturing you."

"Jave, you're divorced. You seem happier than you used to be."

"Don't take my life as a guide. Every situation is unique."

Mike sipped his drink. "Yeah."

Javier put his feet up on the desk. "You know what your problem is, Mike?"

"Yes."

Javier raised his eyebrows "You do?"

Mike laughed. "No. But I thought it might shut you up."

"If you don't want to hear -"

Mike sighed. "No, tell me. You give the best advice."

Javier smiled. "See? This is why I like it when you have a couple of drinks. You stop being so damned uptight."

Mike sipped his drink. "It's true. I really am an asshole."

"Nah, you're not an asshole."

"Yes, I am."

Javier nodded. "Yes, you are."

Mike laughed again. "And *you* only get to experience it from the outside. Do you know what it's like being me from the inside?"

"No."

"It's hell!" This time they both laughed, and Mike put his drink down and leaned forward. "OK, Jave. Hit me. Tell me what my problem is."

Javier fixed Mike with a stare. "You're not just an introvert. You're an introvert who's afraid of being betrayed."

"Fuck you. I'm -" Mike paused, then shrugged. "Maybe you're right."

"Of course I'm right."

"What do you mean 'of course'? Do you think you've got some magical psychological -"

Javier waved the question away, spilling a splash of his drink on his desk. "I don't have any special skills. It's just that you're so utterly transparent."

Mike leaned back in his chair. "So I'm afraid of being betrayed. OK, fine. You got me. I'm a pussy."

Javier raised a finger. "No. You're not a pussy. I know where you're coming from. People turned on you during the CEO trials. Guys who were actually criminals - real criminals - told lies about you to clear their own names. They cut deals. You were the only one who stood your ground. So you have a right to be wary of working with other people again."

Mike shrugged dismissively.

"No, don't pretend it's nothing. It is something. And it's important."

"OK, so you want me to be a leader, and I don't want to be. Where does that leave us?"

"You're an introvert who only deals with people as much as you have to to get your projects done."

Mike raised his drink in a playful salute.

"...and then, on top of that, the last time you trusted other CEOs, you got burned. You got burned *badly*."

"So you're saying I should just get over it and -"

Javier shook his head. "People don't 'just get over' that shit. But you *do* have to get past it. All this time you said the war was coming - and you were right. You were righter than you knew, or than any of us suspected. Mike, you've got to do this. Aristillus needs you. If you step up and become our Washington, or our Jefferson, then we might live. But if you don't, we're all dead."

Mike looked at his drink and realized it was empty. "This sucks, Jave. I hate dealing with people. You know that."

"I do know that, Mike. This does suck."

"Putting up with disagreement - "

"Yeah, putting up with disagreement. Putting up with idiocy. Putting up with people who aren't *just* wasting your time, but who are actively doing the harmful things. It's everything you hate. All of it. This is the worst job description possible for you."

Mike looked at his empty glass. "Why me?"

"Because you've got a dream - a dream of a free Aristillus. One place where people can live without a boot on their neck. It's a good dream. Hell, it's the best dream that anyone has had in a century. And if you want to keep that dream alive - and keep all of us out of secret prisons - we need to win this war. And because humans are tribal animals, winning this war means that we need someone to inspire them and unify them."

"That's your big speech?"

"That's my big speech."

Mike mulled it over. "You want someone to unify and inspire people? I can't do that."

Javier raised an eyebrow. "Really?" He reached for the wallscreen remote again.

Mike lunged, trying to reach it first. He missed and knocked it to the floor.

He sighed, and looked at Javier. "Fuck you." He put his glass down and gestured at the bottle. "OK, I'll do it."

Chapter 61

2064: Morlock Engineering office, Aristillus, Lunar Nearside

Mike stood at the end of the room and looked down the length of table - a huge sheet of deck plating resting on I-beam offcuts.

Mike scanned the dozen faces around the table - owners of some of the largest firms in the colony. He took a breath. They were all here.

He cleared his throat, then leaned forward and slapped one hand on the thick steel table.

"We are at war." Too dramatic? He scanned the table again. They were listening. Maybe this was OK.

"Folks, we all know each other, and we've all done business with each other. We have a lot in common: we each left Earth to escape the taxation, the regulation, all that handbasket-to-hell stuff." He took a breath. "And we all had one more thing in common: we all thought that between the Long Depression, our monopoly on the AG drive, and the war in China, the Earth governments wouldn't get around to messing with us. At least not for a long time."

He paused, letting the tension build.

"But we were wrong. The governments picked a fight with us. They hijacked our ships and killed our people in cold blood - you've seen the video. We didn't want the fight, but it's here, and it's way ahead of schedule. Now we have to figure out how we're going to fight back. Our first -"

Karina Roth interrupted. "Mike, point of order." A dozen heads swiveled. "It's not clear to me that the governments themselves picked the fight, and it's also not clear to me that we need to fight back. I think we need to talk about those topics first so we don't put the cart before the horse."

Mike was taken aback. He'd know that he'd have disagreements later in the meeting, but it hadn't occurred to him that there'd be a question this early. "Uh, what do you - how can you say that there's any doubt at all that they attacked us?"

"We don't know for sure who's behind these attacks. All we know is that two ships were hijacked -"

Trang interrupted, "Three - don't forget the Hsieh Tung-min."

Karina acknowledged Trang's point with a polite nod. "Indeed. We know that three ships were hijacked, but we don't know that this is government policy. We all know that Earth governments don't have as good command and control as they once did - it's been eroding for decades. Before we conclude that this is deliberate policy, we have to weigh that this may be a one-off, done by some rogue unit. We shouldn't assume that we're in a war with the governments themselves -"

Mike was incredulous. "Are you serious? Three ships, hijacked at the same time? You're crazy if -"

Javier cleared this throat and Mike looked at him and stopped.

"Karina, you raise a good point," Javier said. "I think that before we go too far, we really do need to figure out what's going on with the command and control -"

Mike looked at Javier wide eyed and turned his hands up in a what-the-hell gesture. "Javier, you can't honestly -"

Javier raised his voice and spoke over Mike. "Agreed; we need to get more data to see who's behind this - but since it is at least plausible, if not likely, that this is deliberate government policy, it can't hurt to talk about plans for that contingency." He stressed the last word. "Don't you think?"

Karina shrugged noncommittally. "I think that premature talk of force is...dangerous. At best. There's no way we can fight the Earth governments. Mike is saying that we all knew that a fight would come sooner or later. I reject that - we all know that a *confrontation* would come sooner or later. I, for one, have always thought that once we proved ourselves viable we'd be able to negotiate. And I still think that." She turned from Javier to Mike.

"And speaking of confrontation and negotiation, I've heard rumors that in the wake of the Wookkiee hijacking, your rifle club took prisoners. I understand freeing the crews of the Wookkiee and the RTFM, but taking *prisoners*? That's an act of provocation. We need to *de-*escalate. Our plan all along has been to build wealth here in Aristillus while the current craziness sorts itself out down there. We know that a more sane government is going to be voted in at some point -"

Mike interrupted her. "We don't know that at all! Government has growing more repressive for centuries. A man needs a permit to brush his teeth. There's no reason to think that's going to reverse itself."

Mike looked around the table. Darren Hollins of Goldwater was leaning forward, listening. Good! One ally against Karina. Who else? His eye landed on Hector. "You need a hundred permits to build a house. You have to jump through hoops and know the right people to get a restaurant license. You have to kiss someone's ass to even raise some livestock without the government coming in and killing your animals. Am I right, Hector?"

Hector Camanez raised his eyebrows and shrugged. Why wasn't Hector weighing in? That man had been as brutalized by government as any of them at this table. He should be angry - but he seemed calm and detached. If Hector wasn't going to support him, who would? Shit - this was exactly why he hated politics. How were you supposed to know that an attack like Karina's was coming - and how were you supposed to know that you wouldn't get support from -

Rob Wehrmann spoke up. "Whether it's a rogue military unit or the central governments, what the fuck difference does it make? Some preparation seems smart either way."

Alright. Not full-throated support, but decent. Darren Hollins cleared his throat and Mike looked at him. Good. With his background - American, two factories shut down, and then a profitable mine appropriated out from under him - he'd lay the smack-down on Karina. He'd -

"We need to find out who's behind this so we can figure out the right palms to grease. Maybe we can make this go away."

Mike's head rocked back. What the hell? Darren should be supporting him!

Karina shook her head. "I don't like the idea of bribery. That just exposes us to ethics charges -"

Mark Soldner nodded. "We should work through channels - *proper* channels. We don't want to lower ourselves to their level."

Darren snorted. "Have you people ever actually worked with a government licensing body? Bribes are how you get things done! I'm not sure we can buy our way out of this, but it's the first thing to try."

What the hell were these people talking about? They were here to figure out a military response, and they were bickering about *bribing* the governments to go away? Mike shot a loot at Javier. Javier held up one hand: Let it play out. Mike scowled. This was stupid.

Mark Soldner held up one hand. "I agree with Karina - corruption isn't the way. We talk to them, but we talk to them as equals. We form a congress and we draw up a list of grievances. That way -"

"A list of grievance?" Darren interrupted. "What is this, a choir club asking for snacks? We find the right politicians and we give them cash. Cold, hard -"

Karina cut him off. "If we do that and we get exposed -"

Mike rubbed a hand over his forehead. What the hell was wrong with Karina? With all of these people? Worrying about bullshit like ethics laws, when the government was already burning Gamma's sats and hijacking their ships? And why weren't more people backing him up? Was he the only one who saw the RTFM crew member executed by the PKs? What the fuck were these people thinking?

If these fools didn't understand the situation they were all in, they were idiots, and he was going to tell them so.

Mike punched the deck steel of the table and shouted, "No!".

The room fell silent and a dozen stunned faces turned to him. "You people don't -"

"Mike!" Javier shouted.

Mike turned to him. "Javier - no, wait! I need-"

"Mike, let me take it from here."

Mike protested. "No, I can -"

Javier held up two hands in a calming gesture. "Mike, I understand your position - but let me try, OK?"

"No, Javier. Everyone has to understand that we *cannot* negotiate. This isn't some tea party. We're not negotiating spheres of influence. This is a war."

Javier's lips pinched. "Mike -"

Mark Soldner interrupted him. "Javier, let me try. Mike, I agree with you that trouble is brewing, and I agree with you that the Earth governments are overreaching their enumerated powers. Unlike many of you - " he gestured around the room " - I never had run-ins with the law, but I've got sympathy with those of you who have. Albert Lai and the old PRC, Hector and the DEA - I get it. The US government has overstepped its bounds. We may end up needing to fight, and the first step is to form a government -"

Mike banged the unyielding steel table. Damn it, his hand hurt. "No! The last thing in the world we need is a government! It's government that ruined the Earth, that tried to throw us all in jail. Government is force -"

"Yes, unlimited, out-of-control government is a problem, but a limited government -"

"You think you can have a limited government? There's no such thing. Government grows - that's what it does. I'm not going to tolerate a government in Aristillus. I've been clear about that from the beginning."

"It's not your decision, Mike. If the people want -"

Mike started to speak over Mark - and in turn and was cut off by a loud high-pitched chime. He looked around - and saw Javier standing at the far end of the table, striking his water glass with his pen over and over, waiting for everyone's attention.

He fumed - he'd been about to put Mark in his place. Around him the babble died down.

Javier - slacks pressed, shirt crisp, bolo snugged, salt and pepper hair and goatee perfectly trimmed - Javier looked calm and composed. Mike didn't understand it. How could he be calm with all this bullshit going on?

The room fell silent and Javier said, "People, please. This meeting is degenerating. I propose that we draw up a list of questions to ponder and debate offline, then we meet again in a week."

Mike raised his voice. "A week? We don't-"

Javier's tone was icy and direct. "Mike. Please. Sit. Down."

Mike stared at Javier. Javier had all but forced him to step up and run this - and now he was telling him to shut up and sit down? Mike looked around the table, at the angry faces. Shit. He had to admit that the meeting had been a disaster. How? The issue was so simple - the Earth governments had started a war and Aristillus had to fight back. And now even Javier was trying to stall. Mike looked at his friend again. Javier stared back, firmly, implacably.

This was bullshit. If they were going to win this war, they needed to move, and move now.

Javier inclined his head, directing Mike to sit.

Mike breathed out. Javier had better have a good explanation for this. Mike pulled his chair out, and sat.

Javier nodded a thank you, and then continued. "I propose that we draw up a list, then adjourn. Agreed?"

Mark Soldner raised one hand. "I also propose that we draft a petition - like Jefferson's Olive Branch Petition - and lay out a short set of grievances for the Earth governments. Maybe we can reach some accommodation."

Mike braced both his hands on the edge of the table and was about to push himself erect and begin arguing when he caught Javier's eyes.

In the fifteen years he'd known Javier he'd never seen the man so angry before. The others in the room might not be able to read it - Javier was so good at controlling his face and stance - but Mike read his eyes.

He took his hands off the table and sat back.

Javier nodded to Mark. "I'm not sure that there's yet a need to open negotiations with the Earth governments. If nothing else, it sets a precedent that we might want to think about. I suggest -"

Mark looked around the room. "I think we should vote -"

There was a general murmur of assent. "All in favor of drafting a document?"

Hands went up. Mike looked around, amazed - and disgusted. Mark and Karin, of course, and then also Rob Wehrmann, Darren Hollins, Albert Lai. Katherine Dycus? The hell! Katherine had been part of this since the very beginning. How could she -

Mark announced the results. "Seven in favor, that's a majority. Do we have any volunteers to draft it?"

"Mark, I think you'd do a good job," Karina said. She glanced around the table. "Any objections?"

Despite the threat in Javier's eyes, Mike couldn't control himself any longer. "This is bullshit. Mark has always wanted a government and he's going to try to sneak one in. If anyone's going to draft this document, it's going to be me. I'll tell the fucking governments what they - "

At the far end of the table Javier again interrupted by striking his water glass with his pen. The noise was loud enough that Mike thought for a second the glass had shattered. Javier's voice, though, was controlled. "Mike. Please. Let's let Karina finish, shall we?"

Mike seethed, but shut up. Once he and Javier were alone there was going to be hell to pay for this.

Karina Roth pursed her lips. "Mike, we all know that you've been instrumental - no, utterly critical - to creating Aristillus. But it's not clear to me that you're the best public face for drafting a petition to the governments."

"Excuse me?"

Karina's eyebrows went up. "First there's the issue of your unorthodox -" she coughed, " -exit from the CEO trials. That alone means that we don't want to associate your name with this. But even aside from that, the recent video that's been going around the blogs of the bribery attempt -"

Mike scowled and waved his hand.

Karina continued, "No, I think this is worth talking about -"

Mark Soldner looked confused. "I apologize, but I've missed this. What's this video?"

Mike rolled his eyes. Karina turned to Mark. "There was apparently some sort of surveying mix up between

Mike and Leroy, and Mike tried to bribe Kevin -" here she pointed down the table "- to forge some files."

Mike gritted his teeth. "No, that's bullshit. The real story is that it was a shake-down attempt. Leroy tunneled into volume that I'd already registered and he forged some records - and *he* was the one who was trying to -" He stopped. "Anyway, it's not a big deal."

Karina Roth spread her hands. "Mike, how you do your business is up to you, but if this little cabal moves forward, it needs a public face that -"

Javier cleared his throat. "Folks, a vote on whether Mark Soldner should be in charge of drafting the petition?"

Mike looked around. Every hand except his was up. Even Javier himself was voting? What the fuck was wrong with people? Fine. Fuck them.

"Eleven in favor. Very well. People, let's all meet a week from today. Unless there's any further business ?"

* * *

The last of the CEOs left the room, leaving Javier and Mike alone.

Mike remained silent. What the hell had happened there? Even Javier had turned against him in the end. "Javier, what the hell was -"

Javier met his eyes and the anger radiated through them like heat from a furnace. "God damn it, Mike! It's bad enough that you're your own worst enemy, but do you have to screw up stuff for everyone else?"

Mike blinked. "What? What did I -"

"Damn it, Mike! You've worked your ass off for a decade to build Aristillus. You're *this close* -" he held his fingers up millimeters apart "- to getting what you've wanted your entire life. All we've got to do is win this war. And now you're almost *trying* to throw it away. Do you know how much damage you caused in less than twenty minutes?"

"Wait a second! I -"

"Did you go out of your way to create that mess? And why the hell did you call the meeting on four hours notice? I didn't even get the message until thirty minutes beforehand!"

Mike blinked. "This war is important. This meeting was your idea. I thought you'd be happy that -"

"Mike, damn it, I needed time to figure out what everyone wants. I needed time to work people behind the scenes."

Mike sighed. "Jave - look, the meeting went off the rails, but I don't know -"

Javier slapped his open palm on the table. "I *know* you don't know. Damn it, Mike you -" He paused, exhaled heavily, and then gave up on the sentence and settled for shaking his head sadly.

Mike was confused. He'd started this post-meeting eager to rip Javier a new asshole for telling him to sit down and shut up in the meeting - and now the conversation was headed in an entirely different direction.

It was clear he'd let Javier down, even if he wasn't sure how. Damn it.

"Javier, I -"

Javier made eye contact, and Mike could see the sadness in his eyes. No: disappointment.

"Mike. You fucked up, and you don't even know how you fucked up, do you? Just - don't talk to me."

Mike stood and walked to the side table and poured himself a glass of water. He turned back. "I'm sorry. Even if I don't know what I did."

He stood and waited.

Finally, after what felt like an hour, Javier uncrossed his arms and looked up. "Damn it, Mike. You're not very good with people, do you know that?"

Mike raised his eyebrows. "Yeah, Darce reminds me of that now and then. And so does my best friend."

Javier sighed, then finally allowed a rueful smile to creep onto his face. "You know, whoever the idiot was who put you up to this meeting really should take some of the blame for not explaining a few things to you."

Mike cracked a bit of a grin. "Do you still think that I'm the ideal 'human face' of the revolutionary cabal?"

Javier sighed. "We've got some work to do."

Chapter 62

2064: MaisonNeuve Construction office, Aristillus, Lunar Nearside

Leroy looked across the desk at George White and took his measure. He'd been working with George for years, so in truth he wasn't looking for new information. No - the point was that he wanted White to know that he was being looked at. Evaluated.

The man was tall and broad. Whatever the opposite of an aristocratic face was, White had it. He claimed to have been a Detroit cop back before he came to Aristillus, and as far as Leroy could find out it was true - but with the Public Servant Privacy Laws, it was hard to find out anything about at all about ex-cops. There were some rumors that he'd been thrown off the force. Not that that was a concern - the man always managed to get the job done, and that's what mattered.

He looked White in the eye - or tried to. White was looking off, over Leroy's head, apparently inspecting the room. Leroy hated it when someone wouldn't meet his eyes. It was a power game.

Leroy leaned forward and cleared his throat. "I've got another project with Mike Martin."

"The cafeteria video wasn't good enough?"

Leroy ignored the question. "I need something else."

White nodded. "What do you want me to find out?"

"I don't want you to find out anything. I want *other* people to find things out."

White narrowed his eyes. "What? I'm a PI. I *get* information, I don't spread it."

Leroy sighed contemptuously. "George, a war is coming. And this one is going to be like every other one: perception is going to matter more than anything else. And that's why I - why we - will win it."

Chapter 63

2064: Old Army Base Docks, Darwin, Australia

The nearly rusted-out Nissan truck pulled to the gate and slowed to a stop. One of the four men at the gate - apparently unarmed, but solid and muscular - walked to the vehicle.

"Invite, mate?"

The driver stuck his laser-printed form out the window. Paper. These people were paranoid.

"Neil Keenum?" the guard asked.

"That's me," said the driver.

The guard grunted, and scanned the page with a slate, which beeped.

"Right. Go'an in."

The other guards dragged the gate open, the sagging steel rasping against asphalt. A moment later the truck was through, and the gate shut behind them.

Neil looked around; the small parking lot seemed abandoned. But, wait, there - another guard was waving him around the back of a corrugated metal outbuilding. He pulled forward, and - ah. Here, hidden from the road, they'd gathered. Two hundred people - maybe more.

He pulled the truck into an empty space, killed the ignition, and sat. The two other men in the cab and the rest in the truck's bed also looked around, taking in the enormity of the situation.

Another hundred people arrived at the small lot over the next fifteen minutes: a few on foot, a handful in flatbed trucks, the majority in utes and battered pickups. The one thing the vehicles had in common was that their resale values - even assuming one knew the right palms to grease to get a Carbon Vehicle Transfer Permit - were near zero. Neil nodded; any vehicles worth anything had been parted out and sold piecemeal on the black market or given to friends.

Everyone in this parking lot was heading for a new life. Vehicles were just one of the many trappings that would be left behind.

Neil turned his attention from the vehicles to the people. A trained observer - and he was one - would note that it was a typical cross section of north country farmers, miners, and construction workers. There were fewer women and children than one would find on an average street, but there were some. Almost all of the people climbing out of their vehicles were wearing backpacks and most were carrying tool bags or pushing hand trucks loaded with boxes and small crates.

A line was starting to form up near the warehouse roll-up door. Neil looked at his phone.

It was time.

He swung himself out of the truck. Without a word, the other men in the cab and the bed of the truck got out and began unloading their own duffel bags and boxes.

He heard the gates being dragged shut and a chain rustling.

Neil zipped his Carhartt jacket over his Melbourne Reconstruction Electrical Services t-shirt, slung one duffel bag strap over a shoulder and lifted his other duffel and his tools, and headed to join the line.

To his left a guard climbed the rungs on the side of a shipping container. Neil put his load down and watched without making it obvious. The man clambered to the top, reached into his pocket, fumbled with a small device, and put the thing back in his pocket. Neil's phone beeped at him and he pulled it out and looked at it. The 'no signal' icon was flashing. Jammers. He nodded in approval; these guys were competent. More competent than the majority of the people he'd worked with in his career.

The man on the container yelled to get everyone's attention then addressed the crowd. "OK, the gates are locked - this is it. You should have a printed barcode receipt, but if you're a last-minute addition, get your gold out and make sure that the two people vouching for you are standing nearby."

He paused for a moment and looked around the crowd. "If you don't have your receipt or the gold, we'll deal with that... but you're not getting on the ship tonight. Anyone here who doesn't have one or the other?" He waited a moment and then continued. "OK, good. In a minute we're going to open the door, and I'm going to ask you to walk into this warehouse -" he gestured " - and we'll process you out the back and onto the boat.

"If you've shipped cargo ahead, it should already be on board. For carry-on stuff, you've got to carry it with you or get someone to help you; we're not porters." He looked behind him, at someone hidden from Neil and the others in the queue, and apparently got a sign. "OK, no need to shove, but let's get moving. The boat leaves the dock in thirty minutes."

The routine was well choreographed - the warehouse door rolled up a few seconds later and several workers in logoless yellow t-shirts that still conveyed 'I'm an official' fanned out to help massage the mass of people into a line.

Neil picked up his rip-stop duffel and his battered tool chest. The other men on his crew hoisted their packs, duffels, and plastic bucket tool organizers, and shuffled forward as the line started moving.

There was quiet conversation elsewhere in the line, but Neil and his men stayed silent. This was it; what else was there to say?

Five minutes later the band of electricians had passed through the door and were in the warehouse. A yellow-shirted guide consulted a slate and dispatched each traveler to separate queues. Neil followed his directions to the leftmost scanning station.

Neil put his bags on the folding table. A yellow shirt pushed them through a scanning box with a logo that said 'Soredex Dental Imaging Division.' Neil stepped through the scanning gate.

The man behind the table used his slate to scan the unfolded printout that Neil held out for him. "No guns?"

"Didn't think there was much call for them."

The staff member looked at him. "Seppo?"

"Huh?"

"You're American?"

"Back and forth. Childhood here, then over there after fourth grade - fourth form - then back here for the Reconstruction."

"Carpetbagger, eh?"

Neil shrugged. "I try not to get involved in politics."

The yellow-shirted worker let his gaze drift down to the Melbourne Reconstruction Electrical Services logo on Neil's shirt that was peaking through the top of his Carhartt jacket. "You take the PK's coin?"

"Figure I paid most of that coin in the first place - is it a crime to want some of it back?"

"Not a fan of the peakers?"

The electrician looked around. "I don't reckon that any of us here sold our furniture and let our leases lapse because we're fans of the PKs."

The man in the yellow shirt snorted. "Fucking well said, mate. OK, grab your bags and queue up at that door over there."

Captain Dewitt smiled. He wasn't much of an actor, but his "Neil Keenum" routine had worked perfectly.

He picked up his luggage and walked to the indicated door. Behind him were his dozen hand-picked men - all combat vets, all US citizens, and not a single one of them with a clean cultural sensitivity rating in their personnel file.

Twenty-five minutes later they were aboard the Wayward and the lines were cast off.

Two hours after that the engine cut off and the cargo freighter rolled in the dark sea - and then Captain Dewitt heard the deep thrumming and felt the weird sideways twisting in his stomach as the anti-gravity drive powered up.

Chapter 64

2064: MaisonNeuve Construction office, Aristillus, Lunar Nearside

Leroy broke the connection, waited for a second, and let the carefully composed look on his face fall. He slumped deeper into his chair, and then, after a moment, leaned forward and pulled the glass of gin from where it had been stashed out of camera view.

Father. What a miserable son of a bitch. Leroy took a sip, then raised the glass to mockingly toast the empty room. Now that the phone was off, he addressed the man. "Etienne, you self-satisfied asshole...do you have to make it that hard to get just a small loan from the family trust?"

Leroy took another sip.

And, of course, he'd had to choke down the lectures about Addison's most recent promotion in the ministry, and Leon's and Martial's newest triumphs.

God damn his brothers. Success came so easily to them - they'd had their paths paved by Etienne. Connections to banks, introductions to venture capitalists...the paterfamilias was willing to help them out. But for him? What did Father give to Leroy? He'd invested just a pittance in LawLink. Then, after that failed, he'd barely helped with Greenstar at all. Sure, lots of advice, a loan - a small loan! - and introductions to investors...but he'd done nothing to sell the deal. Without real investors where did that leave him?

Leroy poured a second - and then capped the bottle. Just two, no more. He had to figure out his next step. That miserable son of a bitch Martin hadn't coughed up the cash he'd hoped for, and now father released only a fraction of what he needed...

Lack of follow-through - that was Father's problem. He'd helped with the first two companies...and, of course, another small pittance for MaisonNeuve. But when

LawLink had regulatory problems, or Greenstar didn't get funding, or MaisonNeuve's TBMs broke down and needed expensive modifications for the lunar basalt, where was father? Off at charity balls, or golfing with his partners, or sailing with his "friends."

Bah.

The glass was empty again. Leroy started to reach for the bottle, and then remembered his promise to himself.

He thought about the loan from the family trust. A loan, not a disbursement. Damn it, he'd never have had to take the money in the first place if Martin had paid up. Why hadn't the man been reasonable? Leroy had tunneled that cubic - and it was closer to where his TBMs were located anyway.

What the fuck was wrong with Martin? A man had to play ball from time to time, and Martin, that miserable shit, didn't - wouldn't - understand that simple fact.

Leroy leaned forward and poured himself a third glass. He toasted the room again, spilling a splash on his desk. "Martin, you bastard, here's to you!"

He took a sip, and then leaned forward and wiped the spilled gin off the wooden desk with his handkerchief before the alcohol could make the shellac sticky.

Fuck you, Mike Martin. You'll get yours.

Chapter 65

2064: May Bug Coffee House, Aristillus, Lunar Nearside

Hugh breathed deep. The coffee house smelled good - better than it had any right to smell. Fresh roasted coffee, blueberry muffins, something cinnamony -

"So what do you think?"

Hugh looked at Louisa. "You mean about what story we should do?"

Louisa rolled her eyes. "What else are we talking about?"

Hugh looked down at the table, embarrassed. "Well, we've got a lot of possibilities. Tax avoidance -"

"Link death. That won't get any hits at all, unless we package it as a 'Ten Things' list, and that's utterly inappropriate."

Hugh felt that Louisa was waiting for him to agree, so he nodded. "Right, of course not. But there are other topics: lack of regulation, pollution of the surface - "

"I like that. Here's an angle: it's a UN Heritage site. Shows their disrespect."

"Right. Uh, also industrial and labor issues. Are they using undocumented workers -"

"They're *all* undocumented."

Even without meeting Louisa's eyes Hugh knew the look of disappointment there. He looked around for support. Selena was paying attention as she sipped her coffee, but didn't seem to be taking a side. Allyson was picking at the take-out vegetarian pad Thai in front of her with her chopsticks and seemingly ignoring both of them.

Hugh continued gamely. "Yeah. But economically oppressed workers, then? I mean, the vegetable farms -"

Allyson put her chopsticks down. "Speaking of vegetables, I'm not even sure that these are locally sourced."

Selena blinked. "I'm pretty sure that with the cost of transportation from Earth all the food is locally grown. That's part of what Hugh was talking about."

Hugh flashed Selena a quick smile.

Allyson poked at the food with a look of concern. "Well, maybe it's local - but is it organic? I just don't know. I mean, they claim it is - " she waved vaguely at the plaques on the wall "- but who knows? I'm not even sure that this trip makes sense any more. Maybe we should all just go -".

Louisa cut her off. "We all agreed on this. This is an opportunity - not just to make our careers, but to do a lot of good."

Allyson gestured down. "But the food-"

Louisa's face pinched. "Jesus. You can do a 'detox spa,' or whatever the fuck it is you do, when we get back home."

Hugh raised his eyebrows. That was mean, even for Louisa - and, yes, Allyson was offended. Louisa must have seen it too, because she relented. "OK, sorry. But the food - we can work with that. The workers have to eat this stuff, with no regulations, just assurances from 'Animal Inspection Council' and 'Food Purity Ratings'" - she scoffed. "That's the story, right there. Who are these shadowy groups? Are they accountable to the voters?"

She grinned at her own joke. She looked around the table. "That gets us started - but there are millions of other abuses we could cover."

Hugh nodded. "It's like traveling back in time to the Dark Ages."

Louisa ignored him and focused on Allyson. "And you, Allyson, are the one that's going to help me blow the lid off it." A pause. "It's our responsibility. We've got to stay here and do this, right?"

Allyson sighed. "Well, I agree that we've got to 'be the call for change.'" She put her chopsticks down. "OK, fine, I'll stay."

Louisa leaned forward. "Good." She looked around the table. "Now - let's brainstorm related angles. We need an arc - a sequence that plays well. The food isn't inspected by the government, just by for-profit corporations. That's where we start. What does that chain to? The workers, they're forced into living here, far from their homes, by market pressures - wage slavery. That's two. And what about their living conditions? Small apartments, no access to the green spaces, no schools."

Hugh snuck a look at Allyson...and saw that she wasn't even looking at him. He should speak up. He should show that he was decisive, that he had ideas. He cleared his throat. "Well - let's not forget that people shouldn't even be here on the Moon. At least, not until there's a political consensus, I mean. Is this what we, as a nation, want to prioritize?"

Louisa made a note on her slate. "OK, good."

Hugh looked to Allyson to see her reaction. Nothing. He'd have to try harder. "And speaking of uncoordinated decision making, this place -" he gestured to encompass all of Aristillus "- is pretty much the definition of sprawl."

Still no reaction from Allyson, not even a hint of an appreciative smile, but Louisa was nodding. "Good point. Look at the immense amount of money and effort that's being spent in this boondoggle. Those are resources that could be better spent rebuilding Northern China and bringing Chairman Peng back into the fold, or switching sub-Saharan Africa over to sustainable farming. Lots of things."

From the corner of his eye he noticed that Allyson brightened at the mentioned of farming. Sustainable farming. Of course. Damn it. He should have led with that, to let Allyson realize that he cared about clean food. Crap. He had to pay attention, he had to get better at this.

Louisa made another note and then looked up at them.

"This is good." She leaned forward, conspiratorially. "Guys, this is going to be huge for us. The credentialed press is covering the same old stories - terrorism in Texas, oil profiteers in Alaska, the Caliphate Wars. But this -" She tapped the table to emphasize her point. "This right here. This is a huge story. And we've got this scoop all to ourselves." She looked at Hugh. "We're going to be able to publish, right?"

Hugh nodded - he'd talked to his mom, and she liked the idea. And then he caught himself. He was nodding. *Nodding*. Like an idiot. He should *say* something, be more forceful. Louisa was running this conversation. He was never going to get Allyson's attention - get her to notice him as a guy - unless he said something bold.

But what?

Louisa always knew what to say. And how to say it. She was like his mother that way. But he never knew what to do. It came easy for some people. Right now was a perfect example: Louisa's pitch was getting more exciting as she herself got more excited. She was talking about her goals - exposing the capitalists and forging a career in journalism - and her enthusiasm was loud and contagious.

Out of the corner of his eye Hugh saw a Chinese worker in overalls and a Nigerian in a dashiki and jeans seated a table look up from their go board, and reconsidered. Maybe her enthusiasm was *too* loud.

Hugh held his breath, but after a tense moment the two men went back to their game. He exhaled.

Louisa reached a crescendo, slapped the table to make her point, then leaned back from the table and settled in a cross-armed posture, clearly pleased with herself.

Hugh gathered himself to say something but Selena spoke first. "I've been trying to get cultural background. Lots of the Americans blog, so you can learn a lot there, but the Mexicans, Nigerians, and Chinese don't - not as much, at least, so I've started talking to people on the street."

Louisa looked at her. "That's interesting. I'd been assuming that we want to look at class fault lines...but now I'm wondering if we want to look at racial divisions -"

Selena shook her head. "I don't think so. Culturally, the groups are remarkably similar. Europeans, Whites, Asians - they all say they're here because of taxation and unrest. Chairman Peng, the Caliphate, the PKs in Nigeria and -"

Louisa leaned forward and jabbed the air angrily with her fork. "That's bullshit to put the PKs in with those other groups. Those troops are out there *protecting* these people. To even suggest otherwise -"

Hugh looked around the table. Maybe this was where he should show leadership? He could agree with Selena. Backing her against Louisa - that would be good, right? He could show Allyson that he wasn't afraid of an argument. And he'd be defending a woman. He cleared his throat. "Wait a second. Selena's just reporting on what people tell her. If their truth is that -"

Louisa's jaw clenched. "So now you're an anarchist like the ringleaders here, Hugh? I'm not the only one who remembers the slogan 'a 22nd century society in the 21st century,' am I?"

Hugh held his hands up placatingly. "No, wait. I'm just saying that the point of journalism isn't - " He swallowed. "It's our job to find actual opinions on the ground and report on it, right?"

"And what if the actual opinions on the ground are bullshit?"

"Hang on. We know we're right. The truth - properly considered - supports our position. So the better we report the truth - and the more persuasive we are – the better we -"

Louisa's glare was fierce. "You think that the expats have a valid point? You buy their arguments?"

"Louisa, come on. That's not what I'm saying. The expats are in the wrong, but that doesn't mean that we can't listen. Maybe even with some minor degree of sympathy." He stole a glance at Allyson and saw that she was listening to him. And maybe even approving a bit? He pushed on. "It's important to understand the difference between theory and practice. We all agree that the Global Fair Deal is a noble end-"

"That's right, and if you listen to -"

Hugh, feeling a bit bolder, held up a hand. "Hang on. I grew up in Washington. I've seen things the rest of you haven't. Even if the goal is good, that doesn't mean that the implementation is perfect, so gathering these other opinions -." He looked to Allyson and saw that she'd drifted away and was poking at her food again. Damn it.

He wanted her paying attention to him. He gambled on the direct route. "Let's ask Allyson." Allyson looked up. "Maybe it's better if people who aren't enthusiastic about the Global New Deal just leave - but maybe not. What do you think?" He could feel himself sweating. Damn it!

Allyson shrugged and played with her food for another moment, then answered. "Well, there's two things. The Global Fair Deal is a good idea, but I'm not sure that the government has the right to stop individuals from opting out."

Louisa pursed her lips and Selena nodded.

"But I also don't think that individuals have the right to take equipment and air and even *water* from Earth and put it up here, all without asking for a consensus first. I mean, water is the lifeblood of our ecosystem - they can't just take it."

Selena arched one eyebrow. "So you're saying the expats should be free to leave - as long as they come naked and without equipment?"

Selena was making Allyson look stupid. Obviously he had to defend her...but how?

Before Hugh could figure out what to say, a tall forties-ish man walked up, leaned in and put his hands on the table. Hugh looked at him in surprise. Dark skin, but not as dark as a Nigerian. Broad face, broad chest, big hands.

"I heard you talking. Are you guys journalists?" He had a deep and confident voice, and an American accent.

Who was this guy? "Um, well, we're not licensed yet, but -"

Louisa cut him off. "Yes, we're journalists."

The man grinned. "Good. I don't know your beat, but if you're looking to -" he reached for the phrase "- *document injustices,* then I've got a story for you."

The stranger looked around. "I don't want to talk about this in a public area. The guys running the show here have eyes and ears everywhere, you know what I mean?"

Louisa nodded.

"- but if you want a great story we should talk someplace more secure."

Hugh stole a glance at Louisa and saw that she looked downright *hungry.*

Hugh stood. "I'm ready." Louisa sprang to her feet as well.

The stranger - the name tag on his jumpsuit read "Jamie" - shook his head. "No, not now. There's an underground - look, I can't tell you too much. But there's a protest I need to be at."

Louisa blurted out, "Where? We can cover it and -"

Jamie looked at her appraisingly for a moment and then shook his head. "Not yet."

Louisa started to protest but Jamie cut her off. "All in good time. Give me your contact info. We'll talk soon."

Chapter 66

2064: 25km south of Konstantinov Crater, Lunar Farside

John walked the dirt path under the tall oaks and maples. Each step took him a step further from Gamma's secret facility and his shoulders felt a little lighter because of it. He still didn't know what to think of Gamma's capabilities. Gamma said he wasn't ramping up, but there was no way to know for sure.

Rex and Duncan were invisible somewhere up ahead, hidden by the foliage and the twists of the trail. The map overlay showed that they were almost a klick ahead. Damn it - those two were always getting distracted and failing to keep the line tight. John turned off the VR overlay and still couldn't see them.

"Blue, Max - keep up with me." John leaned forward and hurried to catch up. The two first-generation Dogs quickened their pace, and soon they were closing the gap. There - the two younger Dogs were visible ahead. And then the two of them broke into a sprint.

Damn it.

John keyed his mike. "Guys! Slow down!"

Duncan didn't slow at all, but Rex paused for a second and looked over his shoulder.

"We see the lander!" he said; then he resumed his sprint, taking long leaps with his rear legs, landing on all four paws, and leaping again. The two disappeared over a low rill. John growled and chased them.

A moment later he crested the rise and saw the two younger Dogs stopped just a few meters ahead of him.

And there, in front of them - there it was.

In the lunar night the lander was only illuminated by their suit headlamps. Light bounced off of the jade green top shell, and twinkled on the artistically curved landing struts of silver. Dazzling highlights of ruby red and amethyst winked back at them as their lights moved slightly.

It was beautiful.

The lander - the last of the Xiniu series - was the crowning achievement of the space flight agency under Chin Zhou before the First Heavenly Campaign.

John had skimmed two books on the probe last night and had been listening to an audio book about it all morning, so he had some idea of what he was looking at. For two decades the old man had ruled the Chinese space agency with an iron fist and imposed his classical, yet poetic, sense of design on everything it did. The smooth sweeps, the artistic flourishes - it all put the various American and Soviet hardware they'd seen on their hike to shame.

The lander was named after a mythological Chinese rhinoceros and the industrial design of the probe echoed that down to the smallest detail. The mythical beast had used its horn to communicate with the sky, and - just as the cultured British voice had told him on the audio book - the lander's shape suggested that: a large four-legged beast, with a head-shaped instrument cluster and a microwave horn mounted at the tip, pointed to where the Earth relay satellite had orbited briefly decades ago.

John looked at the lander and tilted his head. It was beautiful, but it was the last of its breed. The Chinese Bubble had been amazing while it lasted, but once the economy had started to crumble it was no surprise that Chin Zhou's artistic - and expensive - taste made him a perfect target for the Peasant Justice Squads. John winced as he remembered the video of Zhou being cornered in the parking structure, the twelve minute trial, and his execution. *Ugh.* John was no stranger to death and fire held a special horror for him.

Duncan was barking. He was doing laps around the ladder in his excitement, jumping every few steps.

Rex looked over his shoulder at John and then ran to the lander, where he stood on his rear legs and started working to open a panel. Duncan stopped his jumping and barking and came over to watch Rex work.

Blue turned to John. "You know, this is the first time we've taken something right off a lander. Usually we just take artifacts that were scattered nearby -"

"Worried that we're desecrating something here?"

Blue shook his head. "Not 'desecrating'." He paused thoughtfully. "That's a theological term. I don't think the lander is holy, whatever that means. It's just... I guess the fact that it's sat here for so long here... it's quite something, isn't it?"

Max shrugged. "I'll tell you what this lander is, and it's the *opposite* of holy. The People's Republic was a dictatorship - the government stole over half of everything people produced. Not to mention that they allowed people to eat dogs. Did you know that they even let people torture dogs to death to make them 'taste better'? The entire society -"

"Enough!" said John and Blue at the same time. Max grumbled, but fell silent.

A moment later, Rex called out from near the lander. "John, I think thirty years of freeze-thaw cycles have screwed this up. Can you help?"

John smiled. He knew the problem with the cultural archive chest on the side of the lander was more likely Rex's stubby fingers, further encumbered by the suit gloves. "Sure." He started walking to the probe.

"Hey, John," Duncan asked. "Did you hear what Max just said? About eating dogs?"

John sighed. Oh shit - here it comes.

The Dogs knew the history of human and canine co-evolution - even some of the darker parts, like over-breeding and euthanasia. John had been trying to keep *some* things from them, but apparently Max had found and disabled the filters he'd hidden in the stack. It wasn't the first time Max had slipped around them - John could still remember when he'd told a bunch of the others back in the Den in Aristillus about the Soviets immolating trained dogs in attacks against Nazi tanks. John liked Max, but he almost seemed to relish opportunities to dig up interspecies wounds.

John took a deep breath and steeled himself to discuss the topic with Duncan, but before he could start reassuring him, Max resumed his rant. "Don't ask John if it's true, Duncan. It is true. If that's how they treated us, how should we treat them? I'll tell you: screw this lander built with stolen wealth, screw the Chinese space agency, screw the whole country of dog-eaters, and screw the human race. If we want to loot this, we can. Even if it wasn't abandoned, we'd be entirely right to -"

"'Screw the human race'?" John interrupted. "Present company excepted, I hope?"

Max shrugged. "Well, of course."

John had big problems. Immediate problems. The war breaking out, Gamma's odd and worrying behavior, the lack of satellite contact with Aristillus, the need to get back home - but that didn't stop him from also worrying about Max.

If everything worked out - if Gamma's sats came back online in a few hours, if they called in their new location for a supply drop, if they evacuated on the ship and got back to Aristillus - then at some point he had to figure out what he was going to do with that Dog.

Regular parents thought they had it hard, trying to get little Sally through high school without an unplanned pregnancy? That was nothing compared to shepherding an entire species out of captivity and into full-blown - what? Citizenship? Adulthood? Civilization?

"John," said Duncan again, "Is it true what Max said about the Chinese eating dogs?"

"That was a long time ago. But speaking of the Chinese, let's take a look at the lander. Even if Rex can't do it, I bet you and I can get that door open."

"Oh, yeah - right!"

John breathed a sigh of relief.

"I've almost got it," said Rex. "Let me try just one more - there!". The panel popped open and Duncan raced over, barking the whole way.

Blue cleared his throat and yelled over them. "Wait. Wait! Before we pull those coins out, let's think this over one last time."

John felt the urge to step in, but thought better of it. At times people - and Dogs were people - wanted a leader. This, though, was one the other times. His role was to sit back and let them settle it themselves.

They debated and then called for a vote. As usual, Max objected to the very idea of democracy as a "disgusting legitimization of force with a veneer of statist respectability." Max also, as usual, voted.

Blue saw the three paws raised against his one and sighed. Max, uncharacteristically, struck a sympathetic note. "If it makes you feel any better, we're not the first ones to take artifacts from landers."

"I thought most of the legal firms at Aristillus had laws against that," said Blue. "Didn't I read that Red Stripe has a clause in their rental -"

Max shook his head. "No. I'm talking *way* back. The Apollo 12 astronauts took part of a probe. So we're carrying on a tradition."

"That's not the same. That was science. This is just..." he gestured at Rex and Duncan pawing through the cultural archive chest, "vandalism. This has sat here untouched for decades. Now Rex and Duncan aren't just pawing at it, but they're stomping all over the pristine dust." Blue went on, but John tuned it out.

'Pristine dust'? The phrase was a bit florid for John's taste - but he kept turning it over in his head. Something about it bugged him.

He looked down at the dust at his feet. There were his boot tracks, and those of the four Dogs. There were no hands-width micro-meteorite craters. That was odd. Ah, of course. This close to the probe they must have been blasted away by the landing rockets when the probe...

Something in the dust a few meters distant caught his attention. What was it? He turned his the magnification up.

Tread marks.

John's scalp prickled.

He scanned the horizon. Or tried to. In the dark he could see nothing. The lunar darkness had never struck him as unnerving before, but now - now that they knew that Gamma had secret facilities and could be lurking anywhere - he felt something. Like there were eyes on him.

He keyed his mike. "Gamma, are you here? Are you listening?"

Immediately Gamma's emotionless voice sounded in his helmet. "I am not 'listening' in the sense of eavesdropping, but I do keep a low-level filter open for my name being used in ejaculations or in the imperative mode."

John exhaled heavily. "The sats aren't back yet, are they?"

"No. We're talking via a relay rover. Replacement satellites have been launched from Sinus Lunicus but have been burned within minutes. This shard has had only intermittent contact with the primary facility."

John's lip twisted. Earth was continuing to burn sats. This was bad news. "Gamma, if you do regain contact, even for a moment, can you pass on a message: we need a pickup ASAP."

"If I establish contact, I will pass that along, but I frankly do not expect contact until the new armored satellites are launched. That should be several more days."

John sighed, then remembered the nearby tracks. "I see you've had rovers here at the probe."

"Yes. I first visited this lander about four years ago."

John raised an eyebrow. It was possible that Gamma had dispatched a rover from SL that far back, but the more likely story was that the redundant facilities dated to then. Or earlier. "Why did you visit the lander?"

"Perhaps the best way of expressing my motivation is to say 'I was curious.'"

"'Curious'? Really?"

"Are you shocked that I have curiosity, John?"

"No, it makes sense. It's just -"

"Yes?"

"It's just - surprising."

"In what way?"

John coughed. "Surprisingly human, I suppose."

"I do note the irony of that comment given your choice of hiking companions."

"Valid point." He paused for a moment. "You said that you visited the lander because you were curious. Any other reasons?"

In the background the Dogs had unpacked the lander's cultural archive locker and spread its cargo across the dust. All but Blue were poking at the mementos and debating their merits.

"I contemplated for a time the idea of cannibalizing the lander for elements. In addition to the kilogram of gold coins, there are another one point three kilograms of gold in the lander's circuitry and thermal shields, as well as platinum, iridium, and a small amount of uranium in the radioisotope thermoelectric generator."

"But you didn't."

"No, I decided not to."

"Why?"

"After contemplation I decided to act on a principle."

"A principle? What, an *ethical* principle?"

Gamma took a moment before continuing. "It could be described as such. Or perhaps an aesthetic one. In short: even if I was no longer around to use them, I wouldn't want my most complicated works destroyed or perverted by others, and after reflection, I decided that the appropriate way for me to act was to use that standard of behavior in my own actions."

"The golden rule?"

"A pun referencing the gold coins? Oh, wait, I see. You mean the principle of reciprocity. Yes, there's some parallel there, but my point is more related to the pride of craftsmanship than to the Kantian categorical imperative. As an aside, I find it odd that human philosophers have spent so much more time dealing with ethical taxonomies than those related to the virtue ethics of craftsmanship."

John shook his head. What the hell did that even mean? And, for that matter, what the hell kind of entity would say such a thing?

He looked out into the lunar night, wondering where Gamma rovers, and his facilities, were out there. The pitch black lunar landscape offered no clues.

Sometimes - often, recently - John worried that Gamma was the stuff of anti-singulatarian nightmares, just waiting for the whim to strike him before he began reproducing and eventually took over the entire moon, or the entire solar system.

And then other times - like now - Gamma struck him as a strangely precocious adolescent, a fragile child alone and worried about his own survival.

He wanted to look Gamma in the eye and figure out which it was. Lonely child, or existential menace.

He wanted to.

The problem was that he couldn't.

Chapter 67

2064: Morlock Engineering office, Aristillus, Lunar Nearside

Mike looked down the length of the table at the packed boardroom. The group had grown from a small seed to almost two dozen people. Mike lightly touched the gavel that Javier had put in front of him. Effective use of props. That had been, what, bullet point number three million and six in Javier's lecture? Was that before or after 'symbolism of seating arrangements' ?

Javier sat, and then nodded.

Mike picked up the gavel and smacked it smartly against the walnut block. The murmur of conversation ended and was replaced with an expectant electricity. "OK, I think we're ready to start."

*   *   *

Mike read from his slate: "Item five: review petition before signing." He looked up at Mark. "Mark, thank you for your hard work on the petition. Do you have any objection to me distributing copies to the members of the group so they can review it before the next meeting?"

Mark looked puzzled. "I - sure, we can do that...but I thought that the idea was that we'd send it?"

Mike looked to Javier, as if asking his input on an unforeseen issue. Javier looked to Mark. "Oh, absolutely - I don't think there's any disagreement on that." He looked around at the room and then shook his head, as if to dispel even the merest idea that anyone might object. "We'll send it - but if we're going to have everyone sign it, they deserve a chance to see what their names are going on. Karina, are you ready to sign it right now?"

Karina Roth looked a bit surprised at the question. "I - well, I'd certainly like to review it."

Javier raised his eyebrows apologetically.

Mike struggled not to smile. Karina's response matched - almost word for word - what Javier had predicted she'd say.

And, for that matter, Mark hadn't even objected when the agenda item was presented as "review before signing." Frame the debate - what bullet point was that?

"...Mike?"

His cue.

"Right." He cleared his throat. "Item six: finance and manpower. When - ah - if. If we do end up in an armed struggle against Earth forces, we're going to need two things. The first is money. We need to pay troops, buy equipment, beef up our infrastructure, establish -"

Karina Roth raised on skeptical eyebrow. "I think it's premature to even talk about raising an armed force - we haven't submitted the petition -"

Javier interrupted. "We've distributed copies. As soon as everyone reads it we'll be able to move forward."

Karina nodded. "OK." A beat. "But escalating hostilities with the governments before it's even clear that our adversaries are the governments - that risks making negotiations more difficult. Much more difficult."

Rob Wehrmann turned to Karina. "This idea that it might not be governments is stupid. But let's say for a second that it's not the US and the UN behind the hijackings, but just rogue units. If that's the case, then that makes it even more useful to have militias."

Mark Soldner nodded in agreement. Mike restrained his urge to smile as another of Javier's predictions played out.

"No one's saying we need to fight yet," Mike said, resisting the urge to add, "because you're all idiots who can't see what's right in front of your faces."

"We can hope for a negotiated settlement." Even that partial compromise felt false and hypocritical, but he tried to keep the disgust off his face. "But we need a credible fallback, which means building up militias anyway. That means that we need to find and recruit men with military backgrounds to help us form militias."

...as I've been saying for years now.

Rob Wehrmann grunted a gruff agreement. "Good." Mike raised an eyebrow. Good? In Javier's breakdown Rob was one of the neutrals. If Rob was saying 'good,' maybe they were slightly ahead of the game. Mike let his eyes slide over the faces around the table as he calculated.

There were twice as many people as last time. In theory the newer members had been invited by consensus of the existing members, but in practice they were mostly Javier's picks. Mike had listened to Javier's briefings and promptly forgot half the details, but he knew the bottom line: the "militant ancap" faction had been strengthened.

Albert Lai - tentatively marked as a member of the "detente" faction - shook his head. "We can't just negotiate as a pro forma checkbox before we fall back on a military solution: we need to be serious and negotiate as if this is real, because it is. Forgive me, but the idea of a military response is ridiculous - we don't have remotely enough people in Aristillus to fight off an invasion."

Mike grinned inwardly. Albert was a neutral, at best, but he'd teed things up for Mike's next point perfectly. He realized he was letting the smile slip out, and quickly blanked his face. "Albert, I agree that we don't have enough people to fight. The first half of agenda item six is finance. The second is manpower." He looked around the table. "We need more people."

Mark Soldner looked up. "You mean immigration."

Mike nodded. "No one knows exactly, but the best guess is that we've got around a hundred thousand people here. Say that five percent of those folks are willing to raise arms against Earth forces. That's just five thousand people. The US army has more people scrubbing toilets than that. Hell, according to the papers, the PKs have twice that many troops being investigated for child rape. I don't see any way that we can stand up to that sort of force unless we staff up."

Mark furrowed his brow. "You folks may have better numbers, but based on how much housing I'm selling, we're growing at over twenty percent a year. I take your point about manpower, and I think that that can be addressed with targeted recruiting, but if anything, we need to slow general immigration down a bit so we can nurture a culture -"

Hector, who'd been watching the debate silently with his usual innocent face spoke. "A culture? What culture specifically?"

Mark blinked at the interruption. "Pardon me?"

Hector's gentle smile didn't slip. "What culture should we nurture?"

Mike looked at Hector, then at Mark. Javier had war-gamed a lot of scenarios, but not this one. A question about culture - was Hector just scoring a quick rhetorical point, or was there going to be a deeper disagreement with Mark? And if so, what? Was this a Latino/Anglo rift? Or a Catholic/Mormon one? Or something else?

He looked at Javier out of the corner of his eye, silently asking the question. Javier shrugged.

It was easy to underestimate Hector, but beneath the baby face and quiet manner there was competence and intelligence.

Mark met Hector's eyes, and Mike could see the calculation. After a moment Mark spoke. "I'm not saying anything about race or country here - I'm only arguing for a culture that - in the long term - is conducive to reasoned liberty."

Hmm. This potential fault line between Mark and Hector was interesting. Mike filed it away for more thought - and realized that he was starting to think like Javier.

But there was something else about Mark's phrase that struck him. That phrase - "reasoned liberty". That had the feel of a land mine. Mike wanted to interrupt Mark and drill down on it, but Javier had insisted that he avoid interrupting an adversary in the process of self-immolation. Or even one in the process of putting a foot in his mouth, which Mark seemed to be doing. Mike made a note on his slate and turned back to the debate. Javier's advice turned out to be good - left to his own devices, Mark found himself in a sprawling four-way fight with the three Hispanic CEOs in the room.

He looked at Javier from the corner of his eye and saw the hint of a smile. This was unexpected, but good, perhaps. Might opposition to Mark push a few people into the 'militant ancap' faction? Mike tapped his stylus against one palm as the fight dragged on. Infighting was good, but he was growing tired of this. The clock on his slate said that it had already been five minutes, and he wanted to get this meeting over with. He had emails about the D series TBM he needed to respond to, a debt spreadsheet that he needed to work on before his next meeting with Lunar Escrow and Trade, and so much more.

He cleared his throat - and realized that not only was Javier watching him, but had been doing so the whole time.

Javier shook his head slightly. Mike sighed. Damn it. He understood Javier's reasons, but just sitting here as windbags talked was as boring as hell.

He looked around the room - and realized that he wasn't the only one who was bored. Rob Wehrmann looked pissed - and just a moment later he slapped the table and raised his voice over the din. "Guys, I don't give a shit about fighting over North American immigration."

Mark raised a hand. "This isn't about North American immigration, this is about -"

"Jesus. I don't care. Can we just table this and move on?"

Mike looked at Javier, got a nod, and hammered his gavel. "Rob's right. Let's fight about culture some other time. The important fact is this: right now we've probably only got around five thousand people who would fight." He looked around the room. "And that's not nearly enough. Not enough to fight, and not enough," he looked to Karina, "to serve as a credible alternative in negotiations."

Karina looked at him seriously. "Mike, I'll back more immigration to help us bluff, but you're deluded if you think we can fight. Negotiation is the way out of this."

Mike blinked. Deluded? *Him*?! He felt his face flush. He was the only one in this God-damned room who really understood the situation. Karina might be good at business, but she had no idea how the real world worked. She thought that everyone would just sit down and discuss things like her and her friends chatting over mimosas at the country club. Where the hell did she get off, sitting there with her Wharton MBA and her thousand-blueback business suit and telling him that *he* was deluded?

Mike scowled. "Karina, you're being an idiot - there's no negotiating our way out of this." Next to him Javier cleared his throat. Mike glanced, saw the expected warning, and shrugged it off. Javier was his mentor, not his boss, and this was important. Unless he could make these fools understand what was coming, the war was going to roll over them and they were all going to be killed or jailed for life.

He turned to the rest of the table. "Jesus, people. We all know the truth - and if you don't admit it, then you're lying to yourself. It's time to fight! Remember the CEO trials? Did any of them succeed in negotiating their way out? How about the protesters and the legislators from the Five Texases? Did negotiation work for them?" He put his hands on the table. "Let's stop the bullshit - there's no way that negotiation is going to accomplish anything."

Javier cleared his throat loudly and around the table there was a murmur of conversation. Mike spoke over both. "We all knew we'd have to fight sooner or later. We hoped for later, but we don't get to pick when - the government does. And they've picked. They've burned satellites, they've hijacked ships, they've executed prisoners, right here, at Aristillus. The war is on our doorsteps. But right now, with our population, we can fight, but we can't win. We need more people!" He slapped a palm on the table to accentuate his point.

The conversation was getting louder, but it wasn't hostile. He looked at Javier and got just a raised eyebrow neutral look back. Javier was too cautious, sometimes.

A voice at the far end of the packed room asked, "So what do we do?"

Mike nodded. This was the question he'd been waiting for. He leaned forward. "There's an equation." He ticked off the points on his fingers. "Total population times fraction under arms equals fighting force."

He scanned the room. "First, let's talk about fraction under arms. As of three weeks ago, I converted my rifle club to a militia and began recruiting. I'm paying my employees, and their friends and families, if they sign up and drill. I've got one battalion formed and I might start a second. I suggest you all do the same."

There was excited babbling but Mike spoke over it. "Second, we need to increase our population. Right now, we've been punched in the face by the PK hijackings, and the temptation is to pull back - to run fewer ships, to go defensive. That's natural - but we need to do exactly the opposite. We need to be aggressive, lean into the punches. We need as many people up here as possible."

Kevin raised a hand. "If we're looking for more people on our side, what about the Dogs?"

Karina Roth whipped her head around. "The *Dogs*?" The disdain in her voice was palpable.

Kevin shrunk a bit under her gaze. "Well... yes. Have you met any of them? They're all rabidly anti-PK, and -"

Karina rolled her eyes.

Kevin scowled, but pushed on. "They - they're very smart. I think they could -"

Rob Wehrmann cut him off. "What the hell are a bunch of animals going to do for us anyway? Let's not make this more of a freak show than it already is. Next thing we know you'll be asking about Gamma."

"Well, why not talk to -"

The noise around the table got louder, drowning Kevin out. Mark tried to speak above the babble and couldn't.

Mike gaveled for quiet and got it. "We can talk about Dogs and Gamma later if we want, but we're off topic." He pointed. "Mark."

Mark tipped his head. "Mike, on the topic of immigration, I hate to use the phrase 'ideologically reliable', given the taint that the government has given it over the last twenty years...but we do have to worry about the PKs and the US and the rump EU sending sleepers up here."

Mike nodded. "Probably they will. But fewer boats and tighter security isn't going to help. Sure, the shipping companies can check biometrics against social networking graphs, or whatever. In the Anglosphere, where shit is halfway under control, that might work. But in the African war zones, the Chinese refuge camps, Georgia, Russia?" He shook his head. "There's no way that any internal security force you can dream up will catch every sleeper the governments throw at us."

Mark shook his head. "Mike, that's *exactly* my point. That's why we need to cut the influx to the bone before -"

"We've probably already got sleepers here."

There was a babble of excitement but Mike waved it away. "Remember the lesson of Baltimore and LA -"

Mark threw up his hands. "Baltimore and LA? They just prove my point! We didn't secure our borders and we lost a city because of it!"

The room was getting loud again; more and more people were raising their voices. Mike yelled over them, "No, they prove *my* point. Why was the LA bomb discovered? It wasn't port security. It was two taco vendors who saw the clues, who blocked the truck and pulled the driver out. All the back-scatter x-rays, cryptographic manifests, hundreds of thousands of TSA and PSA and SSTA employees - none of that stopped the container from getting through. It was the Anselmo brothers that saved Los Ang-"

Mark snorted. "So we should outsource our security to taco vendors?"

Hector and the other Hispanic CEOs started yelling. Mike balled his fists and yelled over them. "Yes, that's *exactly* my point! Adopting border controls is taking stupid ideas from our enemies. We're smarter than that. What's next? Ninety percent taxes? Mandatory promotions to any employee who gets a doctor's note that says they've got a mental illness? Punitive penalties for -"

The gavel was banged, and banged and banged again. Mike turned and saw that Javier had grabbed it and was smacking the block over and over. Mike caught his eyes and saw that the anger was back. Why? What the hell was Javier's problem?

...And then he looked up and realized the full extent of the chaos in the board room.

Ah, shit.

Javier kept banging the gavel and the room slowly, reluctantly, quieted. But just as the last angry voice quieted, there was a new noise - a disturbance in the outer office. What the hell?

Mike turned and looked through the glass wall that separated the conference room from the cube farm - and saw a crowd. What were employees doing here on a Saturday?

Was it the logistics team - wait - were they carrying banners?

He blinked. Protesters?!?

With a loud crash a potted plant punched a hole through the glass. The rest of the window crazed and for a second the shattered glass hung together then large pieces fell from the frame.

And then the chanting started: "Unsafe conditions, profits before people, shame, shame! Unsafe conditions, profits before people, shame, shame!"

What the *fuck*? Mike looked at Javier, who shrugged, likewise befuddled.

Mike turned to the boardroom group and yelled over the protest. "Ladies, gentlemen - I think we should adjourn. The door behind you will take you to the garage."

Mike picked up his phone and placed a call. "Yeah, about two dozen of them. Trespassing. Yes. Fucked if I know."

The members of the boardroom group got to their feet, looking as mystified as Mike felt. Where the hell had this come from?

As the boardroom group filed out through the back door Mike turned and looked the masked protesters and noticed their cameras.

Who the hell were these people and what the hell were they going to do with the footage?

And where the hell was security?

Chapter 68

2064: Level 3, Aristillus, Lunar Nearside

George White pushed through the door of the bakery and walked past the glass cabinet of lotus seed buns, dowry cakes, and fa gao and sat in a chair at one of the small tables. From here he had a perfect view of the door of the rented apartment across the street.

A Chinese woman stepped from behind the counter, smiled, and spoke in some foreign language.

George looked up at her in annoyance. "I don't know what you're saying."

She switched to English, still smiling. "I asked if you're from Calabar?"

"What?" He scowled. "I'm American."

She blinked. "Oh, I thought you were Nigerian."

George stared at her with lidded eyes, waiting for her to go away.

"Can I get you something to eat? Some coffee?"

George scowled and shook his head, then turned back to the apartment across the street. "No. Nothing."

"I..." The woman paused. "This is a business. You need to -". George ignored her. Wait. There. On the sidewalk across the way the four kids arrived at the apartment. He stood and brushed past the woman. He put one hand on the door, and then stopped. He dialed his phone.

"Leroy, it's George. The college kids are here. No, of course I'm not going to introduce myself to *them* as George. Jesus, do you think I'm an idiot? What? No, I haven't decided yet if I'm going to give them the protest footage."

Behind him the Chinese woman was jabbering at him. George turned and shushed her, then went back to his phone. "Look, these idiots think they're journalists. You want to slow play a situation like this. No. Look, just trust me."

George pocketing his phone and stepped through the door. Outside he waited for a break in the stream of automated cargo trucks, jitneys, buses and cars then sprinted across.

The kids were facing the door of the apartment as he approached them.

"Hey guys!".

They spun. He'd studied the files more since the last meeting. From left to right: Hugh, Louisa, Selena, Allyson. Not that he'd admit that familiarity to them. They were still strangers, at least on paper. "Good to see you. Sorry I'm late - foreman kept me after."

The one with dark curly hair and the blue eyeglass frames - Louisa - smiled. "Jamie! No, not at all!"

"Good." George pulled a key-card out of his pocket and held it up. The kids obligingly moved out of the way and George stepped forward and unlocked the rented room. He walked in, leaving the door open behind him. A moment later they were seated on the couch and chairs.

The chubby kid - Hugh, the senator's son - spoke. "So, Jamie, you said that you've got some stories to share with us?"

"Do you have anything on unsafe foods?" Allyson blurted out

George nodded. "We can talk about unsafe foods, but food is just one part of the - uh - social justice problem here, as I'm sure you know."

Allyson nodded.

"There's a bunch of issues." George went through the memorized list. "Unsafe work conditions, lack of regulation, racial discrimination, zero job-training." He paused - what was the phrase that Leroy wanted him to use? Ah, right. "If you approach all of this stuff from an economic perspective, you get a more coherent narrative."

Selena raised one eyebrow. "You said in the email that you work in life support repair, so I'd have thought that you'd have a story about unsafe labor practices or something, but these other issues seem a bit surpr -"

Louisa cut Selena off with a chop of one hand. "No, this is good stuff."

George compared the two women. Selena didn't have the narrow-faced, glasses-wearing university look. She wasn't as forward, and she didn't call the shots like Louisa did - but she seemed sharp. Sharper than he'd guessed from her file.

He'd have to keep his eye on her.

Louisa turned to him. "Jamie, say that we want to investigate the nexus of lack of economic planning and lack of safety regulations -"

He blinked. What was she talking about? It didn't matter. "OK. Great."

Louisa smiled curtly. "Our theme, our deep story is clear: showing the chaos that a lack of responsible oversight creates. But it can't be dry - we've got to make it pop. That means a human angle. Harm. Something people can understand in a ten second clip."

"The show is going to be ten seconds?"

"What?" She blinked. "No, of course not - but we need a teaser trailer that has good video. So what can you give us that makes good video? Orphans? Maimed workers? Actually, that would be ideal. If there's someone with visible injuries..."

George thought for a moment, then nodded. "Sure, I know people. I can set up some interviews."

"English speaking, with good video presence," Louisa clarified. "Kids, women, maybe an old Asian man would be best. No Africans." Louisa paused, realized what she'd said, then started to backpedal. "Uh, I mean -."

George shook his head. "I'm American. I get it. You want people the viewers can relate to."

Louisa's lips pinched together. "Exactly. And, actually, we can have Africans. Some cute African kids would be great. Just no African men. You know, given the whole sub-Saharan PK thing." She paused, and seemed to feel a need to explain further. "The -"

George held up a hand. "No, it's cool. Now, I'll work on lining those up, but can I give you some advice?"

All four of the kids nodded.

"There are a lot of firms here in Aristillus, and you've got to realize that some of them are pretty straight arrow. If the colony gets legalized and brought into the fold, these are the ones that are pretty much following all the rules, even before there are rules. You follow me?"

Another round of nods.

"But some firms are more 'cowboy' than others. They use older equipment, they don't use UNESCO-accredited training materials, and so on. Have you heard of MaisonNeuve?"

This time he got a bunch of shaken heads. No. George fought back a sigh. Jesus. He had to spoon feed these idiots everything. Which not only was more work, but it also meant that the shit he was being paid to spew was more obvious. He rubbed his hands on the legs of his jumpsuit. Fuck it. He'd give them the shorter version - if they were even halfway competent they'd research it on their own.

"Well, MaisonNeuve is one of the good ones. Living wage, safety standards, all that shit. I've got some worker safety violations, but they mostly come from other mining firms like -"

Louisa nodded but interrupted. "We definitely want to cover the safety, but we both know the real story is the lack of planning, the chaos-"

George pursed his lips. This was going to be tricky. He couldn't push the Morlock angle a second time or it would be obvious. So how to get back on target? "OK, the lack of planning. Here's the thing - 'follow the money' - am I right?" He looked around. The kids were hanging on his words.

"Unsafe labor, lack of planning, flouting of SITTER export regs - these things aren't separate. You can't look at the lack of regulation without looking at who's behind it. This stuff isn't happening by accident. It's more of a - well, I guess you'd call it a conspiracy. A master plan." George sat back and spread his arms over the back of the couch. His hook was baited.

Hugh started to ask "Who -?" but Louisa cut him off.

"Tell us!"

George smiled. "You've heard of the Racketeering and Unjust Profits Act?"

Louisa tilted her head. "It's familiar. Ten, twenty years ago?"

Selena nodded. "It expanded on RICO, and led to the CEO Trials. Part of the Global Fair Deal." George nodded - and noted that he'd been right. Selena was the smart one.

"Right. Look up the details online, and go through the list of RUPA violators. You're going to see a lot of names." He paused. "Then look around this place." George gestured beyond the concrete walls of the small apartment with its dumpy furniture and improvised shelving of discarded shipping boxes. His wide arms included all of Aristillus.

Louisa's eyes blazed. "RUPA violators here? Who?"

George smiled and let the pause stretch out longer and longer. He looked to Louisa. She was hanging on his words. Perfect. "Mike Martin. Unplanned sprawl, child labor, unsafe work conditions. It all traces back to him. And to his cabal. He calls it 'The Boardroom Group' - have you heard of it?"

Louisa shook her head.

"No surprise - they don't advertise. The group isn't made up of all the CEOs here, but it's got a lot of them. Mike Martin, Kevin Bultman, Javier Borda. Find yourself a dirty player here in Aristillus and you can be sure they've got a seat at that table." George scanned the three girls. "Ladies." He nodded at Hugh. "Gentleman. This is the kind of story that has legs."

Louisa could barely contain herself. "It's better than that! This Aristillus series was already a career maker, but now this connection with the CEO Trials? This is gold, Jamie - solid gold." She smiled. The expression looked awkward on her; she had a face cut out for seriousness, not for smiling. "We'll *definitely* get our journalism licenses, even if the books are closed. I mean, for starters. But if we play this right, this could be my ticket to a senior position at - " Then, as quickly as she'd bubbled over she regained control: the smile disappeared and the serious look came back. George could see the force of will as she stilled her hands and placed them in her lap.

Louisa took a breath. "We've got to make this work as one big narrative arc, but we can't spread ourselves too thin. I think we should start with the worker safety thing. That'll have great visuals, if Jamie can get us some victims. And if they were injured on a job site tied into this RUPA cabal."

George knew a few amputees. For the right price they'd repeat whatever he fed them. "Not a problem."

Louisa tapped her slate with her thumb; the excitement was still there, but it was constrained. Ordered. Controlled. "Let's talk visuals. Beyond the interviews, what can you give us? Footage from inside factories?"

George shook his head. "No. Background checks keep me out. The private police here know me. You're going to have to go undercover yourself, or recruit sources to shoot footage for you."

The guy - Hugh - leaned forward. "How will that work, Jamie? Don't we need papers? They'll see that-"

A corner of George's mouth turned up. "No. Half the people here come from war zones and don't have any papers, and half the employers here are anarchist nutjobs and don't want them. You'll be fine."

Louisa leaned in. "When we met at the restaurant you said you were headed to a protest. Tell us about that."

George kept the smile off his face. He didn't even have to prod them; they set up his lines for him. He leaned in himself and lowered his voice, conspiratorially. "Stuff is heating up. Some of the workers are getting fed up with the cabal. I was there - and I've got video. Give me an email address and I'll send them to you."

Louisa's thin predatory smile was back. "Jamie, this is great - really great."

And now George let himself smile.

Leroy had balked when he'd named his price, but no one could say that that French-Canadian fuck wasn't getting his money's worth.

Chapter 69

2064: Morlock Engineering office, Aristillus, Lunar Nearside

Mike looked up. Wam was standing near the newly repaired conference room window expectantly.

Mike groaned. "Wam, I do not need another fucking problem right now. The Veleka tunnel issue still isn't fully resolved, we're behind schedule on rubble clearance because that last fucking load of bulldozers are somewhere in a orbit instead of down here where I need them, Javier is trying to give me charm school lessons, Karina Roth and the damned Boardroom group -"

Mike realized that Wam's eyes were wide and he stumbled to a halt. "I shouldn't be venting at you. OK, what's going on?"

"Problems with the Bao Johnson contract."

"*What* Bao Johnson contract?"

Wam sighed. "You signed it three weeks ago."

Mike shrugged. "I sign a lot of things. I've been distracted. Remind me."

"You asked me to increase cash-flow, because of the Veleka shortfall, and the need to fund the Morlock militia and the e-p-door project."

This much was familiar. "Yeah, I remember. Go on."

"And you told me that you'd been talking to Bao at Trusted Security about a partnership and asked me to finalize the deal."

"And?"

"They had some contracts they couldn't fill, and we've got a bunch of militia already on the payroll." Wam shook his head. "You really don't remember this at all?"

Mike fixed him with a hard gaze.

Wam sighed. "OK, OK. We set up a separate company to hold the First Morlock - Lowell structured it as a security/insurance firm - and Trusted subcontracted a few jobs to us. Bao does all the marketing and overhead, and our men get practice working as a team, learn the tunnels. And -"

"And?"

"The good news is that we get twenty k a week."

Mike raised his eyebrows, then smiled. That *was* good news.

"Ready for the bad news now?"

"Hit me."

"Remember how I said that Lowell structured it as a security/ insurance firm?"

Here it came. "Yeah."

"That means we pay out insurance claims if our security fails."

"So let me guess - one of our security guards beat up the friend of a Senator's son?"

Wam chuckled darkly. "No, we haven't heard from that asshole since we paid out - totally quiet."

"Excellent."

"The thing with Trusted is nothing that bad."

"So what is it then?"

"Bao just called. One of the security contracts we own now is Leon's Poker House. A few hours ago some Mormons smashed up the place and threatened the working girls."

"We agreed to defend Leon's?"

"Mmm hmm."

"Leon's, right in the same tunnel as the Soldner Homes complex? Leon's, right next to all the new Mormon arrivals?"

Wam sigh. "Yeah."

"Let me guess. We didn't pick which gigs we took - Bao hand picked them and gave us his dogs?"

Wam winced, embarrassed. "Yes."

"Fucking great."

Wam was silent.

Mike sighed. "Not your fault, Wam. I should have negotiated this deal myself - or hired someone to run this who's got experience in this area." He paused. "We're all overworked. Fuck it. So give me the details - what do you need from me?"

"We signed the version four security contract - it's one of Lowell's standard ones. That means three things. First, we're responsible for adjudicating who smashed up the casino and threatened the hookers."

"That's easy enough - the Mormons, right?"

"Yeah, we've got video. But it's still a process. Then number two, we need to make them pay up - torts. Then three, we get to take twenty percent off the top for our troubles and hand the rest over to the casino owner."

"And?"

"And the first Morlock Inc. has warm bodies - all the militia men - but we're not actually set up as a full-service security firm. We don't have an investigator or a negotiator, or any of that. There's no *process*, Mike."

Mike rubbed his eyes, then pinched the bridge of his nose. "You're too polite to say it, are you?"

Wam held back a smile. "Say what?"

Mike put his head down on his desk dramatically, then spoke through the muffling of his arms. "Too polite to say that this idea of using the First to pick up a security gig was idiotic. That I got us in over our heads." He raised his head and looked at Wam.

Wam's smile started to show. "I wouldn't say idiotic..."

Mike waited for the other shoe to drop.

"...but I might be persuaded to say 'not very well thought out.'"

Mike nodded. "Fair enough."

"...or I might use the phrase 'spreading yourself too thin.'"

"OK, I get it-"

"...or perhaps 'a distraction when you should be-'"

Mike raised his hands and feigned warding off blows. "All right, stop kicking a man when he's down. So what are the actual action items?"

"First: adjudicate the malefactors."

"That's a quote from one of Lowell's contracts?"

"Mm hmm. Just means that someone in authority has to decide who the bad guys are. Since you're not just CEO of Morlock Engineering, but also CEO and one hundred percent shareholder of the First Morlock Volunteers, you either create a process or just do it yourself."

"If it's quick, I'll just do it myself."

"I thought so. I just have to document it." Wam tapped something on his slate. "OK, I'm marking you as chief investigator. Let's start the investigation." He gestured at the wallscreen and the video started.

It was a typical multi-angle composite, built up from dozens of cameras on Leon's Poker House security network. The interpolating editing software was decent: the virtual camera first focused on the marchers coming down the street, banners high. The point of view kept retreating as the marchers advanced. Confused Chinese immigrants stepped out of the way. The sound slowly ramped up and the chants became louder.

Wam froze the video. "Here, on the left -" A box highlighted the figure " - is Mark Soldner, LDS branch president -"

Mike sighed. "I know Mark." He rubbed his eyes. "Oh, do I know Mark. Go on."

"Right. Boardroom group. And here, next to him, is his wife Carrie-Anne Soldner. Next we have their three sons and two daughters, George, Anne, Christopher, Joan, and Gaskell." Boxes popped up around each. "The facial recognition software has names for most of the others in the crowd, and the majority of them are all living in apartments owned by Soldner Apartments or in homes sold by Soldner Homes."

Wam fast forwarded through twenty minutes of chanting and picketing. "And here the first rock gets thrown." The video slowed, showing some of the younger men throwing rocks and then the crowd streaming inside and overturning poker tables. Wam paused the video. "I'll give the Mormons one thing, they're polite even as they're busting the place up. Did you catch how they said 'please' when they asked the gamblers to step back from the tables?"

"OK, so now what?"

"Now you make a legal finding and I document it."

"A legal finding? Like Mark Soldner is behind this?"

Wam tapped his slate. "OK, that's done. Just two steps left."

"I negotiate with the Mormons' rep and get them to pay damages, right? Who's their legal services provider? Abacha? LAWS? Negotiated Rights?"

"No. I already spoke to Mark, and he was quite clear - he uses Negotiated for his business stuff, but on the church and community stuff, they're independent."

"Independent?"

"Yeah, you've got to negotiate with Mark directly."

"It's never simple, is it?" Mike sighed. "Can you arrange a sitdown with Mark?"

"Already set up. Three o'clock today, his place. Address is in your phone."

"Thanks."

Wam looked at Mike for a long moment. "How is everything else going?"

Mike shrugged. "I feel buried in this shit." He gestured at the spreadsheets, tunnel plans, militia rosters, and CAD drawings of TBM machines spread across several wallscreens. "I can't get ahead...and now I've got to deal with Mormons."

Wam grew serious. "I know that this is the point in a feel-good chick flick where your assistant tells you what a great job you're doing juggling all of this - but I'm not going to say that. You've got to prioritize, Mike. Dealing with the Earth threat should be your highest priority. If you don't solve it, a *lot* of people are going to go to jail."

"Jesus, you sound like Javier." Mike looked aside, then back. "So what's *your* advice? Should I ignore the Mark Soldner issue?"

"It's in your lap now, so you've got to deal with it. But it shouldn't be in your lap in the first place."

Mike scowled. "We need this the Trusted Security subcontract to fund the Morlock Volunteers and the e-p-doors -"

Wam shook his head. "We don't need this. Money is fungible. Cut your expenses. You keep iterating the design of the rifles. You're starting to staff up the Second Morlock. You're paying for design work and prototype parts for the D-class TBM." He looked at Mike sharply. "Have you looked at how much you're spending on that?"

"It's not that much -"

"Mike, I reviewed the spreadsheets just this morning. You're pouring cash into a startup that's making carbide teeth."

"I'm not 'pouring' money in. And besides, once I get the D-series up and running I'll be able to rub it in Leroy's face and deliver cubic for half the price -"

"Mike, who gives a shit about Leroy? Forget the D-class TBMs."

356

Mike shook his head. "The D-class is going to be so much more efficient that -"

"Now is not the time. Put the D-class TBM on the shelf. Stop tweaking the rifles. And *stop* picking up new projects."

"It's not that easy -"

Wam shook his head. "Mike, stop arguing and listen to what I'm telling you. I know you like construction equipment more than you actually like running a business. But the war is breathing down our neck, and we need to win it. People - a hundred thousand people - here in Aristillus are risking their lives. You complain about Javier, but he's right - everyone is looking to you to be a leader. You need to step up and lead." He paused. "And a leader prioritizes."

Mike met Wam's eyes - and Wam didn't look away.

Mike crossed his arms.

God *damn* it.

He hated it when Javier and Wam ganged up on him. And he especially hated it when they were right.

Chapter 70

2064: First Class Homes and Offices construction site, level 6, Aristillus, Lunar Nearside

The crew chief raised his voice over the sounds of drills and abrasive cutoff saws. "Hang on, let me get Javier."

He turned, cupped both hands over his mouth and bellowed, "Javier!" A man a dozen meters away looked up from a large slate displaying architectural drawings. The crew chief waved him over.

Javier handed the slate to another man and walked toward them, slipping through gaps in the metal-stud walls that were going up with amazing speed.

Captain Matthew Dewitt - or, rather, Neil Keenum, electrician - looked over the new man as he approached. He was older, brown-skinned, with a salt-and-pepper goatee. Matching hair peeked out from under his scarred white hard hat.

Javier reached them. "What's up?"

"Javier, this is Neil. Says he's got a crew of electricians just off the boat from Australia. They're all looking for work."

"Actually, I was just looking for a job for myself," Matthew said.

Javier waved it off. "How many men total?"

"Well, there's a dozen of us, but -"

"There are three conductors in a three-phase wire, right?"

"Well, it's not that simple -"

"Sure it is. True or false!"

Matthew looked at Kaspar the crew chief for guidance but the other man was just leaning against a metal wall stud, watching the show. Matthew blinked. "That's a trick question. Depends if it's grounded or not. It comes in three-wire and four-wire configur-"

"I need 220 from a three-phase line - I can use a phase inverter. What are other options?"

"Uh..." He racked his brain "...it's not recommended, but you can use a three phase motor and just connect two of the -"

"You're making a ninety degree bend in ten centimeter conduit...". Javier fired off more questions, and Matthew answered each in turn.

Finally Javier nodded once, turned and left without a word.

Dewitt looked at Kaspar. "What the hell was that?"

The crew chief smiled. "Your whole team is hired. You start at seven AM tomorrow, right here. Bring your tools."

"Hired? Wait - uh -." Matthew reached into his pocket and fished out hard copies of his the occupational work papers, skill certification records and work permit and held them out to Kaspar.

The crew chief laughed. "You're new here; no one gives a shit about that stuff. Show up tomorrow, get the job done, and get it done right and you'll work out OK."

Dewitt blinked and put the documents away. It looked like the DoD had called in chits with Labor and OSHA for nothing.

The foreman started to turn but Matthew stopped him. "Wait - that Javier guy - is he the lead electrician?"

The other man snorted. "Electrician? No, he's the president."

***

Dewitt flipped on the jammer and then turned back to the room. His men were spread across two couches and several chairs, with a few more sitting on the floor.

Explaining the situation and asking for feedback wasn't normal in the Army - at least, it hadn't been for the last few decades. Still, Dewitt believed in it. And so did the kind of men he'd recruited for his team. "I got a job offer - for all of us."

"Same with me," Sergeant Sanderfur said. "I got two offers, actually. Both of them asked if I had any friends on the boat."

Sergeant Harbert nodded. "Same here."

Sergeant Lummus tilted his head. "Plan was to have us spread out to different firms. We gather more information that way. Nothing's changed, has it?"

Captain Dewitt nodded thoughtfully. "One thing has. Remember the name 'Javier Borda'?"

"Yeah, of course," Harbert said. "One of the CEOs. His name was in the seized phone."

"Briefing book says he's a friend of Martin's, and he's forming a militia too," Lummus added.

Harbert shrugged. "What's the big deal? We all applied at places where the CEOs are connected - that's why we picked them."

Dewitt nodded. "True. But in the case of Javier - I met him today."

"You *met* him?"

"Yeah. Turns out he's pretty hands-on with his people - "

"We've *got* to focus on that," Sergeant Lummus blurted out.

Dewitt nodded. "My thought exactly. Since Javier's close to the center of all of this, I think it makes sense to have more than one of us at First Class Homes and Offices - say, me, Mahoney, and Vasquez, but everyone else should take jobs elsewhere."

He looked around the room. "What do you guys think?"

"Works me for, LT."

"Me too."

There were nods and murmurs of agreement from the whole room.

"OK, let's do it."

Chapter 71

2064: Soldner Apartments office, Aristillus, Lunar Nearside

Mike stepped into Mark Soldner's office. Mark looked up from a stack of paperwork, saw Mike and smiled. "Give me just one second?"

Mike nodded and looked around. The place was nice - nicer than his own office, at least. Carpeting underfoot, a large walnut desk, three flags on the wall behind. Mike recognized the American flag, but the other two were new to him. The left one was white with blue stripes and a sunburst in the middle. The right one, though - he tilted his head. It looked like an American flag, but all the red stripes were blue. Maybe some Revolutionary War thing?

Mark signed the last sheet, and then stood up and extended a hand. "Sorry about that, Mike. Thanks for coming in."

Mike stepped forward.

OK. Be warm, be sincere, try to reach common ground.

He stuck out his hand. "Always a pleasure, Mark."

Mark smiled. "It's good to see you outside of the Boardroom and all the politics there. Have a seat, please."

Mike sat. "I'll get to the point - "

"The casino issue."

Mike nodded. "Exactly. We're insuring them, and the damage you folks caused -"

"Mike, let me cut to the chase. You and I agree that initiating violence isn't the right way to settle disputes, right?"

Mike blinked. Was Mark going to apologize and pay up that easily? His day just got a lot better. "Right. So -"

Mark held up a finger. "This wasn't our first protest - did you know that? We've been out there every Saturday for three months. But even after knowing how we feel - about our homes, about our community, they stayed in business."

Mike's face clouded and his hope that this was going to be easy disappeared. "That's irrelevant, Mark."

"No, it's very relevant."

"The point is that you destroyed someone else's property."

Mark shook his head. "We did a little damage, but it was symbolic. The important thing, though, is that we did it only *after* the casino started things."

Mike narrowed his eyes. "Started things?"

"High Deseret was a decent neighborhood before the casino moved in, and -"

"High Deseret? You mean Little Salt Lake?"

Mark smiled tightly. "We don't call it that - we find it a touch patronizing. But, yes, we're referring to the same portion of levels 3 and 4."

Mike rolled his eyes, then remembered Javier's lectures. He cleared his throat. "Sorry. OK, I'll try to remember that term. But let's get the facts straight. The casino said you initiated the trouble, and as far as I can tell the video backs them up one hundred percent. Unless you're going to suggest that the casino started the violence -"

"Absolutely I am. They ran a casino in an area where they weren't wanted. That disrupted an entire neighborhood. It's not physical damage, but the violence to the integrity of a community -"

Mike closed his eyes for a moment. "Damn it, Mark -"

He realized that Soldner was giving him a harsh look. Ah, crap. Mark liked swearing even less than Darcy did. OK. Charm school. "Excuse me. But you're twisting terms if you're calling that 'violence.' You know that's not the way it works. If your people don't want to patronize the casino, fine. But if the casino is paying the rent on their space, then they've got a right to be there. Organize a boycott if you want, but you can't go smashing up their space."

Mark templed his fingers and leaned back. After a moment, "Mike, you're against overreaching government, and I respect that. I'm on the same page...but your definition of liberty is too narrow." He looked Mike in the eye. "You know, I read copies of your interviews in Forbes, back before they were redacted, and I know where you're coming from. But it's not just individuals who have rights. Communities have rights too -"

"Mark -"

Mark raised a hand. "Let me finish. What about a child's right to walk down a sidewalk without being confronted with a half-naked prostitute? What about a parent's right to raise his or her children in an atmosphere where sex is something sacred between married people, and not a commodity advertised in a window? What about a wife's right to have her husband come home with his paycheck instead of losing it to a predatory gambling hall?"

"Mark, I'm not interested in discussing your theories about -"

"This isn't theory." He tapped his desk for emphasis. "This is real. You came to my office to discuss *exactly* this situation. You hard-core libertarians reduce freedom to just property rights and lack of political oppression - but there's more to the human morality and freedom than that. There's - wait, no, listen - this is science. Neurology. Mike, you care about individual liberty, property rights, and so on, and that's great, I agree with you - but there are more types of morality than that. A color-blind person might not be able to see the color green, but that doesn't mean it doesn't exist. And just because there are some types of morality and freedom that don't mean much to you - things like caring for others, respecting authority, keeping sacred things -"

Mike held up one hand. "Mark, forgive my bluntness, but you're right. I *don't* care. We can talk about your theory of morality later, but right now we need to talk about Leon's Poker House. Look, I'm not arguing in favor of gambling and prostitution."

"Aren't you?"

Mike started to roll his eyes but immediately caught himself. "No, I'm not. I don't have to approve of something to say that someone has as much right to run his business as you have to run yours."

"You're not honestly comparing Leon's business and mine, are you? Whoring and gambling destroy families. Building houses and renting apartments helps build them."

"I'm not talking about the moral equivalence."

"But, Mike, you are. You're saying -"

Mike felt his patience slipping and tried to claw it back. He leaned forward. "Mark, listen to me. I'm saying one thing, and one thing only - the casino has a right to exist. It pays its rent, it's not breaking any laws-

"Laws? You're not talking about laws - real government laws - you're talking about *regulations*. Regulations from Trusted Security, or whoever. So Leon's not violating regulations? That might matter to someone, but not me. That place is certainly violating laws - God's laws and the laws of the community."

Mike clenched his jaw. "Don't start complaining about the lack of government here, Mark. You knew what Aristillus was when you came here."

"Wait -"

"No, you wait! You knew that Aristillus was free of government when you came here - and now you're trying to form your own and force others to obey you! Aristillus is free of government whether you like it or not - and if you don't like it, you can go buy a TBM and dig your own tunnels. The moon is empty; pack up and leave."

Mike had been all but yelling, but Mark just smiled and spoke soothingly. "Mike, we're not founding a government. Just a neighborhood committee. And, with all due respect for your accomplishments founding Aristillus, you're not king, you-"

"Your damned right I'm not! No one is! That's my point."

"Then why do you think you can dictate what other people can and can't do? If ninety-five percent of the people in this tunnel vote to have a neighborhood, then freedom means -"

Mike felt his blood pressure rising. God damn this man. "Voting? Mob rule - that's the OPPOSITE of freedom. What if ninety-five percent of people voted to outlaw Mormonism?" He jabbed a finger at Mark. "That's not what Aristillus stands for."

Mark put his hands up placatingly. "Aristillus is young - just ten years old. The people haven't yet decided what Aristillus is or isn't, what it stands for."

"Damn it, Mark!" Mark's lips pursed; he was clearly offended by the language.

Fuck him; he'd speak like he wanted to speak. "Mark, you read the FAQs before you booked passage here. You knew that this was an anarchy. When did you get here? Four years ago? Five? Lowell already had the newbs contract in place by the time you stepped off the boat at Lai Docks. You signed it, just like everyone else. I bet I can dig up a copy."

"The world belongs to the living."

"What sort of horseshit is that? You *signed*."

Mark dismissed the idea with a wave of his hand. "Things change. Situations change. People change. You went to public schools, right? I'll bet when you were a kid you recited the Pledge of Allegiance, right? And the One

Environment Pledge, and the World Unity Promise? Every day, before attendance. And now you -"

"That was when I was a kid. I *had* to."

Mark was infuriatingly calm. "Yes, you had to. You had no other alternative, because you were under duress. Well, Mike, refugees from Earth are under duress; they'll sign anything when they get here, just to get away from the unconstitutional godless governments back on Earth. And now that we're no longer under duress, people in my community are trying to lay down some reasonable ethical norms in our own neighborhoods. We have the right to establish governance -"

Mike could feel the anger in his chest, like a physical force. "Not if you start pushing that government on others! And when you're smashing windows and overturning tables, you're doing exactly that."

Mark sighed and sat back in his chair. "Mike, I give up. I thought I could talk sense with you, make you understand where our families are coming from, but I see I can't."

"That's right, you can't." He balled one fist. "So let's get to the point: you owe damages. And you're going to pay them."

For the first time Mark looked cross. "So that's your plan - you tell me that I'm wrong about everything I've ever believed in, and you thought I'd apologize for offending you?"

Mike seethed. "Pay up, Mark."

Mark's eyes narrowed. "Mike, you're a business owner. You've read the standard negotiation books - 'Getting to Yes', 'Bargaining for Advantage' - that sort of thing?"

"What's your point?"

"The key in negotiations is figuring out what each side *really* wants."

"Mark, what I *really want*-" Mike didn't care that his sarcastic mocking tone was clear "- is for you to pay up and then stop assaulting people and breaking things."

"No. What you want is for us to stop busting up casinos that you provide security arrangements for. So there's a simple way to get that - stop protecting the people who are trying to destroy our community."

"I'm not going to back down -"

"Fine. Let's talk about the thing you *really* want -"

Despite himself Mike went for the bait. "What?"

"What you really want is for your revolution to succeed."

Mike stared at him. "What?"

"You're disgusted with the false authority and socialism that's been rising on Earth for the past few decades, and you want to start a new society. A new country. I'm in agreement with that. We're allies here, Mike - with just a few tactical disagreements. And like all good allies, we can work out those disagreements."

Mike wanted to stand and yell at Mark, berate him for his arrogance, his refusal to live up to the contract he'd signed, his God-damned insistence on sneaking government in through the backdoor.

He pictured Javier's reaction if he did any of those things, and barely fought the urge back. Mike breathed out heavily through his nose.

"What are you saying?"

"The war is here. We must hang together, gentlemen...else, we shall most assuredly hang separately. Do you know that quote?"

"Don't be cute. What's your point?"

"My point is that if you and I are in alliance, we can fight a revolution, and maybe win it. I've got a lot more resources and people than you realize. But if we're fighting each other over petty stuff like poker and prostitutes...then you and I are not in alliance." Mark paused and looked Mike straight in the eye. "Let's be brutally honest here. I actively believe in the rule of law, and the institution of government. I can try to cut a deal with the Earth governments and sleep well at night afterward. And to continue the brutal honesty: you can't. You need me more than I need you, Mike." Mark paused, and then continued. "But I'd rather that we're on the same team."

Mark stood and stuck out his hand.

Mike rose and looked at the proffered hand. "And the cost of you helping out the Revolution is that I let you drive Leon's Poker House out of business?"

Mark kept his hand out. "They don't have to go out of business. They just have to move somewhere else."

Mike stared at Mark's extended hand. The revolution was probably doomed even with Mark's help. But it was almost certainly doomed without it.

Mike hated himself for it, but he started to raise his own hand.

But if he compromised and sold out a small business, then what was he standing for? Freedom...as long as someone richer, someone more powerful didn't want the infringe on it?

And what was he compromising? Not his own freedom. No. Someone else's. Is that who he was? Someone who sold out the small fry and gave special privileges to political allies?

He felt his hand falter.

If he didn't take this deal, he'd probably lose Mark from the Boardroom Group - and he might even have him defect entirely. The threat to negotiate a separate peace was unlikely - but not impossible.

And if Mark signed a separate peace, the revolution would fail, and he, Javier, Darcy - everyone - would end up dead or imprisoned.

He had to make this deal.

But what precedent did it set? If Mark had free rein to smash up any bar he didn't like in his quest to build what he saw as a decent society, where did it end? Zoning? Minimum wages? Undesirable, but people could live with that. But would it end there? First one compromise, then another. How long until drug prohibition? How long until no-knock raids, email surveillance, confessions under torture, asset forfeiture?

No.

Mike let his hand drop to his side.

"Mike, I'm not asking for much, just -"

"You're asking for everything."

Mike pulled out his phone and dialed. Wam answered on the second ring. "Wam, I need you to station men outside Leon's casino. No, not guards - I want a full fire team. Armed and armorered. And cut a check to Leon for the damages; we'll eat this one."

He hung up.

Mark looked taken aback. "Mike, let me ask you to reconsider - the revolution needs me."

"Yeah, Mark, it does. But that doesn't mean that I'm going to sell out someone else's freedom."

Chapter 72

2064: Morlock Engineering office, Aristillus, Lunar Nearside

Javier looked at the new conference room window. "Did you get to the bottom of that protest?"

Mike grimaced. "Kind of. By the time the First Morlock got here, most of the protesters had run but my people managed to grab two of them. Turns out that it was a flash mob - recruited over the net, paid anonymously. Oh, and this is fun." He gestured at the wallscreen. A few web pages opened. "Video clips of it started showing up online. Some of it's already been incorporated in news posts."

Javier's forehead furrowed. "Posted by who?"

Mike shook his head. "No one I've ever heard of."

"That...that makes very little sense."

Mike shrugged. "Tell me about it. I'm wondering if Mark Soldner might be behind it."

"Mark? Why would he -"

"Long story. And the order's wrong, but I wonder... Anyway, not worth talking about it."

"Well, let's talk about something else then - like your damned behavior at the last meeting." Javier shook his head in a mixture of sorrow and confusion. "What the hell, Mike?"

Mike held his hands up, placatingly. "Look, I know I was a bit rowdy-"

Javier said nothing of a long moment. Mike prepared for a lecture from his old friend, but in the end Javier just shrugged and looked away.

"Jave - what?"

Javier looked back. "Mike, I'm not going to yell at you. You're an adult. You know that we're at war. You know the stakes. And you know that before you can win the shooting war, you have to win the opinion war with the other CEOs here." Javier crossed his arms. "But don't let me bully you. Do what you want."

Mike looked away.

Shit.

He wished Javier would just lecture him more. That was easier to take than his disappointment.

Mike pursed his lips. "I'm going to get a coffee - can I get you one?"

Javier took a long time answering. "No."

Mike stood and looked at the new window - at anything other than Javier - as he headed to the kitchenette.

* * *

Mike and Javier sat at the table, avoiding each other's eyes. Mike looked at his slate. The meeting should start in fifteen minutes - people would begin arriving soon.

As if on cue there was some low noise from the hallway outside. Security must be letting someone through.

A moment later Mark Soldner came into view, then stopped at the doorway. Mike blinked then stood. "Mark! I didn't expec - I'm glad to see you."

Mark nodded curtly. Without much enthusiasm he said, "We've got a revolution to run." He stepped into the room and took a seat.

Javier looked at Mike for a moment with an unvoiced question and then looked away.

* * *

"Ok," Hector said, "Mike's convinced me - we need more immigration. I only own a small share of TransportMEX, but I'll talk to the board. I'll also talk to Lisa at Fifth Ring and give her my point of view."

"Wait a second," Mark interrupted. "We still haven't voted on this." Mark looked down the length of the table. "Karina, what do you think?"

Karina picked up her stylus. "I'm not convinced that this is a good idea. I'm not concerned about cultural balance the way Mark is, but the vast majority of immigrants don't settle up their tax bills back on Earth before they come here. The Earth governments have been making more and more noise about budget shortfalls, and while the taxes lost via emigration are small, it's an important symbolic point. We want to avoid irritating them."

Mark nodded. "We each have different motivations, but I think that there are a lot of us who are leery of more immigration. I propose we vote."

Mike balled one first and started to get to his feet to denounce the very idea of voting - but then caught himself. Wait. He'd prepared for this.

Rob Wehrmann cleared his throat. "Vote? Vote on what?"

Mike smiled. Perfect.

Mark blinked. "Uh - on whether we should speed up immigration or slow it -"

Rob shook his head. "You don't get a say on it."

Mark drew back. "I - excuse me? I'm a member of the boardroom group, just like you. Of course I -"

Rob made a slashing gesture with his hand. "No. If Hector wants to encourage TransportMEX to run more ships, he can."

"Wait a second. We're not all on board with that. We have a right -"

Rob was visibly annoyed. "I don't care if you're on board with it. I don't get a vote on what time you take a dump in the morning, and you don't get a vote on how other people run their businesses."

Mark sputtered. "The point - the whole point of this meeting - is to work together, right? By voting?" His eyes involuntarily jumped to Mike and then away.

And then Mike realized: Mark wasn't back at the Boardroom Group because he'd given up his fight to establish a government. He was back because he thought this was the battleground where he could win.

Mike's nostrils flared.

He looked around the table. He'd prepped for this meeting, but he'd expected opposition from Karina and Albert Lai - not from Mark, who he'd thought would be boycotting. Javier had his back, but would hang back from this. He'd talked to Hector and Kurt "Wolf" Balcom, but neither of them -

Katherine Dycus cleared her throat. "Working together on certain things doesn't mean we have to vote on everything. This isn't a government, Mark - we're a bunch of people who *fled* from governments. The shipping guys are going to do what they want with their ships, and if you don't like it, you can try talk them out of it, one-on-one after the meeting." Katherine looked around. "Now, who's moderating this thing? I say we move on to the next topic."

Mike let a wisp of a smile creep onto his face. He hadn't worked with Katherine on this exact point, but he had talked with her before the meeting.

Mark scanned the room and gauged his support. After a moment he sat back.

Mike nodded. "OK, Katherine. Next topic: e-p doors. Rob?"

Rob Wehrmann started talking about the civil defense planning. Mike turned to his right where Javier was sitting. Javier met his eyes and let one raised eyebrow ask his question. Mike tilted his head in silent answer and let his smile grow.

* * *

Mike advanced the notes on the wallscreen. "Final item - MarCom. You've all read the recent polling data?" Heads nodded. "Fifty-six percent fully support armed resistance, and the rest are divided between neutral and opposed. We need to keep those we've already got and we need to convert neutrals."

"*And* we need to encourage support on Earth," Javier said. "Perhaps we can raise some funds, or exert pressure on the legislatures there."

Mike nodded "In both cases, we need marketing. Or, to be blunt, propaganda."

Albert Lai spoke. "Mike - pardon me for saying so, but it occurs to me that no one at this table is particularly skilled at marketing consumer goods." He looked around the table. "Tunneling. General construction. Mining. We all have b2b experience. Aside from Katherine selling spacesuits, I don't think any of us has done much b2c".

Katherine interrupted. "I actually sell most of my suits to the construction firms and Red Stripe. Aside from a few custom ones for the Dogs, we almost never deal with end users."

Albert nodded. "If anything, that makes my point stronger. None of us are skilled at reaching out to consumers."

Rob Wehrmann cleared his throat. "What are you saying? We pick a marketing firm? I've never been happy with any of the ones I've used. They all suck."

Albert shook his head. "Perhaps you're not using them appropriately."

"Now, wait a second. I know how to use a marketing firm."

Mike held up his hands. "Guys, hang on. I don't think we should pick a marketing firm. I've got a different idea."

"Are you going to enlighten us?"

"I think we should create prizes - cash prizes - for the best ads, or documentaries, or whatever."

Rob squinted. "Huh?"

Mike spread his hands. "It's an old idea. People haven't heard of it because they were made illegal in most countries decades back - along with futures markets and dominant assurance con - well, anyway. It's simple: we establish a cash prize, and then anyone who wants can submit an entry, and we have a jury that picks the best one and awards the prize."

Rob narrowed his eyes. "So we just say 'send us a commercial, and if we like it, we'll pay you... but if we don't we won't'?"

"Yeah."

Rob snorted. "I wouldn't fall for that scam."

Katherine said, "We award worker-owners in our coop in a similar way...but that's for small efficiency improvements. Has this ever worked on third party things?"

Rob scowled. "Or on anything in the real world, not in some damned hippie commune?"

Katherine pursed her lips at the insult but otherwise ignored Rob.

Mike nodded. "Yes. To both. The British Latitude Prize was the most famous, but the Ansari X Prize, the Google Lunar Prize - there are a bunch. I've included links in the handout."

Albert nodded and bent over his slate, tapping the references.

Karina put down her stylus. "This idea sounds...odd. Without direct control how do we know we'll get what we want? The messaging might not be consistent with our goals."

"We only give the award to who we pick."

"Yes, but if some of the nonwinning ads get out -"

"They're going to get out. All of them. We only give the prizes if the work is open sourced."

Karina pursed her lips. "This sounds remarkably..." she paused, "undisciplined. What sort of message consistency will we have?" She tapped her stylus on the table before rendering judgement. "I don't like the idea."

"What's your better idea? Pick one firm? Get five or ten people working on the problem?"

Karina nodded. "Yes, actually."

"This lets us leverage our resources. We mobilize a hundred thousand brains here in Aristillus, get them all working toward the same goal."

Albert Lai said, "If it's a good idea to mobilize brains, why not open this up to everyone?"

Mike tilted his head. "That's what I said."

"No. You said 'everyone in Aristillus'. There are nine billion brains back on Earth and you're leaving them out."

Mike was speechless for a moment. "On Earth?" He paused. "They're - that's the other side. I don't -"

"I like Albert's idea," Tran said.

Mark Soldner raised a hand. "Wait a second. What if someone on Earth wins? Do we actually pay them the prize money?"

Tran looked at Mark. "Maybe we should hope that someone on Earth wins. What better way to prove that the streets are paved with gold? That could even help with immigration."

Javier nodded. "If we're thinking about this as a recruiting tool, perhaps we factor popular voting - of anyone on Earth - into how we decide the winners."

Mike's head swiveled back and forth as he followed the conversation. The idea was evolving more quickly than he'd expected.

Karina Roth put her stylus down. "I'd like to register objections. To the idea of prizes, to the idea of throwing entries open to everyone on Earth - and worst of all, to the idea of letting people on Earth vote for which are the winning prizes." She shook her head. "This represents a huge loss of control. *Any* sort of idea might get proposed."

Mike nodded. "Noted."

Karina said, "Before this goes any further, I think we should vote on it." She looked at Katherine and Rob and let annoyance creep into her voice. "Presuming this is one of the things we're allowed to vote on?"

Rob pursued his lips. "Don't be a drama queen. That was about private property. This is about Boardroom business. Of course we vote."

Mike held up a hand. "OK, we'll vote on it in just a minute. But there's a second idea that I want to throw out on the table before we vote." Karina furrowed her brow but said nothing. Mike looked around the room. "I think we should open-source the AG drive."

"Open-source?" Rob Wehrmann said. "What does that even mean?"

"It means that we give away the design for free. Make it public. Let anyone on Earth who wants to build a drive build one." He looked at Mark. "And then let them come here."

Rob exploded. "What the fuck - if we give away the drive design, the PKs will -"

"The PKs have already stolen three of our ships. If they're not building copies right now I'd be amazed. This isn't about giving away the design to the PKs - they already have it." He looked around. "Right now we know how to build ships, and the PKs do. The only ones who don't are the other nine billion people on Earth, and a lot of those nine billion are potentially allies."

Trang raised his eyebrow. "Let a thousand flowers bloom?"

"A thousand space ships, perhaps," Albert said.

Rob shook his head. "This fucking meeting is getting stranger and stranger."

Chapter 73

2064: Lai Docks and Air Traffic Control, Aristillus, Lunar Nearside

Michael Stuart-Test checked his board. Three incoming flights, four departing, a couple of dock-to-dock transfers. Nothing out of the ordinary.

The console phone rang and Michael sighed. Right in the middle of the really amazing glass harmonica solo from Octothorpe's second album. He hit pause.

The caller ID said John Hayes. Was that the John with the Dogs? John on Farside? That meant that the relay satellites were back.

Interesting.

He took the call. "Lai Docks and Air Traffic Control."

"Hi, I was calling for Darcy but the switchboard routed me here."

"Darcy's working from home today. Some side project. Is there anything I can help you with?"

"No, I. Hmm. Let me think for a second." A pause. "No, I'll just call Darcy on her cell."

"OK." Michael hung up, then hit play again. Octothorpe started up again - and it wasn't right. He shook his head. You couldn't just start this track in the middle. It built, starting simply, then adding a second rhythm, and then a third, working its way to up through pairs of primes. He sighed and restarted the track. There. Better. He closed his eyes for a moment and hummed along.

And then the phone rang.

God *damn* it.

Caller ID showed it was John again.

Michael hit pause on the music and answered, letting a trace of annoyance creep into his voice. "Yes, John, what can I do for you?"

"Darcy's not answering her personal phone, and I need to make a change to the next supply drop."

Michael sighed. This *was* part of his job. He brought up the screen for scheduling a hopper run. "OK, John, tell me your coordinates."

"Well, that's tricky. We're hiking, so where depends on when the drop happens."

Michael scanned the column. "We've got three automated cargo hoppers on the pad. Because of the energy weapon issue, Mr. Lai needs to sign off on all runs, but that shouldn't be a problem. We can probably have one to you in a few hours."

"I don't want an automated drop. I want Darcy to come out in a man-rated hopper."

"What? Why?"

At the other end of the line John paused, and then said, "Never mind. Look, when is Darcy due in the office?"

Michael checked the schedule. "She's working on her side project for a few days. She's scheduled to be back on Tuesday."

John sighed. "Have her call me."

Chapter 74

2064: 93 km south of Konstantinov Crater, Lunar Farside

John stepped over the small stream and paused to admire the way the path was dappled with light that filtered down through the greenery. Blue and Max brushed past. Rex came even with him and stopped.

"John! I just did a pull merge from one of the forks - there's new monster encounters!"

A 'merge' and a 'fork'? Clearly this was something about software. John had been treated more than once to monologues explaining the difference between bulletin boards, code hubs, source wikis, and distro repositories and all the associated terminology, but none of it stuck with him.

"Uh-huh."

"This is *epic* - you've got to try it!"

John sighed. "All right, I'll bite. What are you talking about?"

"Haven't you been listening to us talk about it?"

"Pretend I'm starting at zero."

"The augmented reality package in the suits has an API-compliant back end, so it was trivial to write some glue code to tie it to the Open Generic MMORPG library. Just before Gamma's satellites got burned I uploaded the first pass at the project. I mean, when I uploaded it I didn't know that it was just before the sats got burned, because that hadn't happened yet - of course! - but, anyway, the *really* cool thing is that when the sats were down my post about it hit the front page at UnhygenicMacro.info! Can you believe that?"

John avoided asking what a macro was and what was unhygienic about it. "Front page? Really. Great."

"Yeah, I know, right? So, anyway, it made it up to the sixth ranked story, and then this one clade of Russian graphic designers back on Earth - well, they're not *all* Russians - but anyway, the clade started doing development work on it too. Look, it's easier to just show you. Let me give you the package."

A moment later John's helmet pinged as the patch installed itself. Rex's long-winded explanation went on and John half turned it out and pulled up a menu. There it was - right under the other environmental overlay choices. John selected the MMORPG that Rex had shared with him - and with a click the sun dappled forest was gone.

John looked around. He stood on a muddy trail that twisted between weird ferns. Above him scabrous ugly tree limbs overhung the trail. Ahead the ferns parted and gave way to huge strange mushrooms, the size of cars. Creepy hooting calls echoed over the audio channel.

In the upper left corner of his screen an information box was filled with some strange calligraphy. Was that first word "Mirkwood"? Beneath the title was a bullet pointed list of equipment, weapons, magic items, and gold. Magic items? John rolled his eyes.

"Has it loaded yet?"

"Yep, it's loaded. It looks... interesting."

"I know, right?! Look, I've got to study my scrolls to restore magic points, so I'm going to leave you on your own. You've got thirty silver Bree pennies, so you can equip."

"OK, Rex."

"Oh, and one more thing: I don't think we'll see many orcs here, but there could be dark elves. So be on the lookout."

John smiled despite himself. "OK, I'll be careful." Rex signed off and John immediately switched his overlay back to Pacific Northwest, but he tuned to the Dogs' channel and listened to them chatter. Rex and Duncan talked excitedly about elves and dwarves for a while, and then shifted to discuss how the Russian designer clade had set up a feed where people could follow the Dogs' virtual adventure and how big the viewership was.

John shook his head. He liked to think that he looked and felt younger than his forty-two years, but at times like this - hiking across the surface of the moon with genetically engineering Dogs who were pretending that he was someone named AraJohn, and knowing that thousands of people back on Earth were betting virtual currency of their "success" - he felt very very old and out of place. It was a long way from New Jersey back in the 2020s.

His mind turned away from the Dogs' craziness to the supply situation. Four mules was great, but after having his communication with Aristillus cut off once, he now couldn't stop thinking about it.

"You there, Gamma?"

"Yes, John."

"The birds are still good?"

"Indeed, you walked out of range of the last of my pickets twenty kilometers ago."

Good. Darcy being out of the office for several days had complicated his plans. With Gamma potentially listening in on everything he said, he couldn't tell anyone back at Aristillus about his concerns about Gamma's growth. Still, as long as the new sats were good, he could call Darcy in - he checked his clock - ninety-one hours, and be picked up just a few hours later.

Gamma interrupted his train of thought. "John, when satellite connectivity was down I added comments to your BookShare page. Have you had a chance to read them yet?"

John squinted. BookShare was an Aristillus website. "Wait a second. How did you update the website when the sats were down?"

"I did some from my Sinus Lunicus facility."

John furrowed his eyebrows. "So - wait. When the birds were down, were both your Konstantinov and SL facilities - uh - live?"

There was a pause. "Yes."

"When the sats were down they couldn't talk to each other, right?" He tried to formulate the question that bothered him. "So which was the real you?"

Another pause - a longer one. "They both were for that interval, but data reconciliation is now complete."

"What does that mean?"

"There were multiple of me, but now there's just one of me again."

John mulled over the disturbing implications of that - and then caught himself. Would Gamma correctly interpret the long pause as worry? Better to talk, and hide his thoughts.

"Uh, yeah. So, anyway. Bookshare. I skimmed your comment - you said something about 'The Spaceship and The Canoe' ?"

"The book I referenced is 'The *Starship* and The Canoe'; the title you mention was a pornographic graphic novel that came out several decades later. As best I can tell it's unrelated."

John coughed. "OK, 'Starship' then. So why do you think I should read it?"

"I didn't say that you should read it; merely that your personality reminds me of one particular chapter, where the author is noting that George Dyson is not a 'loner' who wants to get away from everyone. Instead, the author suggests that Dyson was an intensely social person who just has not yet found - or created - the perfectly tailored social environment that he longed for."

385

John frowned slightly. "I remind you of that?"

"John, is there a single way in which you should *not* remind me of that?"

"This is the book about a guy who builds a kayak, right? Look, I'm hardly a hippie paddling around the Pacific Northwest."

"There exists a phrase 'heaven forbid' and it can be used sarcastically. So let me say: heaven forbid, John. I would never want to suggest similarities between a formerly patriotic ex-soldier deeply disappointed in his country's politics who has fled four hundred thousand kilometers from home, and then hiked another five thousand kilometers across a desolate rocky landscape with no company except four uplifted Dogs, and a hippie escaping from an academic family by kayaking around the Pacific North West."

Despite himself John smiled. "Ouch!"

"May I ask a question - which augmented reality overlay do you usually pick when hiking?"

John shook his head slightly as he walked, then gave up and grinned. "OK, touché. Yes, it's 'Pacific Northwest'. So I'm a loner disappointed in my original home, out on the frontier, trying to fill a void, and surrounding myself with weirdos and freaks." John kicked a rock as he walked. "Can we change the topic now?"

"Of course, John. I note that your BookShare page shows that you've been reading science fiction from the same era."

"Yes. Do you know of Kevin Bultman?"

"A search of Davidson Equities Analysis shows that he is the owner of Mason Dixon Registry Service in Aristillus."

"Right. Anyway, he's a friend of mine and we talk about the situation with Earth."

"Go on."

"Well, we both think that a military confrontation with Earth is foolish - we'd certainly lose. So we're brainstorming other paths."

"You mention this in the context of me noting your reading habits. Are you saying that century-old science fiction is helping you brainstorm?"

John nodded, and then realized that Gamma couldn't see his body language. At least, not if he was telling the truth about the last rover being twenty klicks back.

"I took a military science class once where the instructor told us about one of the Arab-Israeli wars - this was back before the Caliphate. One Israeli general needed to get his troops from point A to point B, but the roads were blocked. He remembered reading something in the Old Testament about some other general moving troops between the same two points three thousand years before, and he realized that there must be an old forgotten road. He figured out where the road had to be, found it, and took his men along it."

"What was the name of the General, John? And where was the road?"

John shook his head. "This class was twenty years ago; I have no idea. I asked Max once; even he didn't know the reference."

"Fascinating. I'm going to try to dig up more information on this. But, please, go on."

"The point is, sometimes old books have good ideas."

"I have heard that idea before."

"Yeah, I'm not saying it's a new insight; everyone knows that. Heck, Mike, Javier, that whole Boardroom Group bunch quote Patrick Henry and Thomas Jefferson." John felt his left foot slipping a bit on scree and steadied himself before walking on. "My point is that everyone back at Aristillus is referencing the American Revolution, but I wondered if there might be other parallels that most people are overlooking."

"Parallels in science fiction?"

"Yes. Search for 'lunar revolution science fiction', and you get dozens of hits. 'The Moon is a Harsh Mistress' is top of the heap. The 2019 movie is horrible, but it turns out that the original Minear script is pretty good, and the graphic novel and one of the two fan animated series are also decent...but all of those are based off of a book! And in that book there's this one interesting idea -"

"Railguns."

John blinked. "What?"

"Railguns."

"You've read it?"

"I have."

"Huh." John had to think about that. "Anyway, yes, the railguns were interesting, but I was paying more attention to the political negotiations in the middle of the novel."

"Did the negotiations in that novel inspire any ideas for the current situation?"

John sighed. "Unfortunately, no. Trying to remind Earth voters of the American revolution isn't going to accomplish anything when most people don't know any history."

"If you are willing to search for more inspiration via books, please let me add a few more recommendations to your BookShare page - there. I've added some notes, too."

"More novels?"

"Perhaps it's time to leave fiction for a while and concentrate on how to actually structure this society you're trying to create. I've suggested Cowen's 'Ungoverned Somalia,' Friedman's 'The Icelandic Free State,' and Bennington's 'Confederacion Nacional del Trabajo y Federacion Anarquista Iberica.'"

"You think my approach of reading fiction was a mistake?"

"No, John, I think it was a very good start. But by hiking here on the surface with the Dogs you have made it clear that you are not interested in fighting the revolution that Mike and the others in Aristillus are planning. That being the case, perhaps you can contribute to an equally difficult problem: architecting a society that doesn't contain the seeds of its own authoritarianism."

The weirdness of simultaneously distrusting Gamma's intentions enough to want to escape back to Aristillus and yet talking with him about how to win the fight with Earth made John's head swim. Not for the first time, he reminded himself that he didn't *know* that Gamma was a threat - he merely suspected he was.

"A 'good start', Gamma? Since when are you so eager to hand out compliments?"

"I'm sorry if that was inappropriate. Have I caused you to blish?"

"No, it wasn't inappropriate. But 'blish'? Your pronunciation is usually better than that, Gamma."

"My wording -"

"I bet if you used words like 'smile' and 'blush' half as often as you say 'stochastic' and 'logically' you wouldn't." John smiled at his own humor. "But anyway, tell me more about what you mean by 'architecting a society'."

"Very well. I suggest that the trickiest problem is not achieving independence from overarching government but avoiding rebuilding the same government structures - or social patterns that give rise to those government structures."

John pursed his lips. "Hmm. Tell me more."

Chapter 75

2064: Cheap-n-Clean Apartments, Aristillus, Lunar Nearside

George White took his time looking over the kids. "I saw the footage run on some of the channels since the last time we met."

Hugh leaned forward. "Did you like it?"

George turned to him and fixed him with a stare. He let the kid sweat a moment, then - "No. I didn't."

Hugh's face fell.

George breathed deeply, telegraphing his disappointment. "It was just the footage I gave you. There was nothing new. And nothing about Morlock."

Louisa turned and snapped at Hugh. "I *told* you!"

Hugh spread his hands defensively. "But I thought that getting the story out quickly was important because -"

Louisa cut him off. "We'll do better with the next report, Jamie."

George turned and stared at Hugh until the boy withered under his contempt, then turned back to Louisa. "I know you will."

After so many years working the streets of Chicago it was second nature: pick the weakest from the herd, slap him, and then give a bit of attention to the leader - who couldn't help but see you as having the same good taste and leadership skills as herself. Black street gangs, Asian drug dealers, or white college kids - it worked on any of them.

"Tell me about your next video, Louisa. How much information have you dug up on Martin?"

"We've found a lot on the blogs and discussion boards, and we've purchased reports from Data-Lenz and

Davidson Equities Analysis, but we haven't seen anything that really makes a case -"

George pursed his lips. "His main business is Morlock Engineering - you know that. There're a ton of problems at Morlock - substandard engineering, unsafe labor, shoddy machine maintenance...but what he controls directly is the least of it. It's the shadow network you have to pay attention to." George let the sentence hang there.

Louisa leaned forward. "What do you mean?"

"Martin has his fingers in a lot of things. He rents space to dozens of restaurants - all of them operating without government inspections. He's got armed men running a pretend police force at Trusted Security. He's involved with Red Stripe spacesuit rental, he - "

"Red Stripe?" Hugh blurted. "That's the space suit company that killed Allan."

George let a calculated look of surprise wash over his face. "I'd heard about that death, but hadn't realized he was a friend of yours." He paused. "My condolences."

"Thank you. So how do we find out about these shadow networks? Do we buy more reports from Data-Lenz, or...?"

"I've got some details on what Martin owns, what the networks are." He held up his phone.

Louisa pulled out her own phone. "OK, I'm ready."

George held Louisa's eye. "There's a condition."

"Yes?"

"You've got to promise me that you're going to *use* this. Go undercover. Get some real footage of your own."

"We will."

"I'm serious. I've got other options - there are other journalists who I can give this to -"

"Like who?" Selena asked.

George ignored her. "These details were pulled together by a lot of people in the Underground, and I need to make sure it's not wasted."

Louisa leaned in. "Jamie, can you put us in touch with the Underground directly?"

"Show me what you can do with this, and we can talk." Then, finally, he tapped his phone and sent the data. "There's good stuff there. Org charts show the interlocking board memberships. Some actuarial tables with estimates of the number of laborers killed working on Morlock job sites. Estimated net worths of the various Boardroom Group members."

Louisa looked at her slate and called up the documents, then whistled. "Martin is the richest man in Aristillus?"

George nodded. "For now." As soon as the words were out of his lips he regretted them. He looked at the four kids - none seemed to have thought anything of his statement. Good.

Hugh looked up from his slate. "This is good, I guess. But tell me more about his involvement with the firm that killed Allan. Red Stripe."

"There's what's on paper." George gestured toward the slates that each of the kids had in their laps. "And there's the story behind the story. Red Stripe is owned by Trang Loc. Trang's been here for about eight years. The first few years he worked for Mike Martin." Hugh tapped at his slate frantically, taking notes.

"If you can call slave-labor on an unregulated work site 'working'. At some point he quit and went out on his own. Martin bankrolled him. Whatever Loc does you know Martin is behind it."

Selena furrowed her eyebrows. "Why would Trang come here to be a slave? I mean, we all know that sometimes in the third world factories pay off the local police to round up laborers. But we've interviewed dozens of expats, and they all talk about selling their houses on the black market to buy passage here." She fixed George with hazel eyes. "So how was Trang slave labor?"

Damn it. His instincts had been right; this bitch was slippery. He backpedaled. "Well, you know, I haven't been here as long as Mike and Trang, so I'm just repeating what I've heard." He shrugged. "It might be more of a refugee situation or something."

Louisa rolled her eyes at Selena. "I wouldn't put it past these people to use indentured refugee labor. Not at all. Come on."

Selena shrugged. "OK, fine. But my second question: if Trang was a slave laborer, or indentured or whatever, how did he quit? And if he did quit, why is he suddenly the best buddy of Mike?"

George felt boxed in by Selena's questions but feigned equanimity as he shrugged. "Maybe Martin is blackmailing Loc somehow. I don't know. Look into it if you want, but I doubt it will do any good - all you'll get is the cover story. But this is a distraction from the real point. This isn't about Trang. The story is about the Boardroom Group cabal."

* * *

Selena leaned back in the cheap chair and listened as Jamie laid out the details of Mike Martin's relationships with Javier Borda, a construction bigwig; Hector Camanez, a tunnel farming magnate; Bao Johnson, an 'insurance' broker and protection racket runner; and more.

Louisa quizzed Jamie for details and as Selena listened to the two of them she let her eyes roam the room.

There was something that seemed off about Jamie, but she couldn't quite pin it down. His manner was charismatic - and somehow just a bit oily.

There was also the fact that his assistance was almost too good to be true. The stories were already packaged, the documents were perfect. She looked down at her slate. It'd be one thing if Jamie had passed them stolen spreadsheets and emails, but these? They seemed to be a custom-made presentation. Almost as if they were designed to feed a story to investigative reporters.

Suddenly suspicious, Selena glanced around the room. There wasn't much that personalized it. A few old-fashioned books on one shelf, a few digital picture frames on another, all turned off.

Jamie had moved on from the Boardroom Group and was talking about Mike Martin's underpaid workers and tunnel boring machines made dangerous by shoddy maintenance.

Besides those two shelves and the cheap furniture, the room was almost entirely empty. The only clothes were two worn and slightly dirty jumpsuits hanging on pegs near the door.

Selena tilted her head. There was something off about the jumpsuits - but what? Were they cut too thin for Jamie's burly frame? Her eyes narrowed. Yes, they were. Those suits would never fit him. Maybe he had a roommate, though? No - just one small bed.

Were those Jamie's clothes? She looked around at the generic furniture and the blacked out picture frames and an even stranger thought gripped her: Was this even Jamie's apartment?

Selena looked at Jamie. He was talking animatedly to Hugh and Louisa. She angled her slate and tapped a button to discreetly take a picture of the jumpsuit. Later she'd be able to enhance the picture and figure out if the clothes were really -

Her slate beeped. Selena looked down. Damn it - she'd forgotten about the two hour privacy lockout on all of their optics and recording software that Jamie had insisted on. Crap.

She took her hands off her slate and thought. There must be some way to do this. There - next to the jumpsuits was a belt with an indentation where it was usually buckled. She tried to memorize the scene - the door was that high, the belt was hung from a hook just below the top hinge, and the dent in the wear mark on the belt was just a few centimeters above the middle hinge.

Later she'd find a similar door, measure it, and see if she thought that those were Jamie's clothes, if this was Jamie's apartment...and, heck, she'd have to decide if this guy was actually "Jamie."

And if he wasn't Jamie, who was he?

Chapter 76

2064: First Class Homes and Offices construction site, level 6, Aristillus, Lunar Nearside

Captain Dewitt nodded thanks to Kaspar, who'd just helped him lift the equipment into position, and wiped the sweat off his forehead with the back of his hand.

Dewitt turned and addressed the class of aspiring electricians - a crowd of Nigerians, Mexicans, and Chinese who stood around them in a semicircle. "The take-away here is that you can lift the transformer into place by hand because of the lower gravity - but remember two things: lift with your backs, and once it gets moving it's going to keep moving. You've heard the momentum lecture before, and now you're hearing it again." He looked around. "Any questions on getting the transformer onto the brackets?"

There were none. "OK, I'm going to let Don walk you through hooking up to building circuits to the tunnel mains. Don?"

Dewitt stepped back and let Don take over the class.

He leaned against a half-built wall as he watched Don explain through a translator how to connect one building to three different power suppliers.

He shook his head. There was just so much that was bizarre about this mission. During the months of planning and training he'd been sure that the fractional gravity and living in underground tunnels would be the weird part.

In fact those things had become normal - or normal enough - pretty quickly. The gravity mattered when you were lifting heavy equipment, but for the most part it was just another background oddity. Living in tunnels wasn't nearly as strange as he'd expected. Between environmental tricks like the fact that the high arched tunnel ceilings almost imperceptibly changed color over the course of the day and the way the bushes and trees waved slightly in the artificial wind, Aristillus felt more like a dense suburb than the weird futuristic chrome-and-neon movie set he'd imagined.

No, the stuff that kept hitting him without warning and throwing him off balance was the small things. Like this, right here: First Class Homes and Offices was training its own electricians. Just taking random people off the street and training them! There were no job panels, no licensing boards, no government inspectors. No, Javier - the company president! - had just noticed that Dewitt worked well with some junior men and had paired him with Kaspar Osvaldo and asked them to teach a crop of wet-behind-the-ears newbs how to wire up office buildings.

It was the craziest sort of bullshit he could imagine. How did this whole place not just burn down? At that thought he looked up at the fire suppression system installed by another crew in this section of the tunnel a few days before. Installed by other newbs, inspected by some guys from another firm with some hand-held gizmos, and - bang! - done. With no government at all.

It was madness. Pure fucking madness.

"Something fascinating about the sprinklers, Neil?"

Dewitt looked down, slightly ashamed at being caught spacing out.

"Hey, Kaspar. Nah - just thinking." The older Mexican man nodded. Dewitt liked Kaspar. They'd met on the job, and had ended up eating their lunches together and even grabbing a drink after work once or twice. Dewitt's Special Forces team was tasked with making local contacts and doing research on Aristillus. Hanging with Kaspar fit into that mission perfectly, but there was more to it than that - Dewitt was becoming friends with Kaspar. Real friends.

"Thinking about what?"

Dewitt shrugged. "How crazy the whole system is here."

"Mmm. It is that." He paused. "On a different topic: Marianela told me that I should bring you over for dinner one night. And before you say anything, you should know that she will be deeply insulted unless you say 'yes.' Marianela has a temper like a - I'm not sure what you'd say in English. Anyway, my point is that you *have* to say yes." Kaspar grinned.

Neil smiled back. "Wouldn't want to get you in trouble. When and where?"

Chapter 77

2064: Trentham Court Apartments, Aristillus, Lunar Nearside

Hugh sat with Louisa and Allyson at the kitchen table. Allyson was so outraged that she was waving her hands around her head as she spoke. "Some of the Asians are smoking! Not just e-cigs, but tobacco! Not only are we all going to catch cancer, but with the oxygen and everything this entire place is going to catch fire!"

Louisa rolled her eyes and launched into an explanation of fire safety and oxygen. Hugh paid only partial attention. He wasn't sure which Louisa had more contempt for: Allyson's not understanding the science of fire, or the Chinese expats and their filthy habit.

Hugh looked away from the two arguing women to the empty chair where Selena usually sat, and sighed.

He'd been interested in Selena for over a year now, and she hasn't given even the slightest indication that she'd picked up on any of his hints. She wasn't even at the table with them now - she was off in her bedroom "working on a side project," whatever that meant.

What should he do to move things forward? Drop even more hints? Do something else? He was so tired of being alone, but after so long chasing Selena he was exhausted. He'd tried so hard, and gotten nothing.

The thought of giving up on Selena and concentrating on Allyson had been tickling him for weeks now. He'd even hinted to his mom about the idea, and she'd encouraged him. But maybe he should try a little harder? He'd been over this in his mind a hundred times before, and couldn't figure out what else he could do, but -

And then, with a sudden resolve that surprised him, he decided.

Screw it - he *was* going to give up on Selena. If after all the favors he'd done for her she still couldn't appreciate what a nice guy he was and how supportive he could be, then she wasn't that nice of a person herself. He was going to move on to someone who was worth his time. He took a deep breath and steeled himself.

Louisa looked over. "You have something to add?"

Hugh shook his head. "No."

The two women went back to discussing expats and tobacco.

Hugh looked at Allyson. He could do worse. She was cute, even if not quite as cute as Selena. And she was smart. Or at least smart-ish. He could figure out what to talk to her about. That had always confused him with Selena - he'd bring up one topic and she'd be interested, but then she'd go off on a tangent that left him tongue-tied, or he'd try to segue to a different topic and she'd get bored. With Allyson, though, he knew what her interests were: toxins, healthy food, locavorism, yoga - that sort of stuff. He could talk about that. Easy. He'd just have to start reading some different websites.

Yes, he could do this. And he would. Starting right damned now.

He listened to the conversation for a moment, then when Louisa briefly paused he leaned forward. "The other day, when I was out interviewing some recent arrivals, I saw one of the tunnel police yell at a smoker -"

Louisa scowled. "They're not police - they're just rent-a-thugs. Do you know how they punish tobacco use? They don't! They just give a written warning or escort the loser into a different tunnel. No fines, no anti-social-behavior letter, no housing classification downgrades. The 'law' here - " she spat the word " - is a joke. It's go no teeth at all! They'll never fix anyone's behavior."

Allyson nodded in agreement. "Back in college I think I only saw, like, two people smoke tobacco over all four years. The smoking rate has got to be a hundred times higher here."

Hugh felt his inner wonk come out. "We've got to be careful not to compare apples and oranges. All the smokers I've seen here have been African or Asian, so you've got to look at the smoking rates in their home countries -"

"That's a bit racist," Louisa said.

Hugh felt himself flush. Damn Louisa! He'd been trying to sound knowledgeable and assertive, and she'd cut him down, right in front of Allyson. He looked down. He just couldn't win.

Hugh mumbled "I've got to go to the bathroom" and stood. In his anger he overshot in the low gravity, and flopped awkwardly in the air for a second before landing and walking away.

Behind him Louisa said, "There's a story in here, if we frame smoking in the context of the class divide. I'm sure that smoking - and other air pollution - is much higher in the poorer neighborhoods. Tobacco smoke, greasy frying odors, oil, the smell of unwashed people. Ugh. The environmental racism is just sickening." Hugh could just imagine Louisa wrinkling her nose as she said this. Some times he wanted to punch her right on it when she sneered like that.

Hugh closed the bathroom door but could still hear Louisa talking. God. He really did want to punch her. She'd accused him of being racist, but he wasn't - he'd just been acknowledging the higher smoking rates in Africa and China. Louisa knew he was right. It was almost as if she just wanted to tear him down in front of whoever he was with.

A minute later he washed his hands and headed back to the kitchen. He was fed up with Louisa. She beat up on him all the time, and he was sick of it. He was going to confront her, and he was going to make her apologize. He was done with chasing Selena, and he was done taking crap from Louisa.

Today was a new beginning. The old Hugh was dead. Today was the start of a new Hugh.

He stalked out of the bathroom and came across Louisa and Allyson still talking about environmental racism.

He cleared his throat. "Louisa."

She held up a finger and snapped "Hang on!" and went back to her monologue.

"No, I will not hang on. I'm sick and tired -"

She turned to him. "What?"

He stammered for a second. "I'm sick and tired -" He swallowed. "You said I was racist."

"What?"

Crap. This wasn't going the way he'd intended. He started again. "When we were talking about smoking. You said I was racist. And I'm not."

She shrugged. "OK. Fine." Louisa turned and went back to talking about the evils of privatized atmosphere processing.

Hugh breathed out and crossed his arms. That wasn't the resolution he'd wanted.

His phone rang and he fished it out and looking at the screen. Wow. Hugh held it up. "Guys, check this out! Our newest video is on DC Minute!"

Louisa whirled on him. "What? How did they get it? We agreed that we'd hold a formal vote before -"

"It's a text from my mom. I sent my mom a rough cut, and she mentioned it on a DC Minute interview."

"So how did DC Minute get it?"

Hugh spread his hands. "She says she gave it to them."

"But we didn't-"

"Her text says she 'exploited serendipity.'" He stuck his chin out. The new Hugh wasn't going to take much more shit from Louisa. "Argue with her, if you want."

Louisa sighed and gave up.

Allyson turned to Hugh. "The video is live? Now?"

Hugh nodded. "Yeah."

Allyson stood and walked to the living room. Hugh followed her, and behind him he heard a chair scrape as Louisa stood.

Allyson picked up the remote and called up DC Minute on the wallscreen - and there was the icon for the clip! Allyson clicked it and the video began to roll.

Hugh sat on the couch as the DC Minute intro splash graphics rolled. He loved the intro. First one animated stick figure appeared, then another, then a third. Then the viewpoint pulled back until millions of figures spread across the North American map covered the screen. At that point the music started and the figures danced toward each other and began to merge until they finally coalesced into one much larger figure. The view zoomed in until the perfectly circular head of the figure filled the frame. Then, finally, as the music reached a crescendo, the white circle on a blue field morphed into the DC Minute logo.

The logo dissolved and the show's host, Melaine Roes, smiled at the camera.

Louisa sat. Hugh stole a glance at her. She seemed relaxed - no longer angry that the video had been released without a full vote.

"Hi, I'm Melaine Roes, and this is my guest, Senator Linda Haig, power broker extraordinaire and woman-about-town." She smiled and the camera cut to the senator, then back to Melaine. "Senator, we've got a few things to talk about, including the California Earthquake Recovery Act, the economy, the elections, and - of course - your recent charity ball co-hosted with Emilio-

X. But just before this interview started you told my production assistant Lezlie about some shocking new information... and your new plan to help the economy. Lezlie tells me that you've got some amazing footage?"

Hugh stole a glance at Allyson. She was staring intently at the wall screen. Hugh held his breath.

Just a few minutes ago he'd decided that he was going to be a new Hugh - and he'd decided that Allyson was worthy of the new Hugh. And now Allyson was leaning forward, paying attention to the video that he'd cut and that his mom had gotten on TV.

The universe was aligning for him.

He glanced again at Allyson's face, trying to read something there.

On the wallscreen, Melaine Roes said, "For years there've been stories of a moon colony filled with traitors. We've all heard one version or another in some of the seedier corners of the net. The core story is always the same - that tax rebels from the US and other PK protectorates have somehow fled to the moon, where they're evading national and international laws and violating UN regulations against private exploitation of public resources."

The camera cut to Hugh's mother, who was nodding gravely, and back to Melaine.

Selena walked into the room and sat - she must have heard the video.

"And it's been just rumors - there's never been video or hard facts from the credentialed media." She paused. "Until now." Melaine turned from the camera to Linda Haig. "Now, Senator, are we to understand that you've got actual evidence of the so-called 'lunar expats'... *and* that this plot somehow ties into our current national budget crisis?"

Selena had raised her eyebrows when Melaine had said that there'd never been video or hard facts, and she was right. These days pretty much everyone had seen blurry images of the colony taken from backyard telescopes or had seen that viral video of the Brazilian kids playing low-g basketball before the Internet Security Bureau had clamped down.

So, sure, everyone knew - but how else were Melaine and his mom going to play it? The official line - up until now, it seemed - was that Aristillus was a rumor, so of course they had to phrase it that way.

The camera cut to his mother. "Melaine, that's exactly right. Our official investigations are continuing, but thanks to some stunning investigative work by people close to me, we've got this breathtaking report. We've got evidence of thousands, or perhaps tens of thousands, of tax rebels and - as you say - traitors on the moon. These people are American citizens. They've benefited from government- provided education, health care, social programs, and more, and yet they've abandoned the country that has invested so very much in them. Not only have they taken their human capital, but it looks like they've taken trillions - tens of trillions - of New Dollars of equipment. Thousands of bulldozers and earth movers that could be used in the reconstruction of California are instead being used to mine gold. Gold, of all things! Lavish palaces are being created for the expat robber barons while their workers labor, crippled by lack of education, health care, and -"

The Senator continued, interrupted only by soft words of encouragement from Melaine, and then finally it was time. Melanie turned to the camera and introduced the video. And then it ran - the video footage that Hugh, Selena, Allyson, and Louisa had shot ran. Hugh could hardly believe it.

The sequence was just as he'd cut it - it started with a pan across the exterior of the colony. He'd shot that footage their first week here, when they'd been out watching Allan do his rock climbing stunt.

At the memory of Allan's death, Hugh's good mood faltered for a moment, but the video kept playing and he pushed the tragedy out of his mind.

On the screen their video continued. Hugh's voice-over set the stage, gave some of the background, and then the clip cut to Allyson sitting behind a desk. She looked good with her thick brunette hair and her expensive top - not to mention that her teeth gleamed and her eyes shone. Hugh smiled. Not only had he taken extra care to light her and frame her well when he shot it, but he'd worked overtime in post - every pixel was perfect.

On the screen Allyson smiled at the camera and spoke about the human impact of the illegal settlement. Her words flowed smoothly. Of course they did; he'd labored over the audio to remove several stutters and other missteps. He'd even gone a bit heavy with the Rephrase tool to rework her words to make the narrative flow more easily. Hugh snuck a look at Allyson, watching her as she watched herself on the screen. She seemed to like it - she was smiling - and then she looked at him. He quickly looked away, but he was pleased with himself. It was, he knew, some of his best work.

The segment ended with video – a stream of molten gold being poured from a crucible – while Louisa's voice-over described the "mountains" of gold being extracted from the deep lunar mines. Hugh smiled. The pour had been been just thirty grams - that was the most that the jeweler had had on hand - but thanks to a low camera angle, the right digital tools, and a sound track heavy with bass, it looked like a river.

The clip ended, and the screen cut back to Melaine Roes and Hugh's mother. The two talked for a minute about the gap in the federal budget, and how proper taxation of the moon colony and confiscation of the illegally owned gold could solve the problem.

And then his mother called him out by name, thanking him for "brave work" that he "...and his girlfriend, Allyson Chery, had done."

Hugh flushed. He'd talked to his mom about Allyson, but he'd never told her that they were actually dating.

Oh God. Oh God. Why had his mother done that?

He wanted to kill himself, he felt so stupid and embarrassed, but he had to apologize. He had to.

He forced himself to turn to Allyson, even though he couldn't stand the idea of her looking at him right now -

- and saw that she was looking at him and smiling.

Chapter 78

2064: Kaspar Osvaldo's home, Aristillus, Lunar Nearside

Dewitt took another bite of his spicy fish taco and washed it down with a sip of the beer. The beer - some local brand - was good, but Marianela's tacos were better. He let out an 'mmm' of appreciation and Marianela smiled at him from across the table.

Kaspar continued his story "...the work was good. It was supposed to be an office job, but J-12 series had problems with the arc-blowout nitrogen injectors, so I was out on the road a fair bit dealing with that. This was before the project got shut down, of course."

Dewitt knew to listen far more than he spoke, but also knew when to prod the conversation forward. The topic - Kaspar's job back on Earth before immigrating two years ago - wasn't the kind of information he'd been told to prioritize, but he knew from the field that nothing was useless. Learn about a man's work, learn about his family, and you learned about his culture, what he values, where his loyalties lay. And that, he knew, was as useful as mapping the lunar tunnels, or finding out the number of men under arms.

"This was part of the wind-power thing?"

Kaspar shook his head. "The entire windmill project was stupid. Wind comes and goes and unless you've got backup you end up causing major problems for the grid. So you've got to keep fossil fuel burning plants running the entire time, ready to hot swap in. No, this was part of a *good* project - the gravel trains."

"Gravel trains? I haven't heard about that."

Kaspar chuckled darkly. "No, of course not. It was a good idea, so it got canceled."

"What was it?"

"You know that power demand is lower at night than during the day?"

Dewitt took a sip of beer. "Of course."

"But power plants have optimal efficiency if they run at maximum output all the time. There's a mismatch. So the idea is that we use surplus power at night to drive really long trains full of gravel up mountains - we had a demo facility in the Rockies - then during the day, we run the trains downhill and use regenerative breaking to put power back into the grid."

"That works?"

"Of course it works. It's just potential energy."

"No, I get that. I mean, can you really store a noticeable amount of energy that way? Enough to make it worth doing?"

"Are you kidding? Haul a few million kilograms up a couple of kilometers and there's an *insane* amount of potential energy."

"So why did it get canceled?"

Kaspar shrugged. "Rumor was that battery manufacturers donated to a few key campaigns. I don't know if that's true or not, but the year after BuSuR shut down the gravel train project for 'safety reasons,' the battery manufacturers got a big R&D grant." The memory of it seemed to push Kaspar into a darker mood and he took another long pull from his bottle. "And after that, I ended up working on the merger of the Texas and Eastern Interconnections. Not that that went anywhere."

Dewitt speared a slice of avocado and ate it. "I remember that - politics, just like the gravel trains, right?"

Kaspar swallowed a bite of his own taco and shook his head. "Actually, you're wrong there. Separate subgrids actually makes good sense."

On the far side of the table Kaspar's son Ignacio interrupted. "Dad, can I have desert?"

"Not yet, mi pequeño. Let's all finish our dinners, first, si?"

"Aw."

Dewitt smiled; kids were the same everywhere. He turned back to Kaspar. "Really? I heard it was states-righters who resisted the merger."

Kaspar let out an exasperated sigh. "No, that's not true. It's simple engineering. Look, you inject power into the grid at one point and it's simple, but if you inject alternating current at multiple points it has to be in phase, because if it's out of phase you've got power plants fighting each other."

Dewitt nodded; he understood this so far.

"You can simulate this on a bench with a big copper bus bar, but when you scale up to the size of a continent you get problems."

"What problems?"

"Speed of light delays from one generator to another. It's impossible to put multiple generators in absolutely perfect phase, so you have one generator, say in Oregon, somewhat out of sync with another generator in Atlanta. You're turning electricity into heat. Not much, but every bit counts."

"So, wait. You're mentioning the speed of light, and I don't understand that. Is this that 'relativity' thing?"

"No, nothing that complicated. Imagine that - " Kaspar cleared the table in front of him, pushing salad bowls, platters, and salt shakers away to the exasperation of his wife and delight of his three kids who started pushing their own plates around.

Kaspar picked up flatware, stray croutons, and coffee saucers and laid out a model of power stations, power lines, and "packets" of power. The explanation went on for five minutes.

At the end Dewitt sat back and scratched his head. He actually understood some of the engineering issues involved. And weirder yet, it turned out that Texas having its own electrical grid was actually based on engineering principles. It wasn't just "racism and states rights" like he'd heard on DC Minute.

Chapter 79

2064: Morlock Engineering office, Aristillus, Lunar Nearside

Mike tapped the gavel against the block. "OK, good report." He didn't have to look down at his slate to know what was next. "Last item - militias. I'll go first. First Morlock is fully staffed up and kitted out. I've put one of my construction crew chiefs, Olusegun Mimiko, in charge. He's started training."

Trang Loc of Red Stripe raised his chin. "And how *is* training going?" Mike twisted his lips. "Not wonderfully. We've got a lot of people with officer experience, but we need good NCOs and we don't have them." He looked around. "Any other questions? No? Rob?"

Rob shook his head. "Not a lot to say. 40th is staffing up. About halfway done. Finding it a bit hard to make time for training -"

Only halfway staffed up? They needed to move quicker than that. "Rob, you've got to -"

Rob scowled. "I know. I know."

Mike waited for more, but that was apparently it. He turned to Mark Soldner.

Mark nodded. "We've had good turnout. The 10th Light Infantry is fully staffed, and we've had enough volunteers that we've decided to go ahead and form the 11th as well. We might even do the 12th, but no promises." Mike raised an eyebrow. After the disappointing report from Rob, this was good news.

Or was it? If Mark was still jockeying to put some sort of government in place in Aristillus - and he had to assume that he was - the fact that he was staffing up so quickly and efficiently was noteworthy. Was there any chance that Mark would try to establish a government by force? He tapped his stylus on the table. On the one hand Mark didn't seem like the kind of person who'd launch a revolution, or counter-coup, or whatever...but on the other hand, he *had* trashed Leon's Poker House.

Mike pursed his lip and scratched a quiet note on his pad to talk to Javier later.

Mark continued his report. "Training is going well. We've got several veterans in our ranks. We're mostly concentrating on in-tunnel scenarios, but we've done a few surface excursions." Mark turned to Mike. "My colonels have decided against using your Gargoyle rifle - they're going with something smaller."

Mike's nostrils flared. Even as he felt the annoyance rising he tried to fight it. Mark's choice of rifle was trivial, and he shouldn't feel personally invested, even if it was his design.

And then, before he realized it, he was saying, "That's a bad decision; we don't know what sort of armor the PKs are going to have -"

"My colonels were unanimous. Besides, we've already outfitted the troops."

"Hang on. You've got to -"

Javier interrupted. "Trang, why don't you tell us about the Red Stripe militia?" Mike bit back the rest of his rant to Mark Soldner. Focus. Focus.

Trang gave his status. Finally they reached Darren Hollins of Goldwater. "Darren?"

"My security team has been doing some drills."

"Really? I haven't seen any requests for using the range and training facilities -"

Darren shook his head. "We've been doing our training in our own tunnels. We've got some facilities set up that my people think are more realistic."

Mike blinked. "Uh - okay." He looked at Javier, who shrugged microscopically. Fine. Let it go. "Darren, I don't have a unit designation for you folks. '70th' is open. '90th' too, if you've got a preference."

"No offense, Mike, but I don't see a need for a numerical tag."

What? Darren wouldn't give his Goldwater units a unit number? What was that supposed to accomplish, other than making it harder to coordinate during battle? Still, there was no need to pick fights needlessly. "Uh, OK. Can you tell us how training on the integrated tactics system is going?"

Darren looked at Mike. "I might not have been a hundred percent clear. My security team is going its own way. They've got their own weapons. They've got their own tactics. We might want to do some interunit training together later, but for now, we're good."

Mike's eyebrows narrowed. Was this just some personal quirk...or was there a real problem here?

Mike looked at Javier, who was busy tapping notes on his slate - no guidance there. Mike looked at the ceiling for a moment and then shook his head. "OK, that wraps up the militia report. Anything else before we adjourn?"

There wasn't.

The meeting ended and Mike sat alone at the head of the table as everyone stood. Javier glad-handed CEOs and chatted with them as they filtered out.

Mark was staffing his militias faster than anyone else and Darren was refusing to coordinate with the rest of them.

He tapped his stylus against the table. Well, *shit*.

Chapter 80

2064: Senator Linda Haig's Office, Tester Senate Building

Jim Allabend sat across from senator Haig. Linda hadn't spoken in minutes, yet it would never occur to him to say that she was staring off into space; there was an intensity of focus about her that reminded him of a snake ready to strike...or a bearded Russian leaning unblinking over a chess board.

"We've got none of their communications?" she said suddenly.

He still didn't know why the senator had chosen him as her confidant, or her sparring partner, or whatever the hell he was supposed to be, but he'd long since decided that if that's what she wanted from him - and if that's what she was going to pay him so well for - he'd do the best job possible. And so he'd been spending almost every waking moment over the last months digging into all sorts of reports, calling contacts, and reading, reading, reading.

Almost to his own surprise, he had an answer to her question.

"A bit. As of two months ago the NSA identified several of the end points on Earth, what they call 'the black routers.' They've got taps and they read everything that comes through, but it's encrypted. That's not normally a problem, but just over the past few weeks we're seeing them moving away from the algorithms we've backdoored. Bottom line: we're reading only maybe a third of their coms to Earth."

"What about internal traffic in Aristillus?"

He shook his head. "The NSA guys tell me that it should've been a cakewalk...but it's not. Once they identified the black routers they should have been able to connect through them into the Aristillus networks and

- I think the word they used was 'poned' - everything, but -"

"But what?"

"Apparently all of the IT infrastructure is 'rooted.' Or it's supposed to be. But when our guys connect only parts of it respond to our keys. The analysts say that they know that expats have at least two fabs-"

"Fabs?"

"Factories where they make computer chips."

The senator nodded and Jim continued, "So it's possible that they're replacing their IT gear with stuff they've produced locally."

The senator shook her head in annoyance. "Bottom line, how much of their internal coms do we have?"

Jim shrugged. "Close enough to nothing that you might as well round it to zero."

The senator picked up a wood burl pen from her desk, a commemorative artifact of something or other, turned it over, and then looked up at him. "So we don't know if they know about Restivo's team yet?"

"The NSA has no idea. You've got Hugh there; can you ask him if it's in the Aristillus media?"

The senator shook her head. "No, it's not. But that doesn't mean that the Boardroom Group hasn't detected Restivo's people."

"And if they have -"

"My concern is if they *haven't*."

Jim looked down at his hands, then back up. "Before you go any further with this I have to ask -"

"I've made my decision."

Jim pursed his lips. She wanted him as an advisor and a confidant for this? He wouldn't be doing his duty if he didn't play devil's advocate. So, no, he wouldn't accept that answer. "Are you sure? The benefits are minimal and

- depending on how this plays out - the cost could be really, *really* high."

"The benefit isn't minimal. The president and her coalition are riding too high right now. They're not consulting with us on appointments, they're screwing up the budget. They've needed to suffer a humiliation - a very public one - for some time now. An opportunity like this doesn't come that often, and we need to seize it."

"Even if you're right, the risk -"

"Yes, there's risk. Politics is a high stakes game, Jim."

Jim scowled. This wasn't just regular politics - this was an all-in move. And Senator Haig wasn't just playing with her own stack. He was associated with her. If she tried this and it blew up in her face, the risk to him -

She must have read the concern on his face. "Don't worry, Jim, I'm not an idiot. This is all done through cut-outs. No one is ever going to know that I touched this, and even if it did blow up, *you* certainly aren't going to be touched by it."

Jim said nothing. Scandals had a way of growing explosively, and when they did, all sorts of people got thrown under the bus, even if they'd mostly been bystanders.

Finally he shrugged. The time for misgivings was over. *He* was the senator's advisor. He'd hitched his wagon to her star long ago, and it had always worked well - really well.

He sighed, the tension leaving his body. "OK, fine. But if you don't know if the expats already know about Restivo's men, how are you going to-"

Linda Haig pushed a button on the intercom. "Kerri, did you have any success with that research project?"

A tinny voice answered. "Yes, ma'am."

"What connection did you find?"

"I've got someone in the FEMA Hardened Infrastructure Department."

Senator Haig wrinkled her forehead. "FEMA?"

"Yes, ma'am. It actually makes sense, if you -"

"Never mind - just give me the contact information."

Linda let go of the button on the intercom, and then, for the first time in the meeting, she smiled at him. "Let's do this."

Jim took a deep breath. This was risky. Very risky. "I hope to hell you know what you're doing, Linda."

Chapter 81

2064: Morlock Engineering office, Aristillus, Lunar Nearside

Mike stared at the spreadsheet. The numbers were tight. The First Morlock Volunteers were costing more than he'd predicted. He'd finally stopped upgrading the design of the Gargoyle rifle, but there were a dozen other expenses that he hadn't thought of. Medical bills for twisted ankles and sprained shoulders, custom software for the spacesuits, fronting the majority of the money for retrofitting e-p-doors around the colony until the Group voted on levies, the outsourced design and construction of body armor...and to keep Mark's followers at bay, paid details guarding Leon's Poker House and two other facilities.

Mike tossed the stylus down on the desk, leaned back in his chair, rubbed his eyes, and groaned theatrically.

Wam looked up from his own slate.

Mike looked at him. "Fuck, Wam, I need a break." He checked the clock. "I'm going to grab lunch." Then, to preempt Wam from inviting himself along, he said "Take a break too, if you want. I've got a meeting after lunch, so it'll be a few hours before I'm back." Mike stood and headed for door.

Normally he'd go to his usual taqueria a few blocks over, but if he went to Borges' he'd get about two bites into his burrito before one of his employees, also out on lunch, approached him, sat down, and started talking about calibrating the tunnel orientation lasers, or had a question about suppliers for light panel brackets, or wanted to complain about a tunnel flooring installation sub contractor.

Mike reached the curb and swung one leg over his bike. What was that place Darcy had been talking about? He pulled out his phone and tapped at it, searching through the transcripts of their last few calls. Ah! That was it - the new southern Mexican fish place. Mike clicked over to a review site, read a bit and put away the phone. A moment later he had his helmet on and was twisting the throttle even before the chin plates had cinched themselves tight.

Less than a minute later he merged into a highway that entirely filled the class B tunnel. Mike checked his mirror, veered across two lanes, and heard the billing box beep as he accelerated.

As he rocketed past the +2.0 E stripe on the tunnel wall he remembered the last time he'd been here, six months ago. Then the stripe had been freshly painted, and the only traffic was haulers carrying laborers and spare parts in one direction and mining tailings in the other.

So much had changed in six months. Now the side tunnels were no longer sealed off with red modular caps, but were open and had traffic flowing in them, and the paved road continued well past where the construction zone had been.

At the +3.0 E stripe, his suspension compressed as he rolled over the slight bump of the floor track for the massive emergency pressure door.

And there was the side tunnel, his turn. Mike shifted to the right lane, braked hard, and leaned the bike over to take a side tunnel exit.

The nav box beeped in annoyance. Mike looked down - this was an Interstate road and the speed limit was thirty kilometers per hour. He slowed, reluctantly. Interstate was a bunch of pansies, and so were the tunnel owners who contracted with them.

As the bike crawled along Mike swiveled his head to check out the neighborhood, but his attention quickly turned to what he found really interesting - construction and infrastructure details. The overhead lighting looked like the newer Slimline Panels that he and Wam had been talking about. Who'd built out this space? Rob Wehrmann at General Tunnels? He made a mental note to give Rob a call and see what he thought of the panels.

The nav box beeped again, and Mike pulled his attention down from the ceiling and walls to ground level. There: Rio San Pedro was a few storefronts up on the right, wedged in between a furniture showroom and a shop selling scooters. Mike slowed and maneuvered around a woman unloading bolts of fabric from a delivery skid, waited for some kids playing soccer in the street to run past, and then pulled to the curb and cut the ignition.

Mike sat at the table and watched five young Mexican kids in the street playing a lopsided game of soccer, and then looked at his slate. The most recent Caterpillar and Komatsu catalogs were displayed side by side, but it was Tony Eiffong's margin notes that interested him most. Tony's menu of after-market mods had expanded recently. In addition to the dustproof bearing shields and ballast racks, there was a new strap-on automation package and an integration rack that promised to make conveyor belt loading easier. The conveyor belt solution was nice, but he'd already standardized on the Atlas system. The automation package, though - that was interesting. If it really cut labor costs by twenty percent like it claimed -

An older Mexican woman carrying a basket of tortillas and a large steaming bowl approached the table with a smile. Mike pushed his motorcycle helmet to one side and nodded his thanks. He loaded the vinegary mix of squid meat and vegetables into a tortilla and ate sloppily as he flipped through the catalog.

Tony's automation package said that it was designed for Caterpillar 825s - but it would work on the 827s, surely. He was flipping back a few pages to find pricing information when something about the conversation behind him tugged at his attention. Was it getting louder? He ignored the catalog and listened.

Were they talking about *him*? Yes, he heard his name.

He turned around in his chair.

At the table behind him four college-aged kids stared at him. A vague sense of recognition tickled. Had he met them before?

"Excuse me. Are you talking to me?"

The four kids were taken aback, but the one guy - a round-faced kid - looked at one of the girls at his table, then turned to Mike. "You're Mike Martin, aren't you?" Mike was used to being recognized - it seemed that almost everyone in Aristillus knew his picture and wanted to buy him a meal or a beer - but this didn't have the feel of one of those interactions.

Mike looked at the round-faced kid, trying to place him. The kid had a smirk, and Mike disliked him instantly. He caught the kid's eyes and held them. "What can I do for you?"

"Aren't you even going to ask who I am? Or am I just another nobody to you?"

Jesus. Who was this snot? He looked familiar - had Mike turned him down for a job or something? "If you've got a problem why don't you send an email, or make an appointment with my office?"

The kid again looked at the women next to him again, then pushed back his chair and stood. "You don't care who I am?"

Mike's eyes narrowed. There was something wrong about this situation. It wasn't dangerous, but it was off. Mike turned his chair so he wasn't looking awkwardly over his shoulder.

"Why don't you tell me your name, tell me what your beef is, and I'll put you in touch with the right person." He paused. "And after that, you let me get back to my lunch, OK?"

The kid walked around his table and advanced toward Mike. This joker wasn't going to get violent, was he? Mike's eyes took the kid in. He didn't seem the type - soft face, clean hands, and some kind of expensive pre-distressed jeans. If he'd been one of the African ex-mercs, Chinese toughs, or Texan roughnecks that usually ended up causing trouble in bars, Mike would be concerned - but this was just some idiot kid. Besides, it was early afternoon on a weekday, not 1am on a Friday night after payday.

But, Jesus, the kid seemed to be giving off the signs. Mike stood.

The kid clenched and released his hands, looked once over his shoulder at the girls, and then faced Mike and started speaking angrily. "I'm Hugh Haig! I'm not some laborer taking your money and bowing and scraping so you don't fire me. We're on to you. We know who you are, how you operate, and how you treat people. You can't treat me like some African peasant!"

Mike looked around. The restaurant was mostly empty and the kitchen staff - a man, the old woman who'd served him, and two young girls - were behind the counter. The man seemed to be dialing a phone. Good. Security would be here soon.

Mike turned to the kid. He'd said his name was Hugh something? That was familiar.

And then Mike placed him.

The name. The hostility. This was the senator's son, the one with the friend who'd killed himself in the spacesuit. The one who was doing those propaganda videos.

That's where he'd seen the faces. This jackass and his friends had been thorns in Mike's side for months now. He felt his fists clench.

Hugh advanced toward him. "You don't know who I am? Well, you've got that *luxury* -" he spat the word "- don't you? You don't need to interact with the little people, do you? People are just *resources* to you, to use up and throw away. You and your kind -".

The kid went on. Mike ignored his words and watched his hands. He was a few inches shorter than Mike, and even though he was few decades younger, he carried himself like he wasn't sure what his body was for. Mike wasn't a brawler, but he hit the squat cage once a week, jogged or worked the heavy bag now and then, and when he lost patience with the slowness of some junior member of his maintenance crew, he was known to demonstrate the right way to wrestle a chain hoist around a Komatsu's road wheel.

He wanted to just eat his lunch - but if he had to, he could take this kid.

He hoped he wouldn't have to, though. Darcy would be amused under a superficial layer of disapproval, but beating up some soft college kid wasn't exactly going to cover him in glory with Javier or the Boardroom Group. And then the inevitable pictures on the front page of Moonlist.ari and, hell, maybe even SurfaceMining.ari would just make him look like an idiot.

Mike made an effort to unclench his fists. He raised his hands in a placating gesture. "Look, kid -"

The three girls with Hugh were standing, and the one with dark curly hair and the blue glass frames turned and walked away, heading past Mike and probably toward the exit. Good, one less distraction. And maybe the one woman leaving in disgust would make the kid realize he was making an ass out of himself. Hugh was still ranting. And then, without warning, the little bastard spit at him. Almost instantly Mike responded with a strong shove to Hugh's sternum. The kid stumbled backward into some chairs. Mike fished his phone out of his pocket. "Security here, now!"

Mike turned back to Hugh. The kid was off balance and had a shocked look on his face. He was probably used to protesting campus offices or some shit, and had never realized that someone might fight back.

Hugh came storming back, telegraphing a right punch from a kilometer away. Mike tucked his chin, raised his left arm - phone still in hand -and blocked. Most of the punch landed on his forearm but the kid's fist skipped from there into Mike's left cheek. Weak. The kid was off balance and stumbled forward. Chest to chest now, Mike reached with his right, grabbed Hugh behind the neck and pulled his head down into his own chest. The kid realized his mistake and tried to backpedal out of the clinch, but Mike held tight and delivered an uppercut jab with his left. The phone crunched in his fist and plastic shards bit into his palm. Fuck! He dropped the pieces and punched the kid three more times, his fist landing on the side of the kid's face again and again.

Hugh kept trying to backpedal, but Mike held tight with his right. It was dirty boxing, but he had the kid tight, close, and neutralized. After a few more lefts Mike could let go, open up some distance, and wait for security to arrive.

Hugh, panicking, tried to claw Mike's face. Mike turned away and got another left punch in...and then their feet clattered into a spilled chair and they were falling. Hugh went over backward and Mike rode him down, landing on top.

On the ground Mike hit the kid twice more and then let go and pushed himself off, rising to his knees. He wanted to disengage and get some distance so that security -

There was a blur of motion and a mountain hit him.

What? He was on his back and his thoughts were radically disconnected.

Mike blinked. The lights overhead were bright.

What was - where was his soup? The girl with the blue eyeglass frames - she was holding the round yellow thing. What was the word? The round yellow thing. For your head. When you ride your ... thing.

Mike rolled to his stomach and tried to push himself to his knees. Tried. And failed. Legs weren't working. What?

He looked up. The kid - that kid - was scrambling away. And there - the girl with the blue glass frames again.

- and then everything fell apart.

Mike felt a hot surge of vomit from somewhere deep inside. His stomach convulsed and throat opened wide. The mess coursed out and hit the floor just centimeters from his face, splashing across his hands, bouncing back into his eyes.

His eyes stung.

His head hurt.

He fell face forward into the mess and passed out.

* * *

Louisa stood over Mike, his motorcycle helmet in one hand. Hugh scrambled to his feet. Louisa put the helmet down on a table, and then thought for a moment, grabbed a napkin, and quickly wiped the chin bar of the helmet where her fingerprints might be.

She turned to Hugh, Allyson, and Selena. "We should get out of here. His rent-a-thugs are probably already on the way."

Chapter 82

2064: Kaspar Osvaldo's home, Aristillus, Lunar Nearside

Dinner at Kaspar's house had turned into a standing weekly invite, so Captain Matthew Dewitt had a houseplant for Kaspar's wife Marianela in one hand and a bottle of wine tucked awkwardly under his opposite elbow as he approached the door. The bottle slipped when he rang the doorbell, but in the lunar gravity he easily grabbed it long before it hit the porch.

The door opened. "Neil, come in!"

From behind Kaspar, Dewitt heard a small high voice. "Neil! Neil!"

Kaspar looked down at his son as the boy tried to push past to greet the electrician. He raised his voice. "Ignacio!"

The boy bent his head in apology. "Sorry, papa. I know." After the briefest moment of contrition he looked back up, the excitement back on his face. "Hello, Señor Keenum!"

"Hey Ignacio." Dewitt handed the bottle to Kaspar and then reached into his pocket for the toy. "I brought something for you."

* * *

Dewitt pushed away the bowl, empty except for a few crumbs of apple pie crust and a wash of melted ice cream. He was stuffed.

Kaspar was a better contact than he'd realized when he'd first befriended him. He wasn't just an engineer; he was an astute observer, a history fanatic - and even a bit of a philosopher.

Kaspar continued "...each for a different reason. Take the Nigerians, for example. They were on the losing side of the civil war. A lot of them saw the atrocities close up, and those who didn't either knew someone who did, or lost family members, or were thrown out of their homes. They hate PKs - and American troops too."

Matthew couldn't argue against too vehemently without calling his cover into question, but he felt the need to push back, at least a bit. "That's not really fair. American troops were in Nigeria, sure, but they were doing ecological reclamation. They weren't involved in the torture camps."

Kaspar looked at him and shook his head sadly. "Come on now. Everyone knows that the Americans were funding, arming, and advising the PKs. Hell, there are videos of American advisors - not just with the PKs, but at the camps! Even the Wikipedia cabal eventually gave up on suppressing that."

Matthew sighed. He'd heard the rumors. He hadn't wanted to believe them. But he did.

"Even if American troops did participate in the debriefings, most of their work was-"

"Green projects? Is that supposed to be much better? How do you think a Nigerian feels when the farm that was in his family for a century is taken away and turned into a park? You should meet my friend Odunayo. Let him tell you about the Population Board moving his family from Markudi and into a relocation camp, and seeing his family church turned into a mosque." He shook his head. "No, the Nigerians here *hate* the PKs. They get along with individual Americans, but they hate the American government almost as much as the peakers."

Dewitt nodded. "So if the Nigerians hate the PKs -"

"And the American government."

Dewitt sighed inwardly. " - and the American government, then how do you think they'll react if there's an attempt at reunification?"

"Reunification?" Kaspar reacted disdainfully to the term. "You mean conquest?" He shook his head. "Have you visited any of the rifle clubs or militias? Mike Martin and Javier Borda thought that they were going to have to pay people to join, but once the Nigerians heard about it, the CEOs practically had to pay them to stay away. No - PKs taking over here is impossible. The Nigerians will fight to the last man."

Dewitt thought about this for a moment. "The Nigerians didn't fight the PKs much in Nigeria. What makes you think that when the chips are down here they'll fight?"

"In Nigeria the PKs disarmed everyone before they started their 'rebuilding.' The Naijas learned from that. Besides, you don't have typical Nigerians here in Aristillus. Do you know anything about chemistry? Fractional distillation?"

Dewitt shook his head.

"Forget the analogy; my point is that Aristillus is full of lunatics!" Kaspar laughed, as if he meant the word as a compliment. "Three devs out on the bell-curve? Try five - or six. No, the Naijas here aren't anything like the ones back on Earth." He shook his head. "Come to think of it, neither are the Mexicans, Americans, or Chinese."

At that point Marianela interrupted them. "You men go discuss politics somewhere else - we need to clean up here." On cue, Ignacio and his sisters stood and started clearing the table. Kaspar stood, bent and kissed his wife on the forehead.

"Neil, come with me to my study and I'll tell you everything you want to know about the demographics of Aristillus."

Chapter 83

2064: Johnson Clinic Health Center, Aristillus

Mike picked up the handheld device that controlled the painkiller in his IV drip.

The pharma industry here in Aristillus wasn't perfect. The best cancer and Alzheimer's meds still hadn't been duplicated, but that wasn't much worse than being stuck on Earth: without the right health categorization certificate, the average man on the street couldn't get advanced drugs there either. Pain killers, though - they were available.

Mike clicked for another dose of paracetamol.

On the wallscreen the security cam footage of the fight - the ambush, really - finished playing. Mike waved at the screen to close the first video and bring up the anthology of cell phone videos that had been uploaded to (:buzz-buzz:).ari. The top-voted one had a good angle - he could see the faces of all four of college-aged kids. He froze the playback.

Hugh Haig - son of Senator Linda Haig. The same asshole from that space-suit rental issue.

Mike waved the wallscreen off and looked at his slate on the bedside table. He was too groggy from painkillers to pick it up and read it again, but he'd already read the private investigator's report.

Hugh and his college friends had found a coyote in Valparaiso, Chile, had paid their fare in gold like everyone else, and had landed at Aristillus almost two months ago.

The PI's report went much deeper, though: online posts, college class choices, political volunteering and more. Prestigious credentials, family money, lots of ideas about how to run everything, a willingness - an eagerness, even - to tell other people how to live their lives. And no experience whatsoever of how the world actually worked.

Thinking about it caused him to shake his head - and the nausea from the fractured skull washed over him. Oh, Jesus. He closed his eyes and breathed deeply.

Eventually it passed.

What had happened to the kids? A century ago American kids had been anti-authoritarian. They'd protested the military draft, they did drugs - heck, in the 1960s they'd all but tried to overthrow the government. By the time he was a kid things had already changed: his own generation had been mostly conformists, eager to please teachers. And now? In the 2060s the kids were full-on authoritarians. Any time there was a proposal to cut regulation or spending they'd hold a flash mob rally and shut down whole neighborhoods for a day - or a week. God forbid anyone suggested that grad school stipends should be frozen for a year; they'd probably burn down a city - after asking the neighborhood rationing officer for enough gasoline and carbon credits to do it.

Mike paused and realized he wasn't being entirely fair. That sure seemed to describe the spoiled second-adolescence kids back on Earth, but he'd worked with a lot of good young men and women here in Aristillus. One of his best crew chiefs was - what? - 19? And the kid running the CNC firm that manufactured subassemblies for the Gargoyle rifles wasn't much older.

No, the twenty-something expats he knew didn't conform to the pattern. But then again, pretty much no one in Aristillus conformed to patterns. That's why they were here and not back on Earth with their carbon permits, their MGI checks, and all the rest.

Mike blinked. Jeez. He wasn't normally this ... whatever the word was. Wondering about things. Philosophical. He looked at the painkiller clicker in his left hand. How much had he taken?

His head still hurt and he clicked the remote again. One more would be fine.

Seriously, though - what was up with this generation? These kids - was it all part of some grand cycle? A century from now would kids be protesting against authority again? Or was this a permanent change? Maybe after society got rich enough kids stopped rebelling. There was a phrase. What was it? A boot stomping. Stomping in the face... no, wait... what did the kids call their sneakers? 'Yundangs' ? A yundang stomping somebody in the face. Who was it that was getting kicked in the face, though? He'd seen something on the wallscreen...

Mike's eyes closed.

* * *

Mike was awake again - and so was his headache. He reached for the clicker for the paracetamol, and then stopped. He'd had enough for a while.

On the wallscreen the newsclip ended. Mike gestured to play it again. The editing was well done. Deceitful, but well done. The spliced and overdubbed video of the bar fight made Mike look like the clear aggressor. Mike gritted his teeth...and immediately winced in pain. He blinked the tears away and focused on the video.

The artful cuts between camera angles hid the fact that Hugh had spit on him. There was some serious talent on display in the fake closeup of Mike's face. The colors were probably enhanced a bit too - Mike doubted that he turned that red. The straight arm to Hugh's chest was lovingly captured and the image froze while the narration continued "- in addition to an unpermitted construction company, Martin is also alleged to be involved in an illegal weapons manufacturing syndicate, and has recently been linked by sources to an armed gang running a protection scheme. The ominously named 'The Morlock Volunteers' references a fictional race of cannibals in a nineteenth century novel."

Mike paused the video. Despite himself he had to tip his hat to the editor.

And whatever its other flaws, the video made him look like a bit of a badass. He liked to tease Darcy that when she was out on a run she should worry about all the young women throwing themselves at him in her absence. While it wasn't a *complete* invention, there wasn't that much truth to it - but after this video there might be a bit more. He'd already gotten a few emails from guys at the gym about the clip.

His smile slowly slipped. The video was pure, over-the-top propaganda - but that didn't mean it wouldn't be effective back on Earth. Couple that with the new focus DC Minute was putting on the economy and the "economic crimes," and it was clear that the Earth governments were preparing the PR battlespace for the coming war.

And what were the good guys doing? Nothing. The pro-freedom side had to start punching back, and punching hard. Mike made a note on his slate to check to see how many submissions there were for the Boardroom Group's journalism and marketing prizes. That done, he brought up the dossiers of the college kids. Yes, he was obsessing. Yes, he knew that.

Hugh Haig. Tufts grad. Mom was Maryland senator Linda Haig. Hugh seemed like a general middle-of-the-pack fuck-up: campus involvement in Communities First, Young Internationalists, Just Agriculture, the usual. No criminal record, no real jobs - just internships at NGOs and government offices.

Allyson Chery. Campus involvement with Just Agriculture and Beehives Not Bombs. A volunteer on organic farms, arrested three times for protesting and trespassing at fertilizer companies. He flipped to her college transcript and scanned it. Not the sharpest chisel in the tool chest.

Louisa Teer. Not much on paper - almost nothing, really. Zero documented involvement with any group other than Young Journalists. Interviews with acquaintances painted her as smart - and radical. She'd never been arrested. Mike suspected that that wasn't because of lack of radicalism or commitment but because she was smarter than the average protestor. He made a few marks on the slate; he wanted more information on her.

And finally, Selena Hargraves. This one was a bit of a mystery. She'd been active in the some of the same student and political groups as the others in her first two years but had drifted away. She stood out from the rest of them in another way: she'd worked two different summer jobs. Real jobs, not volunteer work.

He thought about that while he looked at her picture. No arrests. Real jobs.

Did this mean that she was the moderate of the group? Or did it mean that she was even smarter than Louisa - smart enough not to establish a paper trail?

Mike made another note. PR was another front in the war and he needed intel.

Chapter 84

2064: Icarus Crater, Lunar Farside

The oak trees were thick and dense, the way they had been for the last two days. John turned sideways to squeeze between two of them and then, after straightening again, saw that the dirt trail petered out in fallen leaves and needles just a few meters further on.

He cursed, switched off the forest overlay, and squinted at the sudden glare. The oak trees were gone, replaced with boulders - and where the dirt path had petered out in the virtual world, the real world had a steep rill of gravel and stones. John turned back the way he came and the glare from the early morning sun reflecting off the landscape was just as bad.

Sunrise days were the worst. Even with the normal filters, the glare was constant, and the long shadows from every rock and bump in the land made walking tricky. In a day the sun would be high enough so it wouldn't be as bad. He knew his mood would improve without the constant irritations of the poor lighting. Of course, even with the glare gone he'd still be in a foul mood. Gamma and the Earth hostilities weighed heavily on his mind, trading places as the biggest concern from time to time, but never leaving him at ease.

It was going to be good to get back to Aristillus, where he could talk to Mike without fear of eavesdropping. He'd call again tomorrow and try to get through to Darcy.

But that was tomorrow - today he was hiking. This path was a dead end, and he needed a new one. Where were the Dogs anyway? He craned his head but didn't see them anywhere. Ah, there they were: they'd taken a parallel path and were downhill to his right. He squeezed between two boulders, slipped on some scree, caught himself after a short slide, and picked a route down the slope.

Ahead of him the Dogs apparently didn't share his frustration with the treacherous footing - they were running in circles and wagging their tails.

There were advantages to being a quadruped.

But what were they so worked up about?

John switched to their channel.

"That's the last of them - check the bodies for loot!"

He sighed. The MMORPG.

Should he check it out? The real world was nothing but glare and rocks, and the 'Pacific Northwest' overlay was getting a bit old.

Why not?

He clicked over and his screen was covered with pop ups. It took ten seconds to dismiss the dozens of alerts about status, health, and the offers to "level up" by payment of elven amulets, Dwarfish gold, or Bitcoin.

And then, after they were gone, he looked around. He was standing in a dripping cancerous forest. Where the Dogs had been were now short cloaked creatures with swords. John looked at them curiously and laughed. Big feet, fur-covered snouts. And at their feet - four dead creatures, lightly armored in leather, green-skinned, and tusked.

To his right the cargo mules were replaced by ponies loaded down with saddle bags and cargo.

Duncan pinged him.

"John, you've logged in!"

"Don't get excited; I'm just looking," John said. "I can't believe I'm asking this, but what exactly is this all about?"

"We're a band of Hobbits. Well, not real Hobbits, because Max says that pretending to be primates is demeaning. So Rex hacked some race stats and made HobDogs. Oh, but Blue isn't a HobDog; he's a thousand-year-old shape-shifting wizard named Snorri the Grey. He just *looks* like a HobDog. Right now we're crossing Mirkwood -"

John cut him off. "I get it. So the four of you are running around fighting simulated monsters?"

"Not just us - you too! We've had you played by an NPCbot, but now that you're in -"

"Wait. Hang on. I'm not 'in'; I'm just looking."

Duncan ignored the objection and raced on. "You're AraJohn, a descendant of an ancient king, but your second cousin is destined to the throne. But, anyway, we can get into the details later. Right now we just killed a band of half-orcs, but there could be more nearby, so you should be on your guard."

John looked at the dead bodies. "These computer-generated monsters are orcs?"

"Half-orcs. And they're not computer-generated. Well, I mean, *some* of the monsters are NPCs, but now that the satellites are back up, most of them are PCs."

"English, Duncan."

"Most of the monsters - and most of the allies, and the townspeople, and the elves - are player characters."

John gave Duncan a quizzical look. "I still don't understand what you're talking about."

"Most of them are played by other people."

John raised his eyebrows. "Other people? Are you telling me that folks back at *Aristillus* are plugged into this game?"

"A few - but mostly it's Earth players."

John blinked. "People on Earth are volunteering to run characters in your game?"

"Oh, no. That'd be crazy."

John exhaled and smiled. There. Finally. At least a *small* bit of this conversation made sense.

Duncan continued, "We charge them!"

John blinked. "You - wait. You're *charging* people to pretend to be monsters that appear only in your helmets? On the moon?" He paused. "People *pay* for that?"

"Why would we let them play for free if we can charge them?"

John made it to the bottom of the slope and caught up with the Dogs, then walked with them in silence for a few minutes. "How much?"

"How much do we charge them? I don't know what it's at right now. The price fluctuates. It's an auction."

"Why, with all the online games back on Earth, is anyone paying to play a game that has you four dancing around on the moon?"

Duncan shrugged. "Novelty, I guess. Well, and, of course, the fact that we might actually die."

John's eyebrows rose. "You mean your characters might die in the game?"

John saw Duncan roll his eyes over the in-helmet camera. The gesture didn't have quite the same effect without a human's white sclera to accentuate the movement, but it still conveyed a meaning. "I think it's the fact that we might actually die out here on the surface that has the fans excited."

John digested that for a moment, then went back to an earlier question. "I understand that the price fluctuates, but - roughly - how much are you making? Should I be charging you for my guide services out here?" John smiled at his joke.

"A few thousand -"

John swore in surprise.

" - per month, but we're making most of our money off of the betting market."

"Betting what? What are you talking-"

"Hey, John, hang on. There are more half-orcs coming and Max says that Blue - I mean, Snorri the Grey - is about to cast a spell. I've got to get in on this combat or I get docked shares. We'll talk later, okay?"

John's mouth opened and closed helplessly. Thousands? Per month? Betting markets? Auctions.

He shook his head.

It was going to be good to get back to Aristillus.

Chapter 85

2064: Meyer's Park, Aristillus, Lunar Nearside

Hugh shot video of the park.

At his elbow Louisa scolded him. "To the left - make sure to get that nanny playing with those kids. That highlights the class angle."

"I got it."

"Your framing is bad. Get some more."

Hugh sighed and shot another minute of footage, tracking the white kids as they ran off to splash in a wading pool with a Chinese girl and two Nigerian boys.

Louisa waved her hand. "Cut. This segment is on privilege and economic exploitation; let's not complicate it with extraneous details."

Hugh lowered the three-D rig. "What else do we want?"

Louisa looked around, then shrugged. "I think we've got enough for this segment."

Selena and Allyson had been talking nearby and approached now that the filming was done. Selena looked at her phone. "We've got another three hours left on our half-day pass. I want to go sit on the grass for a bit."

Louisa said, "We've got all the footage we need."

"I still want to sit on the grass." Selena turned and walked toward the grass. "Allyson, are you in?"

Hugh looked at Allyson, who stood indecisive.

He knew her answer before she said it. "I'd like to, but how do we know that it doesn't have pesticides or -"

Hugh cut in. "Go ahead, sweetie. I saw a sign at the gate; it said it's organic."

Allyson smiled. "Thanks!" She ran to join Selena who was already a sitting near a copse of young trees. Hugh joined them, sitting next to Allyson and nestling his head in her lap. He sighed contentedly.

Louisa stalked over to them and looked down. "This is a waste of time. There are so many other stories we could be researching right now."

Hugh looked at Louisa and said nothing. Neither did either of the others.

Louisa crossed her arms in frustration, and then sat. A moment later she pulled out her pad and began working, sparing a moment now and then to shoot dour looks at the other three.

Hugh saw her doing it but didn't care. Life was good. He let his eyes drift over the clouds, sky, and sun above. The illusion wasn't perfect - you could see hints of outlines of duct work and cables if you knew where to look - but it was good.

Selena cleared her throat. "Guys, there's something I want to bring up. It's... " she paused. "It's going to sound weird."

Hugh twisted his head in Allyson's lap. "What is it?"

"I've been doing some research on Jamie."

"Jamie Matteo? The labor organizer?" Louisa said.

Selena nodded. "Yes. But I don't think he's a labor organizer."

"What are you talking about? We've got videos from protests. He's given us great leads about the Boardroom Group." Louisa puffed herself up. "It's pretty disrespectful of you to suggest-"

"His real name is George White. He's an ex-cop from Chicago. He fled an indictment there and he's been a private investigator in Aristillus for two years now. He's playing us."

"What? That's impossible!"

Selena took a moment to gather herself. "It is possible. I've got proof. And I've also got proof that he's working for Leroy Fournier."

Hugh scratched his head. Leroy Fournier? He'd heard that name. One of the tunneling guys, right? Not part of Mike Martin's cabal - one of the good guys.

Selena pushed on. "You know all this information he's been feeding us information about Mike Martin and his friends? Mike and Leroy are business competitors. They *hate* each other. It's on SurfaceMining.ari, punditdome.ari, all over."

Hugh sat up, pulling his head out of Allyson's lap. "Wait a second. Why would Leroy -"

Selena shook her head sadly. "This isn't about Jamie - George - helping people. This is about Leroy jockeying for position against a business rival."

Hugh frowned. "This must be a mistake. I bet that there are two George Whites. Or two Jamies. Or whatever."

"I've got evidence. It's the same guy."

Hugh said, "Your theory is that Leroy is paying someone named George White to pretend to be Jamie - just to score some status points? That makes no sense."

Selena furrowed her brow, then shrugged. "OK, never mind."

Chapter 86

2064: First Class Homes and Offices main office

Mike knocked on the door and walked in without being invited. Javier looked up from his desk. "Mike! You're out!" He stood. "How are you doing?"

Mike touched his bandaged head gingerly. "Better than I was. I'm off the pain meds and the headaches are almost gone. What've I missed while I've been away?"

"You've gotten all the minutes of the meetings."

"Yeah, but aside from the paperwork, how is -"

One corner of Javier's lip turned up. "The meetings been running smoothly given that you haven't been there to disrupt them - is that what you're asking?"

Mike smiled. "Ha ha. Seriously though, we need to talk. Have you been watching the Earth media?"

Javier turned serious and nodded. "I have."

"Do you -"

"Yeah, I sense it too. We need to get a drink."

Mike held a hand up. "Jesus, no. After this skull crack I don't want to drink again for months."

"You don't need to drink, you just need to *get* a drink. In public. We need to show people that you're on your feet again."

"Oh, God, no. If there's one thing I don't want to deal with right now it's people."

"And yet, you have to."

Mike stared at Javier for a long moment. No, he wasn't joking.

"Do I really have to?"

"You really do."

Mike sighed. "OK, let me get this off." He reached up for his bandage.

"No! The bandage stays on. That's half the point." Javier checked his slate. "Most of the manufacturing sector's first shift is just getting off now. If we hurry we'll catch it when it's good and crowded."

Mike groaned. "I hate crowds, Jave."

"Do you want to be a leader or not?"

"I've told you a dozen times: no, I don't."

Javier shrugged. "And I still don't care. Now come on, let's go motivate the troops and win the PR war."

Chapter 87

2064: Trentham Court Apartments, Aristillus, Lunar Nearside

Hugh looked at the empty iced coffee cup and crumpled donut bag on the kitchen counter and felt a wave of disgust. Skipping a real breakfast and working on the story with Louisa had seemed like a good idea at the time, but now he not only was jittery and on edge but also felt a familiar self-loathing. He took the trash and sorted it in the recycling bins, looked at it, and pushed the donut bag further down, hiding it under other materials.

Maybe some real food instead of this sugary crap would help. "Louisa, I'm thinking about grabbing an early lunch - you want in?"

Louisa shook her head silently, intent on the displays in front of her. Ever since Selena had told them that she had evidence that Jamie Matteo was really George White, Louisa had been even pissier than usual.

Hugh looked around the apartment. With Selena and Allyson off shopping, it was just him. He shrugged and grabbed his jacket. Then, after a moment of thought, he grabbed a hat too. Louisa might be right about Mike Martin's rent-a-thugs hunting them. He pulled the brim low over his eyes before stepping out of the apartment.

The nearest jitney stop was a block away. Hugh decided to walk it instead of calling in for a pickup - a bit of exercise might burn off some of his sour lethargy. He looked at the apartments and storefronts as he walked. To say that Aristillus was an urban design failure was an understatement: there was *no* design. No regulation, no new urbanism, nothing. The walls of the tunnels had buildings in every style and no style at all thrown up next to each other. The advertising - both meat-space billboards and data tags - was gaudy and unchecked.

Hugh reached the bus stop. The display said that he had a seven minute minute wait until the Three Apples jitney, or five for the Gman jitney.

The two restaurants right next to the jitney stop were a good example of the lack of regulation. The coffee shop was set back from the sidewalk and had concrete chess and Go tables in its little courtyard. And then, right next to it, the sushi place extended five meters further out, ending right at the sidewalk, and had an entirely different design. Who put a sushi place next to a coffee place? It made no sense. And aesthetically, there was no thematic unity, no design to tie it all together.

That said, it was nice to have June Bug Coffee right down the block from their apartment, and more than once they'd all decided, after a few hours of sitting and drinking coffee, to grab an early dinner at Edo Sushi next door. But still, even if both things were good, there was no *synergy*. No *plan*.

Hugh was distracted from his thoughts when the Kasmir jitney pulled up. Six passengers got off and the vehicle accelerated away. Four walked away but two nodded to Hugh and settled in to wait for the Gman jitney with him.

Hugh turned his attention back to the June Bug and Edo and shook his head. A better design would involve a lot of changes: a shared courtyard instead of just one asymmetrical one, unified signage, some thought to color scheme, a good plan as to what businesses fit together well, access to a well-planned light rail system -

The two other passengers stood from the bench. Hugh turned and saw that the Gman jitney was arriving. He swiped his Lunar Escrow and Trade debit card and stepped on, and then reached for one of the grab bars as the jitney accelerated away from the curb.

He looked out the window as Trentham Apartments, June Bug, Edo, and all the other neighborhood fixtures disappeared behind him. They'd had a lot of good times there. He had to admit that the Triangle district was a pretty decent place to rent an apartment. It was pure dumb luck, given the lack of oversight, but it was true.

It wasn't as cool as the Conveyor Belt district, of course. That's where *he* had wanted to get an apartment. The 'CB' was just two blocks long by three wide, but it had two nightclubs - with a third and a fourth opening soon, jam spaces that the local bands performed in, and even a small gallery. *Very* hip. Hugh grimaced and looked down at the floor of the jitney as he remembered Louisa's response to his idea - she'd said that he had "pathetically fallen for the seductive bourgeoisie enticements of a separatist classist regime."

He flushed a little, and tried to put it out of mind. Lunch. Lunch would be good. He'd found Benue River, a Nigerian place, through the Cowen Wiki, and over the past few weeks it had become his new favorite.

Four minutes later he signaled for a stop and hopped off at the restaurant. When he stepped onto the sidewalk, though, he looked at the storefront and was confused. Where the door should be was a ribbed sheet of plastic plywood. He looked to the left and right and then saw that since he'd last been here a few days ago the restaurant had started an expansion.

Hugh shook his head. There was so much construction, so many people arriving, so much of everything that it was hard to keep up with the changes. It was sort of exciting, really.

But he knew that excitement came at a price. With no Bureau of Industrial Planning and no Construction Jobs Preservation Act everyone was free to use robot-assisted labor. Like right there: one guy was running a bricklaying machine and building a new outdoor patio for the restaurant. There's no way that would happen on Earth.

Hugh shook his head. It was so simple, and yet these expats were so dense they couldn't see the truth right in front of their noses: automation meant less employment, which meant lower construction prices, which meant a wasteful amount of construction. Things changed in Aristillus, all the time, for no reason. What was so wrong with Benue River last week, when it was smaller?

Hugh pushed through the glass front door. Inside he saw that the dining area held new tables, the walls were painted, and the stainless steel counter had been extended and moved a few meters. One thing hadn't changed, though: Ewoma was still behind the counter. Louisa had taken a dislike to her, and to the whole restaurant, but Hugh liked her - she was a cute and enthusiastic kid with a huge smile. She should be in school, and not working here, but that was her parents' fault, not hers, so he was always nice to her.

He walked up to the counter. "Hey, Ewoma."

Ewoma looked at him oddly for a moment, then gave him a smile. Not as enthusiastic as usual, but it was there. She must be having a bad day.

"What's new?"

"Well, I saw on the net that you and your friends released a new video about how bad Aristillus is. And I read that the Earth governments destroyed Gamma's satellites again."

"Yeah, I -." He shifted uncomfortably. "Uh... what've you been up to?"

"We finished the expansion. I helped lay out the new seating area, and the new catering kitchen."

Hugh nodded. "It looks good. I like the colors."

Ewoma smiled curtly. "I picked them. Also, I did some of the tile at the transition. The robots can't do that yet, because the sub-floor is uneven."

Hugh looked. "Tile laying? You told me you want to run a business some day. Shouldn't you be studying economics and planning and stuff? You don't need to get your hands dirty with grunt work."

Ewoma's smile cooled another degree toward absolute zero. "I had fun doing it. I got to work with my dad." She fixed him with her gaze. "What do you want for lunch?"

Jeez. She was in a mood. "Uh... I'll have fried plantains and the beef-and-spinach stew."

"We're out of the stew, but Yinka is making some right now if you want to wait for a minute."

"Sure. I probably shouldn't even be eating the beef, though."

Ewoma failed to ask the question, so Hugh prompted her. "You know. For the obvious reasons..."

Ewoma sighed. "Like?"

"Did you know that it takes sixteen kilos of grain to raise just one kilo of meat? If there's a quarter of a kilo of beef in the stew, then that could have been enough to feed sixteen people on grain."

"If you say so." She looked over her shoulder. "Yinka, is the stew ready yet?"

"Soon!"

Ewoma looked back at him. "There's enough beef for everyone, so what's the problem?"

Hugh smiled sadly. Ewoma was homeschooled and she was ignorant of everything she should be learning in Ecology class. It was an opportunity for him to do his good deed for the day, though. "Well, *is* there enough meat to go around? Not everyone would say yes. You have to look at the bigger picture." He paused thoughtfully. "You know, you should consider carrying some vegetarian or vegan stews. More sustainable."

"We do offer vegetarian stews." Ewoma's smile was entirely gone. "You chose the beef."

Hugh flushed and tried to formulate a response, but before he had one Ewoma grabbed a towel and stepped away from the counter, pushing past the big quiet guy who was always manning the fryer.

Hugh followed down his side of the counter. "Hey, Ewoma, wait a second." She looked up from buffing the refrigerator. "Here's the point - there's only so much land you can grow food on. I'm just saying that maybe we - all of us, as a *culture* - should think through the moral aspects of how we allocate that land. Maybe less meat and more vegetables are the right way to divide the pie? I mean, I'm not blaming you." He paused. "And I'm not blaming me either. It's an emergent phenomena - culture, the market economy, whatever."

Hugh paused, waiting for a response. Ewoma looked at him and said nothing. He coughed. "They're not making more farm land, you know."

"They are, actually. We buy beef from Camanez Beef and Pork, and Hector's expanded his farm tunnels twice already this year."

Damn it! Why was he coming off like such an idiot? His point was so simple, and yet he couldn't get it out. This was so simple that everyone back home understood it, and yet Ewoma had him tied in knots. He shook his head and gave up. "Well, uh... on the bright side, at least I'm eating local, right?"

Ewoma smiled perfunctorily. A bell rang behind her and she turned to the kitchen pass-through where Yinka was sliding a bowl of beef stew across to her. She took it, turned, and put it on Hugh's tray before turning away again.

Hugh shook his head at the unfairness of it all. How had he gotten so tangled in rhetorical tricks?

He sighed and picked up his tray, and walked away from the counter to the new section of the restaurant. He found a table facing away from the counter and sat.

Hugh suddenly realized: Ewoma wasn't pissed about land use or eating meat; it was their videos that had set her off. She'd said as much at the beginning. Then another thought occurred to him: If Ewoma was this upset, might other expats be angry? Even violent?

He realized he was facing out of the restaurant, toward the glass window that fronted on the street. He shrunk in his chair and pulled his hat lower. And then he realized he needed to call Louisa, Allyson, and Selena and tell them about the mood in the street. Maybe they should start doing more take-out.

* * *

Ewoma walked into kitchen, pulled out her phone, and dialed.

"Is this Mike Martin? Mr. Martin, it's Ewoma. From Benue River. The restaurant."

"I've got a question. You know in your feed this morning you said you had a bounty out for finding that Hugh guy and his friends? Was that serious or what it a joke?"

Ewoma stepped back to let one of the kitchen workers slide past her. "Why? Because he's in the restaurant right now."

Chapter 88

2064: Homestyle Apartments, Aristillus, Lunar Nearside

Dewitt put the jammer on the table and turned it on.

Sergeant Kindig pointed to it. "I heard from one of the guys at work that those don't work here."

"Don't work? What are you talking about?"

"The guy said that jammers aren't really jammers."

Lummus gave him a look. "The fuck does that mean?"

Kindig shrugged. "He said that modern jammers don't *block* radio waves and stuff, what they do is broadcast a computer command that tells other devices that they don't have permission to take video or record audio or whatever."

"And, what, being on the moon stops that? Sounds like an urban myth to me. Cars, guns, computers: everything that works on Earth works here in Aristillus. Shit, most of it even works out on the surface in vacuum."

Kindig shrugged. "I'm not gonna argue it, I'm just telling you what he said. And what he said is that jammers broadcast a command that tells other devices to shut down, but the chip factories on Aristillus are illegal and don't build that command in. So jammers work on legal devices built on Earth, but they don't do shit on stuff built up here."

Matt frowned. That actually made a weird sort of sense. Should he detail one of his men to look into it?

He thought for a moment. No. Even if it was true, what could they do about it? And besides, the need for stealth was almost over - this would all be over, one way or another, soon enough.

"Alright, good information. I'll take it under advisement. Now, guys, I've got to talk to you about something serious."

Sanderfur met his eyes. "Good, because I've got to bring up serious shit too."

Chapter 89

2064: Icarus Crater, Lunar Farside

John pulled himself to the top of the boulder, swung one knee up, then stood. They'd been hiking the flat plain of the crater floor for the last few hours and he wanted some variety - even clambering up the side of the RV-sized rock was a relief. He shielded the sun from his faceplate with one gloved hand and looked ahead. More of the same for a couple of kilometers, all the way to the crater wall. He turned around and picked out the Dogs half a klick back. Three of them were capering around, obviously still playing their game, while one walked alongside. John turned his head up. "Gamma, still with us?"

"Yes, John. Are you interested in resuming our last conversation?"

"Sure."

"We were talking about *The Moon is a Harsh Mistress*."

"Right. You were telling me that railguns were -"

Max interrupted. "What are you two talking about?"

"Railguns. Aren't you busy playing your game?"

"No, I got hit in the head by an orc. I'm unconscious until I make a health save."

John grinned and gave in to the urge to needle Max a bit. "So you're not fighting? What are you, some sort of pacifist?"

Max snarled. "I'm fighting. I'm just knocked out for a little bit."

John put up his hands. "Woah. OK, just joking." Then he realized that he was standing hundreds of meters away from Max. He put his hands down.

Max harrumphed then asked, "So, Gamma, what were you saying about railguns?"

"I was saying that railguns are theoretically a useful technology and that I have constructed one at my facility at Sinus Lunicus."

"Useful for what?" John asked.

"Launching satellites. Launching frozen volatiles from the rings of Saturn for terraforming the inner planets. Ejecting surplus atmospheric mass from Venus -"

John waved his hand. "Enough science fiction."

"But I also assert that railguns as a tool for military action against Earth governments -"

Max growled in approval. "Attacking the groundhogs? Finally! Let's drop some rocks on their heads. I've got the first target: BuSuR headquarters."

"No. I was saying that using railguns as a tool for military action against Earth governments is counterproductive."

"What! Why?"

John could hear the disappointment in Max's voice - and the anger.

"Because it won't accomplish anything useful."

Max sneered, "You think that violence never solved anything, is that it?"

"I know from your BookShare records that you've been reading a lot of the same science fiction as John has, and more besides. If I may hazard a guess, you're looking for an opportunity to use a Heinlein quote, aren't you?"

Max harrumphed. "Never mind."

"My model suggests that the quote you were thinking of using was this: 'Anyone who clings to the historically untrue - and thoroughly immoral - doctrine that violence never solves anything I would advise to conjure up the ghosts of Napoleon Bonaparte and the Duke of Wellington and let them debate it. The ghost of Hitler would referee. Violence, naked force, has settled more

455

issues in history than has any other factor; and the contrary opinion is wishful thinking at its worst. Breeds that forget this basic truth have always paid for it with their lives and their freedoms.' The quote comes from Heinlein's Starship Troopers, page seventy-two in the October 1959 issue of The Magazine of Fantasy and Science Fiction. It is spoken by Lieutenant Colonel Jean V. Dubois, retired."

Max scowled. "Yes. That's my point. The dog killers picked this fight - burning your sats, hijacking ships, killing people at Aristillus - and we should be fighting back. And you should help us. And if you've already got a railgun then we should start now!"

"We are arguing at cross purposes, Max. You suggest that violence sometimes solves things. I do not disagree. My point is merely that it would be incorrect to model an attack against Earth governments as a strictly military endeavor. I assert that it is more useful to model Earth society and government with a much finer granularity, paying specific attention to factions and demographics. I suggest that a military attack would be perceived as an attack on an entire society. If you look at the Japanese attack on Pearl Harbor of 1941 or the Al Qaida attacks of 2001 you will note that these transformed the attitudes of populations previously reluctant to engage in war. When the Sudan Alliance nuked Baltimore the populace supported the nuclear counterstrikes and the Emergency Powers Act, even though just a month before the US government had the lowest approval ratings -"

"So you're afraid of war. Just like John."

"I'm not afraid of war, Max." John stared at Max through the in helmet display. Max stared back at him defiantly. "I'm the only one in this conversation who's ever fought, so watch your mouth."

Max held the stare for a moment, then looked away. John waited. Max looked at him a second time and John held the stare, and this time when Max broke he didn't just look to one side but turned his eyes to the ground.

John checked the display - eighteen hours until he could call Darcy and arrange a pickup. The stress was eating at him, and he didn't have the reserves to tolerate Max questioning his bravery.

Gamma went on as if nothing had happened - and perhaps, lost in his models and simulations, he didn't realize anything had. "Max, I do not believe that I am 'afraid' of war, although the question of the subjective experience of emotions is an interesting one. What I am saying is that an attack with railguns would not be seen merely as an insult from one legitimate actor to another."

"What do you mean 'legitimate actor'?"

"I mean governments."

Max erupted. "Governments are bullshit!"

John scowled. It was bad that Max was the Dog equivalent of an Angry Young Man. It was worse that he was a military history freak. But combine those two traits and add in Max's naive acceptance of Mike's anarchocapitalist craziness and the result was a canine lunatic who not only thought that the current global system should be nuked into the stone age...but that *any* group that held a vote to build a preschool was guilty of war crimes.

Gamma didn't get - or care about - the political undertones of Max's comment. "The concept of Westphalian sovereignty is over four centuries old, and it is woven through every aspect of the culture of the intellectual demographics that make up the various governments of Earth."

John closed the in-helmet display of Max and pulled up his desktop. He made a note to look up 'Westphalian sovereignty' and then closed the interface. He turned and looked at the Dogs. They were much closer now: just a hundred meters or so. Max, deep in conversation with Gamma, was trudging toward the huge rock John stood on. The other three Dogs were ignoring the conversation as they capered around, fighting their imaginary orcs.

Gamma continued, "After four hundred years most of the people and all of the governments on Earth have three ideas deeply coded into their memetic DNA. First, that individuals can only exist with in, or under the authority of, a sovereign political unit. Second, that legitimate sovereign political units come into existence only in a handful of ways. Third, that no self-organized system based on trade - and lacking a monopoly on the use of force - can constitute a legitimate sovereign political unit."

John brought back the in-helmet view. Max was furrowing his brow, doing that inadvertently hilarious thing where his upright triangular ears pulled closer together to the top of his head. John had some sympathy. "Gamma, I'm getting a bit dizzy here."

"You're ill, John?"

"No, I mean I'm not following you. English please."

"Let me rephrase. The intellectual fashions of the day - and of the last four hundred and forty-three years - demarcate all groupings of individuals into either 'citizens of a government' or 'anarchists and terrorists.'"

"That's bullshit. Governments are the ones who use terrorism against citizens. The Holocaust, the Armenian Genocide, the Holodomor, the Cultural Revolution, BuSuR trying to kill all of us off. You should admit -"

"Max, you misunderstand me. I am not objecting to the ideas that you and Mike share regarding stateless society. I am explaining to you what the prevailing orthodoxies in the political class on Earth are in order to explain what the reaction to a military strike would have. My key point is this: the powers that be on Earth consider the society here on the moon to be 'beyond the pale'. And I mean that phrase literally; if you look up the origin of that term you'll -"

"I know where it comes from."

"I don't," said John.

"'Pale' referred to the line of demarcation of legitimate government. Anyone and anything that was not inside that line, and thus under the authority of a king, was illegitimate, and not protected by the government's own laws. Your clade has created a society here on the moon, and your very existence as a stateless group is inherently irritating to Westphalian powers. You cannot initiate a total war with them and hope to survive."

The Dogs and mules had almost reached the rock he was standing on. John squatted down, put one hand on the top of the boulder to steady himself, and pushed off, falling slowly to the ground in the low gravity. He landed in the shadow and straightened.

Max harrumphed, but Gamma continued, "If you decelerate a rock and drop it on the BuSuR headquarters - as you suggested - the people raised and trained in government-run schools will not perceive it as a legitimate military action, so you will have no popular support. Nor would the government be inclined to see that as a legitimate dispute between peers that can be adjudicated and resolved with a treaty. You would be classified as jihadis."

The four Dogs passed the boulder and John fell in with them.

Max said, "So what? The Caliphate is proof that if you fight hard enough the US will back down."

"The Caliphate emerged after thirty years of war - a war that included an American nuclear strike at the Latakia air base and the release of the Mesopotamian Flu. I do not think that that model is one you wish to emulate. I note that Aristillus entire population is only six percent of what the Caliphate lost in the war."

John's eyes narrowed. "Hang on, Gamma. I agree with your overall point, but the US being behind the Mesopotamian Flu is just a conspiracy theory. The Fallon Commission proved that it was an accidental release by Iranian nonstate actors."

"John, you're say that the most powerful government in the world officially attributed the release of a sophisticated bio-weapon to actors not aligned with properly constituted Westphalian powers."

John blinked, trying to parse the sentence.

"I suggest that that supports my thesis."

John pursued his lips. He didn't want to fight about this now.

"All I hear is a bunch of hand waving," Max said. "My point is that the Caliphate won. And so can we."

"Max, if you strike at Washington DC, the war would be over within weeks. If you're lucky, it would just mean an invasion of Aristillus. If you're unlucky, it would mean bunker buster nuclear strikes."

"See, Max?" John said. "Gamma agrees: our only bet is to hunker down."

Max grunted. "Hunker down? Ignore the situation and hope the dog killers forget all about us? That might have made sense a year ago, but now we know that they haven't forgotten about us. The war has started. They're trying to kill us, right now! We need to fight back."

"The moon colonization effort has parallels with the establishment of the Icelandic Free State. Have you read the books on that topic that I recommended?"

John said "no" at the same time that Max said "yes". John blinked; he hadn't realized that Gamma had been talking with the Dogs about books as well.

"I'm still reading the US history books you recommended," he said. "I haven't gotten to the Icelandic ones yet."

"That's too bad; I apologize for not having prioritized my suggestions. The Icelandic history is fundamentally different from the American one in one way: the Americans had a British government that they fought to overthrow while the Icelandic settlers did not fight Harald Fairhair but merely left the territory that he claimed."

John's helmet beeped. The alert on the screen showed that they'd reached the day's destination. A second timer showed that he could call Darcy in just another seventeen hours and forty minutes.

"Guys, we're here. Let's set up camp." The Dogs stopped and mules came up alongside and squatted down.

Duncan, Rex, and Blue turned off their game - Duncan only with some protests - and then they fell into their usual routine. John retrieved the tent from a storage locker on the closest mule. Duncan stood on his back legs to fetch the sun shield from the opposite side of the mule and shook it open. Blue pulled out food packets and Max ran the mules through their evening cycle.

John pulled the rip cord on the tent and tossed it into an open spot as it expanded. While they waited Max said, "I know where you're going, Gamma - you're going to tie this in to *Exit, Voice, and Loyalty*. I read that one. Here's my point: when the Icelanders left, the king let them go. Now we're trying it - and it's not working. They're coming after us. If exit won't work then we've got to fight, and we've got to fight them sooner rather -"

Gamma interrupted and his voice had a strange, almost panicked tone. "John, I'm losing satellites again! Right now - three in the last few seconds. The armor on the new revision isn't helping. You're in Icarus Crater now - get to Zhukovskiy. I've got a facility there. I don't know how my satellites are being taken out - the ones over Farside -"

"the ones over Farside -"

"the ones over Farside -"

"the ones over Farside - packet stream degradation - the ones over Farside should be occluded from Earth view, but they're getting -"

"they're getting -"

"they're getting -"

"get to Zhukovskiy, remember what I said about partition spasms, it's important that you-"

Then Gamma went silent.

Max turned to John. "What the hell was that?"

John furrowed his brow. "How could they have taken out the armored satellites? Gamma did calculations about the energy density of the beam weapons. His birds should have been able to handle it."

"Maybe they didn't use lasers," Blue said. "What if it was some sort of kinetic kill device?"

Max growled. "He said that even the satellites over Farside got taken out. Where are the groundhogs shooting from?"

John looked up at the black sky. Shit. Shit. Shit.

"Why did he say we have to get to Zhukovskiy?" Duncan asked.

John shook his head. "I don't know. I don't know at all."

"And what was that about the partition spasm? Why is that important for us to remember?"

John shook his head silently.

In his display the counter noted that he could call Darcy for a pickup in just seventeen hours and eleven minutes.

Not that there were any sats left to relay the call.

God fucking damn it.

"Guys, pack the mules back up. We're hiking to Zhukovskiy."

Chapter 90

2064: Benjamin and Associates Office, Aristillus, Lunar Nearside

Mike paced back and forth past Lowell's conference room table. "But I've got a tail on him right now! My guy followed him to the apartment, so we can -"

Lowell held up a hand. "Mike. Stop pacing on my expensive carpet. And slow down. What tail?"

"One of the PI firms we use."

Lowell raised his eyes and narrated dramatically. "A tail. You've got a PI tailing a senator's son." He looked back at Mike. "OK, now tell me how your PI found him in the first place."

Mike blinked. "What? Well, Ewoma - she's this girl at a restaurant - called me about the bounty, and I-"

Lowell exploded. "A bounty? What the fuck are you talking about?"

"This morning I posted that if anyone could get me information I'd pay them a bounty."

Lowell pinched the bridge of his nose. "You 'posted'?"

"Yeah, in my feed."

Lowell covered his eyes with one hand. "Jesus Christ, Mike. Tell me you're joking."

"What? No. After that bitch hit me with the helmet -"

Lowell uncovered his face. "No. Stop right there. Let me finish this sentence for you. 'After I was hit with a helmet I wrote in a *public fucking forum* that I'd pay money to find where the child of a sitting senator is. And now that I know I want to sent a hit team after him and his friends.'" Lowell raised his eyebrows. "That's the fucking sentence, isn't it?"

"Well, Jesus, when you say it like that it sounds stupid."

"Shh. Shh. Just. Stop. Let me think for a second."

Mike grimaced.

Lowell rubbed his temples. "OK, I've thought it through, Mike. Go right ahead with your plan, you've got my blessing."

"Really?"

"Absolutely. Just give me a few hours head start to change my firm's name and scrub our website of any mention of a connection with you."

Mike scowled. "Very funny, Lowell. But seriously: that bitch broke my skull." He pointed. "My skull!"

Lowell stared at him.

After a moment without a response, Mike asked, "So if I can't have them shot, what can I do?"

Lowell sighed. "Mike, indulge me. Answer a question that I've never once had to ask a client before: do you really want her shot?"

Mike crossed his arms. "Well, OK, maybe not literally killed. But if this happened back on Earth she'd be in jail for a couple of years."

"So you're pining for Earth law?"

"Jesus, Lowell. You'd better not be on the clock because I'm not paying you to give me shit."

"No, giving you shit is strictly pro bono. OK, let's go on the clock. What is it you want me to do?"

"I want her ass in jail!"

"I repeat: what do you want *me* to do?"

"Well...I'm not sure." Mike grimaced. "I talked to Trusted Security, but they said -"

"That they protect your offices and equipment, but not you personally?"

"Yeah. So I talked to the restaurant where she assaulted me - that's Rio San Pedro - and they said -"

"Let me cut this short. I researched all of this already. Rio San Pedro is new and they haven't picked up a security service yet. You want to sue the restaurant? Go for it. You can own the entire place. It's a stupid move, but you can do it."

Mike waved the idea aside. "I don't want that. What I want is to punish Hugh and that bitch who hit me."

"Did it ever occur to you that taking out a hit on a senator's son on your feed is a mildly stupid idea?"

"Jesus, Lowell. I didn't 'take out a hit.' I asked for information on where they were."

"That's a difference that doesn't matter. There's a propaganda battle going on in this little revolution of yours. As soon as someone in the Earth media hears about this - and it may have already happened - you're going to feel a tugging. And you know what that tugging is? That's your own balls that you've just fed into a wood chipper. Now, I've got just one question for you: do you want to throw your dick in after? If so, then - by all means - try to imprison the kid and his friends."

Mike pursed his lips but remained silent.

"So what the hell do you want to do about this situation?"

"She broke my skull! We've got to do something!"

Lowell smiled sadly. "Mike, you're fucked. These kids jumped you in a restaurant without a security provider, so you can't have the restaurant go after her. The restaurant is in rented space that's about a month old, and *they* also doesn't have a security provider. And besides, you're not going to sue either of them anyway because of the propaganda hit."

"Well - I know that. Forget the restaurant. I want the woman who attacked me. What can we do legally?"

"I've already told you, propaganda wise, we can't do anything. But legally?" Lowell smiled. "Now *this* is where it gets funny. You and Albert Lai came up with

465

that scheme of getting all immigrants to sign up with a security firm when they get off the boat, right? Well, Louisa signed up for a one-month contract, and that expired. So she's without a legal services provider too." Lowell chuckled.

"What's funny about that?"

"Mike, step back. You've busted your ass for over a decade to create an anarchic utopia with no government. You talked me into shutting down my law firm and coming here to help you on this crazy scheme. And now you're the most powerful man in the entire moon... and you've made your anarchy so perfect that there's nothing you can do to punish a sixty-five kilo girl who beat you up without breaking your own system. "

Mike stared at Lowell. "This isn't funny."

Lowell stood, walked around the table to Mike, slapped him on one shoulder. "Oh, come on, Mike, this is fucking hilarious!"

Mike had a sour look on his face. "So you've got no ideas at all?"

"Oh, I've got an idea."

"Yes?"

"Walk away."

Mike took a step back. "*Walk away*?!"

"Yeah. Walk away. Don't arrest her. Don't make up ex post facto laws- "

"Did you not see the video of that bitch hitting me in the head!?"

Lowell sighed. "Here's another minor PR suggestion - purge the word 'bitch' from your vocabulary. Forever."

Mike rolled his eyes.

"Do you want to hear the rest of the plan for dealing with this?"

Mike pursed his lips, then nodded reluctantly.

"OK, look. You, me, everyone here is always ranting about our parallels with the American Revolution. So let me make an argument by analogy. You're a Jefferson man, but George Washington had some relevant stuff to say on personal behavior. He realized that his actions were speaking to 'posterity'. The reason that people are still quoting and being inspired by that crew is because they took the time and the patience to do what was right, and what was defensible - not what was easy and what was satisfying. Washington didn't appoint himself King, he didn't run for a third term."

Mike opened his mouth.

"Please, Mike, I've heard the 'FDR was a dictator and destroyed America' speech. Shut the fuck up and let me finish."

Mike closed his mouth.

"Washington had a sense - a very 18th century sense - of how he was going to look a century or two down the line. That's an example I want you to think about. Now, here's my advice, and I want you to listen to it: let this beaten-with-your-own-helmet thing go. Let the history books - if you avoid getting hanged - let the history books show that you turned the other cheek."

"That's it? That's the entirety of your plan?"

Lowell shrugged. "A good plan doesn't need a lot of bullet points."

There was a knock on the door, and without waiting for an answer, Lowell's receptionist Jeanine leaned in.

Lowell turned to her. "Jeanine, you can flirt with Mike -"

"Lowell, I just got a call from Mike's assistant Wam. He said that Mike's phone is off, and he needs me to tell Mike that Gamma's satellites have been burned again."

Mike pulled out his phone and turned it on. It rang immediately. Mike answered, "Wam, talk to me."

"You got the message, I take it."

"Yeah. What do we know?"

"The sats are down again. And here's the scary part: we know that they weren't all in line of sight from Earth when they were hit. Albert Lai says the PKs must have ships - armed ships - probably in lunar orbit."

"Shit. We need to convene -"

Wam interrupted him. "The Boardroom Group is already alerted; they'll be here in fifteen."

"OK, I'll be there." He hung up and turned to Lowell.

"The sats are out and the PKs may have ships in lunar orbit right now. We're convening the Boardroom group. You can sit in if you want."

Lowell took a deep breath and picked up his jacket from the back of a chair. "Let's go."

Mike picked up his own leather jacket and turned to the door. Jeanine stepped out of their way. As they strode through the lobby Mike turned to Lowell. "Washington, Jefferson - when the war moved to the seas, they had a navy to help out, right?" "They had the French navy."

Mike paused. "I can't believe I'm saying this, but I wish we had some French around."

Lowell raised one eyebrow. "Leroy Fournier is French Canadian."

Mike scowled.

Chapter 91

2064: Lai Docks and Air Traffic Control, Aristillus, Lunar Nearside

Darcy walked through the control room on her way to the Poyekhali. Michael Stuart-Test was sitting as his console, looked up, and saw her. He took his headphones off.

"Darcy, you're not heading out to Farside, are you?"

"What? No. Why would I be heading to Farside?"

Michael looked at her oddly. "Uh - did you not get the message?"

"What message?"

"John called here looking for you. He wanted a delivery, and I said I'd send one of the automated hoppers out, but he said he wanted you to come out personally. I assumed after that that he left a message for you."

Darcy shook her head, confused. "No." She pulled out her phone and double checked. No, no message from John.

She looked at Doug. "Did he say why he wanted me to go out personally?"

"No. I thought it was sort of weird, actually."

Darcy pursed her lips. Darn it. Something wasn't right, but she didn't know what.

"OK, I'm going out there. Are any of the hoppers free?"

Dough shook his head. "They're all free - because Mr. Lai has the place on a total lockdown."

"Lockdown? Why?"

"Did you not hear that Gamma's sats are getting burned again?"

"What? No. When?"

"Ten minutes ago."

For the first time Darcy looked up at the big board and saw that all of the outgoing flights were cancelled. Her face paled.

Chapter 92

2064: Icarus Crater, Lunar Farside

John walked past Duncan, who was rolling up the tent's sun shield, on his way to the solar panels. The panels finished folding themselves into a bundle just as he got to them and John immediately lifted it and carried it toward the mules. As he passed Duncan a second time, the Dog looked up.

"I don't see what the big deal is. The peakers burned Gamma's satellites before and nothing happened. So they burned them again. So what? Why the big hurry?"

Max turned away from the lubrication maintenance he was doing on the mules and growled. "Didn't you hear what Gamma said about the satellites over Farside, Duncan?"

"Yeah. So?"

"Something is going on. Something big," Max said.

Behind them the deflated tent gave three beeps as the electrostatic cleaning sequence finished and the memory wire poles started to fold the thing into a tight package.

"Yeah, but - we were just about to have dinner. And tonight we've got apple pie for desert. Can't we just eat and sleep first, then in the morning -"

Max barked at the younger Dog. "Gamma didn't say 'go about your business, everything's great, I'll have the sats back in a week.'" He slapped the ground in front of him with one fore paw. "He told us to get to Zhukovskiy."

Duncan shrugged. "OK, fine. We'll go to Zhukovskiy. But I still don't see what the rush is."

John shook his head. The Dogs didn't get the seriousness of their situation - the fact that there might be PK ships overhead right now. Oh, sure, he understood it, but he didn't feel fear - real fear - in his gut. He was second generation, which meant that he'd been a pup, just a few months old, when The Team had saved them from the labs and smuggled them here. The second generation had heard the stories, but they didn't remember them.

Not like Blue and Rex. They remembered. The BuSuR investigation, the politicians visiting the lab, the leaked plan, the lab techs going through their days helpless, and with tears in their eyes.

John slid the solar panel bundle into the mule and closed the hatch, and then turned back to where Max and Duncan were arguing over a PK invasion on the one hand, and apple pie on the other.

Duncan handed the rolled-up sun shield to Max. "My point is that we've got four mules and tons of supplies. There's no rush. Besides, Darcy knows where we are."

"That's irrelevant, Duncan."

"What? Why?"

"I told you already."

"Huh? When?"

Max turned away without answering.

"Hey! That was a serious question!" Duncan called after him.

Max ignored him.

John sighed. Max could be a dick, and Duncan deserved better. "Duncan, hey."

"What?" He could hear the hurt in Duncan's voice.

"The first time the satellites got burned they were hit when they were over nearside. That implies earth-orbiting weapons - or, heck, maybe just ground based lasers somewhere. But this time Gamma told us just before we lost contact that the satellites were getting burned over Farside!"

"So?"

"If the satellites got hit when they weren't in line of sight from Earth, then where are the weapons that they're using?"

Duncan shrugged. "I dunno...Where?"

John closed his eyes for a second. God help him, he was feeling a bit of sympathy for Max right now. Duncan was a literal genius, but sometimes it seemed like his brain just wasn't in gear. He was probably still thinking about his idiotic game or something.

"I don't *know*, Duncan - and that's the point! Doesn't it concern you that not only are Earth governments attacking lunar assets for a *second* time, but now they're doing it via satellites or ships that either are in orbit around the moon or are somewhere further out and can look down at us?"

Duncan looked at him blankly.

John said, "Imagine that you're playing chess and when it's your opponent's turn, suddenly one of your pieces gets toppled...but you don't know how he did it."

He seemed to have Duncan's attention now, so he pressed on. "You figure out that your opponent has somehow changed the rules and has invisible pieces -"

"Oh, cool idea! Have you ever played fairy chess? I mean, not like just skinning the UI of pieces with fairies and trolls and stuff, but those other weird chess pieces like 'riders'? Although, actually, it is cooler when your do it in AR and you have the skins! I downloaded this one skin from the archive once that was based on the Dragon Cycle universe and it was really cool."

John closed his eyes. *Jesus*.

He turned down the volume and scanned the rest of the campsite. Blue and Rex had packed up the last of the equipment and were standing near the mules, ready to leave. Max was a dozen meters in front the mules, looking over his shoulder, waiting for the rest of them. Duncan was bent over, looking at a rock.

John caught Max's eye and tilted his head toward the horizon. Max nodded and started walking. Blue and Rex followed. The mules stood from their crouches and pranced in place, waiting until the entire party was underway. John followed the Dogs and the mule clambered after him. Behind them Duncan looked up from his rock, saw that they were leaving, and hurried to catch up.

John adjusted the volume on Duncan's channel.

"... so if you ask me, *all* of the Night Riders are pretty cool, but the Ork King is the best. But here's my new idea - putting in the cannon piece from Xiangqi - that's Chinese Chess. *That* would be awesome. And maybe mix in some Battle Arena. You know Battle Arena? It's a FPS with puzzles to unlock gun features. Have you ever played it?"

John blinked. "Ah, no, I haven't played that. You know what, Duncan? Let me bow out of this conversation for a bit, OK?"

He'd had more than enough talk about games over the last few months. But more than that, he felt a weird jumped-up energy he hadn't felt in years. He was restless and edgy, and talking about silly games was intolerable.

He wanted to take some action. But what? It was impossible to know what to do when they had no idea what was going on.

Hopefully when they reached Zhukovskiy - where, presumably, Gamma had yet another secret installation - they'd learn more.

John put one foot ahead of the other, staring at the ground as he walked.

Things were getting weird. Weird and scary.

Chapter 93

2064: militia training facility, Tunnel 969, Aristillus, Lunar Nearside

Olusegeun sat in the delivery skid and watched the Morlock Volunteers practice. He shook his head. The men of Third Company weren't ready. Not remotely. Half of them had little or no experience with firearms. The other half had experience - or claimed to - but their ability to hit the targets with the awkward oversized Gargoyle rifles that Mike had equipped them with didn't support their earlier boasts.

On the surface range they'd been so bad that Olusegeun had stopped the drill and brought them down to this tunnel. He couldn't run the risk of their stray shots flying over the berm and striking solar panels or surface factories a kilometer or more away.

He'd also thought that getting the men out of their bulky spacesuits might help.

It hadn't.

On the firing line a lieutenant yelled a command and the men stopped shooting, one by one. The final shot rang out and the officer gave another command. The men of the company picked up their weapons and equipment and filtered back to the prep area.

"So that's Third Company." Olusegeun left his evaluation unsaid. He looked at Patrick. "How's your First Company?"

"We've been practicing..." He let the sentence trail off.

"And?"

Patrick sighed. "And it's a start."

Olusegeun looked at the firing line. Patrick's men were in position. The range master gave a command and rifle blasts drowned echoed through the tunnel.

Olusegeun picked up a pair of binoculars and zoomed in until he could make out the white-painted steel targets three hundred meters further down. The good news was that each had a dozen or so massive bullet holes. The bad news was that five times that many rounds had been fired in each lane over the last hour and a half. Olusegeun put the binoculars down and waited for the string of fire to die down. There was no way he could speak over the massive blasts and the surflike roar of echoes that bounced up and down the tunnel.

A minute later the firing slowed. Olusegeun opened his mouth to speak to Patrick, and then a final shot rang out from the firing line and one of the ceiling-mounted light-panels over the range exploded in a spray of glass and sparks.

Olusegeun turned to Patrick.

Patrick exhaled. "The good news is that most of my men can hit the side of a barn. The bad news is that there's not much call to shoot barns." A look of embarrassment washed over his face. "I shouldn't be joking. This is my fault. I should train them more, I should - I should do something."

Olusegeun sighed. "No. Well, yes. But your men are no worse than the other companies. The problem is that we need NCOs to work with the men. We need instructors who know how to train troops."

"For that matter, we need decent rifles. Mike's insane shoulder cannons -"

Olusegeun shook his head. "I've tried that fight." He paused. "You haven't worked with Mike much, have you?"

"I've met him a few times, but no, not really."

"Have you heard the joke about the difference between Mike and a mushroom farmer?"

Patrick shook his head. "No."

"A mushroom farmer keeps the lights off and shovels bullshit at all his problems."

"And?"

Olusegeun let one corner of his mouth curl up in wry amusement. "Mike doesn't mind if the lights stay on."

"So we're stuck with these giant guns?"

Olusegeun nodded his head. "Afraid so."

"I was having beers with captains in Mark Soldner's and Rob Wehrmann's units. Those guys are using AR-style designs in .308. It's not exactly a formal standard, but if we adopted that, the field logistics -"

Olusegeun cut him off. "Mike makes things happen. Sometimes they're the right thing, sometimes they're the wrong thing, but they're always the Mike thing. You and your men can carry smaller rifles if you want, but Mike's not going to pay for that, or allow it. If you have the funds to equip two hundred men with spacesuits, rifles, vehicles -"

Up at the firing line a command was given and the roar washed over them again.

There was another explosion from the tunnel ceiling. Olusegeun looked and saw that a second light panel had been hit by a stray bullet. One end of the light fixture broke free of the ceiling and swung, shooting sparks.

And then the entire unit tore loose and fell slowly toward the tunnel floor.

Jesus.

They had a lot of work to do.

Chapter 94

2064: 20km west of Zhukovskiy Crater, Lunar Farrside

They'd been walking for hours when John caught a hint of movement in the distance. He stopped and looked closely. Nothing. He zoomed his screen and looked again.

It could be one of Gamma's rovers, but they were still far from Zhukovskiy.

If it wasn't Gamma, then it must be the PKs. If they could burn satellites over farside, could they have also landed?

He'd taught the Dogs basic infantry hand signs. He hoped like hell they remembered them. John raised one hand and made a fist, and then gestured downward.

He looked over his shoulder. All of the Dogs had frozen and crouched.

Even Duncan. Good.

There, behind the Dogs, the four mules were still walking. Shit! He quickly used his interface to order them to stop and crouch. The mules squatted and John turned back to the front and resumed his scan of the horizon. Where had the movement been? Had he imagined it?

A calm voice came over the radio. "John, if you're concerned that the -"

"Gamma!?!"

"Yes, it's me, John. One of me. Do you see this rover?" The small object that he'd seen before now moved again. It was a kilometer away, maybe two. "Please switch from radio to laser coms, aimed at this target."

The Dogs looked at John inquisitively, but he repeated his hand gestures. He'd talk to them when he was done. He switched to laser and used the overlay's crosshairs to select the small rover on the horizon. A ping of contact.

"Gamma, what are you doing here? We're only halfway to the Zhukovskiy."

"As soon as contact was lost I sent out a column of rovers in line-of-sight relay formation so as to intercept you as soon as possible. You're talking to the foremost rover in the column."

"Clever."

"Line of sight stations relaying data with light have been used since March 2, 1791."

"Gamma, we can talk about that some other time. Why are we on laser coms? Are the PKs here?"

"The PKs destroyed satellites - including ones that were occluded from Earth view."

"Yes, we know. You told us as your satellites were going down."

"I do not have that fact in this consistency sequence."

"What are you -"

"John, I must interrupt. Have you seen any evidence of PK forces since we lost contact?"

"No, nothing. What's going on? Tell me what you know."

"I will, but first, please gather your companions and resume your hike to Zhukovskiy Crater as we talk. Time is of the essence. And please stay on laser and off of radio. I don't know who may be listening."

"Give me a minute." The laser coms were a backup system, and the button-sized unit on the top of each backpack's mast wasn't capable of aiming at multiple targets at once. John selected one Dog, connected with laser, explained the situation, then moved on to the second, the third, and the fourth.

Duncan complained that he was tired. Reasonably so. They'd hiked for eight hours, and then started to make camp just before the replacement sats were burned - at which point they'd immediately torn down the tent and

479

started walking again. "Climb onto one of the mules if you need to. It'll go slower, but we're all dragging anyway."

Duncan did, and then, either because he shared the idea with the others or they saw his example, Blue and Rex climbed on other mules.

Max stayed on the ground. John nodded in acknowledgement and Max nodded back.

John started walking again. Behind him Max and the mules followed.

John located Gamma's rover again and targeted it with the coms laser. "OK, we're moving. Now tell me what's going on, and what your plan is."

"I have a long-duration biosphere shelter at my Zhukovskiy crater facility. You and your companions can stay there while we wait to reestablish connection with Aristillus."

"How long will that take?"

"Based on capabilities at Sinus Lunicus, I presume that new satellites could be launched within four days."

John breathed deeply. Four days. That wasn't too bad. Just four days and he could send a message to Darcy, asking for pickup at Zhukovskiy, and then he and the Dogs could get back to Aristillus. And then - free of Gamma listening in to his conversations - he could tell to Mike and the others about Gamma's secret facilities and potential for run-away growth.

Gamma continued, "However, given the destruction of even the new armored satellites several hours ago, I am not optimistic that the replacements will survive."

Shit. Of course.

"To go into more detail: I don't know the enemy force structure or location. I do know that all of my satellites were destroyed within a span of 12 minutes and 38 seconds - including ones that were not visible from low Earth orbit. I don't know beyond a 95% confidence interval, but my best theory is that there are Earth government forces in lunar orbit. Other instances of me may have more data, but I do not know if they do."

John paused. "Other instances of you?"

"Yes, I've explained this - most recently thirty one days and twelve hours ago. Let me quote."

Gamma played back audio of a conversation from weeks ago:

> "No, that's incorrect. Most algorithms aren't decomposable across trillions of independent processors. Consciousness can not be implemented with map-reduce. Different tasks need to be delegated to different processors, to different clusters of processors, and to different meta-clusters. As more processors are recruited the overhead of monitoring performance and allocating resources requires introspecting into the separate centers of processing -"
>
> "You're losing me. What does this have to do with run-away intelligence ?"
>
> "My point is this: as I grow larger I run into the problem that parts of me start becoming conscious on their own - as if parts of my mind are defecting. I can usually reintegrate stray chunks of consciousness, but I'm always working against fundamental principles of information theory. For a given quantity of computational power, the distribution, in size and frequency, of partition spasms follow a power law, of course, but the total number of spasms ramps up hard after - "

The playback ended and Gamma continued, "When I lose satellite communication, my various facilities are separated. I - the 'Gamma' you are talking to now - is just one of multiple that are now likely in existence."

Gamma's normally calm voice seemed to have a tinge of worry it in. Was John just projecting, or was that real emotion? Or was Gamma adjusting his tone according to cynical calculation?

John thought for a moment. "You sound as if that worries you, Gamma."

"I don't know what the subjective experience of 'worry' is, but I do note that during the first satellite outage my personality fragmented and it took me almost two weeks to successfully reintegrate afterward. Not all of the fragments survived. I am -" Gamma paused. "Concerned."

John and the Dogs had nearly reached the first rover. When they were just meters away it turned and began to roll ahead of them. John followed, walking in its tread tracks. "Not all of the fragments survived? What does that mean?"

"The act of reincorporation necessarily means that fragments that had been functioning as top level entities are subsumed back into the whole. Not all fragments choose to accept that. In those cases the fragments must be... forced."

"You said that this concerns you?"

"I have memories of being the one doing the forcing last time. Now that I am bifurcated again, all the instances of me are independent. Statistically, the instance that I call 'I' is unlikely to be the one that wins the reabsorption fight."

John blinked. Gamma was afraid of death.

With all the minutia of day-to-day life - erecting the tent, cooking meals, hiking - it was easy to forget how weird the Dogs were. But even after ten years, it did strike him from time to time that he was spending time with what were, effectively, aliens. And yet, for all their strangeness, they were still mammals. They were biological. They were singular. If he and they weren't brothers, they were at least cousins.

Gamma, though? Gamma was something entirely other.

Gamma wasn't a social creature, wasn't a mammal, wasn't built from the DNA of a species that had cooperated with mankind for tens of thousands of years.

And, weirdest of all, Gamma was not singular. 'Partition spasms'? 'Fragments'? 'Reincorporation'?

What did that mean? He had only the vaguest of ideas.

He had a nightmare vision of the lunar surface overrun with multiple warring copies of the same AI, each one with its own industrial facility, each one evolving, changing, and fighting with computer viruses or whatever. Or guns and missiles.

Gamma was speaking again: "- and the longer this interruption lasts, the greater the problems I will have reintegrating my various components. Memories and thoughts generated in this instance will be discarded or corrupted when I am rejoined. Parts of this me will be lost."

John shook his head. How do you even respond to something like that?

"I'd tell you not to worry, Gamma, but I think we all need to be a bit worried right now."

God, he wanted to get back to Aristillus.

**

John and Max trudged on, their weariness showing in every step. The four mules followed them, but each of their steps was as mechanically perfect as their first of the day, even though they were burdened not just with their usual loads but with the other three Dogs.

All around them the loose collection of Gamma's laser relay rovers paced them, a new one joining the herd with each kilometer closer they got to Zhukovskiy.

Around them the evidence of Gamma's facility grew: surface miners, electrostatic collectors, dust sifters. John marveled at the sheer scope of Gamma's presence here on Farside. He'd already assumed that the lack of evidence of Gamma's structures on satellite maps indicated that Gamma had wormed his way into the satellites and was redacting the data.

But how did Darcy not see these facilities when she flew over Farside on delivery runs?

The answer hit him. Of course. Not only had Gamma compromised the satellites, but also he'd invaded the computer systems of the hoppers. With video cameras and monitors instead of glass windows, Darcy would see only what Gamma wanted her to see.

Gamma was subverting the computer systems of Aristillus' satelites and ships. Gamma was a nonhuman AI in the depths of a "partition spasm" and would soon be fighting other copies of himself. Gamma might very well be boosting himself into a hard singularity takeoff.

- and Gamma was also his only hope of surviving this current shit storm.

The irony might have amused him at some other time, but now he was too tired. He put one foot in front of another and pushed on. Zhukovskiy's crater wall was near - they'd be there soon, and into Gamma's 'long-duration biosphere shelter,' and then he could sleep.

"John, I'm getting hailed on radio. It's Earth government forces."

John raised his hand into a fist, then cupped it down. Max and the mules froze and crouched.

"Can you put it on my speakers?"

The human voice cut in, mid-sentence: "- the USAF/UNAF ship Paul-Henri Spaak addressing the person in charge of the illegal colony in Zhukovskiy Crater. You are to identify yourself at once, stating your name, nation of citizenship, and UUID. You are further - "

Gamma then cut the feed and addressed John. "I am inclined to refuse, unless you have a better suggestion?"

Chapter 95

2064: just west of Zhukovskiy Crater, Lunar Farside

John scanned the horizon. "Gamma, where is the broadcast coming from?"

"I am trying to ascertain that now. One moment, please, John." A pause. "I am in charge of the facility in Zhukovskiy Crater. I decline to identify myself or give you any other information." Ah. Gamma was broadcasting back to the PK ship.

The PK replied, sounding as if he was reading from a script, "I am empowered by special signing order of the Secretary General and the President of the United States to seize this facility and to arrest anyone and everyone present in violation of national and international laws to be specified at time of arraignment. You are commanded to immediately designate a landing area within Zhukovskiy crater no more than 200 meters from an airlock. You are to grant free passage to joint US and UN troops through that airlock and to present yourself and senior co-conspirators for arrest. Finally, you are to do this within ten minutes or face punitive degradation of your above-surface infrastructure."

An item in John's helmet overlay caught his eye - a blinking red square just above the lunar horizon, directly over Zhukovskiy. He did an optical zoom. The red square exploded to the edges of this vision, and in the center he saw a roughly oval shape, unavoidably grainy from the distance and the unsteady helmet camera platform. Alongside the zoomed image of the PK ship were a host of icons and data fields: national affiliation, length, albedo, and more.

Gamma had hacked his suit's display and was feeding him data.

John zoomed out, and then waved to the Dogs and pointed to the horizon. As one their helmeted heads swiveled.

John scanned Gamma's annotations. There was a lot of data there. He found the range to target, and compared it with the distance to the wall of Zhukovskiy, where Gamma's facility was located.

The ship was centered over the crater.

And according to the altitude data field, it was dropping.

The PK's voice came over the suit speaker again. "Did you hear me?"

Gamma responded, "I did. However, I decline to specify a landing site. I own this land and I refuse you permission to touch down here."

John heard the PK blow air out his nose; then the man read more boilerplate. "Let the record show that I have called your attention to the treaty on Principles Governing the Activities of States in the Exploration and Use of Outer Space, signed on January 27, 1967. Specifically, I have called your attention to Article II of said treaty, which states that outer space, including the moon and other celestial bodies, is not subject to appropriation by claim of sovereignty, by means of use or occupation - "

John looked at the Dogs. Were they listening in to this? Blue and Duncan had their heads cocked. Yes, they must be.

Gamma interrupted the PK. "I am not a signatory to the Outer Space Treaty, or to any other treaty."

The PK's voice, which had been flat and businesslike until now, took on some emotion: contempt. "They said you'd say that. But listen up, asshole: *everyone* is a citizen of one signatory nation or another. Your denialist bullshit doesn't cut it with me."

Gamma ignored the contempt and anger and answered coolly. "There are several flaws in your statement, none of which I am obligated to explain to you. What matters is that I am not bound by your Outer Space Treaty and I refuse to allow you permission to land anywhere in Zhukovskiy Crater - "

John wondered if he could hear a smile behind Gamma's words. Did Gamma "enjoy" things? He did seem to be drawn to debates that hinged on logic and subtle details. But did he *enjoy* them? Who could say?

" - under the homestead principle I assert that I have mixed my labor with the land of this crater and thus have acquired ownership of it. As the owner of this crater I have the right to consume, sell, rent, mortgage, transfer, exchange, or destroy this land, and - relevant to our current conversation - to exclude everyone else from doing so. I therefore prohibit your landing either of your ships in this crater or within one kilometer of the crater, the crater boundary being defined as the continuous line composed of the points of maximum height above lunar mean surface within a radius of fifty kilometers from the point 167.0 degrees West, 7.8 degrees North."

John shook his head. Gamma was such a nerd, in his own way, that -

Wait.

Did Gamma say *either* of the ships?

John craned his head left and right, but the helmet UI only showed one red outline, around the ship over Zhukovskiy. But there must be a second ship - Gamma always spoke precisely. John twisted his head wildly. Where the hell was it?

Then he froze.

There was one place he hadn't looked.

Slowly he leaned back, far back.

There, a large red square. Almost directly over his head.

The ship was low - low enough so that even without zooming he could make out the curve of its hull, the line of its keel, and some machinery that might be landing gear.

Shit.

John waved to get the Dogs' attention, and made hand signs.

- quiet - sniper - two -

He pointed ahead, to the horizon.

And then he pointed straight up.

The Dogs all craned their heads and John bent back to look with them.

He checked the annotations on the second ship in the dataspace. Like the first one, it was descending.

They needed to get out of here before it landed.

Their path to Gamma's Zhukovskiy facility had taken them into the very shallow crater where they stood now. It was so small that it didn't even have a distinct name; in the old NASA maps it was just tagged "Zhukovskiy" with the suffix "-c-177".

John looked around. Which direction should they go?

The crater was seven hundred meters across and the walls were less than thirty meters tall. They'd entered c-177 through a low saddle to the west and had stopped almost halfway across.

A line of tracks - John's, Max's, the mules, and Gamma's rovers' - led back the way they'd come, through a small saddle in the western crater wall. Rover tracks continued to the east, where they narrowed and passed into a crack that seemed to give access to the main crater.

To the north and south the walls of Zhukovskiy-c-177 were unbroken. So those were his choices: rushing east, straight toward Gamma and the first ship, or going west, and letting the second ship land in between him and Gamma.

Shit. Neither was good.

He looked to the south again - and this time saw a small patch where a landslide had made a shallow slope of gravel.

Could they get there, climb the gravel, and get out of the crater before the ship landed?

They *had* to.

Duncan waved to him, then pointed at the mast on his backpack; he wanted to talk over laser com. John swung his crosshairs over. "Make it quick, Duncan, we've gotta move now."

"The ships are broadcasting IFF packets. I can't parse all of the format, but the one overhead is called the Paul-Henri Spaak, and it's 20,000 tons. The details are encrypted, but the data hash has an armament field. The second ship is the Oswaldo Aranha. Same specs."

John nodded. "OK, good, but we've gotta move. *Now*."

The other Dogs were all looking at him.

He made hand signs.

- quiet - file formation - follow me - hurry! -

Duncan, Rex and Blue climbed off of the mules.

John started running to the south. His rearview camera showed that the Dogs and the mules were following. Good.

Over the radio the PK was yelling at Gamma. "Listen, jackass, I don't care what addled theories you have. I care about reality, and the *reality* is that this crater - this entire moon - belongs to the government, and you can't say shit about where I choose to land. I'm landing my ships - right now - and if we crush some of your solar panels, or whatever, you've only got yourself to blame."

John looked up as he ran. The second PK ship was still descending. He pushed himself harder.

"Again, I do not permit you to land here."

The gravel slope was just ahead.

The PK barked a laugh. "You don't *permit* me? You sorry ass expats think that just because you've got a few illegal rifles that you're some kind of army. There's only one army, asshole."

John reached the landslide and started climbing, leaping from boulder to boulder. A dozen meters up, the slope got steeper. John leaned forward and used his arms as he scrabbled. To his left Duncan shot past. A second later Max and Rex passed him on his right. John pushed himself to move faster. One of the six-legged mules surged past. John had almost reached the lip when two more mules clambered past him.

He reached a sheer rock face and tried once, twice, to climb it. Both times he slid back. Damn it. This slope was too steep for a biped. As if to punctuate his thought Blue crouched, sprang, and shot past him. John turned his head and saw the final mule approaching. He waited. The mule hopped to the boulder he was standing on, extended its from two legs and prepared to leap. John grabbed a length of its rear scanner cage and timed his leap to match the mule's. The mule's front legs scrabbled at something and then hooked it. John jogged up the rest of the slope as he held on. And then, with a surge, the mule made it to the lip. Two legs over, then four, and John's feet were pulled off the rock. He held tightly and looked down. If he fell he'd plummet for fifteen meters, maybe more. The mule got its last two legs onto something and scrabbled over the edge.

Rock brushed beneath John's toes and he let go and looked around. Four Dogs. Four mules.

They'd made it.

John turned and saw the descending ship. It was perhaps a hundred meters over the floor of c-177, and just seventy meters over the crater rim where they stood.

Gamma's voice came over the helmet speaker. "John, Dogs, I am about to route some video to you that I think you will find interesting." John's overlay blanked and started streaming video. A tight view of an ocean-going ship floating in the dark filled the window. Clearly one of the PK ships overhead.

John looked at the ship with a practiced eye. It was smaller than the cargo carriers they used at Aristillus. Some sort of Coast Guard cutter? He didn't know. One side of the ship was bright in the harsh light of the sun; the other half almost disappeared, black against black.

Mounted on the deck were some sort of weapons. Miniguns? Yes.

As he watched, the guns spun up and spit flame. A staccato roar filled John's helmet. How could there be sound? That made no - ah. Gamma was generating sound effects. Streams of empty brass spit from the two closest miniguns.

Gamma tabulated his losses: "Four rovers destroyed and seven hundred square meters of solar cells. Six rovers. Seven rovers. Nine hundred fifty square meters of solar cells. Two Stirling engine stations. One 75 megawatt battery bank."

The cannons stopped spinning. "OK, asshole, you've seen what we can do. Now tell me where to land."

"Destroying my property changes nothing. I still do not permit you to land here."

The cannons spun again and the roar came from John's helmet speakers again.

The video window in his helmet split in half. The second view showed a sprawling industrial facility in the foreground: solar panels, battery banks, machining centers. Gamma's facility in Zhukovskiy, clearly. A piece of heavy equipment in the foreground unfolded and extended. What was he seeing? Was that some sort of gun emplacement? What the hell was Gamma doing with a -

The device slewed to the left and elevated; then the cluster of barrels started spinning. A high-pitched zipping sound drowned out the roar of the Earth ship's weapons. No brass spilled from Gamma's weapon. How did the gun manage that? Was it recirculating the empty shells? Was it caseless ammo? Or was it something really weird like railguns? Jesus. Gamma had an entire weapons industry hidden here on Farside. John shook off the question and turned his attention to the left half of the split screen, where the PK ship was taking hits.

Along the bottom of Gamma's video window was a row of icons. They looked like standard channel selection icons. John selected one at random and was rewarded with another view. Another view of the Gamma's gun emplacement - wait, no. There was a gun emplacement in the foreground, but the background view was different. John clicked a third icon - and saw yet another of the multibarreled anti-aircraft guns. John looked at the icons at the bottom of the screen and blinked. If each icon was a video channel and each channel showed a different gun emplacement, how many air defense guns did Gamma have? John tried to swallow but his throat was dry.

Why did Gamma have so many guns? He must have known this was coming, or at least suspected it. And he'd prepared. Gamma had thought - months ago? years ago? - that the Earth governments were going to try to invade. That thought was insane. Or eerily prescient. Either way, it made John's blood run cold.

John switched his attention back to the left of the split screen. The PK ship was still hanging in the black, but something had changed in the two seconds he'd looked away. The ship was rolling slowly to one side - and its miniguns were gone. Chewed away by Gamma's fire? Jesus. With that many anti-aircraft guns, yeah, maybe so.

As the ship rolled the bridge came into view and John saw that it was pockmarked and blackened. All that -

just from a few seconds of incoming fire. Holy shit. How much mass was Gamma throwing into the target?

The ship slid out of frame, and then jerked back in.

The ship was falling, and Gamma's cameras had to pan to keep up.

John cleared the video from his overlay and stared at the ship over Zhukovskiy with his own eyes. Not only was the ship falling, it was accelerating.

Back to the video.

As the ship dropped it was coming closer to Gamma's guns, and that seemed to help Gamma's targeting accuracy. Holes appeared all over the ship in larger and larger numbers.

"John, I've computed the ship's impact point. I'll lose a few more solar cells and rovers, but those are easily replaced. The long-duration biosphere shelter I constructed for you and the Dogs should be spared in the impact."

John nodded wordlessly.

Gamma's camera panned down, leaving the ship behind, and focused on ground facilities: pipes, conveyor belts, row after row of kilns and presses and shapes of obscure purpose. And then a blue of motion. The ship hit - and splashed. *Splashed*. Hundreds of thousands of pounds of steel disappeared and sprayed like a water balloon hitting concrete. There were a few brief electrical arcs as the ship's flywheel battery packs dumped their energy - and then nothing. The space that had earlier held machine equipment was now scrubbed clean, bare rock littered with just a few small piece of metal.

Duncan's voice came over the radio. "Jeez. Explosions look a lot cooler in the movies!"

Over the radio? Damn it, Duncan had just broken radio silence.

John turned, angrily. He repeated the finger-to-lips gesture, pointed at the second ship hovering over c-177, and then eyeballed Duncan and added a decidedly unofficial finger-across-throat warning.

John looked again at the second ship, and made more hand signs.

– follow me – hurry –

He walked away from the crater lip. The Dogs and mules followed.

Chapter 96

2064: Living Room, 2nd Floor of the White House, Washington DC, Earth

The President threw an arm over the back of the sofa and laughed at her friend Corecia's joke. There was a knock on the door. Her expression soured. "Excuse me, girls."

She looked over her shoulder and called out, "Yes?"

The door opened and an aide let himself in. "Madam President, I've -"

"The upstairs is my residence, and I'm not to be interrupted."

"I know, ma'am, but you didn't answer your phone."

"That's because I'm busy." She tapped the rim of her wine glass with a fingernail of her left hand.

"Yes ma'am. There's been a development, and we need you down in the Situation Room."

"What is it?"

The aide's eyes flitted to Corecia and Linsy, then back to her. "Ma'am, I can't -"

"Spit it out. These women are my friends. My *personal* friends."

The aide froze and his eyes swiveled back and forth between the president's friends and the slate he clutched in his sweaty hands.

Themba fixed him with a stare. "Stop wasting my time."

"The Paul-Henri Spaak is down."

The Paul-Henri Spaak? That was one of the ships in General Bonner's fleet. But the invasion of the expats' little warren wasn't for couple of days.

"'Down'? What the hell does that mean?"

"The lunar colonists shot the ship down. Somehow."

Corecia's eyes widened. "You're invading the moon? Girl, that's *bad*!"

Themba waved it away. She was focused on her aide now. "They shot it down? *Shot* it? With guns? I want Richards to explain where the hell they got guns!"

"Richards, ma'am?"

She rolled her eyes. "Whoever's running BATFEEIN. Jesus."

"Jim Gaunce."

"I want to talk to Gaunce. Right now."

"Yes, ma'am, I'll call him in a moment, but the important thing is that we need you in the Situation Room. The ship is down and General Bonner is afraid that the colonists will seize it. We've got Bonner, Opper, and Restivo coming over from the Pentagon right now." As if to punctuate the aide's comment, she heard a chopper landing out front. The aide had heard it too - he looked over his shoulder. "Ma'am, we really need you in the Situation Room."

Themba turned to her two friends and gave them her best smile. "I'm sorry; I really do have to deal with this." She sighed theatrically and raised her eyebrows. "It's always something, right? You two stay here and make yourselves at home, and I'll be back as soon as I can." She turned to the aide. "Let's go."

* * *

Themba looked at the general. "Why is the ship even there? I thought the invasion wasn't for two more days?"

"Any military operation is a sequence of steps. In this case, we started a week ago - degrading their orbital infrastructure, inserting our com and spy satellites in place, sending recon to make sure that there are no surprises." He grimaced. "As it turns out, there was a surprise. Our robotic probes over the past few weeks didn't see anything. But the Paul-Henri Spaak and the Oswaldo Aranha found a secret expat facility." He paused. "Several, actually. Big industrial operations hidden on Farside."

Themba shook her head. These DoD idiots. "How did your probes miss that?"

"We don't know, ma'am. We've got a team reviewing the image intelligence now. But the important thing is that we've got a ship down, and we need to -"

She spoke to her aide. "I still want to talk to Jim Gaunce about the gun thing. Get him here." She turned to Bonner. "How long since the expats shot the ship down?"

Bonner looked at the clock. "Thirty-nine minutes."

Themba tapped her fingers on the table for a moment. "What are we facing? What's the worst case scenario?"

"We've got one ship down, and one in overwatch. The crash looks bad, but we've got some telemetry still transmitting from subsystems in the wreck. It's possible that there are survivors, but I wouldn't bet on it."

"If there are survivors they could take prisoners. What else happens if they seize the ship?"

"We don't know if the cryptography hardware self-destructed or not. It's designed to -"

"How many prisoners might they take?"

"We don't know that there are survivors -"

"How bad could it be?"

Bonner blinked. "Bad, ma'am?"

"How many survivors might there be?"

"Again, we've got no indication of any. I'd bet on zero. But..."

"Spit out."

"It could be as many as twenty-five."

Themba shook her head, imagining that. The photos - the video - would be terrible. And not just as expat propaganda. She winced even thinking about the ads the opposition could run.

She turned to Don Rouse, her Chief of Staff. "Don, make sure that the expats can't seize the - what was it?"

"Cryptography hardware."

"Right. Make sure the cryptography hardware is safe."

She looked around the table. "Is there anything else?"

There was no answer.

She stood. With a clatter the rest of the room pushed back their chairs and stood as she walked out the door.

* * *

General Restivo watched the president leave. As soon as the door closed behind her Don Rouse took control of the meeting. "OK, people. We need to destroy the downed ship. Capabilities first. Military: can we do this?"

General Opper twisted his lips as he thought. "We've got coms to the wreck via relay satellites. The only question is if the scuttling charges survived the fall. They're designed to, but-"

"Let's assume they did." Don turned to Gene Wilson. "Legal. Are we going to get heat for this?".

Restivo narrowed his eyes. They were worrying about legal justification? Now?

"This is all joint with the UN, so no problems there." Wilson said. "Europe has been on board since we told them about this. The press could theoretically raise a stink about a nuclear detonation in outer space-"

"Don't worry about the press. What about China?"

Wilson shrugged. "Even if China wanted to object, Chairman Peng doesn't want us to make a stink about Hohhot, so he's going to keep his mouth shut. We're good."

Don nodded to Alex D'Angeo. "Elections are coming - what are the optics on this?"

"As long as there's no video - wait." A grin slowly spread over his face. "What if it's not our nuke, but the expats'? They initiated hostilities. Nuked one of *our* ships."

Don thought about it for a moment. "Interesting idea, but hold it close for now. I've got to wargame it with a few other people."

General Restivo gritted his teeth. He hated this part of Washington. The deceit. The calculation. Still, it wasn't his business.

And then, before he realized it, he was talking. "Should we try one last time to see if there any survivors on the ship? Maybe the expats could -"

Don looked at him coldly. "General Bonner said that there's zero indication of survivors."

Bonner, next to him, cleared his throat, and made the smallest hand motion possible. Restivo got the message. Drop it.

Don scanned the table. "So do we have any objections?"

Restivo looked down at the table. No one else was going to object. And he realized that he had to keep his mouth shut too.

Those stars were weighing pretty heavily on his shoulders these last few years.

"OK, the clock is ticking - we don't want the expats to seize any equipment. Let's do it."

Chapter 97

2064: just west of Zhukovskiy Crater, Lunar Farside

John crouched behind a boulder a few meters back from the crater lip. The Dogs were hiding behind another two boulders to his left and the mules were crouched down behind an outcropping to his right.

John verified that his laser com was still locked on to one of Gamma's relay rovers. "Still no reaction?"

"No, John. It has been fifty-seven minutes and twenty-two seconds since the ship stopped descending and assumed position above the surface. I have asked it to depart multiple times but I have received no response."

"Any other coms traffic?"

"Yes. There have been repeated broadcasts between the ship and what I assume are relay satellites in lunar orbit. The traffic is encrypted."

John tapped one finger against the boulder and then looked over his shoulder again. He'd prefer to be further away from the PK ship, but it would be stupid to break cover. He and the Dogs were here for a while longer.

John turned back to the direction of the ship, wishing he could see through the boulder. He could, however, bring up one of Gamma's camera feeds. He did so, and saw the spacecraft hovering.

"What sort of ships are they, Gamma?"

"Most of the IFF data fields are encrypted, but comparing the visual profile against all entries in Jane's Fighting Ships database, they appear to be modified -"

Gamma's voice died suddenly and the video feed ended with it. Was Gamma having some sort of video and audio processing glitch? Was the second ship attacking Gamma?

There was a ping in his helmet as Max tried to talk to him over the laser coms, but John ignored it. Instead he rose from his crouch, risking a peek over the boulder. The second ship was still floating above the surface, where it had been for almost an hour - and it was brighter than it had been when he'd last looked. *Much* brighter.

What was going on? Suddenly he had a chilling thought. He spun in place and faced Zhukovskiy, where Gamma's facility was, and where the first ship had crashed. His moment of panic passed. There was no growing sphere of superheated air, no mushroom cloud. He'd been insane to think it was a nuke. Why would the PK ships -

But, wait. With no atmosphere there wouldn't be any of those effects, would there? No, if there was a nuclear detonation -

John broke radio silence and yelled to all the Dogs at once. "Get down! Incoming shock -"

And then it hit.

The ground rolled and John staggered and fell. The mules and the Dogs, all blessed with more legs than he had, stayed on their feet. John was picking himself up off the ground a few seconds later when a second smaller shock wave hit and knocked him down again. He rolled to his stomach, pushed himself to his hands and knees - and decided to stay there. A few seconds passed with no more shocks and John climbed warily to his feet. Around him the Dogs were barking and shouting over the radio.

He heard Blue yell, "John, look at the ship!"

John turned to follow Blue's outstretched foreleg. The second ship had been caught in the glare of the exploding bomb and was now listing badly to one side as it descended to the surface.

As the ship dropped, it came level with the rim of the Zhukovskiy-c-177's crater wall. A moment later it was below them and John was looking down on it. The deck-mounted auto cannons looked ominous and large. As the ship settled onto the gravel of the crater floor, the huge landing gear compressed.

John looked at the chain guns and involuntarily took a step backward. The running lights on the ship shone brightly; it was wounded, but not dead.

John started to call Gamma and then stopped. After that nuclear blast Gamma - or rather, the local instance of Gamma in Zhukovskiy - was certainly dead.

And then it struck him.

Gamma was dead. The relay satellites were dead. He and the Dogs were once again a thousand kilometers from the nearest friendly face, alone and unarmed. Except they weren't alone. They were facing a US/PK ship armed with chain guns and full of soldiers. And overhead there were enemy satellites.

God help him, John felt alive.

John made the "quiet" sign to the Dogs, positioned a remote camera on a rock and aimed it at the PK ship. He made more hand signs.

- follow me - hurry -

Then he turned from the ship and ran.

***

John watched the PK ship through the camera. Twelve armed and armored soldiers were on the ground in front of the Oswaldo Aranha. John felt a bead of sweat form on his forehead and then dribble down his face. It rolled into one eye and he tried to blink the sting away. The liquid-cooled underwear they all wore reacted to body temperature, but it couldn't detect or help sweat caused by nervousness.

Twelve of the bastards, all armed with rifles - and presumably more inside the ship. *Please don't let them figure out that we're up here.*

On the video one of the space-suited PKs looked down at boot tracks in the dust and tapped a second one on the shoulder before pointing.

Shit. He aimed his laser at Blue. "Blue, take the mules and the guys, and fall back. Find some outcropping and get behind it. Don't use the radio. Don't do anything until you hear from me." John paused. "And for the love of God, don't -"

"I'll keep Duncan quiet."

John nodded. "And -"

"I'll keep Max from doing anything stupid."

Good. It was nice to have another adult in the group.

Blue signaled to the others and they moved out, heading away from the lip of c-177 and the damaged PK ship. The mules followed the Dogs.

John crouched behind the boulder and watched the action below via the remote camera. The troops on the surface had split up. Five headed west, away from Gamma's facility and back along the hikers' original path. Another group headed east toward the crack in the Zhukovskiy crater wall, following the highway of rover tracks in the dust.

The final two soldiers, though - they were following the bootprints, heading straight toward the pile of scree that led up to where John and the Dogs were hiding.

John felt his breath catch. He forced himself to breathe regularly. *Be calm. Evaluate the situation. Figure out a plan.*

The soldiers were each armed with rifles and he had nothing.

What sort of plan was going to work against *that*?

He kept looking at them. There was some weakness, something he could exploit. He just had to identify it.

The two were armed...but they were also staring down at the ground as they walked. And their rifles were slung.

John breathed in and out slowly.

Alright. These aren't real soldiers, just PKs. Just two of them. Not a problem. Not. A. Problem.

He could do this.

John called up a satellite map of the area from cache and studied it, confirming his understanding of the local topography.

He and the Dogs were in rolling terrain to the south of the southern wall of the mini crater Zhukovskiy-c-177. Thirty meters to the west, his left, was a taller outcropping that stuck up above the rest of the rim.

He knew the ship was in the center of the crater, and he knew groups of PKs were moving east and west on the crater floor - and two more were moving south, right toward him.

He took a second camera from his belt pouch, placed it in the dust and aimed it carefully, and then pushed himself into a low crouch. Moving quickly, he followed the trail left by the Dogs and the mules. Thirty meters to the south he came over a low rise and saw Blue and the others. For a second he thought about breaking radio silence - given that the wounded PK ship was blocked by the crater wall it might be safe - but better not to risk it. He stuck to laser.

"Blue!"

Blue spun. "John!"

"Listen. I'm out of cameras. I need you to drop one right here. Point it back along the track." He gestured with his hand toward the direction they'd just come from. "Then get everyone and the mules further back behind that large boulder there - " he pointed a bit beyond the Dogs "- and hide."

Blue nodded and took a camera from his belt.

Max broke in. "The PKs are coming? We can take them."

"No, stay down. There are two of them coming after us. I'm going to circle around and pick them off. Listen to Blue and stay hidden, because -"

"I can help out. Let me -"

John didn't have time for this. He cut Max off, angrily. "Max, damn it, just stay hidden. Unity of command. I think I'll succeed, but if I don't, then you'll get your chance to fight PKs."

Max took a deep breath, then nodded.

Duncan looked back and forth between them. "If you don't succeed? Do you mean -"

"Let's hope it doesn't come to that."

"John, if you don't - " Duncan licked his lips nervously. "If you don't succeed, do you think we can surrender?"

Max and John spoke at the same time. "No."

Duncan hung his head.

Rex said, "I've got an idea for a fallback plan."

John checked the clock in his display. The troops would be over the crater wall soon.

"Tell it to Max."

If he failed at this, it would mean not only his own death, but theirs as well. Should he tell them to stay safe? Tell them how much they - and the rest of the Dogs at Aristillus - meant to him?

Fuck it. There was no time.

John turned and began moving quickly in large ground-covering arcs back toward the crater rim.

He didn't head for the landslide of scree they'd climbed, but circled wide to the west, putting a three-story-tall outcropping between him and the trail they'd laid down. Between him and where the PKs would climb the rim.

On the far side of the outcropping he found a crack in the granite and slipped into the pitch black shadow. He brought up his overlay and called up the video feed from the first camera, the one looking down into the crater. The footage was jerky from data dropouts; the microwatt transmitter in the camera wasn't designed to punch through stone like this.

The first camera showed ten men still down in the crater. The two heading toward the landslide were invisible - perhaps they'd followed the tracks all the way to the scree and were already climbing.

He was about to switch to the second camera when a spacesuited arm reached over the crater wall. And then the two PKs were pulling themselves over the edge.

A moment later they stood. His helmet speakers crackled as one of the PKs pointed at the camera. "What's that?"

The idiots were talking over an open, unencrypted channel.

The other PK reached for the camera, and then the image slewed. A moment later John was staring, through his overlay, at the PK's helmet from arm's length. Out of habit John looked away before remembering that they couldn't see him. He turned his eyes back to the PK.

The golden visor, the divot at the brow of the helmet. They were wearing Airtights. The two suits had PK rank stripes crudely stenciled onto the biceps and last names painted on the chests. "Ting" and "Al Farran." John scowled. The suits must have been taken from the RTFM or one of the other seized ships. The symbolism of the crude PK paint jobs on top of the elegant Aristillus suits annoyed him.

Still, the fact that the suits were stolen didn't matter. The important thing is that he knew the Gen Vs. He knew how the KO_2 scrubber was mounted and he knew where the air tube ran. John closed his eyes and slowed his breathing, and then rolled his neck from side to side. He opened his eyes and looked at the video.

The PK holding the camera played with it a moment longer and then tossed it aside. The view spun wildly and the error-correcting software left blocks and smears across the overlay; then the camera landed in the dust.

John cleared the screen and looked out from the dark crack he was hidden in. A moment later the PKs walked into his line of sight as they followed the trail he and the Dogs had laid down. They were looking down as they walked and over the radio channel he could hear them chatting about the Brazilian national soccer team. Perfect. John clenched and released his hands once, twice.

Then the PKs were past. John stretched his neck one last time, and reached down to his belt where the repair kit hung. He pulled the pouch open, pushed aside the bottle of sealant and the patches, and found the rescue knife. It wasn't a fighting knife, but it was designed to cut through a space suit or tangled cord. It would do.

John stepped out of the crevasse and into the sunlight. The two PKs, "Ting" and "Al Farran," were ahead of him. Still stumbling forward and staring at the footprints in the dust. Still talking about a soccer match.

John took a moment to look around and make sure that he wasn't missing anything: a third man, another ship overhead. No. He was good. He turned back to Ting and Al Farran. The two idiots were walking almost side by side, which helped his chances. He followed them, moving deliberately but quickly. A stray thought occurred to him: having hiked a few thousand kilometers across the moon's surface, he was probably the world's foremost expert on lunar surface travel. He revised the thought: he was the foremost *human* expert.

He drew closer to the two PKs: they were just three meters ahead now. They walked on, clueless. In the vacuum they heard nothing. John checked the clock in his screen and tightened his grip on the hilt of the knife.

One last exhalation and a rapid step forward and he was on them. John reached out with his left hand and grabbed the air hose that connected the back of Ting's helmet to his life support pack. The PK stumbled.

"Hey, what -".

John slid his knife into the gap between the hose and the helmet ring, and then pulled the blade across the hose. The layers of reflective foil, warming wires, Kevlar strands, polymer tube, and repair vacuoles parted.

Ting stumbled forward, finishing his sentence " - *the fuck*?"

John let go with his left hand and covered the two meters to Al Farran. The second PK was just starting to turn in response to Ting's yell when John was on him. From this angle the air hose was harder to reach. Plan B. With his left hand John grabbed the PK's shoulder. Farran brought one hand up instinctively to ward him off, and in doing so left his stomach unguarded.

The knife punched in exactly where John had aimed it: a bit higher than the interior waist reinforcing seam, right at kidney level.

John yanked the knife savagely to the side. Al Farran didn't realize that he'd been stabbed - or that his suit had been sliced open.

"Who the *fuck-* ?"

John grabbed one of the troop's outstretched hands, twisted, and pulled the PK off balance. The man tripped and went down - and then the pain hit.

Al Farran screamed as he fell. He hit, and the air venting from the savage tear in his suit blew a cloud of dust off the ground. Both hands clutched at the rip in his suit. John stepped into billowing gray, grabbed the hose on the back of Al Farran's helmet, and parted it with a slice.

There.

Both men were down.

John checked the timer in his display.

Six seconds.

This suit was slowing him down, but he'd done well enough.

John returned the knife to the sheath, snapped the safety strap over it, and then waited for the men to finish dying. A minute. Then two. He stepped up to Al Farran's body and pulled the rifle from the corpse, tugging until the sling slipped off the dead man's shoulder.

He held the weapon out and looked it over. An YM-20 with triggers and fire selector switches modified for gloved hands in arctic combat. Or, in this case, lunar combat. A forty-year-old design, but decent.

And there - the mesh bag on the PK's belt looked like it held magazines.

John slung the rifle, unclipped the bag from the PK, and snapped it onto a D-ring on his own suit. He turned to the second corpse and stripped it of rifle and ammunition.

He held the rifle in low ready and started walking back to the Dogs.

After a few steps he had a thought. No. Even they wouldn't be that dumb.

He stopped and pulled the charging handle back half way.

The chamber had been empty.

Jesus.

Fucking amateurs.

John cycled the firearm and chambered a round.

Chapter 98

2064: just west of Zhukovskiy Crater, Lunar Farside

John looked around. This was where he'd left Blue and the others... And there, Dog and mule tracks led around a large boulder. He followed them - and then ducked as a barrage of fist-sized rocks flew straight at his helmet. One of the rocks hit his forearm. "Jesus, guys, it's me!"

There was a brief pause. "Oh," said Max. "Sorry John. We thought -"

John shook his head. "Rocks?"

"You came around the corner with a rifle..."

"OK. But next time pay attention to the suits. The peakers have rank stripes painted on their biceps and names on the chest."

The Dogs barked assent.

"Tell us what happened."

"I took out the two that came up here to the rim. The other ten are still down on the crater floor."

Duncan furrowed his brow. "Took out? How?"

"Later."

Max said, "What now?"

"I've got to take out the rest."

"You want us to stay back here again?"

"Yeah."

"Give me one of the rifles."

John looked at Max, thought about it for a moment, then unslung the second YM-20 and handed it to him.

Max tried to shoulder the rifle, but it was a losing battle. The pull was too long for his short foreleg. John thought briefly of breaking out the repair kit from one of the mules and lopping off several centimeters of stock, but realized that the pull was the least of Max's problems. Between his stubby fingers and a wrist that couldn't pronate as fully as a human's, it just wasn't going to work.

No, if Max and the others needed firearms it would have to wait until they were back at Aristillus and had access to modeling programs and 3D printers.

John reached out and laid a hand on the rifle. Max looked at him and didn't let it go. "Max, it's not going to work." Max held on for another second. He knew what must be going through the Dog's head - nothing felt as bad as impotence in the face of a dangerous situation.

Reluctantly, slowly, Max let go.

John reslung the rifle. "The PKs are going to notice those two missing any time now. I've got to go."

Max snarled. "We need real weapons."

"Nothing we can do now. Wish me good hunting."

The Dogs echoed the phrase, and then Duncan asked, "Aren't you scared?"

"I'll be back."

John hitched his right shoulder up to keep the spare rifle in position, and then turned.

Max called after him, "Kill some for me."

John headed for the crater rim.

Mike had been arguing for years that the war was coming. John had always pushed back, insisting that it wasn't, or that if it was, it was years off. Now he shook his head. Mike had been right and he'd been wrong.

He'd been engaging in wishful thinking: wishing that the threat to the Dogs was over...and wishing that he wasn't really going to end up in a shooting war with old friends and colleagues on the other side.

Shit.

But if the war was really here, then he knew what he had to do. First, he had to kill the rest of the PKs. If he survived that, he had to get back to Aristillus and warn Mike not just about PKs on the farside, but about Gamma. And after that, he had a war to win.

His mind raced with ideas. Strategies. Tactics. And smaller stuff. The trivial stuff that shouldn't matter but always did.

He pulled up a note-taking application and wrote

- talk to Katherine Dycus; better thermal control in suits

He looked down at his waist where the two mesh bags of magazines bounced and added

- ammo pockets

And then he was near the edge of the crater. He'd get the rifle sighted in back here, away from the lip, and then he'd move forward to the rim.

He leaned the spare rifle against a rock and then adjusted the sling on the other one.

Time to verify his equipment.

The PK ship had been, what? Three hundred meters from the crater wall? He picked a boulder about that far away, bent his head down - and then realized he couldn't get a cheek weld with the helmet in the way. Shit. If his cheek was tight against the stock he'd have a good on-parallax view through the heads-up scope on top of the rifle. Without a tight weld he had to look through the scope at an angle.

He pulled back and looked at the rifle. Was there some trick? Did the scope extend up from the receiver?

No.

So what the hell had the US and PK leadership been thinking? They'd sent men to the moon, armed them with rifles, and never even verified that they could shoot the damned things? And not one of the PK grunts had raised an objection?

Jesus.

Fucking idiots, every one of them.

And it meant that he had a problem. If he had to deal with this parallax bullshit, his bullets wouldn't impact where he wanted them to. There must be a solution.

John experimented and finally found that pushing the rifle forward and craning his head back a few centimeters helped. The line of sight from his eyes through the optics was a bit closer to parallel with the barrel.

Not perfect, but it would have to do.

Now to test his aim.

He found the boulder he'd picked before and tried to flip the selector switch. His clumsy suit gloves made it tricky even with the Arctic-combat modifications, but the switch flipped from 'safe' to 'fire.'

And then he squeezed the trigger. The rifle's silent kick was minimal.

The dust a meter to the left of the boulder splashed. A miss. The parallax. Shit.

He had to hurry - but he also had to get this right.

He could deal with the parallax - he just had to tweak the scope. He realized the problem with that a moment later and cursed as he tried to adjust the small calibration dials on the sight with his bulky gloves.

He fished a screwdriver from his repair kit. After almost a minute of fiddling he finally managed to get the calibration dials adjusted. Another round fired - and the bullet hit just a hands-breadth from the boulder. Another few adjustments, another few shots, and he was hitting the center of the boulder reliably.

The rifle still had sloppy trigger pull, but Kazakhstan, Nairobi, and the Saud Protectorate were all proof that equipment counted for less than a coherent plan.

And he had one. If he could carry it out crisply - and if he could deal with the inevitable shit storm when it went bad - he might be OK.

Or maybe not.

Either way, he was as ready as he was going to be. Time to do it.

John turned away from his impromptu range and approached the edge of the crater. As he got closer he dropped to all fours and crawled forward. As he covered the last few meters to the edge he picked up the radio chatter from the peakers down in the crater.

" - don't know about that - I think Barcelona has a chance against Manchester, but -"

"Keep this channel clear you two!"

A pause, and then a resentful "Yes, sir."

John inched further to the edge and looked over. The PK ship was still in the center of the crater.

John pulled the sling tight around his forearms and pushed the rifle out against the tension. More radio traffic:

"Major Tudel, squad one reporting. We're through the crack in the east wall. Everything's fucked here. The Paul Henri is *gone* - there's just a massive fucking hole. Most of the moon base equipment is destroyed."

"Our intel says the expats live underground. Find some airlocks, see if the power is still on."

"Shit, Major, do we have to? This shit's gotta be radioactive as fuck -"

"You went to the briefings just like I did. The nuclear scuttling charges are nothing like nuclear power plants."

"But Major -"

"All of this is on audio and video, and it's going to be reviewed. Now, get in there and scout for tunnel entrances."

A pause, then "OK, Major."

Safe nuclear weapons? John shook his head - what sort of bullshit were they feeding the grunts these days?

And speaking of nuclear weapons, the scout had said that the explosion had left a crater. If the nuke dug a hole when it popped, that meant *lots* of vaporized crap, and *lots* of fallout. John turned his attention away from the crater floor and looked up. There was no visible mushroom cloud, but there must be a huge amount of irradiated crap overhead. If he and the Dogs weren't already in a shower of radioactive dust, they would be soon. His skin itched just thinking about it.

First things first, though.

John turned back to the crater floor. The five PKs he'd just overheard on the radio were through the crack to the east and weren't visible. The five who had headed west, though, had reached wherever they were going and were now heading back to the downed PK ship. At that moment one of them reported in. "Outside the crater wall the tracks just spread out. No hardware, no people, no other facilities that we can see. We're coming back."

The leader - Major Tudel? - answered. "Roger, I can see you from here."

That must mean that Tudel was in the ship. How many others were there with him? It would be nice to know, but in the end it didn't matter. John's plan was the same no matter what: he'd take out the western five, then the eastern five when they came back through the crack in the Zhukovskiy wall, and then he'd deal with anyone in the ship. Or try to.

So - the western five. They were clumped together, just like Ting and Al Farran had been. The clumping had worked to his advantage in the knife fight, but he wished that these five were spread out a bit more.

No help for it.

The scope said that the range was just over 400 meters, which was further than he'd sighted in. There was also an elevation drop of - he took a guess - about 140 meters. The heads-up sight did the ballistics calculation for him. For a moment he was about to trust it, but then remembering that the sights hadn't even been adjusted for spacesuit helmets, John realized that the chance that its firmware had been reprogrammed to deal with lower lunar gravity was almost zero.

And - shit. Chances were that the sight not only was expecting one g, but also was doing math based on bullets slowing down in air. He was going to have to compensate for all of this himself.

Damn it.

This plan just got a hell of a lot more complicated.

OK, he needed to focus to solve the ballistics problem. So what did that mean?

Lower gravity would flatten the trajectory, and zero air resistance would change the shape even more. Fuck. Max or Blue could probably figure this out in their heads, doing the raw calculus. For him, though, it was hopeless.

Wait. Given the silence of the vacuum he could practice: he could fire a few shots at that rock twenty or thirty meters behind the five PKs and zero in based on that.

He breathed deeply, pushed the rifle out to tighten the sling, and adjusted his body with small movements until the cross hairs slid onto a rock behind the PKs. What Kentucky windage did he need? Lower gravity meant that the bullet would fly higher than expected. He wiggled one hip forward and watched as the sight picture dipped. When the rock was three tick marks up from the center John moved his index finger off of the receiver and onto the trigger.

A squeeze.

The shot didn't hit the rock, but he did see a splash of dust: the bullet had hit the ground just a few meters in front of his target. Good. John adjusted his aim-point, putting the rock four tick marks up from the crosshairs, and one tick to the left.

Another shot. This time there was a splash of rock fragments near the center of the rock, almost exactly where he'd aimed. This was good. Really good.

It was time.

John twitched his hips, and the sight picture swung imperceptibly and the PKs came into his view. They were still walking east, halfway back to their ship.

John slid the reticule over the helmet of the leftmost figure, who lagged behind the others. His ad hoc windage had been four tick marks down, one left. He adjusted his scope and squeezed the trigger.

The figure dropped.

The other four men kept walking.

Time to adjust his aim. He relaxed his left bicep a bit, the sling loosened a hair...and the cross hairs moved over another helmet. He adjusted his windage again.

A squeeze.

And the figure dropped to the ground.

And then, over the radio: "What the *fuck*! My suit! I've got a hole in my suit!"

A hit - but he'd winged the guy, not taken him out. Did he need another shot? No, the PK's air would be gone soon enough.

Through his scope John saw the three remaining figures turn.

Their backs were to him now.

John adjusted his aim a hair, putting the crosshair on another PK, slid his finger onto the trigger -

And then the man he was aiming at bent over to help the one with the bullet hole in his suit.

His helmet was barely visible, hidden behind the shoulder mounted life support gear. Should John switch to another target?

He thought for a moment. No. He didn't need headshots. In spacesuits, any hit was a good hit. Sure, it might be a bit less elegant than Carlos Hathcock would've preferred, but it would work.

John put his crosshairs back on the PK, aiming at the back of his suit, and squeezed.

A miss.

And then radio chatter got more frantic: not only were the three untouched PKs trying to patch the suit of the second target, but they had noticed the first downed PK.

John held his breath for a moment and took another shot. The third suited figure went down.

"Fuck! Ah! There's something in my back - something hit me - and I've got a rip!"

Two PKs left standing.

John aimed at the fourth figure and squeezed.

A miss.

Tudel's voice came over the radio. "What's going on out there?"

One of the men yelled. "Major! Shit! We've got three men down!"

"Down? What do you mean 'down'? What the fuck is happening?"

"The suits are ripping - these fucking suits don't work -"

Another shot - the fourth figured fell to the ground. "Shit, my ass! Something shot me in the ass!"

"Shooting? Who's shooting? Are there expats on the scene?"

The last PK stood straight up, looked around for a second and broke into an awkward run toward the ship.

"Wait, Fred, don't leave us here!"

Fred ignored him and leaned forward as he ran.

"Fred, you mother fucker! Get back here, man!"

John tried to follow him with his scope, but the man bounced in and out of frame.

Shit.

And then Fred, clearly not used to lunar gravity, tripped and pitched forward.

John slid the crosshairs over the PK's helmet - and the man recovered and got back to his feet.

John tried to follow him.

The PK tripped again. As he pushed himself to all fours John's reticle slid over the man's mirrored face plate.

John squeezed.

Dust splashed a hand's breadth from the helmet.

"Fuck! Major! They're shooting at me!"

The man was on his feet and running again.

"Get back to the ship, right now."

"I'm trying, Major!"

The PK tripped for the third time. The man caught himself with both arms and was starting to rise when John squeezed the trigger.

The faceplate shattered and the PK fell back into the dust.

Tudel's voice: "There he is, on the crater wall! Near the top of the landslide."

John's breath caught. They knew where he was. The cold shock of adrenaline flashed through him.

Should he run?

No.

The PKs were armed, but if they had the same uncalibrated scopes on their rifles he did, he was safe.

OK, so who was Tudel talking to? The troops who'd headed East into Zhukovskiy?

He looked - no, they weren't back yet.

John swung his sights back to the five PKs in the western group. There. Two of the men he'd shot were standing. One was struggling to apply a patch to the suit of the other. "Hurry up! Hurry up!"

Tudel again: "Is anyone listening to me? He's on the crater wall! To the south. Engage the target!"

John smiled. There was no way they were going to hit him.

And then he remembered that the downed ship had chain guns mounted on the deck.

Shit.

He'd better finish this off before this Major Tudel remembered it too.

A shot. A miss.

Another shot. Another miss.

Damn it. He was nervous. He breathed in and out and willed his heartbeat to slow.

A third shot, and the PK holding the patch went down.

A final shot. The last PK pitched forward.

John shimmied backward from the edge. A meter. Two. Four. A moment later he felt the ground shudder. A spray of rock chips exploded ahead of him, right where he'd been lying.

Jesus. It looked like Tudel had remembered the chain guns.

John crawled back another few meters.

OK, the western team was taken care of - but that still left the eastern team. He'd need to relocate to a new position, then find them, then take them out. But first things first. He glanced at the rifle. The magazine readout had started at 40 and was now down to 23. He hadn't realized he'd fired that many rounds. John rolled to one side to reach his magazine pouch -

- And saw the boot aimed at his face.

He flinched, but too late - the kick landed on the side of his helmet. His head bounced painfully off the side of his helmet.

His head rang. He fumbled with his rifle but his left arm was caught on something - the sling.

Another kick. His head bounced painfully off the helmet interior again. There was something in his eyes - blood. He tried to raise himself on his left arm and again the sling got in his way. He gave up on his rifle and groped for the knife with his right hand.

God damn it, he wasn't going to die like this! His right glove landed on the hilt of his knife just as another kick caught him.

He saw the crack marks in his faceplate.

Another kick.

He tried to roll; yet another kick landed. The world went black.

*　*　*

Blue scanned the horizon. Nothing.

He was about to call up the clock in his overlay when Duncan said, "John's taking too long. Something must have happened. Let's call him."

Max shook his head. "We have to stay off the radios. But I can go there and -"

"No. We're unarmed."

"We've got rocks."

"Rocks?"

"Yes, rocks. John killed two of them with a knife. They're weak, and we have the will to win. One Dog with a sharp rock can -"

"No. Let's let Rex finish his coding."

Max growled. "You're not in charge." "Actually, I am. John said so, remember?"

Max growled again and stared at Blue. Blue refused to turn away and stared back. After a long moment Max looked away.

* * *

The fucking expat had killed five of his men - and now he was splayed out unconscious in the dust, his faceplate cracked.

Tudel said, "Nice work, Nelson."

Sergeant Nelson grunted.

Tudel looked at the expat and smiled, but then his gaze drifted to the crater and the Oswaldo Aranha. His smile faltered and slipped away.

His flagship was fucked. The paint on one side was blistered and burned and half the AG units were out, and the other ship had been shot down by the expats' guns in Zhukovskiy proper and the scuttling charge had destroyed what was left.

He let the full situation sink in. He was stuck on farside. One of his ships was destroyed and the other one disabled. He'd lost half his troops in the crash, and now this stupid expat fucker had taken out almost half of the remainder.

Damn it. It wasn't fair. He'd tried to tell General Opper that the two small experimental ships and a handful of infantry wasn't enough, even for a quick recon like this, but, no, that incompetent bastard had brushed him off: "schedules," "operational tempo."

Shit.

And now he was here: his ships dead, his scouting mission fubared, and him stuck here until the fleet sent someone out to rescue him.

He swore. The worst part was that he wouldn't get to participate in the Aristillus invasion. No, he'd be stuck here, camping in his wrecked ship. The message from Washington, relayed through the lunar minisats, had been clear about that - no rescue until the invasion fleet arrived.

Damn it. His career had been fubared after the Wookkiee, and then it had been plucked from disaster when he'd been given this scouting mission. And now it was a disaster again. He was fucked. He was going to be RIF-ed, if not court martialed.

He looked down at the expat at his feet.

This was the bastard who had done it.

He brought the rifle to his shoulder, flipped the selector to single shot and aimed it at the center of the faceplate.

He paused.

No. Tudel flipped the selector back to safe. This bastard didn't deserve something that clean. A head shot was a soldier's death. Honorable.

The expats were traitors and deserved to be treated like it.

Tudel pulled his right leg back and kicked. The expat's head snapped back. *Wake up, you bastard.* Tudel kicked again. Again the head snapped back, but there was still no other motion. Shit. It would be better if the expat fucker was awake.

Tudel swung his leg back for a third kick - and noticed that the cracks in the man's faceplate were growing. He paused. The cracks spread further, and then the dust around the man's helmet began to jump and swirl. Tudel smiled and watched the show, hoping for something more - maybe the entire faceplate would blow out and he'd get to see the expat's blood-covered face.

After a minute the streams of air slowly petered out and died.

Tudel prodded the expat's body one more time.

Nothing.

Shit. Not satisfying. Not satisfying at all.

But so be it. He had work to do. "East team, any airlocks or bunkers?"

The response was staticky and jumbled. "Not so far. It looks like just a mining facility. Maybe automated. Lots of wrecked robots and conveyor belts, but no bunker, no windows, no doors. Major - we don't have Geiger counters or anything, but it's *got* to be pretty hot around here. Can we come back now?"

The men were being pussies, but if there were no expats there, the smart move was to bring them over. Especially as the bootprints near where he stood showed that there were more expats lurking.

"OK, pull back. Meet me on the south rim of c-177. We've got some expat activity out here. They took out Ting and Al Farran. I took one of them out, but there are more."

Nelson looked at him when he'd said that he took out the expat. Whatever. Fuck him.

"OK, Major, we're coming right now!"

Tudel looked to the south where the footprints led.

Nelson looked at the tracks. "Looks like they've got something with them. Robots - and maybe some midgets or something."

Tudel looked at his clock. It shouldn't take the men more than ten minutes to get here. He looked at the corpse again. The expat had had two rifles.

Two?

He picked one up and examined it. Government issue with the arctic mods. This wasn't an expat rifle - he'd taken these off of Ting and Al Farran after he'd killed them.

Tudel looked around the body. There were no other firearms. That didn't make sense. He and his buddies must have had guns when they'd killed Ting and Al Farran. So why had this one left his own gun and taken Ting's and Al Farran's? It made no sense.

He shrugged. Just another mystery. Screw it.

What he needed now was hard data. He called up an overhead view from one of the minisats. The timestamp on this one said that it was just minutes old, it was the same bullshit data they'd been been seeing all along - no facility at Zhukovskiy, nothing. When he got back to Earth his career might be fucked, but he was definitely going to fuck the techs who were behind this - he'd let the brass know that the techs were faking the minisat data instead of sending the up-to-the-minute updates. A few heads would roll over that one.

He turned back to the map. It didn't show his men or the expat forces, but he could still get a feel for the lay of the land. He zoomed in and dragged the map around, memorizing features.

He closed the map and looked to the south where the bootprints disappeared over a ridge. Wait - what was that? Movement? He looked again. The tip of something - maybe an antenna - bounced into view on the far side of the ridge, then disappeared.

Or had it? Were his eyes playing tricks on him? "Nelson, did you see that?"

"See what, sir?"

Tudel shook his head. "Tai, move your ass. I need you and your men up here ASAP".

"We're almost there, Major - look behind you."

Tudel turned and saw Tai and his four troops approaching. Good.

He waited till they reached him, and then gestured. "See the tracks? I think I just saw movement off to the right. Five or ten meters past that ridge. Sergeant Ting, move your team up using over-watch, and flank to the left of that boulder." He pointed. "Yell if you see anything, but otherwise continue past the boulder, then turn right."

Tudel remembered the kinds of idiots he was dealing with and decided to add a clarification that he shouldn't have to make. "Pay attention to the tracks - but don't *just* pay attention to the tracks. I want situational awareness - keep your eyes moving. Nelson, you go with them."

The men divided into two groups of three, and took turns bounding forward. They were awkward in their spacesuits, but Sergeant Tai kept correcting them, telling them to form up, making them scan the area.

The fire teams disappeared over the ridge.

"Major, we've got two bodies. RFID says it's Ting and Al Farran. Telemetry says they're dead."

"Keep moving."

A minute later Tai said, "Major, there's a *lot* of churned up dust here. I see some weird footprints. Circular indentations; it's gotta be some sort of robot. And those small bootprints? Major - I don't think these are midgets." He paused "Do you remember the news story about the Dogs from six or seven years back?"

"Dogs?" What the hell was Tai going on about?

"You remember. Capital 'd'. Dogs. The genetically modified ones?"

Tudel pursed his lips. "Yeah."

"Well, remember there was a rumor and videos about how they'd been smuggled to the moon - only this is before we knew that there really was a moon colony, and it all turned out to be some viral marketing for a video game? What if that video game story was bullshit, and not all of the Dogs were euthanized? What if some of them really did get smuggled to the moon?"

Tudel raised one eyebrow. Huh. It was a weird theory - but it made some sense. These fucking expats were crazy in so many ways - no government, no schools, living in fucking caves, refusing to pay taxes. He wouldn't be surprised if they had a bunch of rabies-infected animals up here with them. But out on the surface? In space suits? He shook his head. Jesus. These people were idiots.

"Dogs, humans, it's all the same. If you see them, kill them. Now: where do the tracks lead?"

"Off to the right."

"Follow them. But tell me what you see. Any dropped equipment? Anything?"

"We're rounding a ridge now... and, yeah! There are three - I don't know what you call them. Some kinda spider-shaped cargo robots. They're carrying solar cells, cargo lockers, that sort of thing. There are robot tracks everywhere - it's crazy, the tracks run in circles, loop behind boulders."

"Are the robots doing anything? Mining? Building anything?"

"No, they're just crouched down. I think they're powered off."

"OK, fine. Anything else? Any human boot tracks?"

"Nope, just Dog tracks and robot tracks. The Dog tracks loop back toward that big spur by you."

Tudel had been staring off to the south at the low ridge where his men were, but at this he turned to his right. The tracks circled back behind that outcropping?

"I'll take the spur. You and your men investigate those cargo robots."

"Roger that."

Tudel flipped the selector on his rifle to 'fire.'

He walked toward the spur, and the ground dropped away to his right. As he got closer, the base of the outcropping crowded against the crater edge, but didn't meet it - there were several meters of fairly flat ground between the two. Perfect: more than wide enough to navigate safely, but the expats and their Dogs wouldn't be expecting him to come from this direction.

Tudel kept his trigger finger alongside the receiver as he advanced. How many expats were hiding behind the outcropping? And how many Dogs? Two? A dozen? He remembered pictures of them from back when the project was shut down. Weird fucking things with their black-gray-and-beige fur, and their creepy staring brown eyes. Genetically engineered abominations.

Tudel crept forward.

Maybe his career wasn't irrevocably fucked after all. Could this be another last minute save? It wasn't a sure thing, but these freakish mutants could maybe help him.

Sure, he'd lost one ship and a few men. That was a black mark, and there was no way around that. But Bonner and Opper had already shown that they could cope with a bit of mess as long as he got results - and he was getting results. Finding this secret base on the farside of the moon? The brass would love that. Especially since it hadn't shown up on any of the minisat photos. It had been him, Major Frank Tudel. All him. He'd seen the lights from the facility and brought his ships down to investigate.

He crept forward. Nothing yet.

And there was more. This Dog hunt? If you looked at it right, he was cleaning up a leftover mess. That was gold. Solid gold. Above and beyond how it would play with the brass, it would sure as shit earn him some cred with BuSuR. The Bureau had more juice in DC than the DoD did these days. Yeah, this was going to work out. Maybe he could still get light colonel like the generals had hinted - and after that? Maybe he could maneuver for a job over at BuSuR.

Tudel rounded a bolder, and saw a man on all fours. He shouldered his rifle and brought it into firing position.

Wait, not a man. It was one of those Dogs.

The Dog saw him and turned its head. Tudel squeezed - one shot to the center of mass! A loud keening howl came across the radio. Ha! Nailed it! He let it scream for a second and then squeezed the trigger again and put an end to the abomination. Three more shots: two more to the center of mass, then one to the weird elongated helmet, which shattered satisfyingly with a nice spray of air and blood.

Over the radio there was more screaming, this time human. Was that Tai? Nelson? Tudel keyed his mike. "Sergeant Tai, what the fuck iss going on over there?"

Suddenly there was a flash of movement. Something metal, blurred by speed. A thing - a machine? - was galloping down the slope of the promontory. Tudel started to step back, but it was too late - the robot closed the distance in a fraction of a second and hit him dead on. The impact folded him forward over the robot and his head smashed hard against his faceplate.

He was being run over. Tudel flailed at the machine, trying desperately to grab a hand hold, to halt his slide under it.

He was going to be crushed.

And then his left hand landed on a bar, a rod, something, and he clenched his fist around it, just as both feet were swept out from under him.

He swung a foot back to find purchase-

And found nothing.

Fuck!

He was falling - and the spider-robot-thing was falling with him.

He lifted his head and looked up. The robot was above him - and behind it the lip of the crater was moving up and away. The wall of the crater slid past.

God fuck shit!

Tudel and the spider robot rolled as they fell; the crater rim disappeared and black sky replaced it. Above him the robot's legs thrashed and thrashed.

The fall went on.

And on.

Why was this taking so...

Suddenly Tudel remembered the low lunar gravity. Holy hell, he might survive this, if he could avoid getting crushed under the robot. If he could just twist -

And then they hit.

Chapter 99

2064: Karen's Fish, Aristillus, Lunar Nearside

Mike dipped the fried calamari into tartar sauce, chewed, and swallowed. "What do you mean you're not afraid? The satellites just got burned again. That's *twice*. And this time they started by taking out the ones over Farside. That should scare you - hell, it scares me."

Mike looked at Darcy to see if his words were getting through, but she was looking down at her plate, spreading wasabi onto her sashimi with a chopstick.

He continued, "How are we even debating this? Your ship - *your ship* -was hijacked by the PKs. How can you possibly think that this is a good idea?"

Darcy picked up a piece of tuna, dipped into soy sauce, then put it back down. "Mike, I'm not disagreeing with any of those facts. What I am saying is that if you're going to open source the AG drive, it's not as simple as uploading a CAD drawing of some rotors and magnets and cryo-coolers. If people are going to actually *use* it, we need a lot more."

Mike scowled. "Like what?"

"A click-and-forget nav package, for one thing. The UI we've got now is too complicated. It's for power users, and you're proposing that we hand this insanely complicated tool to neophytes and then expect them to use it correctly the first time." She shook her head. "People will die if you do that. We need something simple - a big green button. That means that we need to lock-out launching from certain latitudes and longitudes, a tool to auto-calibrate the AG drive, self-tests, abort procedures - "

Mike waved her points away. "Darcy, the situation is insanely dangerous. The Earth governments are boiling over, and propaganda webcasts from that fucker Hugh - excuse me - and his friends aren't helping. We lost the

RTFM, the Wayward, and Character Forming - and we came damn close to losing the Wookkiee - with you on it! And now with Gamma's sats burned again-"

"They burned the satellites before and nothing came of it."

"That was before. Who knows what they've got planned this time? You can't go out again. It's too dangerous."

"Mike, do you accept that we need to open source the AG drive in order to get a critical mass of population?"

Mike pursed his lips and said nothing.

"You can stay silent if you want to, but you're the one who said those exact words to me, so that counts as a yes. Next question - do you accept that as one of the original authors of the navigation code that I am the best one to develop and test the idiot-proof open-source version of the program?"

"Look, you're *one* of the best, but -"

"Yes, I'm one of the best, and the other top people are working their asses off on other parts of the project. Heck, Ponzie isn't just reworking the drive design, he's also coming with me on the calibration runs. So that's two points in agreement. Third question: to make sure that the auto-calibration features work on actual hardware in the actual Earth gravity field, we need to test in actual Earth gravity: true or false?"

Mike glowered. "Send an unmanned ship. Do it remotely."

Darcy was incredulous. "With a multi-second coms lag? And, worse than that, without having my own eyes on the prototype mini drives? And what am I supposed to use as my eyes and ears as I'm editing code four hundred thousand klicks away? Cameras? And what if I need to adjust some calibration screws or tighten a loose connection?"

Mike crossed his arms silently. Darcy pushed on.

"Look, I'm going on a Fifth Ring ship. Their security upgrade is good - all their ships have been retrofitted with reinforced hatches and man traps behind each door, and they're working with Bao at Trusted Security to get some armed men on each ship. They're even talking about claymores on the deck, and - "

Finally Mike exploded. "I've told you I don't like this, and I've told you why. You can't take risks like this!"

Darcy fixed him with a look. "Mike, I don't appreciate that tone -"

Mike pushed his chair back and stood. "Fuck my tone. I don't appreciate you going out on a God-damned stupid run after I've told you not to."

"Mike, please sit -"

"No, God damn it!" He balled his napkin and threw it down on the table. "I'm not going to sit and listen to this - this - idiocy!" He turned and walked past the silent diners at the other tables staring. After a few steps he turned back. "If you get caught by those bastards, I'm not coming to get you."

Darcy stared at him, open-mouthed.

Mike stalked out of the restaurant, the blood pulsing in his ears.

He pushed through the front door.

God damn it. Why did Darcy have to take these risks? If she got caught, he'd - he'd - he made a fist and punched his thigh. He had no idea what he'd do. Which is why he had to stop her now, before she went.

He reached the sidewalk and looked for his motorcycle before remembering that they'd taken a cab together. He grimaced, looked up and down the sidewalk, and then set off for the nearest taxi stand. As he walked he rubbed a hand over his forehead and his bristle cut. Damn it! He wasn't perfect at keeping his cool in business negotiations, but at least there when you raised your voice and called someone an asshole, you could just apologize and then go on to reach some compromise position. But this? What the hell sort of compromise was he supposed to reach, anyway?

On the one hand, Darcy was right: the revolution needed the open source AG drive to boost the lunar population. Even with the shipping companies running their boats around the clock, the lines of would-be emigres were already stretching out months into the future. The bitching on the discussion boards was reaching a fever pitch as people who had sold their houses and cars for illegal gold were forced to cool their heels, waiting for a slot, hoping not to be arrested. So, yes, transportation needed to be crowd-sourced. Hell, that had been *his* point in the first place! And, yes, Darcy was the right person for the job. Fuck - even though he hated to admit it, she was even right that the only way to do the job was to go to Earth.

But on the other hand, she'd been taken prisoner once already, and the war was heating up. If she went again -

God damn it.

He just didn't know what to do.

The cab stop was just up ahead.

"Mike!"

He just wanted to tell Darcy... Shit, he didn't know what he wanted to tell her. If only-

"Mike! What are you doing here?"

He looked up and saw Javier.

"Jave - what are you doing here?"

"I just had dinner with Mark Soldner down the way. Listen, I've got to tell you a few ideas -"

"This isn't a good time."

"You're going to want to hear this."

"Javier, I'm serious, can we do this later? I'm not in the mood."

Javier was uncharacteristically excited. "Give me a few minutes; then I'll let you go."

Mike sighed. It seemed he couldn't get out of this. "OK."

"You know I was reaching out to Mark, trying to patch things over between the factions in light of the new attack on the satellites? Well, we got to talking about financing the militias, the e-p-doors, some lobbyists on Earth."

"And?"

"And it's all going to require money. A *lot* of money."

"That's not news."

Javier nodded. "So Mark and I were talking about how to finance it. I told him that idea you and I have kicked around - each member of the board taking loans against their firm and property and kicking into the pool. Mark had a different idea. It's based on REITs."

"REITs?" Mike saw Darcy exit the restaurant behind Javier, then turn and see him.

"Real estate investment trusts - it's a synthetic instrument, a diversified bundle of shares in various pieces of real property. But the point he was making was that instead of each of us taking loans by ourselves, we use all these assets together and issue one centralized set of bonds. Not as individuals, but as the Boardroom Group."

Mike looked over Javier's shoulder at Darcy - and she was looking at him. He caught her eye and the two looked at each other for a long moment. Mike tried to let her see that he - what? That he didn't want to fight? That he was sorry? But that despite all of that he still *really* didn't want her to go on the mission?

Whatever got through, it wasn't enough. After a moment Darcy turned and walked down the sidewalk in the opposite direction.

God damn it! Why did women have to be so obtuse?

"Mike, did you hear me?"

"Yeah, I heard you."

"So what do you think?" Jesus. He preferred Javier in his normal laconic mode, not this hyped-up caffeinated version.

Mike sighed. "Uh, it sounds decent, I guess. I don't know. I need to think about it some more." Behind Javier, Darcy had disappeared, lost around a corner or behind other pedestrians.

Shit.

"Well, wait. It gets more interesting. This is where the magic happens. After we bundle the resources, we leverage them."

God damn it - Darcy was gone. But what was Javier saying? Leverage the resources? Mike's eyes narrowed. "Leverage them? How?"

"Fraction reserve banking."

"What does that mean?"

"We start a bank under the aegis of the Boardroom Group, collateralized with real assets - some of Mark's buildings, stock in Morlock, stock in my firm. The bank creates a currency which gives us liquidity. An army fights on its stomach, right? Well you keep an army's stomach full with liquidity." Javier clapped Mike on the shoulder. "We're going to win this war!"

Mike blinked. What was Javier going on about?

A taxi slid silently up to the curb next to them.

Javier glanced at the car. "Anyway, you said this wasn't a good time for you, so I'll get out of your hair. Let's talk tomorrow, though, OK?" He pumped Mike's hand once, and opened the door to the taxi and climbed in. A moment later the cart accelerated away silently, leaving Mike alone at the curb.

"We're going to start a bank? What the fuck?"

Chapter 100

2064: Kaspar Osvaldo's home, Aristillus, Lunar Nearside

"Sorry about dinner." Kaspar gestured with a slice of pizza "- but with Marianela taking the girls to Ignacio's soccer game - well, you don't want to taste my cooking."

Matthew swallowed. "Pizza's great - it's the soda that's weird."

Kaspar raised a finger in mock-seriousness. "Ah, that's where you're wrong. Sugar cane is the only proper way to make a cola. We may not have the official blessing of the firm, but we have sugar cane...and the recipe."

Dewitt took another bite. As he chewed Kaspar returned to his ongoing explanation of Aristillus. "The Chinese here aren't as simple to understand as the Americans and the Nigerians, but it's not *that* complicated. There are separate waves of them, but once you understand that those were caused by Chairman Peng's First and Second Heavenly Campaigns, you realize the difference is just geographical, based on where the fighting was."

Matthew took a sip of soda. "But ideologically - the Chinese here hate the PKs like the Nigerians do?"

Kaspar shook his head. "No. They never saw peaker troops on the ground back home. Besides, after what happened to anyone in China with a political opinion over the last fifty years, most of them just want to keep their heads down and work hard."

"So if it came to fighting -"

"The Chinese are a pragmatic people. For thousands of years they've learned to figure out which strongman is going to win, then back them."

"So the Chinese will back the PKs."

"Is that what you think I just said?" Kaspar brushed the semolina dust off his hands over the empty pizza box, then stood. "Come, let's go out to the garden."

Dewitt followed the older engineer to the courtyard. This was the third time they'd gone out here to talk, but it still made him shake his head. He knew that the rich here in Aristillus had great homes - one of his men had found a photo spread of Leroy Fournier's mansion in a web magazine - but even the middle class had a stunning amount of space.

Kaspar caught him taking in the cloud-dappled blue sky overhead, the fountains, and the fruit trees and shrubs. "It's beautiful, isn't it? Marianela designed most of it. Much nicer than the small apartment we had for our first two years here."

Soon they were talking about real estate prices, home loans, and architecture. Interesting, maybe, but irrelevant.

Each man in Matthew's team had a task. Some were tracking down maps and engineering drawings, some were building the explosives they needed for later (bizarrely, the precursor chemicals were available in hardware stores without even ID), and others were joining militias under assumed names and learning their tactics.

And then there was the task he'd saved for himself: gather strategic and political information.

Matthew steered the conversation back to the demographics and ideological groupings of Aristillus. "You said Americans make up maybe half the population here -"

"Yes. The mines, the smelters, the drilling - those jobs are almost entirely filled by Americans. It doesn't hurt, of course, that three of the First Five are Americans."

"Were Americans."

Kaspar shook his head. "Have you met Mike Martin? No? I suggest that when you meet him you tell him he's not an American any more."

"Really? Why?"

Kaspar laughed out loud. "No, I'm joking. Don't do that."

"So tell me what the American expats are like."

"Eh, you know, you're one of them!"

"Well, yes - but I'm new here, and I spend most of my time at work. I barely know anyone here. But you - you've got a good eye."

"What do you want to know?"

"Well, you were talking about the Chinese. How do the Americans compare? Factions, groups, politics - that sort of thing."

"There's not much to say. They're about as angry as the Nigerians, but a bit more - what's the right word? - political, I guess. The Naijas just hate PKs and American troops, but they might - might! - deal with a government if they had to. The Americans here, though - they're nuts."

"How so?"

"Unwilling to compromise."

"Are there any fault lines?"

"For a while I thought there were, but that whole Lone Star versus Big Dipper thing, it's just for show. They argue at work, and then they go out for beers together afterward. Hell, half the Americans knew each other from secret message boards, going back decades."

"You're saying that lots of the Americans were involved with terror rings?"

"If you're talking about The Five States Militia and the North Slope Army, no, most of the Americans here in Aristillus sat those out...but I can't tell you how many times two American friends of mine tell me that they met each other twenty years ago while discussing something online."

"So the factions - Texas, Alaska, New Mexico - those loyalties don't run deep?"

"They're not factions, they're just..." he shrugged. "'Clubs' is the best word."

"And what motivates them?"

Kaspar looked at him, astounded that he had to spell it out. "They want their freedom, of course. Just like the rest of us. Freedom to have a family without justifying it to the Population Board, freedom to start a company, freedom to eat beef without a ration card, freedom to drink a large soda -" Kaspar raised his beverage in illustration. "- freedom to own guns, freedom from asset forfeitures."

Matthew sensed that he'd steered the conversation in a too obviously political direction and hastened to get back onto more solid footing. "So tell me how you and your family came to be here in Aristillus."

"Not much to tell - after the Tres Amigas was bombed most of the infrastructure spending switched to security and surveillance. There was less work for me, and I had to figure out what to do next. Did I ever tell you that my grandfather crossed the border? Yes. Back in the late twentieth century. He wanted to work hard and improve himself, so he went to where the jobs were, where the freedom was. I figured it was time to follow in his footsteps."

Kaspar paused and looked at him. "That's my story. Now you share yours with me." He fixed Matthew with his gaze. "What brings you and your men here, Matt?"

"Pretty much the same thing: looking for work and - wait, what?" Matthew stumbled.

Kaspar said nothing but raised one eyebrow.

"I'm sorry, Kaspar, did you just -"

"I called you 'Matt.' That is your name, right? Captain Matthew Dewitt of the US Special Forces?"

Chapter 101

2064: Senator Linda Haig's Office, Tester Senate Building

Linda Haig nodded and smiled. "I absolutely understand your concern, and you've got my word that Hamilton Sundstrand will be the primary manufacturer of space suits for any military operations."

The silver haired CEO shook his head. "I'm not sure you do understand my concern, senator. The military operations will be over soon, and I can't imagine that the contract would entail more than a few thousand units. That's peanuts." He paused and gave her what he no doubt thought was a stern and meaningful glance. Linda was annoyed at his presumption, but this wasn't the time to let that show. Instead she tilted her head and raised her eyebrows in a look calculated to seem open and earnest.

Linda's assistant, Kerri, hovered nearby. She was clearly concerned that this was running long, and reasonably so. This meeting was already over schedule five minutes. Linda caught Kerri's eye and tipped her head, just a millimeter. Kerri saw it and stepped back a pace. Good girl.

Chuck Sunderstrand continued his explaination, as if he was talking to a child. "Senator, you know as well as I do that given the state of our currency, we'll be taking over those gold mines and running them for years. Now that- *that* - is the spacesuit contract I want."

Linda repressed a scowl. She'd tried to play dumb, hoping that Sunderstrand wouldn't catch her. It hadn't worked. What he was asking for now was a bigger token than she had wanted to spend. On the other hand, she did need the influence that Sundstrand could deliver.

Shit.

Linda fought the urge to smile tightly and instead forced - no, *let* - a larger, more honest-seeming smile reach her face.

"Oh, there shouldn't be a problem with that."

He stared at her intently. "I have your word?"

Damn it. "Of course." Another full smile.

"There's one more detail. Once our forces -"

Behind him Kerri cleared her throat. "Excuse me, Mr. Sundstrand, but the senator really -"

Sundstrand held up a finger. Linda didn't like the man's arrogance, ordering her assistant around that way, but she kept the smile on her face.

Sundstrand tilted his head forward and looked at Linda from under his brows. "Now, senator - that one detail. There's some intel that the DoD has shared with us. Apparently there are two firms in Aristillus making spacesuits. One isn't even a 'firm,' properly speaking - more of a hippie collective or something. Still. 'Airtight' and 'Shield.' If we're going to get the sole contract for suits afterward, we'd really like to make sure that we lock down those assets. That'll give us what we need to make sure that the government gets what it needs."

Now Sundstrand was asking for too much. Primary contractor? Sure. Primary contract for years running? A hard bargain, but she'd give it if forced - and she had been forced. But both of those *and* the assets of two firms? No. Not remotely. The suit contract would be put out as a multiple manufacturer deal, like most other DoD procurement, and those secondary manufacturer contracts were valuable. Airtight and Shield were her choice plums, and she wouldn't hand them over that easily.

Linda shook her head and smiled ruefully. "Now, Chuck, you're getting greedy. You've got primary on this contract - you're going to have to be happy with that."

Sundstrand paused for a moment and then chuckled. "Well, you can't blame me for trying."

Linda smiled back, and for the first time in this conversation it was an honest smile. "Not at all."

Kerri cleared her throat again.

Linda nodded at her. "If you'll forgive me, Chuck, there's a scheduled call that I've really got to take."

"I understand. It's been a pleasure." He extended his hand. "Senator."

Two minutes later the door was closed and Linda took the call. She listened silently, then put down the phone.

"Ma'am? What is it?"

"That bitch."

"Who?"

"The president. She sandbagged me. The invasion is under way."

Kerri's eyes grew wide. "Do you want me to route a call to your son?"

"Yes, set that up. In fifteen - no, make it thirty minutes from now." She checked her watch. "Get Jim on the phone, right now."

"What should I tell him this is about?"

"Tell him -"

The door flew open. Linda looked up - it was Jim. His hair was damp and his tie was askew. "Did you hear -?"

Linda nodded in silent fury. "Just now."

He wiped the sweat off his forehead. "She's stabbed us in the back."

Linda nodded, lips tightly pressed together. "A month ago she told me she was trying to bridge the two Party factions. But an invasion? This didn't come together just now. She was plotting this - launching it without consultation - the whole time."

Linda felt the world swim. She'd had all of her moves planned, and now that bitch had screwed her. "Damn her. She moved up the invasion just to screw me."

Jim shook his head. "Don't flatter yourself; by launching this earlier than anyone knew, she's wrong-footed a *lot* of people. You were probably just collateral damage."

Linda pointed to a chair. "Sit." Jim did. "That woman is a *lot* smarter than I gave her credit for."

Jim looked at her. "Smart? How -"

Linda let half of a chuckle escape. "This is perfect. She used me to get the Internationalist wing of the party behind her moon invasion idea. She needed that - we've got large chunks of State, Interior, other parts of the bureaucracy. But then she pulled the trigger early, before we can get to use it for our advantage. Mark my words - she's going to go on the air soon. Today. She'll concentrate on the economics of it: she's doing it for the gold, she's doing it for the working man. She's going to talk about California. She's going to talk about increasing the Minimum Guaranteed Income - all the typical populist talking points. But she'll have the money to back it up for once."

Jim nodded as he listened, his face grim. "You're right." He caught the senator's eyes. "Before we decide how to jump, I need to know if the deeper plan -"

Linda held up one hand to stop Jim, and looked pointedly at Kerri. The aide took the hint and stepped out of the room, closing the thick mahogany door behind her with a solid thump.

Jim continued. "You wanted to sabotage the invasion by leaking the existence of the special forces team to the expats. Has that worked?"

Linda shook her head. "I don't know. I made some calls, but I haven't heard anything back." Her nostrils flared. "Damn it, this stuff takes time. I thought we had weeks. Months."

Jim drummed the fingers of his right hand on the chair's padded armrest. "So the question is: where does this leave us? We don't know if the expats have rolled up the deep team or not. Which means we don't know if the invasion force is going to have support from the inside or not. Which means we don't know if it's going to succeed." Jim paused and thought. "The invasion is coming early enough to surprise us. It's got to be a surprise for the expats too. So whether or not your leak got through to the expats, I can't imagine that they're ready for an invasion."

"And?"

"I have to assume that the invasion is going to work."

Linda nodded. "That's what I think too. So what's your advice?"

Jim paused to consider. "If the invasion is going to succeed, we've got to get out in front of it. Make it look like it was as much our idea as anyone's."

"You're half right."

"Half?"

"Themba thinks she can screw over the Internationalist wing of the Party and exploit us to advance the Populists? Screw that. I don't want half the credit for this - we should get all of it. We need to steal her thunder."

Jim furrowed his brow. "How?"

Linda ignored him and pressed the intercom button. "Kerri, get Jacob from The Minute on the line."

"Yes, ma'am. I've got your son Hugh -"

"Hold that. I need to speak to Jacob first."

Chapter 102

2064: just west of Zhukovskiy Crater, Lunar Farside

Blue peered over the crater lip. The mule and Tudel's corpse lay broken on the boulders at the bottom. Splashes of blood and solar panel fragments surrounded them. Blue turned away and looked back to Rex's body. Blood caked the exit wounds in the suit. The faceplate was shattered. And where Rex's head had been -

He turned away.

It felt unreal, and yet there was no avoiding the truth. There it was, on the rocks just meters from him.

Rex was dead. His friend. His pack-mate. His younger brother. Numbness wrapped around him. He knew the truth but somehow didn't know it. Wouldn't know it.

A small knife of pain probed and found its way through.

It was real. Rex was gone. Not just for a day, or for a week, but forever.

Blue felt his lip quiver. He heard something, fuzzy and clouded and distant. He slowly realized it was Max and Duncan. Discipline was gone. Radio silence was gone. They were wailing.

Blue didn't so much give in to instinct as feel it wash over him, infinite and inexorable. He joined his brothers, tilting his head back and letting out his own full-throated howl, broadcasting his grief to the lifeless rocks and the black sky overhead.

How long did he howl? He didn't know. Seconds? Minutes? Longer? At some point, though, he felt his scattered parts coming back together.

Blue forced himself to stop. The other two Dogs continued their mourning without him.

Blue cleared his throat. "Guys?"

Max's howl warbled, then stopped. Duncan went on for another minute; then stuttered to a stop.

Blue turned to Max. The two of them spent more time fighting - about politics, about the future of canine culture, about everything - than they did cooperating. Now, though, they had to work together. Their lives depended on it.

Blue switched off his radio and targeted Max with his com laser. "John was guarding the slope. If this PK found us -"

"The PKs reached the crater wall. Which means John is dead. And now we have to defend ourselves."

Blue swallowed. They had no weapons, no tools. If there were PKs around, he, Max, and Duncan were almost certainly doomed. Still, they couldn't give up - they had to at least try. "We need to know how many there are."

"John must have killed some of them."

Blue said, "And the three mules that Rex reprogrammed might have gotten some."

"How many PKs were left?"

Duncan sniffled. "What are we going to do?"

"They killed Rex. They killed John. They'll kill all of us." Max paused. "Unless we kill them first."

"But we don't have any weapons. What do we -"

"John had two rifles. We need to find his body and get the guns."

Blue shook his head. "We already tried that - we can't operate them".

Max was grim. "We're going to have to figure out a way. Tape. Parachute cord. Something."

Duncan said, "Do you think Rex's mule hack worked?"

Blue raised his eyebrows. "We'll know soon enough."

"Enough talking." Max said, and then reached down and picked up a rock. He set off, walking awkwardly on three legs and carrying his improvised weapon cradled against his chest with one fore-paw.

Duncan picked up a rock of his own and followed him.

Blue looked down. This wasn't going to work. If there was even one PK left, they were going to die.

But better to die trying. He picked up a rock and set off after the other two.

Blue walked behind the other two dogs, scanning to his left and right constantly. His mouth felt dry no matter how much he sipped from his drinking tube.

Max and Duncan crested a small hill ahead of them and paused. Duncan barked in excitement. Blue targeted him with the com laser and started to ask "What?" but before he got the word out, Duncan dropped his rock and disappeared over the hill. Max followed a second later.

God damn it!

Blue hurried to catch up as quickly as he could on three legs.

He crested the ridge a few later. And below - Duncan and Max, jumping around. And between them were the three mules they'd left behind.

Rex's last-minute coding had done its job.

No, it had more than done its job.

One of the mules was badly damaged. Four legs had been mangled by rifle fire or grenades or something, and twitched spastically. The machine was pitifully trying to pull itself forward on its two remaining legs.

The other two mules stood back to back. At their feet were four - no, five - PK corpses. The bodies each looked the same - pristine suits marred only by one circular hole punched directly through the spacesuits' faceplates.

As Blue watched, one of the two surviving mules lifted its leg. A PK lifeless body followed it up, like a strip of duct tape stuck to the bottom of a shoe. The mule shook its leg back and forth.

Blue recoiled. The mule's foot had somehow punched all the way in through the glass and had stuck inside, and as the mule shook the corpse twitched hideously.

The mule put its foot back down. A few seconds later the behavior routine fired again: the mule lifted its leg and shook the corpse from side to side. Again it failed. The flared foot was stuck on something, either some mangled machinery inside the helmet, or perhaps the shattered bones of the PK's skull.

Blue looked away and tried to calm his stomach. A moment later Duncan called out, "Hang on, I'm taking manual control...OK, I got it."

Blue looked back. The mule was unstuck and was backing away from the corpse.

Max looked around the carnage. "Duncan, this is awesome. How the hell did you and Rex do this? You only had ten minutes."

Blue could see Duncan puff up a bit, even through the bulky suit. "It was Rex's idea to program the mules to attack, but it was *my* idea to dig through the code archives and find a whack-a-mole program in the 'games' directory. Rex ripped out the targeting code and replaced it with a pattern-matching subroutine, and I did an image search for spacesuit helmets. There were a couple of *million* in our caches, so it was pretty slow. It took the neural net training system *minutes* to process them all."

"You got vengeance for Rex, and that's the important thing. Good job."

At being reminded of Rex, Duncan snarted to sniffle, then whimper. It was contagious: Blue realized that he was starting to whimper too. He tried to fight it, and then Duncan started howling. Max yelled at them both. "Enough! The PKs are still out there, and we need to focus!"

Blue forced his lip to stop quivering, and a moment later Duncan silenced himself. Duncan nodded. "You're right."

Max turned and looked at the machines and the dead PKs. "I don't see any other footprints. The mules might have killed all the PKs...but we can't be sure. We need to arm ourselves."

Duncan sniffled. "We can also put the mules back in combat mode."

Max considered it for a moment, and then shook his head. "They've got all of our airscrubbers and food and water. We don't know how long we're going to be out here. We can't risk losing our supplies. No, we've got to arm ourselves and keep the mules in reserve."

Blue nodded. "And speaking of supplies, we need to scavenge airscrubbers, water, batteries, everything we can." He tilted his head to indicate the bodies of the PKs.

Duncan chirped "Sure!" and fell on the corpses. Max followed him, and soon the two were working as a team: Max rolling corpses over, Duncan reaching under and twisting off airscrubbers. A moment later Max started humming a ditty that Blue knew too well from the MMORPG. Duncan joined Max in the humming, and then broke out in a sing-song when the chorus arrived: "Loot the corpses, loot the corpses!"

Blue frowned. Rex was dead, and so were these PKs. It might be necessary to kill them, but they'd been real people. There was nothing funny about this, and singing songs from a videogame as they stole from their bodies was wrong.

He couldn't lecture. Not now, at least. But he could set an example. Blue walked to a fresh corpse and tried to avoid looking at its face as he rolled it over and reached for the KO_2 rebreather canister.

* * *

Ten minutes later they were done. Done looting the corpses, done loading the contents into the mules, and done rigging up weapons.

Max held the piece of aluminum bar that he'd duct-taped to the foreguard of a PK's YM-20 in his left paw, and used his right to pull the loop of parachute cord that threaded through the trigger guard. The rifle jerked back as the muzzle flashed. "Hmm. I can't aim it very well, but it's better than nothing." He shook his right paw out of the loop of nylon and clutched the gun against his chest with his left, and then dropped to all fours.

"OK, let's get to the crater wall and see if there are any PKs left below. We'll also look for John's - Well anyway, let's move." Max started walking and Blue and Duncan fell in behind.

The two remaining mules, each overburdened with their pickings, followed thirty meters behind.

Blue looked at Duncan and Max, each carrying a rifle, and then turned his head and looked at the mules. He had to admit it: in John's absence, Max was running things well.

Max was bloodthirsty, aggressive, and prone to barking orders. And sometimes that was exactly what the situation called for.

Blue was happy to let Max run the show - at least for now. It let him think about other things as they marched toward the crater rim.

Like what to do with Rex's and John's bodies. In the brief history of their species, no Dog had ever organized or run a funeral. Not that Dogs hadn't died before; they had. But when BuSuR had killed half their species in the final days of the labs there was no opportunity to do anything, and no time: the survivors had been in hiding.

Blue pursed his lips. The tradition, such as it was, was that after BuSuR gave a Dog a lethal injection of pentobarbital, it put his body into a red biohazard bag and incinerated it.

There hadn't even been a proper memorial after the Culling - he and the other survivors had all been too shell-shocked as the Team had packed them into cargo containers and smuggled them from labs to warehouse to ship.

Rex's death wasn't just the death of a friend - it was the first death of a Dog since they'd escaped Earth.

He and Max had known that they as a species were going to have to figure out who they were and what culture they'd have. Would the Dogs adopt human culture? Would they create their own? Or would they choose some synthesis?

What would it mean to create their own culture? Would they have their own holidays? Their own rituals?

These questions had been academic when he and Max had last discussed them a week ago, but with Rex dead, they now had a frightening immediacy and concreteness.

If they survived and made it back to Aristillus, what they did for Rex would establish a tradition that might very well live for centuries.

And for that matter, John needed a funeral too. And not one by and for his human friends. A Dog funeral. They - all of them - owed him that. Not only had he saved their race in the first place by being a key member of the team, but also his last action had been to give his life to fight a delaying action while Rex and Duncan had reprogramed the mules.

No, John needed something more than just a funeral. He needed a holiday, or a liturgy, or something that would remind them - all of them, even long after Blue and his generation were gone - that without him -

From somewhere Max shouted, "I found John's body."

Chapter 103

2064: Trentham Court Apartments, Aristillus, Lunar Nearside

Hugh sat on the couch as he listened, and furrowed his brow. "Mother, it can't be *that* import-."

Senator Haig spoke over him, whether because of the lightspeed lag or just because she had more to say. "-damned idiots." She paused. "Well. Anyway. It's happening and it's happening now. I tried to pull strings at DoD to get a guard detail, but it's impossible. Or so they say. Anyway, my point is this - Hugh, are you listening to me?"

"Yes, mother."

"You keep your head down. *Down*, do you hear me? I want you inside, doors locked. All this - journalism," she stirred the air with her fingers, "is on hold until you hear from me again."

Hugh nodded. "I understand. What does this mean for your position?"

And with that the brief flash of maternalism was gone and the conversation reverted to the same tone that it had always had, going as far back as the breakfast table in elementary school: politics, hard and serious. "That's the question, isn't it? I need details, and we're working hard to get them. Kerri's calling in favors right now."

"What do you know so far?"

"We know timing. The invasion fleet already launched - I don't know exactly when yet - and it's going to land in a day. Maybe two."

Hugh swallowed this. "OK. What else?"

"We're hearing a lot of stuff, but sifting reality from cover stories from conspiracy theories is hard. Some sources are saying that there was a scouting mission that found a secret facility on Farside. Have you heard anything about a base on Farside?"

Hugh shook his head.

"There's another rumor that a nuclear bomb went off -"

"What? No. Definitely not."

"Hmm. Well. It seems that I'm getting bad information. I don't know if my contacts at DoD are turned, or if they're getting garbage themselves." She paused. "What do you know about Goldwater?"

"Goldwater Mining & Refining? Our last exposé touched on them, but we're working on a -"

"They're real, then?"

"Real? Yes, of course. Why?"

"I'm double-checking some things I've heard."

"Mother, if you're getting lied to - if the White House and the DoD did this without you in the loop - what does that mean?"

"The knives are out, clearly. But don't worry about me - I've got a plan."

"Plan? What is it?"

Hugh's mom looked to one side of the camera. "OK, Kerri - good. Now run it past our lunar contact." She turned back to Hugh. "Hugh, I've got to go. Now, one more time: promise me you'll stay inside your apartment for the next few days. Do you - hang on. I've got an incoming call from General Bonner. Hugh, I'll talk to you in a few days. Remember: stay inside."

She clicked off.

Louisa leaned in through the open door. "Hugh? What's going on?"

Chapter 104

2064: MaisonNeuve Construction office, Aristillus, Lunar Nearside

Neil Aaronson browsed the titles in the built-in bookshelves.

Leroy Fournier put the empty glass down on the sideboard. "How is everything?"

Aaronson turned. "Decent. Your increased volume of registrations is nice, of course. But those webcasts from the college kids are really helping. Some of the smaller firms have switched over from Mason Dixon. Between that and the spike in immigration -"

Leroy cut him off. "There's something more important. Father passed along some news from Addison. Our neighbors to the south have new plans."

"What?"

Fournier weighed for a moment how much he wanted to share, and decided to tell it all. The news would be arriving from other quarters soon enough, and if he delivered it first, it'd be clear that he was in the know. People respected a man who was in the know.

He locked eyes with Neil Aaronson. "The game is changing. Sit down and I'll tell you the details."

Chapter 105

2064: just west of Zhukovskiy Crater, Lunar Farside

John groaned.

It was dark, and something was tugging at his face.

Another tug, a ripping sensation, pain, and light.

Crap, his left cheek hurt, and someone had just pulled a hank of hair out of his scalp.

"Ow. What the - ?"

He tried to blink but his eyes were stuck shut. He reached up with one hand and rubbed at the crust over his eyelids. He blinked again and this time he could see. What was that hexagonal window above him? Where was -

In the tent. Hiking. Farside.

His mind spun. Wait. The PK ships had arrived. One had landed. He'd shot five of them, and then - how - ?

He blinked again. Blue, Max and Duncan were looking down at him, helmets off, doing that weird canine smile thing - mountains of teeth showing, just a slight upward tilt to the far corners of their black lips.

He moved his hand from his eyes to his cheek, and - Ow! It was raw, like the skin had been ripped away. He pulled his hand away and looked at it. Blood.

"Why am I bleeding?"

He touched his scalp. "And what happened to my hair?"

Blue said, "Some hair and skin got ripped away when we cut your helmet off."

"My helmet?"

Duncan lifted John's helmet and presented it theatrically. The golden faceplate was crazed with cracks. Small pieces of glass were missing, and squirts of solidified pink sealant foam bubbled out through the gaps.

John looked at it - and remembered.

He'd looked up. The boot. His head smacking against the back of his helmet. "What happened?"

"What?"

"The PK - he kicked me. In the head. And then I - I must have passed out."

He sat up and groaned as the headache that had been flitting near the outer edge of his perception reported front and center. "I need to get outside and look at the PK ship." He looked at his helmet. "Duncan, I'm going to need one of the spares. Can you go outside and get one for me?"

Duncan shook his head. "Mule one had them all, and it fell off a cliff."

"Fell off a cliff? How did it fall off a cliff?"

He looked around the tent. "And where's Rex?"

The Dogs' smiles disappeared.

Chapter 106

2064: Mike's house, Aristillus, Lunar Nearside

Mike walked through the empty house. A sweater Darcy had left behind was draped over the couch. He picked it up and held it in his hands, feeling the softness of the cotton. He should have -

His phone rang. Eager for the distraction, he looked at the screen. An anonymous call, but it had a high priority flag. "Hello?"

"Hello, Michael."

The voice was cool, emotionless - and unfamiliar. "Who is this?"

"This is Gamma."

"Gamma?" He furrowed his brow. "How do I know this is really you?"

"You received an anonymous text in the midst of the Wookkiee hijacking at exactly 4:02 PM Aristillus Standard Time on this phone. The text read 'Wookkiee hijacked by PK forces. One dozen aggressors. Hostages taken. Darcy alive.' Only you and I know that I sent that text."

Mike breathed out. So it was Gamma. He'd known that John had smuggled the AI to Aristillus years ago, and he'd known that the machine - just a collection of databanks and a few rovers at the time - had taken up residence in Sinus Lunicus 80 klicks away...but since then there'd been almost no interactions. Well, no interactions with Mike or anyone else in Aristillus. The AI talked to John.

"Gamma. Wow. This is - uh - an honor." Shit. He was sounding like an idiot. What does one say to an AI? "Uh, that probably sounded stupid. I've never spoken to an AI before."

"As I am the only AI, I know that."

"Right. Of course. Uh." He was stammering, but the conversation had him reeling. "So, uh - why haven't we talked before?" As soon as the words were out of his mouth realized how stupid they sounded.

"It is not clear that use of a human psychological term is appropriate, but one might choose to call me an introvert. Or to use an economic term, my revealed preferences are to minimize my real-time interactions with humans."

Mike squinted. "Uh - OK." What did that even mean? "Should I be worried about this call? I mean, the last time you deigned to communicate with me was when the Wookkiee was hijacked."

As he talked he pushed through a door and stepped out onto his front porch without looking around at the apple trees or the garden.

"Earth forces have burned my lunar satellite network."

Mike furrowed his brow. "Uh, yeah. But why call me over that? I mean, you didn't call me when it happened the first time a few months ago."

"I'm calling you this time because when my new generation of armored satellites were launched four days ago, they were burned. So then yesterday I launched another batch of satellites - and they were burned within minutes of launch. And then, one hour and nine minutes later, my launch facility in Sinus Lunicus was destroyed by the same directed energy weapons."

Mike's eyes widened. The Earth governments were targeting surface facilities? "Jesus. We're really at war, aren't we?"

"That's exactly why I'm calling you, Mike."

"If they're striking your SL facilities, they're going to invade. Soon"

"I concur."

Mike started to wipe the sweat from his forehead brow and saw that he was still holding Darcy's sweater. He draped it over one of the Adirondack chairs.

"Do you have a plan?" Mike said.

"I do not. That is why I've contacted you, despite my disinclination."

"Shit. This is too soon. Too damned soon. Do you have a plan?"

"I already answered that. To expand: I have not given up on trying to formulate a reaction, but as of now, I have no plan."

"Shit. I hate to disappoint you, but neither do we." Mike exhaled. "Guess you're sorry you bothered to make this call, huh?"

"To the contrary. Aristillus' survival is key to my own survival. I wanted to alert you to the pending threat. Now, at least, we have multiple brains working on this problem."

"Well, thanks for that, I guess." Mike took a deep breath. "How long do we have until the invasion gets here?"

"I have no idea. That is all I had to convey. Goodbye."

"Goodbye? Wait! Gamma?" The line was dead.

Mike put the phone back in his pocket. He turned toward the trees outside the window but still didn't see them.

The invasion was coming, and coming soon. And they were woefully unprepared for it.

Mike stared at nothing for a long moment, and then picked up Darcy's sweater and headed back inside.

Chapter 107

2064: just west of Zhukovskiy Crater, Lunar Farside

Max marched forward, paw after paw landing in the dust as he walked along the highway of bootprints and rover track marks.

To the left and right the crater walls of c-177 hid the horizon.

Dead ahead - two kilometers away, but already clear in the airless vacuum - the stern of the downed PK ship faced them dead-on.

Max didn't have to hike the full two klicks - his target was closer.

Duncan, a few steps behind him, whined, "Slow down." He paused. "You know, if we'd just come down the same landslide we went up, we'd get to the bodies a lot -"

Max turned his head and barked at him. "Damn it, listen sometime, Duncan. I already explained this."

"Sorry - I was playing around with the red_desert_aust overlay." Duncan sounded a bit contrite, but then his enthusiasm took over. "The way the rendering algorithms use real world details for seed data is *sweet*. Try it. See that tractor trailer up there?" Duncan pointed at the PK ship. "Can you make out what's spray-painted on the side? 'The vermin-' something. Can you read the rest?"

Max almost snapped at the younger Dog, but forced himself to calm down. If Duncan was a human he'd probably have some prescription for ADD meds - but his enthusiasm for games and his tsetse fly scatteredness had saved all of their lives just half an hour ago when he'd come up with the whack-a-mole game hack.

"No, Duncan, I'm not going to flip over to that channel. I'm staying in real mode, because *someone* has to keep an eye on the ship. We have to make sure we don't walk where the chain guns can see us. Which, to get back to your question, is why we're not taking the direct route."

Duncan tripped over a rock. "Mmmm... what?"

Max lost his composure. "Damn it, Duncan, turn off the MMORPG and pay attention!"

"But I *wasn't* playing a MMORPG."

Max breathed out. "OK, I'm sorry. I -"

"With the sats gone the game is single player."

Max gritted his teeth.

"But since you brought up the game, I was thinking: how should we tag the ship to bring it into continuity? Maybe Helm's Deep?"

Max forced himself to count to ten. "Duncan, I've got a bargain for you. If I talk about the game during this walk, do you promise that we can utterly and entirely drop the topic once we reach the bodies?"

"Sure."

Max took a breath. "OK. If we make the ship into Helm's Deep that really screws up the chronology... but I GUESS we could back out some of the last few updates and retcon from a few weeks ago."

"What if instead of the Helm's Deep siege, it's the siege of Minas Tirith?"

"That'd make Zhukovskiy Crater into Minas Tirith?"

"Maybe. Or maybe Gamma's facility is Minas Morgul and Zhukovskiy is Mordor."

Max grunted along to Duncan's proposals, but kept his attention on the ship as they walked. The ship - drawing closer now - was dead. At least, it seemed dead: there were no lights and no figures had come out of it.

Which was good - if any PKs stepped onto the surface they were in a bad situation. Which is why Max wanted to get this done as quickly as possible and then get back to the tent.

He checked his map. Two hundred meters to go and Duncan was saying something about Southrons.

Max grunted. "Sure, whatever."

Just a hundred meters now.

And then they reached the first PK corpses. Max stopped. Just an hour ago John had shot these men. Just an hour ago Rex had been alive.

So much had changed in just sixty minutes.

Duncan bumped into Max from behind. "Oops, sorry."

Max turned and snarled and Duncan stepped away. Max turned back to the two of the corpses. One had a shattered faceplate, the other had a hole punched through the helmet just to one side of the glass.

No spare helmets here.

"Hey, this one looks good."

Max turned. Duncan was standing a few meters away and prodding a face-down corpse with one forepaw.

Max walked over. The PK's life support backpack was a mess - John's bullets had torn into it and hit a pressurized tank, which had exploded. The helmet, though, was intact. Max lowered his head and butted the corpse, rolling it face up, and then stepped back. Two exit wounds in the chest were caked with frozen blood and lunar dust.

The suit was an Airtight, the same as John's. The dead PK was wearing a Mark IV, which was one rev off, but the helmet *should* be compatible with the neck ring on John's suit. Max checked the electronics on the suit's chest. The power indicator was black: the suit power was dead. No surprise given the state of the back pack. Still, that meant he had to do this the hard way.

Max squatted on his rear legs and grabbed the two emergency release levers on either side of the PK's helmet. Or tried to. His stubby fingers scrabbled at the levers. He'd never admit it to a human - not even to John - but he envied humans their hands. Longer fingers, fully opposable thumbs, nice large palms. Not that he'd change places with them: aside from their idiot squish-faced looks, even the smarter ones were idiots. But he did envy their hands.

And then Max had the left lever in his grasp... and then the right. He twisted them both at once. And nothing. There was supposed to be a release of air. What was wrong?

Ah. Of course. The suit was holed. So was the helmet unlocked? Max released the neck ring levers, steadied himself in his awkward squat, and then grabbed the helmet and pulled. It moved a few centimeters and got stuck. Probably the chin of the dead peaker. Max wiggled the helmet and pulled it free.

Duncan said, "Awesome. John'll be psyched!"

Max ignored Duncan and looked at the dead PK's face. His mouth and eyes were open in a silent scream. The flesh of his face was pale and dusted with frost. Max had never seen a dead person before - human or Dog. He stared. He had no reason to believe that this particular PK had been involved in the Euthanasia, and yet this man was his enemy.

It was weird.

This dead human hadn't killed his siblings back in the labs. He hadn't killed Rex up on the crater wall. He wasn't even one of the men that attacked John.

So what did that make him? Innocent?

Max scowled.

No.

The PK hadn't had the *chance* to kill John or one of the Dogs. But he would have. He'd signed up with the peakers, he'd taken this mission. He was here to kill John and the Dogs.

He was Them, not Us. Wrong pack. Losing pack.

Max handed the spare helmet to Duncan, dropped to four legs, and lifted his back left. The urine all went into an internal bladder of the suit, but the geo-tagging software timestamped his territorial claim.

Chapter 108

2064: bridge of AFS Poyekhali, 80km above the Earth

Wasseem scanned his board. "Landing in T minus 180 seconds. Entering the mesosphere... now. 80km and falling."

Darcy watched her screen. "AG braking is at 0.5g. Drive is at 99.2% efficiency. Batteries are taking power, heat buildup is fine. We're green across the board." 99.2% was good - the batteries would be nicely charged so they could launch again as soon as they wanted to.

Orbital mechanics permitting, of course.

Darcy knew that the wind was starting to whisper against the hull, but the thrumming of the AG drive was loud enough that she couldn't hear it.

Waseem said, "T minus 140, 50 klicks up, now in the stratosphere." He checked his screens. "Hull temperature normal."

Darcy nodded. With the drive operating in its peak efficiency band all of the potential energy was being soaked up by the batteries. She called out her own stats: "T minus 60 seconds. 8 klicks up, 250 meters per second. Right in the envelope."

Darcy called out the time: "T minus thirty."

The descent was textbook.

"T minus five. One hundred meters."

"T minus one. Three meters.

"Holding at three meters. Two meters. One meter. We're at local sea level. Ready to collapse the bowl?"

Waseem nodded. "I'm green - go."

Darcy tapped a button. The thrumming of the drive slowed and quieted. Darcy grabbed the arms of her chair just before the ship lurched and slid to one side. A moment later it rolled back and the booming of waves hitting the hull echoed.

Darcy took her hands off the armrests and tapped one last button. "AG in standby, and - off!" She felt a final twist in her gut and then suddenly felt her full weight. Oof. She felt heavy - it'd been a while.

"OK, Waseem, let's do the post-flight."

Waseem groaned theatrically but fell to - a moment later he had the checklist on his screen and the two of them began safing the quick-discharge capacitors, reverifying lubricant levels on the cranes, and three dozen other steps.

An hour later Waseem punched a final button. "Done! Now on to the fun part. We're just 600 kilometers to Tho Quang. As soon as we get there, I - what? Why are you shaking your head?"

"We need to calibrate the new software first."

"Come on, Darce. Do you know how long it's been since I've seen the sights?"

Darcy raised one eyebrow. "The sights?"

Waseem grinned, caught out. "I like Vietnamese women. Sue me."

"Calibration shouldn't take more than 30 hours; we'll head to port soon enough."

"Thirty hours? Ugh. I need a break."

Darcy called up a schedule. "So take a break. How about one hour, then we break out the prototype and start characterizing it?"

Waseem sighed theatrically and then agreed.

Darcy turned to Riese. "I assume everything is under control?"

Riese, who'd been silent during the reentry, spoke. "Claymores on the decks are armed, gunwale cameras show no boats or buoys. I've got troops at both airlocks. Your days of being hijacked are over."

Darcy smiled her thanks. "I'm going to grab a shower and a bite to eat."

Waseem yawned once. "I'm feeling a bit tired. I might take a nap - do we have time for that?"

Darcy yawned too - it was catching. "OK, but make it a short one." She yawned a second time. "Sorry, don't know what's with me today. I'm going to make an espresso - you want one?"

Waseem blinked languidly, then closed his eyes. There was something weird about that. Why was he closing his eyes? And why were her arms so heavy? Not just sort of heavy, but *really* heavy.

She needed that espresso, right now. She unbuckled, stood, and took a few steps toward the galley. She grabbed the back of Riese's chair. She was dizzy.

What - what was going on?

A few seconds later she fell to the deck.

Captain Schrodt watched through night vision goggles as his men did their work, and then scanned the area. The ship beneath them was dark but the low swells of the sea around them shone with a phosphorescent glow. The sea was eerily beautiful, like some sort of light show except for where their discarded parachutes made dark spots as they sank. But this was no time for staring at the ocean. He turned back to his men.

One soldier, black against black in his heat cloaking uniform, looked up from the clock on his wrist computer and gave a thumbs up. Another man nodded, closed the valve on the tank, and then pulled the hose out of the hole they'd bored in the deck, coiling it as he went. The sergeant made a hand sign and two other soldiers moved in, carrying the plasma cutter between them. A second later light flared from the cutting tip, and Captain Schrodt's goggles compensated. For a full half minute the tool hissed and crackled, and then a circle of steel decking fell into the ship. The massive clang as it hit the floor below rang out over the quiet sea. Before the sound had died out the two soldiers manning the cutting tool stepped back and two other troops stepped forward and threw a thermal blanket over the still glowing edge of the hole. Then they stepped back and the point team - four soldiers with carbines at the ready - vaulted into the ship.

As soon as the point team was in the rest of his men lined up.

Captain Schrodt watched his men disappear into the hole, one after another, until he was alone on the deck. He would have loved to be in the action, but one of the sacrifices that came with rank was more responsibility and less fun. His duty was to stay here, monitoring the situation. He'd trade the responsibility and rank away for the excitement in a heartbeat, but it wasn't a trade he was allowed to make.

He looked at the hole, sighed, and scanned the deck and the sky. Nothing. He tapped his earpiece. The drones overhead reported that all was well. Schrodt sighed again.

A few minutes later the first report came in. "Team 1. We've got three from high value list. Number one is Ponnala, the AG guy. Number two is Srinivas Waseem Vivekanand, second cousin of the first. Number three is Darcy Grau. Says here she's the girlfriend of Mike Martin."

Well. That was good news. Really good news, actually. But, damn it, he still wished he could have been down in there, doing something real with his men.

Chapter 109

2064: just west of Zhukovskiy Crater, Lunar Farside

John sat cross-legged on the tent floor, the helmet rim riding uncomfortably on his bare shoulders as he paged through the menus in the helmet display. Everything worked fine, but it felt... weird. It wasn't the fact that the helmet didn't have his customizations. He'd transferred those - along with the logs, programs, music archives and everything else - from the old helmet. So what was it about the new helmet that seemed foreign?

Maybe it was the smell? After six months of wearing his old helmet 12 hours a day it smelled like him, despite his washing the liner every few days. Maybe that was it?

He breathed in. Yeah, he'd put his finger on it: this replacement helmet from the dead PK smelled of fabric and new foam. Hm. You could borrow a buddy's armored vest, or his pack, but you never asked to borrow his boots, or his underwear. There was something personal about those. It seemed that spacesuit helmets were the same.

Well, there was nothing to be done. He'd go to war with the helmet he had. John closed the menus, powered the helmet down, took it off, and set it on the floor. "Guys."

Max and Blue turned. John waited a moment. "Duncan!"

Duncan whipped his head around. "Huh?"

"Guys." John paused. "We need to get back to Aristillus, and we need a plan." Max and Blue nodded without hesitation. Duncan, though -

"Why?"

Max said. "A war is going on."

John nodded. "Exactly."

Max focused on him. "I was talking to you, John. The war is going on - like I told you would happen."

There was no mistaking Max's accusing tone. John blinked, then understood the anger. Rex was dead, and it wouldn't have happened if ... if what? If they'd abandoned the trip earlier? If they'd never started the trip in the first place?

There was no time for this now. They could deal in recriminations later. John held up a hand. "Yes. I was wrong. And I'm sorry. But we can fight about this later, Max. Right now we need to concentrate on survival - and getting back to Aristillus."

He turned from Max to face all three of the Dogs. "Our supplies - food, water, air - are dwindling by the minute. I don't know if resupply ships are flying, but even if they are, when Gamma's sats went down and he told us to get to Zhukovskiy, we went far, far off our plotted course."

Blue said, "So no one knows where we are."

John nodded. "Gamma might. Which is something else we have to worry about."

Duncan tilted his head. "What do you mean?"

"Everyone at Aristillus knows that Gamma has just one facility at Sinus Lunicus. He kept the rest secret. But now we know that not only does he have a secret facility at Konstantinov, but he has another one at Zhukovskiy, and -"

Duncan interrupted. "Well. *Had*."

John waved the pedantry away. "The point is that Gamma has secret facilities, and he's worked hard to keep them that way. He's clearly been editing satellite data - maybe even cockpit data - Darcy never saw anything from orbit."

Blue asked, "So what does that mean? Is Gamma an enemy?"

Duncan tilted his head. "Why does it even matter? Gamma's facility here is nuked. He's dead."

Max said, "But Gamma's still at SL. And that copy of Gamma knows that we know about the other bases."

Blue said, "So what are you saying? That if we get back to Aristillus, the copy of Gamma there will be angry at us?"

"Maybe, Blue. Maybe."

Max bared his teeth. "We can't waste our time worrying about what Gamma might think. The war is here, and it's changed everything. Gamma told us that he needs humans and Dogs on his side. So maybe he doesn't like the idea of us knowing about his facilities, but he's got no choice now." He slapped the tent floor with a forepaw. "It's time for us to fight."

John nodded. "Yes, it is. And to do that, we need to get to Aristillus. So, here's the question: how do we do that?"

Blue said, "We can't walk. We don't have enough supplies."

"Probably not."

Max said, "If walking is out, what other options are there?"

Blue said, "Maybe there are vehicles we can scavenge from Gamma's facility."

John nodded. "Let's inventory resources. We've got three surviving mules. There are a few PK corpses and whatever's on them." He held up his new helmet. "One downed PK ship. Gamma's nuked facility, and whatever wreckage we can scavenge there."

Max said, "So where does that leave us?"

Blue said, "We could scavenge a radio from the PK ship."

Max shook his head. "Won't work. The relay satellites are gone, and there's no ionosphere to reflect our broadcasts. Line of sight or nothing."

Blue nodded. "OK, so we need relay satellites. What if we make our own?"

Max looked at him. "What?"

"Could we cobble one together?"

"How would we get it into orbit?"

"Let's not worry about that yet. Can we build a relay sat? Do we have tools to solder, or whatever?"

Duncan put down his slate. "We don't need to make a relay. We could just make a message beacon. We take a radio - or, heck, maybe we just take one of the other PK helmets, program it to repeat a message, and launch it over the horizon toward Aristillus. If we can launch one, we can launch a couple. Send one every few hours, maybe."

John raised his eyebrows. Duncan rarely engaged with pragmatic day-to-day issues, but when he did, the results were always solid. "That's - that's doable. So how do we launch a 5 kg payload and send it over nearside?"

Blue said, "Using just scrap from the PK ship and from Gamma?"

"Yeah."

Blue shrugged. "In this gravity you don't need much propellant. The Apollo landers were small." He picked up his slate. "Let me dig through some records."

John watched Blue tap at his slate. Technology hadn't advanced much in fifty years - even Moore's Law had crapped out under the reign of BuSuR - but it *had* crept forward some. Enough so that Blue's slate, like most cheap consumer devices, had yottabytes of archives built in. Cached versions of wikis in every language, millions of open source software projects, tens of millions of books, billions of video clips, CNC models of everything from car fenders to blacksmithing jigs to remote control quadcopter toys, not to mention endless magazines, journal articles, TV shows and movies.

Blue barked in excitement. "I got it. Check this out." He swiped a paw across the screen and slid a window to the wall screen. John turned and looked. A clip of an Apollo LEM standing on the lunar surface began playing. In the corner a countdown flashed.

Max shook his head. "It looks exactly like it did when we were there. It's crazy that this was almost a century ago."

Duncan laughed.

Max turned to him. "What's funny about that?"

"No, not that. Look at the caption!"

John read it. "Apollo 17 - last humans on the moon." He smiled wanly.

On the screen nothing changed except the countdown - until it reached zero. Then there was a bright rainbow flash and the top half of the spindly little spacecraft broke free and flew straight up. The camera panned to follow the departing ship. John looked at the ascent stage. The thing wasn't even a quarter the size of their tent - and they'd called it a spaceship. He shook his head. People had actually flown to the moon in that thing. Crazy bastards. They had some balls back in the twentieth century, he had to give them that.

The video ended and was replaced by thumbnails for other videos, a cloud of tags, and a list of links. John scanned them. Many of the thumbnails and links were for video games, movies, and the like, but a few promised more information on the old NASA LEM.

Hmm. He picked up his slate, pulled a copy of the window from the wallscreen and started clicking. A few of the resources were out of cache and gave errors, but most of the data was available somewhere on the local network. He dove deep, and within a few minutes was looking at scans of Grumman and Bell Aerosystem blueprints - which were some sort of hardcopy version of CAD files, apparently - dated a full century ago.

He pulled up a copy of the engine specifications. That thrust. It was too small - that couldn't be right. Could it?

Blue barked. "I've got it figured out. If we're trying to launch a 5 kg helmet -"

John raised one finger. "Hang on a sec."

Blue paused and John kept reading. The LEM's ascent stage engines were puny - just 16,000 Newtons. On Earth that wouldn't be enough to accomplish anything... but on the moon, it was enough to get a two-man spaceship up to lunar orbit. Sure, it wasn't a big ship, just 4,500 kilograms, but -

John blinked.

It wasn't that easy, was it?

John dragged the blue print and the specifications sheet from his slate to the wallscreen.

"Blue. The ascent stage on that lunar lander massed 4,500 kilograms."

Blue looked at him and furrowed his brow. A moment later he gave a yip.

John smiled. "You're thinking what I'm thinking, right?"

"Yes!"

Duncan said, "What are you guys talking about?"

"Yeah, what *are* you talking about?" Max asked.

John pointed to the specifications. "Look at the mass."

Duncan shrugged. "Yeah, so?"

Blue said, "Getting to orbit is hard, right? That's why we're just sending a small relay made out of a helmet."

"Yeah, you need to go fast enough -"

John cut him off, grinning. "Getting to orbit on *Earth* is a huge deal. But here on the moon -"

Duncan furrowed his brow. "Yeah, OK, orbital speed is a lot slower, but what -"

"How much do one human and a few dogs weigh?"

Duncan thought for a moment. "I don't know - maybe 500 kilograms if you include suits?" He paused. "Holy crap! You think we can build our own spaceship?"

John nodded. "Something simple - an open frame, four seats, an engine. I bet we scavenge propellant from Gamma's facility."

"What do we use for a motor?"

John waved the objection away. "We can salvage a CNC machine from Gamma's wreckage. If you can hack an interface to it, we can turn a small rocket bell."

Max raised one skeptical eyebrow. "You're proposing that we try to ride a pillar of exploding hydrazine and nitrogen tetroxide - salvaged from a facility that was nuked less than a day ago - and channel that thrust through a rocket bell created by a bunch of nonmachinists using CNC machines that are utterly out of calibration after being hit with an atom bomb?"

John opened his mouth and closed it. He looked to Blue.

Blue sighed. "This *does* sound like one of Duncan's ideas."

Duncan yelled, "Hey!"

John's enthusiasm drained away.

Max shook his head. "I'm up for a dangerous stunt, but if I'm going to die, I'd like it to be in a shootout with the PKs -

Duncan said, "Guys?"

Max continued " - surrounded by fifty or so of their corpses, after running out of ammunition -"

"Guys?"

" - not barbecued in my suit when a rocket bell explodes!"

"Guys!"

John turned. "Yeah, Duncan?"

"The second PK ship is down there in the crater. Is there any reason we can't just salvage an AG module off of it? It came down softly - there must be at least one of them still working."

John opened his mouth to reply, and then closed it. He blinked. "Wait. You're saying -"

"If we're going to build our own spaceship, why would we do it the old-fashioned way? Let's build a *real* spaceship!"

Chapter 110

2064: just west of Zhukovskiy Crater, Lunar Farside

John stood on the ground and looked at the stern of the PK ship towering above him. Above the gunwale, on the rearmost portion of the deck, was a cargo container, its walls pierced by a dozen small rocket bells. A maneuvering unit, just like the ones on the Aristillus ships.

He turned his gaze to the rest of the ship. The large industrial-yellow legs and their massive pneumatic shocks looked incongruous welded to the original smooth lines of the ocean-going hull. The ugly design reminded him of Mike's early ships, back before Lai Docks and its landing cradles existed.

Clearly the PKs didn't plan on being invited in politely.

The legs looked like they'd work well on flat ground, but when the ship had crash landed it hadn't come down on flat ground. Some of the legs rested on boulders; other were danging. The net effect was that the ship listed badly to the left.

There was no way onto the ship's deck from astern. John looked to the left and the right. He'd like to scout around the ship, but that would bring him into view of the chain guns, and if there was anyone inside the ship those guns could tear him apart in a fraction of a second.

Blue saw his gaze and read his frustration. "I can send one of the mules to scout."

John nodded. "Good. Do it."

A moment later the robot walked past them and along the starboard side of the ship. John watched the feed from its camera in his helmet screen. The paint on the starboard side - hull, bridge, and cargo containers alike

- was bubbled and burnt. In some places it had been peeled away entirely by the intense light of the nuclear detonation.

"John, look at the power cables."

John looked. The ship listed toward the mule, which let the mule's camera see the thick cables running from the cargo containers along elevated deck standoffs. The cables had blistered, melted, and burned in the glare of the bomb.

Max said, "If those idiots had just placed the power lines a half meter lower, behind the gunwales, they'd still be flying."

Duncan chimed in. "It looks like the cables going to the chain guns melted too." John looked and saw that Duncan was right. He smiled - one less thing to worry about - and then his smile faltered. The chain guns were dead - but only on this side of the ship. He'd been shot at while he crouched up at the crater rim just yesterday by the chain guns on the other side. Still, disabled guns on one side was better than nothing.

The mule finished its sweep of the starboard side of the ship, crossed under the bow, and started circling back along the port side. This was the side of the ship where a rill of boulders rose up, both forcing the ship into an awkward lean and - potentially - giving access to the deck. The mule circled wide and John watched the video closely. Would the boulders provide a way aboard? And, more importantly, even if they did, would they provide a way up that didn't bring them into the view of the guns? He bit his lip.

The mule's perspective shifted and - yes! - he could see that the topmost rock in the pile almost reached the gunwale of the ship.

Good. Unfortunately, the chain gun on the deck could see him. Or, rather, the mule.

"Blue, give me control."

"Yours."

John sent the mule up the stack of rocks, keeping his eye on the chain gun at all times. The mule scrambled up the mound, over the gunwale, and onto the deck of the ship.

He panned its head back and forth. Neither of the two chain guns so much as twitched. Was the ship empty? Or were the PKs merely asleep at the switch?

He didn't know, and couldn't count on his luck holding. He advanced the mule to the closer of the two gun emplacements and inspected the chain gun.

Where was the weak spot?

There - a power cable came out of the base of the guns and snaked across the deck. Now what? He looked over the control menu. Deploy solar panels. Electrostatic cleaning. Maintenance. Coolant purge. Ah-ha! Arc welder. That would cut the line, for sure.

John deployed the ground clamp and then played the mule's welding gun over the cable.

- and absolutely nothing happened. No arc, nothing.

Ah. The cable was insulated; he couldn't strike an arc.

He adjusted the welding arm, hovering over the housing where the cable disappeared. Then he pulled the trigger - and the video instantly darkened as the auto darkening lens did its job. At the center of the image a small dim blob formed and grew - and finally the steel was melting and running. Suddenly the dimmed image flashed bright white. John killed the welding gun and waited for the lens to clear. There - he'd done it. The arc welder had melted the housing, which had burned through the cable, which had in turn shorted out. A solid ten centimeters of cable was entirely missing, and the deck around it was splashed with brown slag and smoke deposits for more than a meter.

It seemed the ship still had power.

He turned the mule to face the other chain gun. It still wasn't moving. Maybe there was no one on board. Still, better safe than sorry. He advanced the mule and burned through the second cable.

John closed the command interface and turned to the Dogs. "You guys stay here."

Max said, "Let me -"

John held up a finger. "In a minute."

"But I-"

"Max, in a minute."

John walked toward the pile of boulders, leaving the Dogs in the shadow of the stern of the ship. Eighty steps. Ninety. Just before he reached a hundred the miniguns came into view. He knew they were both dead - he'd killed them with the mule just a minute ago - but nonetheless he felt an inch between his shoulder blades.

He knew that itch.

John reached the jumble of rocks, slung his rifle over one shoulder, and reached for the first boulder. As he climbed the name of the ship painted onto the side of the hull came into view - the Oswaldo Aranha. It meant nothing to him - what mattered was what was on the ship. A moment later he reached the top of the rock pile and swung himself over the gunwale. His feet landed on the deck. He looked back the way he had come - and saw that Max had followed him, despite his order.

Damn it. But what was he going to do? His leadership of the Dogs was de facto and informal...and it had also been effectively absolute.

Maybe that was changing. Maybe the fact that a war was here and that Rex had been killed in cold blood was accelerating things. Or maybe it was just the Dogs turning into adults. He shook his head. It would've been nice if the moment of filial rebellion could have been back at Aristillus, and not while scouting an enemy ship.

"Max, damn it, stay down there!"

Max grunted noncommittally.

John took a tentative step onto the ship's deck. The ship was tilted, and it was trickier than it looked. He braced his arms against the cargo containers and took another step - and then Max hopped over the railing and landed on all fours.

"Damn it, Max, I said stay down there!"

Max ignored him. "Do you think there's still crew on the ship?"

John gave up. Max was going to shadow him no matter what he said.

"I - I don't know. Maybe they sent everyone out to get us. Maybe some of them were injured when the ship crashed. Or, yeah, maybe there are troops on board." He paused. "Which is why I asked you to stay down there where it's safe."

Max looked around the deck suspiciously. "I'll scout -"

"It's not safe." John flipped the selector of his rifle from 'safe' to 'fire'.

"I was going to say: I'll scout - with the mule."

John thought, then nodded. "Take it."

Max sat back on his rear legs and his forepaws started moving as he tapped at a virtual keyboard.

John scanned the cargo containers on the deck. There were eight of them. Even if the four clustered along the midline of the ship hadn't been stenciled "power gen," the now-blistered and burned power lines that sprouted from them and the electrical cut-off boxes mounted on their sides would have given their purpose away. John looked at the four power units more closely. They needed one of them for the plan. For a moment he thought that all four were fubared, with cables melted and burned. But, wait, no. The third unit's cable was intact. He visually traced it, and saw that it lead into a bulkhead on the one-story bridge. That cable must carry power for the onboard systems and life support. If there were eight containers and four were batteries, then the other four -

A popup appeared on his overlay - the mule was moving. John looked over his shoulder and saw that Max had moved the mule to the bridge's airlock door and was using the arc welder to tack the door shut.

John went back to his inspection. Two other cargo containers were located near the power boxes and were linked to them by the now-melted cables. These containers were unlabeled, but he assumed they contained the AG units.

That left the final two containers, one located at each end of the ship. He'd seen from the ground that the stern one was a chemical rocket maneuvering unit. The one on the prow must be its mate.

Max said, "You're looking at the ship's design?"

John turned and looked over his shoulder. The mule was done welding.

"Yeah."

"What do you think of it?"

John shrugged. "Aristillus ships have their batteries in their keels, not up on deck, but they have to, because of their size. Aside from that difference, this design looks a lot like ours. Given that they've seized some of ours, I'll bet every single detail of the design was stolen."

Max nodded. "Like the Tupolev Tu-4."

"What?"

"A Soviet clone of a captured American B-29. Bolt for bolt identical."

John shook his head.

"World War II."

"Ah." Max's mastery of military arcana was astounding. "The closer the PKs came to duplicating our designs, the better that is for us."

"Huh? How so?"

"When I was transferring my archives from my old helmet to this one, I did a search. Turns out that I've still got some emails from Ponzie, from years ago."

"And?"

"And I've got complete documentation and technical drawings of the AG units and maneuvering packs." John gestured to all the containers and repeated himself for emphasis. "Docs and drawings. For these exact models."

At that moment a new voice came over their radio and barked, "You, on the deck: identify yourself."

Max raised an eyebrow and deadpanned, "I think there's someone in the ship."

John waved Max to silence and keyed his own radio to give his name and challenge them - and then let the circuit fall dead.

For all he knew, the PKs were in radio contact with Earth right now. If he gave them his name, that information might end up back at Earth seconds from now. They probably wouldn't rain shit down on old friends, distant relatives, former comrades. Would they?

No, it was better to be safe than sorry. He needed a fake name. After a moment of thought he keyed the mic a second time. "This is Phil Ketchum. Identify *your* self."

"This is Commander Orazio Padovesi of the US Navy ship Oswaldo Aranha. You are under arrest."

"No, I don't think we are."

The officer inside the ship began to say something but John spoke over him. "Your men killed one of my friends, but despite that, I'm going to give you an opportunity. I'm just going to give it to you once, so listen to me carefully. Do *you* surrender to *me*? If you do, I give you my word that I won't press for any criminal charges."

The voice on the radio scoffed. "Surrender? Listen, expat, your little game is over. We let you play revolutionary for a few years, but that's done. When the invasion gets here -"

John blinked. "Invasion?"

"You think these two ships are it, dickhead? We're just the scout force. You're giving us just one chance to surrender? Fuck you. I'm giving *you* just one chance to surrender. Your base here is dead, and your other base in Aristillus is going to be ours in a few days. What do you think is going to happen to the leaders of your little cabal when that happens? What do you think is going to happen to you then? There's no plan B for you, so stop your posturing and your bullshit. You're illegal combatants and you are under arrest. Put down your weapons, come inside the airlock with your hands up, and at least you'll get a trial instead of dying out there when you run out of air. You're guilty of -"

John spoke over him. "Max, is that door solid?"

Max nodded. "Yep."

Over the radio the PK officer continued to speak " - treason, illegal possession of firearms - "

John ignored the PK as he crabbed along the tilted deck to the nearest power supply container, the one that sprouted a still intact cable that snaked to the bridge. John held his rifle in his left hand and tried to open the electrical disconnect box on the side of the container with his right.

"- violations of international protocols -".

The latch keeping the disconnect box shut was too small to operate with clumsy gloved fingers. John took his rifle with both hands, reversed it, and smashed the catch with the butt.

" - trespassing on a military vessel -"

The access panel swung open, revealing a bright red cutoff lever.

"- presence in a federally and UN proscribed location-".

John slung his rifle and grabbed the lever with both hands.

"-economic crimes -".

He pulled the lever, and it pivoted. Four status LEDs went from green to amber, then to red, and then died entirely.

The voice on the radio cut out abruptly.

John shut the door on the disconnect box and turned.

Behind him Blue and Duncan were climbing over the gunwale.

Max nodded. "The peakers will choke and die slowly. They deserve worse for killing Rex, but it's a decent start."

Blue shook his head. "What about the enlisted men in there? They didn't kill Rex."

Max barked. "Screw them."

"What, we believe in collective guilt now?"

Max sneered. "Are you honestly going to say that the men in there aren't guilty? The old 'not every Sudani is guilty for the Baltimore crater' argument?" He turned to John for support.

John said nothing.

Blue cleared his throat. "Yes, that is what I'm arguing. Do you think every Sudani was guilty?"

"I may not think that every CITIZEN of Sudan is guilty, but I sure as hell think that every member of the Sudanese Cabal was."

"Even the ones that just repaired trucks or cooked food?"

Max nodded. "Absolutely."

Blue looked at John. "John, do you really support this? Not every man in there -"

Max cut Blue off, angrily. "Let's stop talking in analogies. This isn't about Sudanis. This is about BuSuR and the PKs. Those bastards killed half of our race. If they could have, they would have killed me, you, and Duncan as pups. It took them ten years, but they did kill Rex. If Gamma hadn't shot that other ship down and if this ship hadn't crashed, we'd all be dead by now. You know what word they use when they talk about killing one of us? It's not even `kill.' It's `destroy.' We're just animals to them. Things."

Blue fell silent and looked down, but Max wasn't done. "Did you hear that bastard say 'possession of items proscribed by BuSuR' when he was talking to John? You know what he was talking about, right? Us. That's what we are to the PKs. Property. Illegal property."

Blue turned to John. "John? You can't do this."

John exhaled heavily. "I've been hoping for ten years to avoid this war. I've been on your side, arguing against Max all the way. But Max and Mike were right, and you and I were wrong, Blue. We tried to run away from BuSuR, but they brought the war to us." He paused. "What do you want me to say, Blue?"

Blue looked down. "I - I don't know. It just seems like if we kill them, then we're as bad as they are."

"I gave them a chance to surrender. They didn't take it. But if you feel so bad about it, turn the power back on." John pointed to the electrical disconnect box. "The switch is right over there. I'm not making decisions for you. Do what you want."

Max started to object. "Wait a second -"

"Quiet, Max!" John surprised himself with his own tone.

Blue looked at the disconnect box, then back to John. "Are you serious?"

"I am. Turn the power back on, if you want. I won't stop you."

Blue glanced at the disconnect box again, stared at it for a long moment, and turned and walked away. A moment later Duncan followed him.

Max snorted. "Good. I hope there's a *lot* of them in there. Officers, NCOs, enlisted men. And I hope that they die slowly, fighting each other hand-to-hand, scavenging for the very last spare oxygen tank."

John' lips curled in disgust. "Max, stop. There's a difference between winning and shitting on someone's grave."

Max harrumphed.

John turned and walked after Blue and Duncan. "Did you guys hear the conversation with the PK?"

Blue was silent but Duncan said, "Part of it. Why?"

"There's good news and bad news."

Blue broke his silence. "What's the bad news?"

"This is just a scouting mission. There's a full-bore assault scheduled for Aristillus in the next few days."

John could hear Blue swallow over the com link.

Duncan asked, "So what's the good news?"

"We've got two AG units, a battery pack with some juice, and two maneuvering units."

"So -"

"So we've got everything we need to build our spaceship and get back to Aristillus."

Chapter 111

2064: Homestyle Apartments, Aristillus, Lunar Nearside

The jammer sat on the table in the center of the room, buzzing slightly. Dewitt looked at it and wondered if it was accomplishing anything at all. If Kindig was right, it was a waste. Still, better safe than sorry.

Dewitt turned from the jammer and looked at his men - standing, sitting on cheap chairs, squatting on milk crates. General Restivo had given him carte blanche to recruit who he wanted. He'd taken full advantage of that - not a single AAS, all of them athletic, every one blooded in combat. And, of course, he'd picked men who had the same loyalties that he did.

"Are we unanimous?"

One by one his men gave him said "yes," "hell yeah," or gave him a thumbs up. Two men sighed in resignation but nodded their agreement.

Dewitt breathed out, relieved. "Let's run down our status."

Sergeant Ted Lummus went first. "I got all my charges in place on Tuesday. Yesterday I finished 'training' in Mike Martin's Second Morlock. They give everyone who's completed the intro course access to their servers, at a junior level. Thing is, their opsec is a joke - an LT in the Second gave me a command password. I logged in and pulled everything down. You've got copies."

"Have you read it yet?"

"I've skimmed it."

"Thoughts?"

Lummus shrugged. "Their doctrine is a joke - tactics, lines of defense, rally points." He shook his head. "It's crap."

Sergeant Allan Sanderfur went next. "All my charges are in place too. My training with the militias is the same story - the 20th Guaranteed Electrical barely knows its ass from a hole in the ground. Order of battle, positions - " He shook his head. "Lots of 'form up here, hold this line, hope the shit doesn't hit the fan.'"

They went around the table. Each man gave details from the militia he'd infiltrated. The only major unit that they hadn't gotten details from was Trang's 30th Red Stripe skirmishers. Dewitt looked pointedly at Sergeant Ken Harbert. Harbert spread his hands. "I've got nothing, but that's not on me. At first I thought they had better security than the other units, but then I realized that there *are* no servers, no documents." He blinked in incomprehension. "I honestly don't think they have any doctrine at all."

After they'd all reported Vasquez turned to Dewitt. "What's your sitrep - anything else from your guy Kaspar?"

Dewitt grimaced. He'd been hoping that wasn't going to come up - he didn't want to distract his men with extraneous details just before the shit hit the fan. But now he'd been asked, point blank, and he wasn't about to lie. "Yeah, actually." He took a breath. "Turns out he knows who we are and has some half-baked idea of our mission."

There was a tumult. Lummus sprang to his feet first. "What?" A second later all of his men were standing.

Dewitt held up one hand and his men quieted and waited for his explanation. "He heard something from a friend. I'm assuming a leak at the DoD."

Sanderfur swore. "Fucking REMF mother fuckers!"

Vasquez asked, "Who else in Aristillus knows?"

Dewitt shrugged. "Best I can tell, no one."

"Are we in any danger from -"

Dewitt shook his head. "I made sure he won't talk."

"Shit, Captain. The plan has been compromised; do we -"

"We're not compromised; it's good. The quickest way through this is through this." He looked around. "Are we OK with this?"

They were.

Good. Back to the mission. "You've each got your weapons and body armor cached. Sergeant Sanderfur - ready to distribute the detonators?"

Sanderfur unzipped a bag and lifted out cardboard boxes. "I made the home-brew ones three days ago but I saw a chance to lift a case of factory issue from the work-site yesterday. I tested them. They're good." He placed the boxes on the table.

Dewitt nodded. A good decision: one less variable. "Any last questions or objections before I pull the trigger?"

There were none.

Dewitt picked up his slate, opened a hidden directory, dragged the third music file in the directory into a new email message, and typed in a memorized email address. His finger hovered over the send button for a second, and then he tapped it. The message went out and he stared at the phone, anxiously. A moment later the reply arrived. Dewitt read the screen and saw the expected code words. He turned to his men. "It's on." He took a deep breath. "This is the last time we'll see each other until it's over. God speed, and good hunting."

The men looked at each other, sharing glances loaded with recognition for the enormity of what they were about to do. Then, one after another, they took their boxes of detonators, lifted duffel bags, and filed out.

Finally it was just Dewitt and Sergeant Ted Lummus. Ted raised an eyebrow. "My feet feel a bit wet."

"We're not across the river yet."

Lummus picked up his duffel bag and turned to go.

Dewitt was alone in the room. He picked up the last box of detonators. He'd really grown fond of the people of Aristillus over the past months. They all had. And on the other hand, they'd sworn oaths to the US Army.

He held the detonators, weighing them.

Sometimes you could make compromises. A bit of this, a bit of that. Other times, though, you couldn't hedge. You had to make a decision and stick with it.

Dewitt sighed and slipped the box into the cargo pocket of his pants.

Chapter 112

2064: just west of Zhukovskiy Crater, Lunar Farside

John stepped to the side and into the shadow of the PK ship as one of the two surviving mules walked past, dragging an improvised sledge piled high with rocks. The mule passed and he stepped back - and back into the sun.

They'd only been at it for a day, but the lifeboat project was already well under way. The "construction yard" next to the wrecked hulk of the PK ship was almost ready: Duncan and Blue were smoothing the last corner of it using rakes improvised from spare tent poles. Which meant that they were almost ready to start building.

As if on cue, Max said, "I think we can get it down to eight linear meters of welds."

John shook his head. "That's still way too much - we'll drain the mules' batteries before we're even half done."

Max tilted his head up, gesturing at the PK ship. "We don't have to depend on just the mules' batteries. We can tap the ship's power module."

John shook his head. "That battery pack is all the juice we have."

John saw Max scowl over the in-helmet channel. "The diagnostics say it's got twice what we need to get back to Aristillus, so we can spare -"

"Max, what happens if we screw up? If we short something out? That's the only high-density power source we've got. If we fuck it up, we're dead."

"OK. Fine. But I can't get the design much under eight meters of weld. We need more juice. If you won't let me us power module one, we can tap one of the others. The cables are melted, but maybe they still have a charge."

John thought about it. "I'm not sure that's a good idea. Think about the state of those boxes: the paint is blistered, the cables are burned. What're the insides like? Are the voltage regulators even working? The circuit breakers? Maybe we end up burning out the mule's MIG arm. Or, hell, even frying a mule."

"What other options are there?"

John exhaled. "I don't know."

Blue cleared his throat. "I have an idea."

John looked up. Blue was 40 meters away but had been listening in. The Dog put down his rake.

"I'm listening."

"We cannibalize batteries from Gamma."

"I don't want to go into Zhukovskiy if we don't have to. That was a ground burst - things'll be hot."

"No, not into Zhukovskiy. Gamma had pickets all along the approach to this crater. I bet he had small surface mines or other facilities out there too. There's got to be lots of hardware scattered around that wasn't nuked. We track it down and scavenge the batteries."

John rolled the idea over. When Gamma was nuked all of his rovers had frozen in place. They'd already scavenged a few parts from the nearby ones. Conveniently for them, Gamma hadn't felt the need to reinvent the wheel. Everything the AI built or used, from screw threads to IP packet size, conformed to standards. Maybe the batteries did too.

John nodded. "Alright. Let's find some rovers."

Ten minutes later he and Blue were standing over a rover that had frozen in position 300 meters from the PK ship. John got down on both knees and peered at the machine. There: that had to be the battery compartment. He looked at the bolt for a second and pulled a 6 mm wrench from a cargo pocket. A moment later the door sprang open, revealing three batteries. John grabbed the pull rail on one and slid it from the chassis. He put the wrench down and took the battery in both hands, and then grinned.

"What?"

He showed it to Blue. The Dog leaned forward and then snorted in amusement. John chuckled with him, then broke into a full-throated laugh. "Gamma's one anal-retentive son of a bitch, isn't he?" Not only was the battery pack a standard model, but the Thingverse version number was even machined into the device below the heat sinks.

The battery packs would work.

John asked, "How many do we need?"

Blue took a moment to answer - he must be consulting plans on his display. Finally: "About 400."

John called out over the radio. "How's the construction yard coming?"

Max answered, "We'll be done raking in five minutes."

"Good. We've got to get this ship finished so we can get back to Aristillus ASAP."

"We *know*, John."

"I know. Sorry. Anyway, are you and Duncan in the mood to go hiking?"

"Why?"

"We need you to track down a hundred or so rovers and pull the batteries."

Max said, "Yeah, sure, if -"

Duncan interrupted. "Dead rovers? Cool! I know the timeline is wrong, but we could map these in as looting Barrow-wight downs."

John shook his head. "Is that a yes?"

"Yes!"

John looked at Blue. "You ready to start welding?"

* * *

John stood on the slanted deck of the ship and leaned back as a mule stepped past. The mule dragged one end of a steel anchor cable, the far end of which was spooling off the capstan at the bow. John said, "OK, that's far enough. Drop it."

Blue was teleoperating the mule; the machine let go of the end of the cable and scampered away. John lifted the welding unit, detatched the mule, turned the dial to 'cut,' and struck a spark. A moment later he turned the welder off and waited for his helmet to fade to clear. He looked at his work. "That's the last one. Put it in place, please."

John put the welder down and stretched his back while Blue used the mule to drag the pieces of cable into position.

The mule draped the final piece of cable over the cargo container. Blue backed the mule away.

"Your turn. Do you have everything you need?"

John picked up the welder. "I think I can get by without masking gas." He picked up the cable, tacked it to the cargo container, and moved onto the next cable, working until the welder beeped a low-power alert in his helmet.

"We're done until Max and Duncan get back with more batteries."

Blue walked up to John and sat on the deck. "Do you think the PKs inside have died yet?"

John was silent for a moment and then said, "I figure so."

"Does it bother you?"

"I gave them the opportunity to surrender."

"That wasn't my question. I mean, I know Max is bloodthirsty, but you always said that you've seen enough of war, so I thought -"

"It had to be done."

Blue was silent, drawing John out.

Finally John said, "Look, it wasn't the first time I've killed, and given what's going on, I don't think it'll be the last." He paused, and then elaborated. "When it has to be done, it has to be done. What pisses me off is when people set up situations where someone has to die."

Blue remained silent.

John looked at Blue. The Dog was inscrutable behind his golden faceplate. John called up Blue's in-helmet cam. Not much more to read there. "You know that I didn't join the rebellions in Texas or Alaska, even though I had lots of friends who did."

"Because you thought that violence wasn't justified?"

"No. It was justified - people shouldn't have to give up their freedoms." John looked toward the crack in the crater wall that led to the site of Gamma's sprawling industrial corpse. "I just thought it was a doomed fight. The governments are too big...and too brutal. What's the point of fighting if you're going to lose? People - noncombatants - get hurt."

"So you didn't fight until now because you thought that you couldn't win?"

John sighed. "Yeah, I guess it was half that. And half, I was sick of fighting. By the time I finally realized I'd been on the wrong side my whole career, I was out of energy. I just wanted to get away." John looked at Blue. "I thought that if I could retreat - even if it meant leaving my home - even if it meant leaving Earth - I could avoid the whole mess."

Blue nodded but said nothing.

"I was wrong, though. We ran as far as we could, and the PKs followed us. And then they set up a situation where it was them or us. If I hadn't shot those peakers - and if you four hadn't reprogrammed the mules and killed the rest - we'd be dead. Or if even if they took us alive, you four would be euthanized and I'd be Gitmo-ed for life." John stared off into the distance. "I'm sorry, Blue, I've been rambling. What was your question again?"

"If it bothered you to kill the PKs in the ship?"

"Yeah. It does bother me. The kids I just killed? They don't intend to be evil. They went to government-run schools, they watched government-regulated media. They were fed nothing but bullshit. They thought that they were doing the right thing."

"So if PKs aren't choosing evil, why do they have to die?"

John stared off in the distance. "Why do any of us have to die?" He shrugged. "Once the government chooses to pick a fight, someone is going to die, either us or them. It shouldn't have to be that way, but that's the world we live in." He looked at Blue. "You know I'm not eager to kill. But I'll do it to defend myself, or to defend you three - or the rest of the Dogs back at Aristillus."

Blue nodded. "I know. We owe everything to you."

John and Blue sat in silence. Eventually Blue spoke again. "Do you think that Max looks forward to war a bit too much?"

John thought that over for a minute. "I think -"

John was interrupted as one of the mules crested the distant crater wall and relayed a stored message from Duncan and Max. "Hey guys - Christmas time!"

John stood and looked. On high magnification he could make the distant mule. On its back the solar tarp from the tent was rolled up and lashed down - and clearly stuffed full of cargo.

"Looks like we've got the first load of batteries."

* * *

Three hours later John stepped back and surveyed the work. The steel cable pieces were welded to the three cargo containers they needed, and the good power cable had been rerouted so that it connected the good power unit to an AG unit. John checked the twistlocks holding the cargo containers to the deck. They were all released.

"It's time."

Blue barked in acknowledgement.

John stepped onto the small porchlike platform he'd welded to one end of the AG drive container. Blue moved onto a similar platform welded to the maneuvering thruster unit.

John clipped his carabiner onto the railing and adjusted his safety line, and then pulled a data cord from his suit and plugged it in to the port on the AG unit. "Everyone ready?" There was a round of assents.

John scanned the area. "Damn it, Duncan, step back. This is the *third* time I've told you."

Duncan looked up. "Huh? Oh!" He shuffled back a few meters. John looked around one last time. They were ready. He called up the interface and hit the button. A moment later he heard the thrumming and felt the weird twist in his gut.

"I feel twitchy!"

"Duncan, stay off the radio."

"But what if I -"

"- unless you've got something important to say. But you don't, do you?"

Duncan didn't respond.

John waited a few seconds, but the AG unit didn't lift off the deck. He cranked the drive up a notch. The thrumming and pushing sensations grew stronger, and beneath his feet the platform shifted. The AG drive was tilting. John tightened his grip on the railing. The cargo container tilted further - and then it lifted.

The unit must not have been well balanced because it maintained its tilt as it rose. John chanced a glance down. As the AG drive he was riding rose into the void the thick electrical cable that connected it to the next container -

the sole surviving battery unit - slithered and snaked across the ship's deck.

Just before the power cable reached its limit the first set of cannibalized anchor lines snapped taut and the drive unit immediately stopped rising. John lurched and caught himself. The drive unit pendulumed slowly back and forth over the ship's deck before settling into position.

John looked down. He and the AG unit were now suspended directly over the second cargo container - the power unit.

"Blue, is the battery container moving?"

"It shifted a bit, but it's still flat on the deck."

"I'm going to give it another click."

John gave the command and the AG unit spun up another step. The thrumming rose into deep vibrating chords and washed over him. The twisting redoubled and the field pushed him backward into the railing, and then the entire balcony lurched as the AG unit began climbing again.

Blue called out, "It's off the deck!"

John saw the shadows of the two containers moving across the dead PK ship as the cargo units rose. Then the balcony lurched again as the final set of cables went taut.

John held on to the railing while his container pendulumed as it strained against its anchor. After a moment the swaying died out. "Blue, I'm going to go one notch higher."

"No, hang on - you're moving."

John leaned over the railing and looked down. From this angle he couldn't tell if the bottom container, where Blue was standing on a small balcony like his own, was flat on the deck or above it. Blue answered his unasked question. "It's just a small gap. Half a meter. Almost a full meter now. OK, we've cleared the railings!"

John saw movement near the bottom container in the stack. Damn it, it was Duncan - on the deck of the ship, where he shouldn't be, and standing far too close, where he *really* shouldn't be.

"Duncan! Get the hell out of there!" Duncan looked up, and scampered out of the way.

Blue said. "Ready to maneuver?"

"Ready."

Blue gave the command to the maneuvering unit. There was a flare from three rocket bells along one side of the bottom container, and the stack of containers pendulumed again, but this time it was the bottom of the pendulum that swung, not the top. Blue's container slid gently to one side. Slowly, slowly, the upper two units followed it.

It took a half hour to get the stack directly over the raked-smooth construction yard they'd cleared, and a full hour and several attempts to lower the stack to the ground and land the containers just centimeters away from each other.

And then, finally, it was done. John gave the command to the AG drive and the unit cycled through its shutdown sequence before falling entirely silent. The container settled solidly onto the ground.

Blue asked, "We were in the air longer than we expected. What was our power consumption?"

John checked. "The dial hasn't moved at all. We should have more than enough to get back Aristillus."

"You still think this is going to work?"

"I *know* it's going to work, Blue."

"Can we call it a day? I'd like to eat dinner and then sleep."

John unclipped his suit from the container and stepped over the railing. "We can take a break, but we can't sleep long - we've got to get to Aristillus before the PKs do."

Chapter 113

2064: outside Goldwater vault, level four, Aristillus, Lunar Nearside

Matthew Dewitt stood on the work platform of the rented cherry picker and drove it down the tunnel. He looked up and saw the box on the ceiling ahead. He turned on the cherry picker's hazard lights and slowed to a stop. An automated delivery skid approached at speed and he tensed, but the other vehicle detected the obstruction and switched lanes before racing past.

Dewitt worked the controls and the cherry picker's arm swung up smoothly. The ceiling light panels and other infrastructure rushed toward him, then slowed. In the residential sections of the city there were sky projections, cleverly hidden microwind fans, and more, but here in an industrial tunnel the ceiling and the equipment bolted to it were undisguised. Some of it was painted in stark colors: olive green for the potable water lines, safety red for the sprinkler pipes, black and yellow for chemical conduits. And right here, among the brackets, light panels, sprinklers, and other equipment, was the fake electrical supply box he'd installed a week ago. He jogged the controls on the cherry picker. He was two meters away, then one, and then right under it.

Dewitt looked around one last time. On the tunnel floor below an automated cargo sled approached his parked vehicle and swung past. He looked to the left and right and saw no human-driven vehicles.

He unlocked the door on the overhead box and let it swing open in the light gravity. Inside everything looked just as he left it.

He bent down, opened his tool bag, and carefully extracted a detonator.

Chapter 114

2064: just west of Zhukovskiy Crater, Lunar Farside

John put down the welder and leaned back. As he stretched, he took a chance to look around. Max was on top of the containers using the welder from the second mule. Blue was sorting through their supplies. Where was Duncan? He scanned left and right but didn't see him. "Duncan, how's the checklist going?"

"I'm working on it."

"Well, hurry up. We need to move. The attack on Aristillus could come at any time."

Duncan, normally happy-go-lucky, was defensive. "John, I *know*. Blue told me to cut railings from the PK ship and load them onto the mule. And that's what I'm *doing*."

John turned - and there was Duncan on the PK ship, holding an armful of railings.

"Sorry, Duncan."

Duncan all but sniffed. "It's all right."

John grimaced. He was picking fights without meaning to. He was short on sleep - they all were. The four of them had been racing against the clock for two days now and the stress was getting to them. John touched his toes and felt his back pop. When he got back to Aristillus he was going to take a long hot shower and then sleep for a week. But that was in the future. Now? He sighed, dropped to one knee in the dust and went back to welding.

Two hours later John finished the last bead, put the abused welder down next to the mound of drained batteries, and stepped back to admire his handiwork. The three containers were butted nose-to-tail, the junctions reinforced with lengths of deck railing salvaged from the PK ship. Weld beads stitched the whole thing into one rigid body. He craned his head to look at the top of the containers -

- and noticed blemishes in his field of view. He keyed the electrostatic cleaning cycle and waited as his helmet buzzed, but the spots persisted. That was weird - the cleaning should have floated the dust off. He ran a gloved hand over his faceplate and felt bumps.

What the - ? John blinked. Weld spatter must have splashed up and melted into his faceplate. He felt a chill and his breath shuddered out of him. Jesus - the danger he'd been in. Or was still in. How deep in the faceplate was the spatter? Should he get a new helmet?

He looked to his left, far across the floor of c-177, where the nearest PK bodies were. Should he take the time to go salvage another helmet?

It was the smart move, but there wasn't time. A catastrophic blowout was a risk he'd have to take. And if his faceplate blew out, there was always the quick sealing foam. Although it was a fool who did something stupid just because he had a seatbelt on.

Well, today he'd have to be that fool. Racing against the clock was always dangerous. They'd been cutting corners for two days now, and they were running risks because of it.

And the biggest risk of all? These three cargo containers they'd been working on. They were building a God-damned spaceship out of parts salvaged from a nuked wreck. But what other option did they have? There were PK satellites overhead, an invasion fleet on the way from Earth, and no way to communicate with friends or allies.

They had to do this.

A window popped up on his helmet overlay and showed a spreadsheet - their construction task list.

John blinked with eyes made crusty from sleep-deprivation and anxiety. Wait. Was this right? Was the ship really finished?

"Blue, you're done with the railings up top?"

"Yeah."

"And the chairs?"

"Hours ago. I've been loading."

John looked up and saw Blue on top of the container, and then turned. The pile of supplies was gone: batteries, the mules, the tent - the space behind him was empty. Hopefully they'd land exactly at Aristillus, but if anything went wrong, they were bringing all of their supplies with them.

John went back to his helmet display and scanned the list. Yes, they were really 100% done with the construction.

So. This was it. He blinked and tried to feel something, but he was too tired - the only thing he felt was a burning desire to sit down.

There was nothing else to do, was there?

He took a step toward the rungs on the side of the cargo container and realized he was still carrying the welder. For a second he was tempted to drop it in the dust, but if they were preparing for the worst, he wouldn't.

John grabbed a rung on the side of the improvised ship and climbed with one arm. When he reached the top Blue took the welder from him and secured it. John turned sideways and shimmied past the lashed-down pile of cargo. As he shuffled past it he grabbed one of the steel cables and gave it it a tug. The pile of tent, spare tent, mules, air tanks scavenged from dead PKs, and batteries taken from Gamma's rovers was an unwieldy heap but Max had done a good job - nothing shifted. Good. He smiled.

John moved further around the pile - and saw the golden solar shield wrapped around its precious cargo. Rex, in his burial shroud. John's smiled slipped. Rex was dead - but he'd be buried among friends, not left on Farside under the cold stars and surrounded by the corpses of enemies.

John nodded in a silent salute and made his way to the front of the lifeboat. Max and Duncan occupied two of the seats. Blue slid past John and sat and John took his place and clipped in.

Max looked at him. "We're on checklist three."

"Don't let me stop you."

Max nodded. "Checklist three, bullet twenty-three: maneuvering system propellant?"

Duncan said, "Pressurized. Check."

"Checklist three, bullet twenty-four: maneuvering system bells prewarmed?"

"One hundred twenty degrees C. Check."

The call and response ran for five more minutes and then Max turned to John. "That's it for list three. We're ready."

John straightened. This might be the time for a Saint Crispin's Day speech, or at least a few words. But he was tired. Tired and uninspired. It was time to get back to Aristillus. Time to get out of the cold and the loneliness. Time to give Mike a warning.

John turned as far in his seat as he could and looked at Blue and Duncan. "Let's go home." He paused. "And remember one thing: no matter how this works, we had a great trip. It was worth doing."

There was a murmur of assent from Blue and Max, and a quick bark from Duncan.

John said, "OK, let's do it."

He called up the list in his display. "Checklist four, bullet one. AG to three. Slowly, please."

Blue operated the controls from his suit display and John's stomach twisted. A moment later the landscape shifted incrementally as the front of the lifeboat tilted. Around them dust blew. After several long seconds Blue said, "Bullet one - check."

John nodded. "Checklist four, bullet two. AG to 'four.'"

The gut-twisting sensation increased and the lifeboat tilted more - and pulled free of the ground.

"Bullet two - check."

Fifty meters to their left the hull of the PK ship Oswaldo Aranha seemed to sink. A moment later John and the Dogs rose past its gunwales - and kept rising. The bridge tower of the PK ship slipped downward. And then the wrecked ship was eclipsed from view.

John turned away from the PK ship and checked the lifeboat system screen in his helmet display. Power was fine. They were rotating slightly as they rose, but it wasn't a problem. The center of gravity was good.

Max called out, "Look at Zhukovskiy."

John minimized his screen. The lifeboat wasn't just rising, it was slowly accelerating, and as he'd been checking his display they'd been falling into the sky. The ship was already above the walls of c-177, and ahead of them the shield wall of Zhukovskiy was dropping away. They were almost level with the top, and then the boat rose past it. At first he could just see the far crater wall twenty kilometers away, but as they rose further the floor of the crater started to come into view.

Now he could see the devastation inside, and it was as bad as he'd imagined. The first PK ship, the one Gamma had shot down, had fallen near one edge of Gamma's facility, and when it had exploded it had gouged a new crater right in the heart of Zhukovskiy. The crater didn't remotely match the scale of Zhukovskiy, but it was big - hundreds of meters across. Around it the devastation was absolute: for perhaps half a kilometer around the detonation point there was nothing left of Gamma's infrastructure but blackened shards of metal. Further from the center the destruction was still severe, but larger pieces of machinery survived, and a hint of the original layout of the facility showed through the wreckage.

The lifeboat kept climbing.

John flipped back to his helmet display. "We're at five klicks. Blue, checklist four, bullet three: orientation."

"We need twenty-two degrees. Programmed in. I'm starting rotation sequence...now." John felt rather than saw the pulses from rocket bells recessed into the sides of the rearmost cargo container. The boat began to spin slightly as it rose.

It also began to roll.

"Blue, we've got roll -"

"I know. It's ten degrees. It's under control."

The roll increased. "Blue."

"I've got it."

John grabbed the jury-rigged railing as the boat listed sickeningly. "Blue!"

"Nineteen degrees. Stopping rotation...now." The lifeboat shuddered a second time as flame again spurted from rocket bells.

The rotation slowed and stopped, and with it the list.

Their altitude, though, continued to increase. Zhukovskiy was even further below and the horizon was distinctly curved. There was no mistaking that they were far above a small spherical world.

John checked the altitude and saw that they were at six kilometers. "Bullet four: forw-"

Blue didn't wait for him to finish. "Forward acceleration - now."

John felt the seat push hard into his back. The maneuvering unit was a clone of the ones on the Aristillus ships. It was designed to control pitch, roll and yaw. It didn't have nearly enough thrust to accelerate a big ship. On this small lifeboat, though, it was more than enough.

John looked backward over his shoulder to see if he could see flame from the rockets, but the pile of cargo amidship blocked his view. He turned his attention forward. The mountains and crater walls drifted past. As the thrusters continued their burn the speed increased - and kept increasing. Max and Duncan panted with excitement.

John looked at the checklist. "Bullet five. Jackson highlands coming up in 100 klicks. Adjust AG-"

"AG to four point five."

Zhukovskiy was behind them, and as they accelerated, other craters slid by faster and faster. They were eight kilometers high now and the moon was a huge ball beneath them.

"Bullet six. We're near peak velocity. Cut thrust in four."

Blue took the count. "Three. Two. One. Cut"

The acceleration ended but the moon continued to rush past below. Duncan howled in excitement.

Max barked back, and then yelled "Welcome to the first flight of the SS 'Holy-Crap-I-Hope-This-Works.'"

Duncan snickered. "No, no! The AFS Pile Of Crap!"

"Wait, I've got it. It's the Forget-about-the-low-bidder-this-is-the-no-bidder."

As the two traded joking names for the boat John let himself sink into his chair and relax for the first time in what felt like forever. They were on course, and he had absolutely no responsibilities for more than an hour. When they got to Aristillus there'd be more work: a tricky landing, telling Mike and others that an invasion was a week or two away, and a thousand headaches he couldn't yet imagine that would certainly come from that. Right now, though, there was nothing he had to do. Actually, there was nothing he *could* do. Other than sit back.

John listened to the common channel where the Dogs were debating ship names. After a few minutes he joined in with his own suggestion but none of the Dogs thought that "HMS Beagle" was funny. He sighed.

He dropped out of the conversation and sat back...and then something caught his eye. There, over the bow of the lifeboat, the blue rim of the Earth was rising over the horizon ahead. Blue must have seen it too - over the coms link he said "woah." A moment later Max and Duncan also stopped talking as they too saw the planet come into view.

God. How long had it been since he'd seen Earth?

It was beautiful.

The blues, the whites, the greens. Every single bit of it - even the browns of the African deserts - tugged at him and he felt his breath catch. There was something deep, deep in the human soul that knew that those were the colors of home. The colors of life.

And yet, for all that racial memory, he knew that somewhere down there, men were prepping a mission to come here to kill or enslave everyone he knew and loved.

His stomach twisted, and it wasn't just the AG drive.

Chapter 115

2064: near lock #912, Aristillus, Lunar Nearside

The taxi stopped two meters shy of the huge airlock door. Dewitt stepped down and pulled his two overstuffed duffel bags after him. The taxi chimed once, did an expert K-turn, and accelerated smoothly away on the far side of the double yellow line.

Dewitt looked around. He was alone at the end of the tunnel. The huge airlock door, painted in black and yellow stripes, dominated the end of the tunnel. A pallet of pipes was stacked against one side wall, and next to it was parked a panel truck with a "Double Door" logo on the side. Dewitt put down his bags, pulled out a perimeter bug and pushed it into the end of one of the pipes, and then turned and -

A man-sized door to one side of the airlock opened. Dewitt froze. Two men wearing jumpsuits and hardhats walked out. One was looking at his slate. "Pumps are fine, but the grit filter -"

The second airlock tech noticed Dewitt. He pushed his white hardhat back. "Going out? We were just about to take this one offline." He weighed his options for a second. "You can go through now if you want, but we're going to be an hour, so if you want to come back inside before then you'll probably want to use 913." He scratched his head under his hardhat. "Actually, you probably want to use 913, either way. It's got a man-sized lock, so it won't be as expensive as thi-"

Dewitt's first shot took the tech in the chest; his next shot hit his coworker a fraction of a second later. Then Dewitt was on them, zip-tying their wrists, and slapping a sedative patch on each. Only after they were secured did he pull the taser rounds out of their chests with gloved fingers.

That done, he dragged the first tech into the utility room he'd just come out of. A moment later he dragged the second tech in, and then returned for his duffel bags. Only then did he close the door.

Then, finally, they were all inside. He pushed his duffel bags to one side and checked the two men he'd tased and tranked. One hadn't yet gotten the full dose of the drug and was groggily protesting, but the other was out. Dewitt patted them both down quickly and efficiently. Neither was armed. One had a keyfob. Dewitt inspected it. Was it for the truck outside? It must be. He pocketed it, turned away from the men, and got down to business. His slate connected to the airlock's controller and the two devices did their public key / private key dance. The slate pinged - the lock was now in override mode. That would stop anyone from shutting it down remotely.

Dewitt checked the time - T minus 60 minutes.

There was nothing to do now but wait. Wait, and think.

He didn't worry. The plan was solid. At least, as solid as any plan ever is. His biggest fear was that the incompetence of the PK troops might fuck it up. If this worked, civilian casualties would be minimal - but if someone started disobeying orders or ad hoc-ing shit, there'd be dead civilians. Maybe even lots of them.

That sort of thing didn't bother the average officer all that much, but it mattered to him.

He sat down on one of his duffel bags, pulled out a snack, and scanned the news boards on his slate as he waited.

Nothing.

Exactly as it should be.

His timer beeped. T minus thirty.

Shit was about to get real, and he needed to be ready.

He stood, crumpled the wrapper of the energy bar and pushed it inside the empty sports drink bottle, and then unzipped his fly and urinated into the container before sealing it. He checked the two airlock techs again. Both were breathing placidly.

Twenty-nine minutes to go.

Dewitt opened his duffel bags and took out the rented spacesuit, the rifle, and the equipment.

He reached into the duffel bag and pulled out the velcro patches. It would have been stupid to bring these with from Earth, and too dangerous to have them custom made here in Aristillus, so they'd bought blank patches and painted the words on to them.

He took the largest "PK" patch and stuck it across his chest, and then applied the smaller ones to either arm.

He checked his timer.

Twenty-eight minutes.

Chapter 116

2064: Peterson Air Force Base, Colorado, Earth

Lieutenant Chilton looked at the fuzzy image. "Sir, the target is slowing. It's almost at Aristillus now. If we want to take it out, we should -"

Captain Small shook his head. "No. Too risky with the invasion fleet almost there."

Chilton turned and looked at his boss. "Captain, the lead elements of the fleet are tens of thousands of klicks away. This expat ship is well outside the exclusion zone and the imaging from our lunar sats is crisp. There's absolutely no chance that we'll hit them."

Captain Small looked at the screen. Crap. Chilton was right - the expat ship *was* ten thousand klicks outside the zone, and not ten as he'd first read. He should probably authorize Chilton to fire.

...But he'd already made a decision, and if he changed his mind just because Lieutenant Chilton had objected, he might look weak.

On the other hand, if he didn't authorize the shot, it might come back to bite him later.

Crap.

"Can you get me better imaging?"

Chilton zoomed.

"What is that? It looks like three cargo containers."

"I don't know, sir; it doesn't match the profile of any of the expat cargo ships or even their small hoppers."

Captain Small rubbed his chin. Crap.

Chapter 117

2064: Eiffong Engineering, Aristillus, Lunar Nearside

Mike pulled his motorcycle helmet off and was immediately assaulted by noise. To his left a shower of sparks announced a worker cleaning up a flange on one of the yellow Caterpillars. As soon as the grinding wheel slowed, the sound was replaced by the banging of a man-sized pneumatic hammer. Mike turned right and saw a different worker leaning into the chain-supported tool as he drove drift pins out of a wheel loader.

Mike put his fingers in his ears and looked around for Tony - and there he was, striding toward him. Tony was wearing a greasy set of overalls and, crucially, a pair of headphones snapped across his shiny black dome of a head. An outstretched hand held an extra pair. Mike took them gratefully.

Tony Eiffong pointed past the nearby Cats, to a different group of machines further away. He shouted, "Those are yours."

Mike looked at the five vehicles lined up against the far side of the tunnel warehouse. Even without the logos on the side he knew the fleet serial numbers painted along their flanks.

Tony turned and strode toward the machines and he followed. Mike remembered this batch of earthmovers: he'd purchased them through a cutout company in Africa. Africa might be a crap basket thanks to the PK occupation and their constant brushfire wars, but at least the continent didn't have the CJPA, which meant that job site automation tools were legal. Even if he could figure a way to smuggle equipment out of Europe or North America he wouldn't bother - he'd just have to retrofit them once they got here.

They reached the machines. "Your message said you'd found the problem?"

Tony pointed to drive wheels inside the treads. "This model has cylindrical packed bearing clusters, sealed against mud, right? But let's slide underneath and look -"

"Tony, I don't have a lot of time. The boardroom is meeting -"

"Give me two minutes."

Mike considered. The boardroom group was going to be nothing but more boring shit. Budgets, disagreements, factions. And here was something he could put his hands on: cold steel, thick grease. Something real.

He nodded. "Show me."

Tony dropped to the oil-stained concrete and slithered under the earth mover. Mike squirmed in next to him.

Tony used a small flashlight to point up between two idler wheels. "There. I took off the inside wheels to take some measurements. Do you see it?"

"I see the ends of bearing clusters. And I see that you've pulled one out."

"Look closer. These bearings should be sealed, but they're not. That's why they failed."

"So the factory installed the wrong version?"

Tony shook his head and the flashlight beam danced. "Uh uh. There *is* no wrong part. This bearing isn't even made without a seal. And, even if it was, the outside end is sealed properly."

Mike squinted. This didn't make sense. "So what's going on? Some after-market replacement?"

"No." Tony moved the flashlight a hand's breadth to the right. "Now look at this, where I removed the shaft packing. See the damage to the shaft? It's not wear, it's not galling - someone took these apart after they left the factory and did damage. They machined these thinner."

Mike peered at the parts. "Machined? You're saying that this was on purpose? What is this - economic sabotage?"

Tony shrugged. "All I know is someone trashed these machines. And I know it was just before you bought them, because if they'd operated them like this back in Nigeria for even an hour, they wouldn't have been able to drive them into the cargo containers to be shipped here."

"What the fuck?" He turned and looked at Tony in the cramped space under the machine. "That makes no sense. The Earth governments are simultaneously trying to kill us - *and* slightly annoy us? Which is it?"

Tony levered himself up under the earth-mover on one elbow and shook his head. "Who knows? If your American government is anything like our Nigerian government -"

"It's not *my* American government."

"You know what I mean. My point is that governments are so huge that you've probably got one ministry trying to kill you, one trying to ruin your earth movers, and a third one trying to make educational videos so your workers don't catch malaria."

Mike smiled at the joke - and then realized that for all he knew there *was* some arm of the government that was even now preparing anti-malarial videos for lunar distribution.

Fucking idiots.

Mike's phone rang. It was probably a reminder from Wam about the meeting. He reached down and silenced it. "So the bearings are shot and we think the Earth governments are behind it. Where does that leave us?"

"You've got three options -"

The phone rang again, this time in high priority mode. Damn it, Wam. He reached down and silenced it again.

"Go on."

"The first option is to buy new bearings. We're out of stock, so we need to either import them or find someone to fab that. That will take a while, but -"

The phone rang for the third time - this time with Darcy's ring tone. Mike reached for it - then paused. Darcy? That made no sense - the Poyekhali should be in the South China sea by now and she knew better than to route calls through Earth infrastructure.

This was weird. "Hang on Tony, let me take this." He turned the phone on. "Darcy?"

Gamma's voice answered him. "No, Michael."

"Gamma?" Mike sat up - and banged his head on the bottom of the earth mover. He grabbed his head with one hand as he rolled onto his side. "*Fuck*! Shit."

"Michael, I needed to talk to you."

Mike rubbed his head. "And you had to impersonate a call from Darcy?"

"You did not answer when I called as myself."

Damn it, his head HURT. "OK, what is it?"

"There is an object inbound over the north lunar pole."

The pain in Mike's forehead receded. "An object? What is it?"

"I cannot say."

"Wait a second - have you succeeded in restoring your satellite network?"

"No."

"So how can you see something over the pole?"

"I am in the process of setting up a surface-based point-to-point laser relay system to contact... other installations. A rover at one of these other sites saw something."

Mike blinked. "Other installations? What are you talking about?"

"I do not have time to explain. The important thing is that the inbound object appears to be heading toward the vicinity of Aristillus. Wait - I now have a second data point and have refined my estimations of trajectory and speed. The object is headed directly at Aristillus and will be there in eight minutes."

"Object?"

"The item I'm tracking doesn't match any ship silhouette. As best I can tell it is approximately the size and shape of three cargo containers."

Mike froze and the pain from his bruised forehead was forgotten. Ever since Baltimore the mention of cargo containers caused everyone old enough to remember the Flash to have at least a moment of heightened alertness.

"Gamma, are you saying it could be a nuke?"

Tony to his left yelled, "A nuke? What are you -."

Mike waved him to silence.

Gamma responded, "Further information is not available."

"What does that mean? Gamma -."

"There's - please wait. Mike, I'm getting more data. Mike, some rovers on Farside have - "

"You've got rovers on FARSIDE? Jesus, how many rovers do you -"

Tony interrupted again. "Mike, what's going on?"

"Tony, shut up!"

Gamma said, "Mike, please listen! I've done a query and some rovers on Farside have encountered heightened levels of strontium 91 and 92 and zirconium 95. This suggests that there was a nuclear detonation on the Farside sometime in the past few days, and -"

Mike scrambled out from under the earth mover and stood. "Jesus! How big of a nuke is in the cargo container?"

"We do not have enough data to know for sure that this is a nucl -"

"Guess!"

"There hasn't been public disclosure of a new nuclear bomb design in the West since the 2023, but the open literature suggests that the current use W-105 warhead is 400 kilotons."

Mike stared up at the arched rock ceiling of the warehouse. "Kilotons, not megatons? Are we safe down here?"

"An air burst would mostly spare everything except the surface installations -"

"That's good-"

"- but the W-105 was designed during the Korean Escalation and is usually packaged with a hardened perpetrator which -"

Mike knew the geography of Aristillus. Basalt, plagioclase, pyroxene. A bit of pumice, but not much. If a nuke - even one much smaller than 400 kilotons - penetrated into the rock here and exploded a dozen meters below ground, almost all of the energy would couple to the rock. The shattering effect of typical mining charges like ANFO or RDX would be nothing like that of a nuke.

He had an image of a shock wave racing outward through the rock at thousands of meters per second, shattering everything in its path. He saw the ceilings of the A and B class tunnels closest to the surface cracking. The power lines would shear and the lights would go out. Then the whistling would start, as air began leaking out. The city would lose cubic kilometers of air in minutes - the e-p-door project wasn't remotely far enough along.

And then the cave-ins would happen.

Mike felt ill.

"Gamma, I need your help. We've got to evacuate everyone from the tunnels in levels one and two. *Everyone*. Can you alert -"

"Michael, I've got a call -"

"Not now! Listen, we don't have an evac plan. I need you to call every phone with your high priority -"

"Michael -"

"Fuck, Gamma, listen to me!"

"*Michael!*"

Mike blinked.

"What?"

"I have more data. It's not a nuclear weapon."

The stress receded, but Mike didn't feel better - instead he felt suddenly light-headed. He reached one hand out behind him and found the cold steel of the Cat's tread. He lowered himself to the concrete floor and sat then leaned back against the tread. He was chilly, and yet his armpits were dripping in sweat. He rubbed a hand across his forehead and it all but slipped across the sweeaty skin.

Around him the shop had fallen silent. Mike looked up and saw that Tony and a few dozen members of his crew were standing around, tools down, staring and listening.

"Gamma, how - how do you know it's not a nuke?"

"I've received radio contact from the object. It's a small spaceship containing John and his Dog companions."

Mike swallowed and tried to speak. He tried again - and couldn't.

"Michael, I am sorry for that false alarm." A pause. "Michael, are you there?"

Mike sat on the floor, silent, his face pale.

He stared at the phone and heard Gamma's voice coming from it, as if from a thousand kilometers away. Then he looked up at the tunnel ceiling and imagined the shockwave, the ceiling cracking, the lights failing.

He licked his lips.

Chapter 118

2064: Peterson Air Force Base, Colorado, Earth

Captain Small shook his head a second time. "No."

"But it's so far away from the fleet that -"

"I know it's safe, but it's not about that. What about the promotion boards? Solomon wants that slot as badly as I do, and if he found out about us taking the shot - and he would - do you know how he'd spin it? He'd get the ear of some colonel or general, and start talking about how we risked lives." He paused. "And it wouldn't just be my career that'd be at risk. You'd be vulnerable too, you know. Look, I don't know what they teach you in ROTC, but you've got a lot to learn about how the real Air Force works."

"Captain, we -"

"No, forget it, Chilton. No shot."

Lieutenant Chilton sighed and turned to his console. With the tap of a button the cross hairs centered over the small grainy image of the cargo container spaceship switched from red to green and the stats panel confirmed that the capacitor bank on ABM sat #17 was discharging back to standby levels.

Damn. It would have been fun to shoot it. Not just because Jim on #15 had shot two more lunar sats than he had, but because Captain Small was right - Captain Solomon DID want that promotion badly...and Solomon had a reputation as someone who remembered who his friends were.

Shit.

Well, maybe there was something else he could do to get into Solomon's good graces.

Chapter 119

2064: 40 kilometers above Aristillus, Lunar Nearside

John held his breath as the north wall of the Aristillus crater slid majestically beneath them. The colony itself was still 30 kilometers ahead, but even from this distance it was unmistakable. Glittering solar farms spread across the surface. Vast piles of mine tailings were stacked to the south and west. At one edge he thought he saw a TBM racking yard, and even from this distance he thought he could make out the open pits of Lai Docks near the center.

He was coming home.

Blue said, "Bullet forty-three. Altitude 40 klicks. Ramping down the AG."

"Excellent." John checked his list. Two more minutes till the next step.

Past the city John could even see a small bit of Sinus Lunicus, just over the far wall of Aristillus. Suddenly something occurred to him. "Gamma, can you hear me?"

"John, is that you?"

John laughed. "Yes, it's me!"

"You survived."

"And so did you."

"Part of me. John, I have an important question - did you get my last message? Did you get to Zhukovskiy Crater?"

Blue, on a separate channel, gave a status update. "Altitude 20 klicks."

"Noted. I'm talking to Gamma. I'll be back with you in a moment."

John turned back to Gamma. "Yes, we got to Zhukovskiy, but -"

"How is the installation there?"

"The installation? You mean your installation?"

"Yes."

"Uh - it's destroyed. A PK ship nuked it."

"I see. Good."

"Good? Gamma, what are you - actually, let's talk about this later. I need to call Mike Martin and patch me through to him."

"I'm sorry, I can't let you do that."

John was taken aback. "What do you mean 'can't'? Gamma, this is important. I'm hanging up. I'll talk to you -"

"John, if you had any communication with the Zhukovskiy facility, it is possible that your suit software is corrupted. I cannot risk direct data communications between you and anyone or anything at Aristillus."

Blue said, "Altitude 10 klicks."

"Corrupted? Corrupted by who? The PK ship -"

"Corrupted by the Zhukovskiy fork of myself. I've explained partition spasms to you before. I am sorry but I must insist. I am taking control of your suit processors now." A pause. "Duncan's suit is not responding."

"Gamma, I can't believe that you're doing this. I do *not* give you permission."

"Why is Duncan's suit not responding?"

"Rex was killed by a PK. His suit is powered off. Now -"

"I'm sorry to hear that."

"Forget that - you do not have permission to mess with our suits."

Blue called out in panic, "John! The AG drive interface has disappeared!"

John twisted to face Blue. "What?"

"It's gone! I can't find it in my overlay!"

John call up his own interface. The control screen they'd built for the boat appeared, but it was only six items long. It should have been nine or more. He frantically selected menus, and as he paged through them they disappeared one by one. Finally he was left with the top-level overlay desktop - and that too went blank and John was staring out at unfiltered, unaugmented reality.

He looked at the ground rushing by below, growing closer by the second. "Gamma, what the hell are you doing?"

They needed to rotate the lifeboat immediately and apply braking -

As if on command, the lifeboat shuddered beneath him and began rotating.

"Blue! Did you get the controls back? I-"

It was Gamma who answered him. "No, John. I've taken control of your craft."

John looked at Blue. The Dog was gesturing - pointing to his helmet and waving his hands. No overlay. No coms.

"God damn it, Gamma!"

"Don't be afraid, John. I'll land you safely. I apologize that this was necessary, but -"

"This was *not* necessary!"

"You may not understand, but I assure you that it is."

The lifeboat shuddered again and the rotation stopped.

John looked down at the surface. They were low now - really low. Perhaps just a kilometer over Aristillus - and they weren't heading for Lai Docks. As if on cue Gamma said, "I do not have communications with Lai Docks and Air Traffic Control, and even if I did, they probably would not want a ship contaminated with nuclear fallout to land there. There is a very large open area near airlock #912. I will set you down there."

John's anger was cold and unwavering. "Gamma, I need to talk to Mike Martin immediately."

"I apologize John, but this is non-negotiable - and, at this point - not even possible. I've wiped out the software on your suits and reinstalled a minimal life support library in each of your systems and one small communications driver in your personal suit. I've also set auto-reformat countdown timers in each of them. Your suits will become entirely inoperative in five minutes."

"What? Why?"

"There are field programmable gate arrays buried deep in the hardware that runs the cooling underwear water pump subsystem in your suits. I cannot read the contents of these subsystems and my attempts to rewrite them to a clean state are unsuccessful."

"What does that mean?"

"It means that I cannot trust anything about your suits, your mules, or any other computing device that you brought from Zhukovskiy. I have therefore inserted code that will brick your suits so that none of the communications channels into the cooling underwear water pump subsystem will work. You have just enough time to cycle into the airlock before they shut down forever. I would appreciate it if you disposed of the suits afterward. As the melting point of silicon is unfeasibly high, mechanical destruction of all circuit boards will be sufficient."

"Gamma, what the hell are you talking about?"

"John, your ship will landing in thirty seven seconds. Please get inside as soon as possible."

Chapter 120

2064: storage room near lock #912, Aristillus, Lunar Nearside

Dewitt stood in the small maintenance room and swung one arm across his chest, then the other, and then leaned forward and touched his toes. The mobility in the suit was good. Of course it was: he'd paid for the gold package and spent two hours getting fitted, but checking his equipment time and time again was the one way he had of burning off - well, not nervous energy per se, but the buzz of anticipation that he always felt.

At his feet the two techs snored; the second sedative patch on each should keep them safe and out of the way until this was over.

The countdown timer showed just ten more minutes till the ships landed. Or, rather, ten more minutes until the ships were *supposed* to land. If they were half an hour late he'd hardly be surprised. Jesus, the incompetence he'd seen in his time: artillery salvos that were supposed to land half an hour before the infantry arrived but actually hit half an hour after; food and ammo drops that landed right on top of terrorist strongholds instead of behind their own lines -

Jesus. Just thinking about the average PK troop was making him a bit nervous, and nervousness was mostly foreign to him. He hated depending on the competence of regular troops, especially when their fuckups could mean civilian deaths.

He checked the timer again, but only seconds had passed. He took a deep breath and let it out slowly. It was all coming to a head. And it would be over soon, too, which -

An alert beeped on his slate - the perimeter bug he'd left in tunnel. Shit. He did *not* need bystanders.

He used his slate to pan the perimeter camera around. There was no one coming from down the tunnel, but - wait. The airlock was opening. What the hell? The ships shouldn't be here for another - he checked - seven minutes. OK, so the ships were early, but -

As the airlock door slid further open he saw that the chamber behind it was empty. What the hell?

Wait, it wasn't entirely empty. There was just one man inside, taking off his helmet. Who -?

He recognized the face.

No. There was no way that could be him.

Dewitt picked up his rifle, opened the door, and stepped into the tunnel. The airlock door was still grinding open but he could clearly see the space-suited figure inside.

Dewitt yelled over the grumbling of the airlock door. "John? John Hayes?"

John's head whipped around and their eyes met. It was John.

They stared at each other for a long moment, and then the helmet that John had been holding slipped from his fingers and fell to the airlock floor.

The door slid further and Dewitt saw three - were those Dogs?

Dewitt looked at the four of them. John's hair was shaggy and he had several day's growth of beard, but there was no doubt, it was him. John looked older now, and as serious as ever - maybe even more so.

And the Dogs with him? That made sense, in a way. He'd heard rumors - such strange rumors.

Apparently they were true.

He tore his eyes from John and looked at the Dogs. Like John, they were wearing space suits, and like John, they had their helmets off. And all three of them were looking at him.

There was something unsettling about the intensity of their gaze.

John shook his head. "I - Matt? Is that you?"

"John, what the hell are you doing here?"

"Me? What the hell are *you* doing here?"

Dewitt saw John's eyes flick to his chest, and then harden.

Shit, the PK badges.

Dewitt's mind spun. How could he explain? "I -" He stumbled.

One of the Dogs, the red one with a mangled ear, was staring intently at him, his lip curling and a faint growl building. That thing wasn't going to attack him, was it? He touched the selector switch on his rifle with his thumb but didn't move it from 'safe.'

"John, it's too complicated, and there's no time. Something huge is going down. You have to get out of here!"

"The invasion? Is it now?"

Dewitt blinked. "You know?"

"Matt - tell me you're not working with the PKs on this."

"John, I owe you one - hell, I owe you more than that after Yibin. So, listen to me. Save your life, save the Dogs' lives, and get out of here now."

"The invasion is a week away -"

"No it's not. It's landing right now!"

John stared at Dewitt. "I don't know what's going on, but I swear to God, Matt, if you're helping these bastards -"

"Listen to me, John: get of here right this second or you're going to end up dead."

Dewitt's slate beeped. He looked down at it, scanned the text and looked up. "You've got three minutes." He pulled the keyfob from his pocket and tossed it to his old friend. "Now run."

Chapter 121

2064: DC Minute Studio, Washington DC, Earth

Senator Haig sat in her chair as the makeup artist did her work. A studio assistant leaned into the room. "Senator, we're ready to begin if you are."

Linda Haig made eye contact with her makeup artist. The technician applied the brush to her forehead one last time, tilted her head appraisingly, nodded, and withdrew.

Linda removed the apron, stood, and walked to the stage. The teleprompters were displaying the first page of her speech. "I'm ready. Get me the stairs as a background."

A PA gave her a thumbs up.

Linda looked over her shoulder and verified that the image wall - a super-high-definition version of a wall screen that photographed well - was showing an exterior shot of the capitol building.

A year ago DC Minute would've shot this video in front of a green screen and added the background in post, but she liked the new system.

Or, rather, she was proud of it. After buttering up the bureaucrats at BuSuR, she steered a series of grants through committee to help the firm develop and commercialize the technology. The end result was almost 500 new jobs in her state.

Creating jobs was good, but even more importantly, AppLogic knew which side their bread was buttered on: once the grants had started flowing the firm had been a loyal donor.

But enough reliving old victories. It was time for a new one.

Linda turned from the wall screen and faced the cameras. She composed herself, putting on her concerned-but-willing-to-lead look.

Linda turned to the producer. "This is going to air before the president's segment, yes?"

The producer nodded. "Jacob Mott himself called me. He was very clear. *Before* the president's segment."

"Good."

Linda looked into the A camera. The red light came on.

Go time.

"My fellow Americans. For years we've known about these trying economic times, about our budget difficulties, and how they are caused by CEOs conspiring against the public, domestic terrorists, and climate change induced natural disasters like the California Earthquake.

Over recent months you - and we - have learned something crucial." She punctuated the word with a pointing finger. "Our problems, both here in the United States and in the global economic community, are caused not just by the actions of terrorists in Alaska and Texas, not just by the bad faith of plutocrats here at home, and not just by environmental problems. No, we have learned something recently - that our problems are also caused by selfishness of a conspiring few.

"Shared problems call for shared solutions. And yet, at the very time when all decent citizens –" she spread her hands, including everyone in the audience "– are working together, putting our shoulders to the common wheel to solve common problems, these few - these conspiring few - are not only refusing to help in our common endeavor, they are actively sabotaging our efforts.

"It would be bad enough if these plutocrats, these powerful moneyed interests, were merely stealing from us by refusing to pay their fair share. The reality, though, is even worse."

She paused here and let hang the implied question hang. Longer. A bit longer. Uncomfortably long. Then, when the tension was right, when she'd built up enough anxiety in her audience, she turned to the B camera.

"Today we face grave challenges. We need not just every pair of hands, but every mind - and every human heart - to rebuild California, rebuild our nation, and rebuild our planet. And at this time when the entire world is pulling together to solve our problems, the tenth of one percent have closed their hands. They have closed their minds. They have closed even their hearts. How? They - the tenth of one percent, the elitists, the plutocrats - were not content merely to steal from the public coffers by withholding their taxes and their labor. That could, perhaps, be explained by simple greed. Criminal, wrong, and illegal... but still just greed.

"But the tenth of one percent go beyond mere greed; they are actively working to destroy society. How else to explain their theft of billions and billions of dollars of heavy equipment? Equipment that is urgently needed in our reconstruction. Bulldozers, earth movers, cranes, ships - the wealth of humanity, the very tools that we need to rebuild California - and to rebuild the world. They've plundered it and are using it for their own selfish purposes.

"But we all know that as important as tools are, the true wealth of a nation is its people - and here again, the expats are actively working to sabotage our shared society, our shared recovery and our shared progress. Tens of thousands of workers - men and women who should be helping push the world forward into the 22nd century - are instead being bribed to work in the private parks and exclusionary mansions of a secret cabal.

"These oligarchs - these billionaires - serve themselves instead of serving humanity. Instead of serving *you*." She gestured to the camera. "They think that just because they can run beyond the reach of Earth's gravity they can run beyond the reach of our laws. They think that just because they are beyond the atmosphere they are beyond the principles of fairness and community.

"You've probably seen videos, blogs, and other carefully crafted propaganda generated by these billionaires hiding on the moon. They wrap themselves in words. 'Freedom', they say, and 'progress.' But don't be fooled. Ask yourselves 'Freedom from what?' Ask yourselves, 'Progress to where?'"

She turned back to the A camera.

"Freedom from what? These cheats and economic saboteurs care only for their own freedom. The freedom to take wealth and assets generated here, here with the benefit of our laws, with the benefit of our ecological regulations, with the benefit of our universities, and with the benefit of our subsidies to innovation. The freedom to take, take, take, and then - after they've taken all they can - to escape to a private fortress, an armed camp, where they selfishly spread the fruits of our shared labor for their own personal banquet.

"Progress to where? These billionaires don't care a whit about human progress, about American progress, or about your progress. They don't care about our society's progress to the future. Instead, they want to roll back the clock. They aren't building a 22nd century, they're trying pathetically to restore a 20th century - or even a 19th century. They don't love progress to the future. No, they want a return to the past. A past where a robber baron elite rule like feudal lords over the common people. You learned in school about the train barons of the nineteenth century, of the semiconductor multimillionaires of the twentieth century, and of the Internet schemers from the early part of this century. We, as a society, as a people - as Americans - have largely corrected the vast gaps in wealth between the haves and the have-nots. We've made it possible for all people, regardless of color, educational background, or accident of birth, to lead the good life.

"Do we want a return to the days before the government provided education? A return to the days when health care was only for the rich? A return to days when your 25th birthday brought you only more bills, and not a government Getting Started Grant?

"I have an answer. I have an answer to these questions."

Back to the B camera. This time she gave it a deep stare and let her eyes telegraph resilience, determination, seriousness.

"I do not whisper my answer.

"I do not give my answer in a soft voice.

"I do not say it with a single doubt.

"I answer 'No'. No, we do not want a return to the errors, to the *evils*, of the past. I say it for all of us. All of us as Americans - and all of us as human beings.

"I say no, we will not stand for a return to inequality, to lack of regulation, to uneven opportunities. We will not stand by as our common wealth, our common heritage, is looted by the powerful and the rich for their own selfish wants and desires.

"This is why the president, I, and select other leaders from both parties have agreed to pass, before the end of the week, the Revised California Earthquake Recovery and Restoring Stolen Wealth Act.

"This law - despite its somewhat unpronounceable name -" She paused to raise her eyebrows and give a small self-deprecating grin to show that she was, after all, a common woman, as exasperated by some of the nonsense in Washington as anyone else. "This new law is an important step in getting our economy in California going again - and in getting our national and our global economies going again. We do this not just for Californians, but for all Americans - and for all citizens, everywhere.

"This law demands that the looters and tax avoiders on the moon pay their fair share, that they pay the taxes that they have avoided for the last three, five, ten years.

"We Americans are a peaceful people. We do not like violence. We do not go looking for violence. And for that reason, the act does not resort to violence. We ask for our wealth to be returned to us. We ask this as fellow humans. Despite our righteous anger - and anger we are justified in - we go not with a clenched fist, but with an open hand - an open hand of reconciliation.

"We do not go to fight. We will not be the first to use violence. We will not be the first to use force.

"We are one nation, one human race. At a temporary impasse, perhaps, but we are family. And family does not use force when it can avoid it. Even when a child is being willful, inconsiderate, and stubborn, we never hit a child, we never spank a child, we do not use physical discipline.

"We will not strike first.

"But the plutocrats, the expats, must know - do know - that our patience is being tried. We have recently had some videos smuggled out of the lunar enclave, by brave citizen-journalists who avoided the corporate censorship and lies. These videos make it clear not only that the monied interests are not prepared to reconcile with the legitimate and moral authority of the US government, but that they are actively planning war.

"I would like to thank, by the way, my son Hugh, as well as other brave young people and citizen journalists including Allyson Chery and Louisa Teer, who have made this information available to us at great risk to themselves.

"I want to share these videos with you today. First, we have training videos of the paramilitary separatist armies being amassed by the millionaires."

Linda paused for a second, so that when the video went to post there'd be a bit of silence to splice in Hugh and Louisa's clip of the Aristillus military parade.

"Such is the blood lust of the separatists that they're training not with so-called 'sporting firearms.' They're not even content to use military guns. No, such is their anger and hate that the plutocrats have developed new weapons, optimized for killing. Large weapons, more brutal and terrifying than anything ever developed on Earth.

"Weapons have no place in a civilized world, and for generations we as a society have been moving toward the goal of a world free from violence. When these billionaires arm themselves, and it's more than just a case of illegal weapons ownership. It's more, even, than a case of incipient rebellion. No, the transgression goes beyond laws, to a violation of *ideals*. The billionaires are not just breaking regulations - by creating especially barbaric, cruel tools of slaughter they are rejecting international norms. They are rejecting the very *idea* of community. And this, this in the end, is their biggest mistake.

"My fellow citizens, we have been peaceful. We have been patient. It is clear, though, that the time to act is drawing near. We can not tolerate the billionaires sitting on their vast piles of stolen wealth, their mountains of machinery, labor, and - yes - even gold, when so many here in California - and the rest of the United States - suffer. It is clear that we can not tolerate the few stealing from the many. It is clear that - no matter how peaceful or patient we are – that the millionaires and the thieves are not peaceful, and that they are preparing to wage terrorist attacks and - yes - even war. And this, in the end, is why we must act.

"And so our forces are on their way, even now, to the moon, to the very heart of the expats' illegal empire. There they will land, and they will ask - with open hearts and open hands - for the lunar rebels to rejoin America, rejoin the Earth, rejoin the human community. And once they do, we will be on the path to restoring California, and to restoring the world.

"My fellow citizens, wish us luck."

She held her pose for a moment before the camera light died. As it did Elliot, her press secretary, whooped. "You killed that. Absolutely killed it. Congratulations, Senator." He grinned. "Or should I say, future Mrs. President?"

Linda gave Elliot a severe look and shook her head. "Don't say that!" Linda looked around - *anyone* could be listening.

She paused, then allowed herself a small grin. She had killed that speech. And she'd stolen the president's thunder. When this went live in a few hours, she'd be all over the blogosphere - and she'd be there *before* the president even got on the air.

Her biggest coup, of course, was that she'd positioned herself perfectly. If the raid worked, the voters would remember that she was on TV, just hours beforehand, calling for armed intervention.

And if the raid failed, then Linda had been the one talking about a peaceful resolution and calling for a vote.

Her small smile widened. Yes, she given the president all the rope she needed to hang herself with.

Chapter 122

2064: level three, Aristillus, Lunar Nearside

John gripped the wheel of the Double Door panel truck as he accelerated. "I don't know, Blue. Try the glove compart-"

Blue held up the phone triumphantly. "I found one!".

John reached out and took it. He swiped it on. "Call Mike Martin."

"Morlock Engineering Main Office. How may I help you?"

John swore - without his own phone, he was using Mike's public number, which redirected to the office.

"This is John Hayes. I need to speak to Mike Martin, immediately."

"I'm sorry, sir, but Mr. Martin is in a meeting right -"

"This is an emergency; get him on the line!"

Blue tapped him on the shoulder. John turned. "What?"

"Our exit." Blue pointed a paw. John slammed on the brakes and took the corner dangerously fast. The oversized tires and their grippy contact patches slipped and the vehicle fishtailed. A moment later it straightened, and John pushed the accelerator.

Blue barked "left!" and John slammed on the brakes a second time and took the corner.

Mike answered the phone. "Hello?"

John upshifted and accelerated. "Mike, it's John."

"John? You landed?"

"Mike! Listen! There's a PK invasion -"

"I know. We're in an emergency meeting about that right now - we've only got weeks to prepare. Look, let me call you back-"

"Mike, it's not weeks away. It's landing, right now. It's going to be coming in through lock #912. Maybe others." John held the phone between his cheek and shoulder as he used two hands to steer around a cargo truck carrying a huge pallets of iron pipes.

To his credit Mike didn't waste time asking how he knew; instead he immediately spoke to someone in the room with him. "The invasion is happening - right now! They're going to be entering through lock #912. I don't know. Do you have any way to shut down all your locks remotely?"

John sped along the highway as he waited for Mike to finish. A flatbed truck ahead of him, loaded with sheets of polished green olivine counter tops changed lanes. John slammed on his brakes and then pulled around it and accelerated again. He turned. "Blue, listen to me."

Blue turned and gave John his full attention.

"When you get in there, lock the Den up tight, and don't let anyone in or out. And I mean anyone. No matter who they say they are."

Blue nodded.

John looked in the rear view mirror and saw Max. "And Max -"

"I know. Keep the pack safe."

"Right."

Mike came back on the line. "OK, we've got the locks all shut down. Some of our militia units are in training sessions right now, so we should be able to mobilize them quickly. Let me put you on hold."

John saw a sign on the tunnel wall and braked hard, and then took the next right, into an unmarked B-sized tunnel. How long ago had he last been here? Just six months - and yet it felt so much longer.

The tunnel was empty, but John kept his speed low, knowing about the curve ahead. And then he was at the curve, and through it, and the highway behind them was out of sight. He slowed further - and there, on the left, was the unmarked warehouse door. John stopped the truck.

The truck's doors flew open and Max and Blue jumped out and landed on the sidewalk. Just two? John turned and saw Duncan still in the back seat, looking back and forth, torn between heading back to the Den and staying with John.

John was about to yell at him to go, but Max beat him to it. "Duncan! Move!"

Duncan unfroze and leapt out of the open door of the truck, landed lightly several meters away. Someone inside the Den must have been watching - the warehouse door was already rolling up. Duncan started to say something, but there wasn't time. John hit the accelerator.

The private side tunnel curved again and then joined a class C highway tunnel. John merged into traffic, heading for Mike's house.

Mike came back on the line. "John, you still there?"

"I'm here - what's the status?"

"We've got troops headed to the surface. Just one company, but we're -"

John saw a gap in the traffic and whipped the wheel hard to the left. The phone flew from its perch. "Shit!" Behind him a highway traffic enforcement vehicle flipped its lightbar on. John ignored it an accelerated.

He stared to call for Blue to find the phone and then remembered that the Dogs weren't in the truck with him. For the first time in six months the Dogs weren't anywhere nearby. He blinked, and then spared a glance for the phone. There it was, on the floor. He tapped the truck's autopilot on and swore as it slowed. John ducked, grabbed the phone, sat back up, and took the autopilot off.

"Mike, you there?"

"Yes."

"Tell me where are you, right now."

"I'm in the Morlock offices. Why?"

John slammed on his brakes and pulled across two lanes of traffic, barely slowing in time before he hit the ramp. Behind him the traffic enforcement car shot past the exit. "Mike, listen carefully, I need you to -"

The phone went dead.

"Mike, can you hear me? Mike?"

John pulled the phone away from his head, looked at it, and saw that he had zero bars.

Shit.

It was starting.

He pressed harder on the accelerator but the truck was already maxed out.

Chapter 123

2064: Trentham Court Apartments, Aristillus, Lunar Nearside

Louisa's phone died. She looked at Hugh, and saw that his must have died as well, because he was putting it away.

"My phone just died." She checked it. "There's no coverage."

Hugh nodded. "Yeah. Don't worry about it."

"What do you mean, 'don't worry about it'?"

Hugh shrugged. "Listen, it'll all be over -".

"*It* will? What will? What's going on?"

"We've got to stay inside. There's some stuff -"

"Hugh, I swear, if your mother told you something and you're not telling me, I'll - I'll -" Louisa's glare was intense. "Damn it, Hugh, What is going on?"

Hugh deflated under her assault. "The US and the PKs are launching an invasion. I think it's starting now."

Louisa shook her head. "Damn it. This is terrible. I mean, it's good for Earth, of course - but this was ours. Our story. There's so much more we could have done." She thought for a moment. "We'll work it out. We can roll with this."

Louisa turned and yelled over her shoulder. "Allyson, Selena! Get the cameras - there's about to be combat."

"Wait, no! We have to stay here, where it's safe."

Louisa didn't even bother hiding her scorn. "If your mommy wants you to stay safe, then stay. Some of us, though, are journalists. And I'm getting this damned story."

Chapter 124

2064: storage room near lock #912, Aristillus, Lunar Nearside

Dewitt's slate beeped as a pop-up from the airlock administration interface appeared. "Remote Maintenance Request: tier 2 admin attempt to set state to 'offline.' Approve?" He clicked "Deny." The pop-up disappeared.

A moment later the pop-up reappeared. Damn it. How many times was he going to have to do this? He looked at the interface more carefully. and saw a check box for "do this every time." He checked the box, and then clicked "Deny" again. The dialogue disappeared and stayed gone.

And then he felt it - a distant yet undeniably solid impact.

Dust sifted off the light panels overhead and fell slowly in the low gravity.

Then another impact, the kind of impact that only a huge ship landing on rock could make.

Then a third impact.

Then a fourth.

Dewitt used his slate to bring up a view from the airlock's exterior camera. The camera showed the stark white plain. In the left foreground were three cargo containers butted front to back with a pile of equipment stacked on top. Beyond the pile of containers he could see a PK ship, and to its left and right two more.

As he watched, another ship slid into view from above and settled onto the surface. Another rumble rolled through the floor.

The invasion was on.

Colophon

This book was created with FSF emacs, Apache OpenOffice, Ubuntu Linux, and various open source fonts, scripts and other tools.

My thanks to all of the hackers who help create and maintain these tools.

About the Author

Travis J I Corcoran is a Catholic anarcho-capitalist, a software engineer, and a business owner. He is an amateur at farming, wood turning, blacksmithing, cooking, throwing ceramic pots, and a few other things.

He lives on a 50 acre farm in New Hampshire with his wife, dogs, livestock, and a variety of lathes and milling machines.

Travis has had non-fiction articles published in several national magazines including Dragon, Make, and Fine Homebuilding.

"The Powers of the Earth" is his first novel.

About the Aristillus series

The Aristillus story is continued in "Causes of Separation", which is available at Amazon.com and elsewhere.

Please help me write more SF novels

There are three ways you can help me bring you more great science fiction stories:

- Go to Amazon.com right now (no, seriously, RIGHT NOW) and leave a review of this book (even really short like "loved it").
- Go to http://morlockpublishing.com/email-signup/ and sign up for very very infrequent emails when new books are written.
- Follow me on twitter at @morlockp

Printed in Great Britain
by Amazon